A Marriage of Lies

By

Sheila Da Lae

2008

How many will you have to tell…?

REAL Straight Publications
Southfield, Michigan

A Marriage of Lies
Copyright © 2008 Sheila Da Lae

ISBN 13: 978-0-9825125-0-0

Cover and interior design by More Graphics

Printed in the United States of America

Table of Contents

Acknowledgements

First and foremost, I give honor to the Creator for the gift of creativity. Without him, there would be no me.

The work of fiction that you will enjoy was made possible through the cooperation, love and respect of my family who acknowledges my need for time to create and encourages me to follow my dreams and explore my options. I could not do this without their love and support. To my husband who allows me to be me and provides me with all of the *research* I need to stay creative. I love you and thank you for your support. To the *Fabulous Four* you are without a doubt the best children on the face of the planet and I would not trade any of you for anything. For my research readers who wait patiently for me to complete composing and who are truthful with their critics, you are very much appreciated. To my sister, wherever you may be who once told me that my alter ego would make me money some day, thank you for reminding me that she lived! To Ms. Marie, thank you for the edits, advice and validation. I could not have done it without you. To Chocolate M.D., Thank you for the medical homework it was well worth all of the call backs! To my designer, you are and forever will be the best in your field…Thank you for a chance to work with the best! Last but certainly not least….My Host, thank you for sharing your personality with me along with your flavor Diva "L", you make it possible for my existence.
I love you all.

Sheila Da Lae

Chapter 1

The Lies Began

Today started just like any other day, I mean why would it be any different? He was still the man I loved but hated all in the same breath and I was still the woman to afraid to be free that he despised but pitied too much to leave. I guess you might say we stayed together out of convenience…you know equal partners in what most viewed as a loving relationship built on mutual trust and respect, but we both knew it was train wreck in progress. Love is the weirdest emotion…I mean you feel it for another but once it's extended past the point of no return, its really just going through the motions. I don't know, what was the alternative? Split up? Leave? Cut our losses, while we were ahead? Our Son was grown…No, I guess we both thought it would be best to continue the lie instead of facing what we both knew would be uncertainty.

Now I could continue on in this train of thought, or I could begin the day as always it would be a full day and time was slowly slipping away…and no matter what, I had to get to him even if only for a little while.

She's my wife good, bad or indifferent. Those are the facts and nothing shy of divorcing could change that, would change that. No, it hadn't been all bad; there were some great times behind in the past. She didn't always have contempt for me when she looked into my eyes and there once was a time that I didn't wish she was her…There was a time when 5:00 o'clock p.m. did not appear to be my sentence beginning, but the anticipated close of my day of separation from her. Now more than ever home felt like a place of doing time rather than making time…you know its funny a man can have so much but view it as very little…especially when, well lets just say what I have I no longer want, and what I want I can't seem to have…

Good Morning. Morning. I have a meeting after work so I probably will be late getting home; I see no reason why you should hold dinner for me. Really? Yeah, sorry I forgot to mention it yesterday, it must have slipped my mine. No problem, I was thinking about meeting up with Tina a little later, maybe I'll just have dinner with her. Cool, at least you won't be home alone. I guess…You did remember that we are expecting Angel and Craig this weekend for dinner? I tried to reschedule but this is the only time that Craig's calendar would be free. He said, he and Angel really needed to see us and it has been a while since they were home last. "God knows I hated having the kids for dinner and putting on all that false pretense, but it meant a lot to our son to spend time with his mom and dad showing his lovely wife that marriages could last the test of times…its unfortunate that he used his parents as an example if he knew the truth it could probably kill him". Yeah, yeah, yes is that this weekend? Yes Curtis, this weekend…don't tell me you have a meeting? No…I just forgot that's all. "Damn, just what I need a weekend in hell with this woman, just so I could continue to lie to my son that his mother was the only woman on earth for me. The whole thing made me sick inside…the fact that I've always told my son to be a man, love his wife, be faithful and true to his marriage, beliefs and principles…and here I sit counting the minutes that I could hold her in my arms. Just one touch from her made it all worth while…the lying, cheating, the hidden sacrifices, just one".

Well I better be going, busy day, don't want to get stuck in traffic. I guess…don't work to hard give my best to Vanessa and do thank her for the flowers they were lovely, Reneea said with a smirk on her face that said fuck you loud and clear. Curtis turned and glared at Reneea as if he could have shot her dead with his eyes, smirked jingled his keys grabbed his brief case from the marble counter top and walked to the kitchen door as fast as his feet could carry him. Reneea's birthday had past just days ago and as Curtis always did, he had his loyal to death secretary send a dozen long stemmed red roses with a card that read, *All my life, all my Love Curtis Happy Anniversary* needless to say she was a little careless this time.

As Curtis proceeded to the garage to make his get away in his black on black 745I BMW; with Reneea looking on, she thought of the embarrassment Curtis suffered in front of their friends as the matter was discussed over drinks and dinner with their long time friends and associates Rick Neal, and the Vaughn's and how she could hardly control her own anger at the fact that he couldn't even take ten minutes to make sure that it was correct but part of her also knew it was Vanessa's small victory in destroying the day for her as she had known for quite some time that Curtis and Vanessa were more than just boss and employee. She remembered the day she found out about his infidelity, how she was hurt but, could never let herself become to upset as Curtis had been unfaithful before during a time when she needed him most back when graduate school was ending and they were engaged. This unfortunate incident lead to a vulnerable time in her life where she did something at the time so unspeakable that it was never discussed, mostly because the person she turned to had to much respect for her but if it came out many lives would be turned upside down. Placing the coffee cup into the sink she shrugged off the memory and made preparations to start her day when she was startled by the ringing of the phone.

Ring, ring. Hello? Ump, ump, ump the deep sexy voice replied on the other end of the receiver. And just who might this be? I think you already know…Curtis? Whatever! Open the door the voice commanded with confidence and force. She hung up the receiver and moved without hast to the door she could feel a smile developing from deep within her. As she opened the door and took two steps back, in front of her appeared the very object of her affection, the desire of her heart took on a whole new meaning and perspective whenever he appeared before her dressed and/or otherwise.

Hey Baby, the tall sexy chocolate muscular man reached out his hand and pulled her toward himself and before Reneea could respond, he kissed her so passionately, and forcefully holding her so tightly she could barely catch here breath or bearings. Baby, baby wait, ooh bay wait. Rick wait Boy! Acting as if she didn't approve, playfully pushing him away only to be handled with love and toying. Rick stop it, what if Curtis doubled back for something we would be caught. Girl Please…you and I both know that brother is in far too much a hurry to get to his office and play HNIC to be worried about the crown jewel he has left here at home for my benefit. At least shut the door…the neighbor. Fuck the neighbors; everybody knows that as much as the two of you pretend, you are not Ward and Joan Clever. Fuck you Rick okay…That's what I've got in mind…they both laugh and commence holding hands. Rick Neal, the finest man God could have created. He had a way of making Reneea feel as if she were the only woman in the world. He stood a towering 6 foot 8 inches with the complexion of a blended Carmel and milk chocolate with the body of a ball player still in tact. He was Curtis' best friend and the Godfather of their son, and the man Reneea had grown to love over the years as she and Curtis began to slip further and further apart.

Innocent enough as it was in the beginning; Rick really just tried to be a good friend. He never approached Reneea although you could see that he was very fond of her from the beginning. He always displayed the brother character. The clean up man whenever Curtis would let his desire for Vanessa get the best of him and leave Reneea feeling bruised and torn, he was the friend who's shoulders became something to cry on later becoming something to lye on. Neither one of them wanted this to be the case especially since Rick's wife was a friend to Reneea…but her untimely passing created a bond between Rick and Reneea which started out innocent and platonic that could not be severed and rekindled their friendship of the past. While Reneea was trying to help Rick get over his grief, Curtis saw this as an opportunity to spend more and more time away from home, never even noticing that his best friend had become his competition and ultimately his successor.

Reneea, Reneea, Rick could see here mine had wondered…Baby, hum, we don't have much time. If we are going to be together this morning, we better be on our way, I have a late morning meeting and I can't be late. He looked at her with wanting eyes, the way a man in love looked at a woman. Well Mr. Neal, I do believe you remember where the bedroom is? Right this way my love. Rick guided her through the halls of her own home as if he had a right to her there. He maneuvered the stair case carefully, and calculated making each step slow and seductive, almost cat like as if he were a thief preparing to take another mans wealth…after all he was.

They entered the bedroom of Curtis Anthony Rae, engrossed in passion kissing one another removing articles of clothing and allowing them to fall where they may. Whispering sweet nothings in each others ears, touching each other in places reserved only for the owners of private property. As they reached the bed, Rick laid Reneea down slowly and began to remove her silk black laced thong with his teeth. After exposing the very treasure he sought, he began to kiss her between her legs slowly, using his tongue to make her surrender her soul, mind and body to his every command. He methodically moved his way up where he entered her and began to stroke away every anxiety, every pain, and every thought of unhappiness that may have entered her mind. Yes at that moment she was loved, in love and experiencing what she had come to believe was real love.

After a vigorous session of love making Rick noticed the time and whispered that he had to leave but looked forward to seeing her later. He kissed Reneea softly. I love you, you do realize that don't you? Of course baby, why else would I risk coming here in broad day light to make love to you when we could be exposed at any time? They laughed in unison. Yeah, I guess so. What time will I see you tonight? I'm meeting Tina for Dinner so whatever time you can be free after that is cool; Curtis has another one of his meetings. Baby why don't you just leave this nigga? Rick don't, not now; let me hold on to this please? Sighing heavily as he knew it was not a topic up for discussion, he grabbed his tousled clothing swinging them over his shoulder, caressed her shoulders made a pouted face and began to speak in a sad voice, I've got to go… I'll call you latter. Love you. Love you more…Yeah? Prove it.

With a slow stagger, Rick went to the master bath shower grabbing Curtis' body wash rinsing away the scent of the love he had just made. Talking about adding insult to injury, not only had he had his wife, but showered away his sin with his friends belongings. Watching him she couldn't help but think of how she loved that man; she thought to herself that she should probably change the sheets and make the bed, but on second thought she decided that she would just spread it up instead so that the scent of her lover would be with her through the night good Lord what he does to her, no one could ever understand.

Chapter 2

The Office

Damn! Those were the words that rolled around the thought process of Curtis A. Rae, owner and CEO of Rae Enterprises, who entered his office only to be received by his long legged tight skirt wearing, almond joy beauty of a secretary and a hot cup of coffee in hand.

Good Morning Mr. Rae, I trust you're feeling well this morning? I am now! Good, I'll take that as a compliment. Vanessa smiled shamelessly as she walked toward Curtis glaring at him as though she had won the lottery. Take your pick. Excuse me? Take your pick, coffee or kiss? Hum, how about this? Curtis took the coffee from her hand, sat it on his desk and pulled her close to him. All in the same motion, he kissed her as if he hadn't seen her in years. Ooh, jugging by that, looking in the direction of his zipper, you are happy to see me? Curtis had an erection that could possibly keep him from sitting for the next half and hour. Don't worry; I plan to take very good care of you and it later this evening. I'm counting on it…Curtis whispered as he backed slowly away from his secretary who could hardly get herself composed to begin the work day.

What's the agenda for today? You have the Briggs account at 11:00, Mr. Wallace at 12:30 and a 1:30 lunch with Mr. Neal along with a racquet ball court reserved for 3:00 and finally…Dinner at 6:00 with me at the Embassy. I trust you told the good Mrs. that you'd be out late tonight. I'm not trying to hear "A couple of hours are all I have" Baby I need to be with you tonight…Please?
Curtis looked at Vanessa, and all he could feel was love and desire. Smiling, he responded immediately. No worries tonight is your night, I will be with you until I'm ready to let you go or vice versa. That's what

I'm talking about. Vanessa turned to exit the door. Oh, by the way Craig called he ask me to have you return the call, he also checked me about the flowers, see that he doesn't do it again please. Vanessa, don't start...my son, my wife...you fucked up on purpose...Whatever, see that he doesn't do it again, huh baby?

The door closed and Curtis laughed to himself thinking of the way that woman made him feel also thinking of the things his son was probably going to say to him. He picked up the phone and began to dial his son and wait for a response on the other end. Craig Rae, may I help you? Yes Mr. Rae, Mr. Rae here you phoned? Hey dad hold on a second...Curtis could hear his son in the background commanding his troops and it made him proud that his son had chosen a career in business even if he decided not to be placed comfortably in his father's company where he felt the way would be paved instead of curved and earned, he was a fine man and despite all of Curtis' short comings he knew that he had instilled in his son the best he had to give. Yeah! Dad sorry about that I was just finishing up a meeting. No problem son, you are working business first, I can respect that. Vanessa said that you called, was there anything you need especially? No, can't a man just call his father? Of course, I just thought that there was something that you needed. No, you do know that Angel and I will be down for the weekend, hoping we could take in a game if you have any tickets. If not, I'm sure you could score some from Uncle Rick. Oh yeah that would be great, I've got four around that I haven't given to clients. Will this be just us or did you want the girls to come. No man! I want to watch the game. Laughter erupts from the two. If you want, ask Uncle Rick if he wants to tag along. Okay, that's cool I'll see him for lunch today, I'll ask him then. Cool alright dad I better go got work. A...uh Craig? Yeah? Vanessa said that you came down on her about mommy's flowers? And...And you probably should let me handle my staff. Dad, she's been your secretary for years, I think she knows the important dates by now...it didn't look good for you or mom. Her birthday man and you didn't buy'em yourself? Craig I got this. Okay dad, but I'm not apologizing. Curtis listening to his sons response noticing the similarities they had smiled and shook his head and slowly reminded his son...you really are a Rae...Takes one to know one. Love ya man.

Curtis hung up the phone and began the day with periodic interruptions from the secretary who captured most of his attention during the day.

Before he knew it lunch was upon him where he and Rick would spend time hanging out just like the old days.

Mister Nicks, best bar burger in town was always their choice of poison. Mr. Neal! Mr. Rae what it is man? Awe I can't call it. The two men affectionately shake hands and sit at their usual table. Hey fellas how's it going? Hey Sherrie! Sherrie baby! Start you guys with something to drink? Why not? Usual? You know it. Dave two drafts, bottles! Sherrie was a waitress with the body of a Goddess, who had a thing for Rick since he became a widower, but he never gave her the time of day despite the urging of Curtis. Man, she is hot! Yeah she is, young though man too much drama for a brother. Man please that's what you need in your life…Now see if I was not a married man I would definitely want a crack at that. Nigga Pleaseeeeeeee. You could be her daddy! Yeah, in more ways than one. Thunderous laughter broke out between them. Seriously man, you should check out the advertisement. You amaze me. What? You got prime grade A choice at home…and you would honestly consider hittin that? Come on Rick don't go there, you of all people know, it has been a little raggedy with me and Reneea for years. But man it doesn't have to be. Look man no lecture now you gone Bitch up or we gone eat. Cool man lets eat. Thank you, beside I don't need no guilt trip tonight. Vanessa right? Rick don't judge me. No judgment man, just an observation. But I will not be able to run interference for you. Not asking. Cool. Rick just looked at Curtis sheepishly smiling reminiscing over the morning's events and preparing for tonight's adventure.
Oh before I forget, Craig is coming down this weekend and wants to catch a game with us you up for it. Yeah, whenever my man is town I'm with it. Curtis never said anything but he secretly resented the closeness Craig and Rick shared. Even though he chose Rick as his Godfather for that exact reason, he always felt as though Rick intruded on their bond.

Cool it will be great. Just like old times. The two finished their lunch and headed for their court time. Rick was a talented athlete as well as Curtis and the competition between them on the court always made the other men at the gym take notice. Little did Curtis know that his rival on the Court was also the rival in his bed? Game! Boy you getting slow, man please you only got me on that last one because I needed to save some energy for tonight. Oh I keep forgetting about your meeting. Rick looked at Curtis with disapproval. Rick you just don't understand? What if Reneea was cheating on you? How would you feel? Man every time I needed her to be my wife and understand my needs as a man she couldn't so I had to make do for myself. Beside, she doesn't want me any more either...You're not in those four walls with us its like being in hell and neither one of us knows how to get out. Besides Craig wouldn't understand that the parents he thinks are so together aren't. I'm not hurting my son for nobody. So kill Reneea instead. Look she's fine just fine. The two shook their heads and called truce and retired to the locker room to shower.

Chapter 3

Two's Company

6:00 on the dot! I knew you wouldn't keep me waiting baby. Curtis entered the hotel room to find Vanessa dressed only in a red satin bra and thong. He could hardly contain his excitement. Dropping his briefcase to the floor along with his jacket and keys, he grabbed Vanessa picking her up in one swooping motion tossing her on the bed. Curtis, stop. What about dinner? Baby right now I only have an appetite for you! Curtis tore off his clothes with urgency with only one thing in mind.

Baby love me, love me now. Vanessa clawed at Curtis drawing blood from his back. Curtis moaned in sweet agony. Damn bay your nails! But he didn't care he grabbed her and forced his manhood into her hands telling her what do. Curtis what would you like? Baby you know what I need. Suck me, he moaned. Vanessa went down on Curtis with a vengeance as if she would tear his parts completely from his body. You know I know what to do bay, lay back let me love what belongs to Nessa…with every stroke she made Curtis feel as if he were the only man alive. He could not remember ever feeling so alive.

Ooh Vanessa, yeah bay, fuck me bay, do it…do it bitch do it! He screamed over and over again, and when Vanessa knew she had him hooked, she turned the tables and made him her Bitch! Fuck Me! She commanded. Put that shit to work hoe. She commanded. Over and over Curtis would make Vanessa climax with everlasting joy and he knew at that moment he was loved.

The hours went on for ever appearing as if the night would never end. Time and time again they made love telling one another how they felt,

what they needed and what they craved, but the end was inevitable... "If only for one night" played softly in the background as Vanessa had to watch Curtis dress and prepare to return to his world in which she was not apart.
Baby?
Yes?
When?
When what?
When will I be number one, when will I be the one you run home to? Curtis let out a long winded sigh and turned to Vanessa with a look that could melt butter and responded.
Soon, soon baby I just need time...but don't ever forget how much I love you and need you. I promise. He swaggered over to her in a playful motion as always kissing her forehead, both eyes and then slowly seductively her lips. He focused on her eyes and said...I promise you are number one in the dark and you shall be number one in the light. Curtis felt bad about lying but as his daddy always said "a lie ain't nothing for a Negro to tell." He knew he would not leave home, but he played the game, and played it well.

10:00 o'clock had rolled around and Reneea and Tina were still nursing the apple martinis they had purchased, laughing and agreeing about their day when Reneea noticed the time. Girl, I need to be on my way...surely Curtis has finished his meeting and I need to make a stop on the way home. Bullshit, you and I both know what that stop consists of Ms. Bitch. Whatever! Whatever my ass! Tina looked solemn for a moment and hesitated before she began to speak. Girl do you think Bea can see you with Rick. T, Bea is dead and let's leave her out of this. I know but you are fucking her man...Tina smiled and smirked in the same motion waiting for a reply that would make sense. Tina, come on, you and I both know it wasn't suppose to happen this way? I can't help that I fell in love with Rick. I didn't plan this shit! Baby girl...I know. I just can't help myself. I mean I know why you do it and yet I still see Bea...you know? I know I was sick for a week when I realized that I was boning Rick. But girl, my body needs him. You don't understand what he does to me. His lips, his eyes, his tongue! Ooh girl stop before I fuck'em. Laughter arose from the table as if a world famous comedian had entered the joint.

Will you call when you make it home? I will. Well…don't keep love
waiting…Remember if he calls don't answer. Mike knows something is
up. Well fuck your husband and keep his mind off us. They smiled as they
parted and walked toward their cars.

She couldn't help but be excited about all she had accumulated over the
years…a beautiful home, a Mercedes Benz and she knew it was a direct
result of being Mrs. Curtis Anthony Rae, but what the hell she deserved a
few trinkets after all he had made her suffer year after year as she tried to
be the wife he needed. There was no time to think about her unhappiness
with Curtis now, her man was waiting and she could keep him no longer.
Reneea pulled into the drive of the hotel smiling as if she knew she had hit
the jackpot. The sound of her engine was familiar as Rick came to the
window when he heard her enter his drive. Anxious, but not hurried, Rick
opened the door as if he was the one in control. He stood at the door
gazing at her angrily but not enough to rock the boat. Do you know what
time it is Mrs. Rae? She hated when he tortured her in that manner. She
spoke slow and methodical….Just past 10:00. And what if anything can
we do now he scowled at her turning her on more than he realized angrily
waiting for a reply. Acknowledging his anger, she opened her coat
exposing her nudity which she had managed to achieve on the drive over
and sheepishly replied…I'll leave if you prefer, licking her lips to make
them moist while at the same time making him want.

Rick looked at her with hunger, not saying another word grabbed her by
her neck pulling her inward while exposing his manhood forced himself
into her as if she were a common street whore calling her names and
demanding that she cum instantly and he was seconds from sprouting like
a river. They went on and on back and forth entangled in bondage of love
that could not be mistaken. Rick, I love you so much and when I think of
having to return to that house and continue to pretend with that man it
drives me insane. You have no idea girl…I'm the one that has to sit by the
phone praying for a call, hang out with a man who has everything that I
want but can't have and know for a fact that he's mistreating her; not to
mention the fact that we all have to hang out with each other and for
appearance sake sit there as he holds you and kisses you on what I
consider to be my lips…it's just not fair baby. Looking away from
Reneea's beautiful oval shaped face, Rick notices the time and cautions
her of the hour. Well it's about that time babe. I know, don't remind me.

Want to shower with me? No I don't think that will be wise. You know how much I love your body wet…we might just start back up again and you won't make it home before day break. They both smile lovingly into each others eyes as he watches her leave the room. Rick laid back on the pillow and thought of his friend, he thought of Beatrice and how he knew she would disapprove, but he couldn't help it he loved her…

Keeping Secrets

Curtis looked over the top of his reading glasses as he heard Reneea climbing the stairs to their master bedroom suite, as Reneea entered the room he noticed her hair was down as opposed to her signature pull back style he had become accustomed to her wearing. She was a woman full of grace and sophistication and she carried herself in that manner at all times. Curtis also noticed that she was wearing makeup; not overpowering but just a touch to accent her natural beauty. She had always been a beautiful woman, even in pregnancy while gaining weight from carrying his son, she still remained fabulous. He thought to himself how he use to be head over hills in lust and love with her, but somewhere along the way that feeling started to die. Could it have been all of the long nights he worked trying to develop Rae Enterprises into the fortune five hundred company it was today which kept him away from home alot that drove a wedge between them, or the fact that he had started this thing with his secretary who appeared to understand him and be there for him on the lonely nights away from home…In any event he knew that their love had suffered a devastating injury and by now he wasn't sure if he wanted to repair it or not. To a man like Curtis A. Rae, image was everything and reputations in this town were too hard to come by to ever attempt to rebuild it again.

You're awake? Yeap, hesitating, that I am. Its late I wanted to make sure you got in safely. Thank you I'm fine. Reneea turned to face Curtis who was laying in their king size Cherry Oak bed, the very bed she had earlier made love to Rick in and she smiled inward with the thoughts she had. Looking at Curtis she could not help but notice that he was shirtless, he was still very handsome and viral. He took so much pride in his appearance; he ate right, exercised and jogged every morning at the crack of dawn. She had almost forgotten how sexy he could be. She must have stared a little too long because Curtis took notice to her eyes probing him. Nea is there something wrong? Uh oh uh no, no um not at all, smiling trying to hide her embarrassment. I'll be damned she thought to herself, this Negro caught me checking him out! The sheer thought of this embarrassed her as if she had cheated on Rick, after all, Curtis was her husband she was still his wife she had every right to have those types of thoughts about him; however, she had no clue where this could all be coming from, especially since she had just made love to Rick for hours.

Oh the thought of it all made her cringe the secrets that bedroom held if only it could talk? Nea, he hadn't referred to her as Nea in months, possibly years why tonight? Nea? Yes? Where have you been, he asked inquisitively knowing that he himself had just arrived and half and hour prior to her arrival. Tina and I did some shopping and then we went to the Martini Grille and talked for a while when we noticed that we had had one to many and decided to just hangout there until we felt comfortable enough to drive. Oh, I see. Reneea begin to disrobe to change into her night apparel when she noticed that Curtis was standing directly behind her, he moved so cat like she hadn't noticed that he had gotten out of the bed. She felt a slight warming sensation run through her as he stroked her hair. He always loved her hair it was shinny, black and long with a natural curl if wet. The reflection of the two of them in the mirror was something that was never shared anymore only to be witnessed tonight. Yes Curtis? Nothing you know I've always loved your hair I'm just curious to find in down tonight. Oh I began to develop a slight headache on the way home so I took the band lose to ease the tension. The truth of the matter is Rick Neal enjoyed her hair down when they made love and she hadn't bothered to put it back because he asked her not to.

Still remaining in close proximity, Curtis watched Reneea shuffle through the dresser to find a gown of some sort to retire in for the night. There were very rare occasions when Curtis and Reneea would sleep together it appeared as if tonight would have to be one of those occasions as Curtis did not appear to be backing down from his advances. Nea, a man has needs and if I am not mistaken you are still my wife. And? She answered swiftly. And…I find myself in need tonight. Knowing that she had found herself intrigued by Curtis as well tonight, she figured that it was going to be one of those for appearance sake nights. She said nothing but found herself being fondled and kissed by Curtis. She felt the swelling of his genitals against her backside as he rubbed his hands ever so gently across her breast and she knew that her nipples would respond to the touch of his hand after all he was familiar with her body and what she liked. She turned to face him and saw a softer gentler man, one with longing and wanting eyes and to her surprise, directed toward her. He kissed her and she felt herself kissing him in return. Standing nude before him, she felt herself being lead to the marital bed but had no understanding as to why this was happening. Curtis knew that he was engaging the enemy, but tonight was different; he had desire for her something that had long left their marriage. This marriage of lies he thought but tonight he needed her, no, he wanted her.

Nea, come to me baby. She wanted to resist him but the way he called to her made her want him all the more, what in the hell was happening, she screamed internally? Curtis…what are you doing? He stopped looked her in the eyes and responded I'm about to make love to my wife. With that being said he kissed her laid her back on the bed, spread her thighs one from another and kissed her so sweetly between her legs, probing her with his tongue until she moaned his name over and over and over again. Once he saw that he had captured her mind and body he begin to use his fingers to warm the area he would soon penetrate. With every stroke Reneea knew that she would climax one harder than the next. Curtis smiled as if he had conquered Mount Everest and begins to whisper sweetly in her ear. You like it don't you? Yes baby, yes. Do you want me to stop? No, not yet, please not yet. He could feel her warm breath against his skin as she panted for breath…That's it baby make daddy cum, make me cum ooh yeaahhhhhh, shit damn girl! Their love making grew intense, sweat beads began to form indicating the amount of work they were both putting forth to satisfy one another. Curtis could not believe how bad he wanted her. Lost in passion he found himself speaking the words I love you, I love you OH GOD I…. Curtis came hard and strong, he had forgotten how good her body felt to him. They both lay there tired to the point of exhaustion with feelings of guilt as they both had cheated on the people they were cheating with and neither one of them were sorry at that moment that they had.

When they came to themselves, silence fell over the room with thick tension to match. They had not done anything wrong but both lay still feeling as if they had. The light from the TV flickered enough to display shadows of their silhouettes. Reneea attempted to rise from the bed thinking that maybe she could escape the guilt that she was feeling when suddenly Curtis grabbed her arm shook his head no in disapproval while pulling her back to him. She closed her eyes laid in his arms and slept.

Chapter 5

Wearing Guilt

The sun light appeared through the bay window of the breakfast nook and it appeared as if the day was going to be beautiful. Curtis had long before showered away the love from the previous night and left for his daily jog before Reneea arose from her slumber. Once she had, she glanced around the room and decided to change the linen before she would shower. She moved without haste and decided that if she wanted to avoid Curtis she had better leave before his return. She picked just the right outfit and fragrance to match. She dressed and hurried down stairs deciding to skip coffee but still must have taken to long or miscalculated the hour for she failed her mission as Curtis jogged up the long circular drive before she could make her get-away it was inevitable that she would have to face him. The door slammed and show time began.

You're up early. I have a busy day planned with the kids coming down this weekend I want to make sure everything is in order, shopping to do and all. I see. Even with all of the activity of the previous night it seemed as if the Rae's had returned to the normal activity that kept their house from being a home. I see your headache's gone. Excuse me, Reneea was puzzled? Your hair, the band its back. Oh yeah the headache…it disappeared last night. Curtis smiled how he did have an amazing smile. I hope that I had something to do with the loss of tension and if so, looking at her smugly, it was my pleasure. Reneea grabbed the back of her neck and clinched her lips together as if to be embarrassed. Don't worry you don't need to respond…he walked close to her and whispered softly, *"Your juices told me everything you couldn't say"*. Curtis backed away from her with an air of confidence; he was good in bed, he knew it and he made no bones about it. As he continued to back away from the smiling

Reneea, his cell began to ring. Rae here. Good morning, your 8:00 a.m. was pushed back this morning so how about breakfast first. The sultry voice inquired on the other end of the receiver. Oh, ah yeah, thanks for letting me know…I was just leaving. Shall I take that as a yes? No problem, I can make that. Good see you soon Curtis, don't make me wait long. I'll see you shortly. Curtis hung up the cell phone and holstered it on his side. Reneea knew it was Vanessa and the thought didn't seem to bother her at all. Well Curtis that's your cue… What? The call, shouldn't you be leaving or getting ready to? Oh yeah I'm going to head into the office after I shower. I should see you at 6:00 for dinner. Try not to be late remember, Craig's coming. Right, see ya later.

Despite the events of just last night or even prior to his playfulness just moments before the call…it was all just a memory after his shower and change Curtis left the house without so much as a goodbye kiss or an acknowledgement that he was departing from his wife.

It was at this time, Reneea knew she had to make her get away as well. She knew what needed to be done and procrastinating wouldn't help matters. Reneea felt perplexed as she drove along the road, she knew that things weren't normal in her home but for that one night it all appeared to be so very real. She was mixed up inside with a flurry of emotions storming inside of her. She knew that Curtis was her husband, but Rick was her lover. She knew she had to tell him as she would rather he hear it from her and it be down played before he met up with Curtis and in one of their male bonding moments he told him and made it appear as if he had rocked her world and he was king of the hill. However, she did have to admit to herself that she did enjoy the love making even if it were only for one night. Nervously, she called out to her voice activation system in the car. "Phone Rick Neal" the phone instantly started to dial and before long she was engaged in conversation with that smooth mellow voice that made her feel all was right with the world. Good morning. Good morning, did I interrupt your session? No, not at all; as a matter of fact I just finished up. Rick I need to talk to you can I stop by the office for a moment? Sure baby that would make my day actually. I was already preparing myself for two whole days of being without you alone. Reneea smiled knowing that it was hard on both of them when they couldn't be together. Great I'll be there in ten minutes. See you soon.

She drove quickly knowing that she had to get to him before Curtis called. However, she knew that by now he had made it to Vanessa and pampering her for the morning would keep him distracted for quite sometime. Meeting my ass, she thought. Reneea arrived at Rick's studio which was housed in a beautiful brownstone with beautiful landscape all around. As she exited her vehicle she could see him in the window waiting for her to enter. They exchanged pleasant smiles with Rick making a kissing gesture in her direction. The lobby was soft and welcoming she remembered going shopping with Bea to help her remodel the lobby soon after Rick decided to move his studio from the family home. So much love went into that room. She had to keep moving as each time she entered she felt the guilt rise up in her and sometimes it was just to much to bare.

Oh aren't you a sight for sore eyes. Hey baby. They embraced one another and rendered a slight peek on the check as she wasn't sure where Rick's assistant was. Come on back, can I get you a cup of coffee or something. No, no thanks I'm fine. What's wrong baby? You seem tense. Good Lord tense was definitely not the word for what she was feeling. It was more like gut wrenching sickness. Rick…she started to speak slowly. Rick, I need to tell you what happen last night after I got home. Rick's face was confused and puzzled but he knew he needed to hear her out. Baby what? Curtis…Curtis and I…oh Lord she mumbled clasping her forehead in her hands. Bay, you're scaring me what is it…did he hurt you? No, What I'm trying to say is we slept together last night. He smirked…that's not news I don't like it but you sleep together every night, he is your husband…Damn Rick, are you trying to make this difficult for me? Babe what are you talking about. Suddenly, it appeared as if a light went on in his head his smile turned instantly into anguish…You mean to tell me that after we made love you went to that house and fucked him? Rick…what in the hell would you have had me to do? I am his wife! Yeah true enough, but couldn't you get out of it? How in the hell do you think I could have done that? Both at this time were screaming at the top of their voices when Reneea began to cry.

Baby, baby, wait, I'm sorry baby reaching to pull her close to him…I'm sorry, you are so right Honey but, I'm human and though I may have no right to be, I'm jealous…okay I said it. I'm jealous, he has everything and yet he has no idea what he has in you. I love you and I have been in love with you for some time and this is just hard for me to handle. Trying to regain her composure as tears were still rolling down her cheeks, with a trembling voice she proceeded to try and explain. Rick, I only told you so you could hear it from me and not hear it from him and he makes it out to be more than it was. I needed you to know, how bad I felt as if I were cheating on you...my lover, but my hands were tide. They kissed and embraced one another. Slowly he pulled back and looked in her tear stained eyes and begin to wipe her tears away. I'm sorry but I really need to know this. Rick hesitated but managed to get the words out. Yes? Did you enjoy it? Was it reminiscent of your past life together? Reneea knew she had to answer this question with care or risk loosing him to further anger. She wrapped her arms around him, looked him dead in the eye and lied. No. It was pure agony and I had to fake an orgasm just to make him go away. Besides baby how could I have enjoyed him after being drained by you, playful grabbing at the crotch of his slacks? That's what I held on to, remembering how you had just made me feel so damn good all over, that's how I got through it. Rick let out a sigh of relief and kissed her passionately becoming aroused by her words, her touch, her sent and the way she magically made her tongue move with sensuality along with his.

They held each other for a while and Reneea racked with guilt knew she had lied. She knew that there were parts of her that enjoyed the love she had made with Curtis maybe even more than she wanted to admit, but she had to make a good showing so that she would not loose what she felt she had with Rick. He was just far too important to her and she would not hurt him if at all possible. Reflecting on her damage control, she was glad she had told him before Curtis could, because no matter what he would say now, she had laid the foundation and Rick would take the word of the woman he loved over the word of a man who had become his rival any day of the week.

Chapter 6

Life's Masquerade

Curtis arrived at Vanessa's apartment and knew that he was going to have to make love to her in order to calm her down. He wasn't pleased with her demanding tone of voice as if she were in control, however, he wasn't worried. He had her number and knew all the right buttons to push to make her behave. He entered the colorfully decorated apartment, which by the way he was paying for, her taste was different from Reneea's chic and elegant was his home and loud and sassy was his haven of sin he stood thinking as he took off his coat. Laying the coat across the chase lounger he looked at Vanessa and waited for her to respond. Well? Well what? I'm waiting. Waiting for what? Girl, if you don't get your ass off your shoulders and bring those lips over here this minute and properly greet me, there is going to be a problem up in this piece. Vanessa smiled and moved slow and cautiously toward Curtis, licking her lips giving the indication that she was more than willing to bring her lips, hips and anything else he wanted his way. Wrapping her long slender arms around his neck she gave him a slight tug toward her and his body immediately followed. They kissed long, hard, and hungrily for what seemed to be forever. You know you make me crazy right? Ness, you were crazy long before I even entered the picture. They smiled and continued to give one another soft sweet kisses about the face and neck area.

Well did you really ask me here for breakfast, or did you have something else in mind? Vanessa took Curtis by the hand and glanced toward the empty dinning room with a smirk she began to explain. Oh, your going to do some eating, however, the only thing on the menu will be me! How Curtis did love the dirty side of this woman. Everything he wanted to do to her he generally could and did. She was the woman that he used to fulfill all of his lustful desires and fantasies. Some of the ways they made love he would never consider asking Reneea to perform. No Reneea was a princess, the mother of his son…there was no way in hell he would ever ask her to perform such disrespectful acts, not his wife. Yes, as far as Curtis was concerned anal sex was reserved for his nasty girl. Even though there was a part of him that felt love for Vanessa and craved her continuously, he knew that the majority of those feelings were built around lust.

As they approached the bedroom Vanessa turned and faced Curtis, drop to her knees removed his belt, exposed his penis and began to suck him as if her life dependent on his satisfaction. Curtis's eyes rolled to the back of his head as he found himself forcing her head in a downward motion with one hand while he used the other to hold on to the door jamb. Damn baby! Yeah. Suck it…he moaned to her. Vanessa knew what he liked and she was never shy or timid about delivering the goods. Yeah boy, Momma knows what you like. Lay down so I can really do you right. Curtis was so turned on by her he could hardly wait to be inside of her. On the bed Curtis took control and begin to show her just why she loved him so much. Ooh, ooh, damn daddy…wait, bay, Vanessa's breath was staggered to the point that she thought she just might pass out. Curtis had laid her down on the bed and licked her clitoris with a force, gnawing at the lips of her vagina. He knew this drove her absolutely wild. I'm cumming baby, I'mmm Vanessa let a loud shriek, tightened her long legs around Curtis neck and begged him to stop. Whose pussy is this bitch? Who's your daddy hoe? You! You are! It's yours Curtis it's yours bay. You damn right! After making her loose total control he forced himself into her without concern of whether he was gentle or not. He fucked her angrily everywhere there was an opening to receive him. Curtis continued in this manner until he could no longer hold back the eruption that was destined to come. As he ejaculated, he called out her name and made promises of love. Vanessa being too weak to respond had a clear perception that though she may have started out in control, it was Curtis who had won that round.

As the day progressed Reneea had completed every activity on her to do list with time to spare. She felt somewhat better after leaving Rick's studio and confessing what she considered to be her sins, however, she still had mixed feelings regarding the events of the last evening. She knew that after making love to her, Curtis was at this moment with his mistress probably doing the exact same thing to her as he had last night. Shrugging that away from her mind she would have a passing thought of how Curtis had touched her so gently and though she lied to Rick when he asked her if she enjoyed it, she remembered the climax they shared together and how at that moment in time it felt wonderful. Startled by the ringing of her cell phone, she came to herself and answered. Hello? Where are you baby girl? Tina shouted in the receiver. Tina was her best friend and knew her so well…she was the one person that she did not have to pretend with. She knew her inside and out, flaws and all…it didn't matter she was just her friend with no judgments even though she wasn't exactly thrilled about her affair with Rick, she still tried to understand. Hey you, I just left Hiller's Grocery and I'm actually headed in your direction. Good, stop and grab some Chinese and have lunch with me. Chinese again, what up with that? There are other food selections you know. Yeah but that's what I want and since I came up with the idea, that's what we're eating. Tina was such a smart ass, but Reneea didn't mind. Whatever, call it in at Fongs and I'll see you in ten. Cool.

Tina was the owner of a temporary staffing company in the suburbs which actually did quite well. Her plan was to become the agency that was a household name and without a doubt, it definitely was. Reneea envied her friend for that at times, she loved the fact that she worked, ran a house hold, and was large in the business sector without the aid of her husband. She was proud of her friend who worked her way from being the help to employing the help. Curtis always thought it best that Reneea was a stay home mom, who ran the house took care of his son and feed his ego. Why had she given him her life? Why didn't she work? Yes, she was comfortable as Mrs. Rae financially but in the eye of everyone it was Curt's money. But never get it twisted; if ever she decided to leave…she was leaving with half if not more! Vanessa would have to have her leftovers and it would not be in her home.

Come on in here girl, I'm starving, Tina yelled from her office. What's up with you? I'm tired. Dealing with these damn clients can sometimes make me want to scream. Here's your order. Thanks. Aren't you going to eat? Yeah, my stomachs a little upset right now. I will in a minute. Reneea pushed the cartons of food away. Tina hesitated in mid movement, studied her friend and spoke matter-of-factly. Hell naw! What is it?

Girl I'm fine. Fine my ass! Let's hear it. Reneea didn't know if she had the strength to relive the whole sorted tale but because she knew Tina, and she knew she would not let it go, she told the story all over again.

After hearing her friends story, shock registered all over her face...Oh my God are you serious? Yes...Tina began to laugh uncontrollably spilling food and gasping for breath. What in the hell do you find so funny T? You, bitch! Only you could get caught up in some madness like this. Reneea was obviously annoyed, and Tina noticed and immediately began to make amends. Baby girl, I'm sorry, I didn't mean to make fun. It's just that this is just so unbelievable. You and Curtis made love right after you left Rick? She shook her head from side to side made a slight smile and began to speak to Reneea in a somber tone...Girl I know your kitty-cat was wore the hell out! Silence fell across the room and almost immediately laughter erupted from both women simultaneously. Tina, you have no idea. Damn girl. Well how do you feel? I don't know? I still love Rick, my feelings haven't changed, my body still wants him...but Curtis did make me feel good on the other hand, and I am his wife. Do you think he stopped seeing the secretary hoe? No, are you kidding...she dropped a booty call this morning. Uh what? Yeah. I think it was just one of those things. He was up and I was available. No I don't think so...I think he took notice last night for a reason. Probably to see if he still had it like that. I don't know Nae-Nae, just be careful. I will. Look I've got so much to do before tonight's dinner I've got to run, you and Mike are still coming right? Girl wouldn't miss it; I haven't seen my God son in so long I need to make sure that he is still the same boy. They both smiled hugged and Reneea left.

The intercom buzzed and broke Curtis' train of thought. Mr. Rae? Yes Charlotte? Your documents have arrived for signature and if you have a few moments I need to discuss a staffing issue with you? No problem come on up and we'll take a brief meeting. On my way.
Charlotte was the manager of Rae Enterprises, she was responsible for every employee employed with the firm they all answered to her with the exception of Vanessa Winters, she was Curtis' assistant and needless to say there was no love loss between the two women. Charlotte had worked hard for Curtis in the early years and it was known to all that her hard work and allegiance had pretty much earned her permanent fixture status at the company, as Vanessa had asked Curtis to let her go on numerous

occasions only to have her request fall on death ear. Curtis was a smart business man and nothing, not even his mistress would tamper with that. Charlotte knew that Curtis was sleeping with Vanessa but chose to keep silent though her disapproval was dutifully noted. Not that she had a love interest in Curtis herself, but that she was fond of Reneea and her loyalty was devoted to her. Though she did not work in the firm, she was always very good to her and members of her staff for years.

Annoyed by the very thought that Charlotte would not reverence her presence, her pit-bull instincts always kicked in where Curtis was concerned. Where are you going? Vanessa snapped as Charlotte walked past her desk to enter Curtis' office suite. Excuse me? I think you heard me? You don't just barge in…your announced. Mr. Rae is expecting me and these important documents in my hand, and since I just hung up the phone with him just seconds ago, I do believe that it would be senseless to announce what he is waiting for. They glared at each other with an intensity that could have been fatal. Charlotte smirked and pushed past Vanessa. Vanessa turned to return to her task, mumbling "bitch". Charlotte who had heard the remark smiled because she had ultimately gotten under her skin and knew it, and as history always had a way of repeating itself, knew that the opportunity to get her back for this little remark she made under her breath would present itself.

Curt, you really need to do something about your watchdog out there. Come on now, lets not go there…Curtis she is rude, disrespectful and clueless. Char…No Curtis, your business with her is your business but please inform her that there is only one Mrs. Rae and until I am informed other wise, she ain't it. Curtis amused at the rivalry did as always smooth it over by reassuring Charlotte that he would take care of the matter. Okay Char, I will handle it. Now may I have those documents? Allowing her a moment to get a grip, he looked over the paperwork and found everything to be in order, but then again he had no reason to believe that they wouldn't be as Charlotte was one hell of an enforcer and he knew when she was assigned a task, it was done and followed to the letter. Alright, as always this is good; let it fly. Very well, consider it gone this afternoon. Charlotte looked up to see Curtis looking past her shoulder with a stunned look on his face and turned to see what the distraction was. To her pleasant surprise, she saw a vision of loveliness entering the lobby in a crisp white linen pants suite with rhinestone studded pumps with long flowing hair that commanded attention, and at that point could not help but wonder why a man who had steak at home for the last 25 years had decided to settle for chopped liver? All of the employees greeted her with the utmost respect and were genuinely pleased to see her and often got a kick out of what her presence did to Vanessa's ego.

Vanessa. Mrs. Rae. Is Curtis inside? Yes bu...Before she could finish her sentence, Reneea smiled moved past her and opened the door but stopping short of entering turning around to engage Vanessa in brief conversation. Oh Vanessa? Yes Mrs. Rae? I just want to thank you for the beautiful flowers you sent for Curtis, they really were lovely, but keep in mind my birthday is in June, our *Anniversary* is in August sweetie and with another year rolling around, I can hardly wait to see what you will come up with next. Reneea gracefully smiled and shut the door on a stammering Vanessa.
Charlotte thought that she would piss her pants she wanted to laugh that bad, but kept her composure for Curtis' sake.

Charlotte, how are you dear? The two of them hugged, it was a genuine greeting between the two. I'm fine, don't you look lovely, and that hair...I would kill for hair like yours. Girl, stop. Doesn't she look beautiful Curt? You took the words right out of my mouth. Curtis was stunned to see her, but at the same time pleasantly surprised. She was a beautiful woman, there was no denying that. Reneea turned to face Curtis and her hair swung in motion with her body movement and he found himself attracted to his wife once again and confused all at the same time.

So, babe what brings you to the office? At that moment Charlotte sensed that she should make her exit interrupting a conversation that looked as if it would borderline on flirtation and sincerity, Guys; I have work to do so will you excuse me please? Charlotte it was lovely to see you again dear we should do lunch at the house soon. I look forward to it. Charlotte had purposely opened the door so that Vanessa could hear the conversation. As she left the office suite, she smirked at Vanessa and openly uttered the words, "*Check Mate Bitch*" laughing out loud as she proceeded down the hall. Vanessa was furious but needed to pay attention to what was going on behind closed doors at this moment.

Curtis, I'm sorry to stop by unannounced but there is something wrong with my credit card and I was wondering if you could check it out? No problem which one? My business account card, they say it's closed. Closed? Um hum. Let me see it. She move seductively toward Curtis and he almost became aroused but knew that Vanessa was just outside the door. Why are you so dressed up? Well I didn't want to come into the office looking a wreck. Your hair is down again, another head ache? No, not at all, this was deliberate, Angie my stylist wanted to do something different today. It looks great; she should do it more often. Holding in the smile that she felt forming as her husband showered her with long overdue attention and compliments, she managed to speak…Thank you. Just at that moment the accounting department came on the line and replied that Mrs. Rae closed the account according to the credit company and that she would have to wait ten business days to received another while they fixed the mix up. As she knew she hadn't closed her account, she had a good idea as to who had. Vanessa had struck again.

Sorry baby, I don't know what happen, but the accounting department will get to the bottom of it rest assured. No problem, I was trying to buy items for the party and was declined. Luckily, I had cash on me. Ooh, here let me give you some money. No that's alright. No, I insist, will $500.00 suffice until I get home? Curtis, hesitating as though shocked at the amount that will be more than plenty. Then here you are. Curtis gave her the money in her hand, playfully snatching it back as he watched for her reaction. At that moment he decided to playfully move closer to her slowly leaving very little distance between them. What do I get in return? Beg your pardon? Reneea shocked at his question looked intrigued by his bold actions toward her. He moved up close to her touching her on her cheek softly repeating the question. *"What do I get in return? I don't stutter last I checked"*. Flirtatiously licking her lips she replied, Well, what is it that you would like? He took the money placed it in her hand and with his other hand he gently stroked her vaginal area causing Reneea's eyes to widen and her lips to part. Curtis, are you suggesting that I sleep with you for money? Curtis smiled with that ever so beautiful million dollar smile and replied; don't make it sound so dirty…besides Nea…sleeping is not what I had in mine.

Reneea took the money put it in her purse, and thought to herself. Damn, I killed to birds with one stone. Vanessa hates me a little bit more and

Curtis wants me even more. She smiled kissed Curtis on the lips and
backed away turning slowly and allowing her hair to cast that spell she
knew it would. She looked over her shoulder to find Curtis smiling with a
longing in his eyes and knew she had achieved her objective. Reneea?
Yes? Walking toward her slowly with his wallet in his hands, here's
another $500.00 buy something sexy to wear tonight in public and private.
Reneea slowly removed the money from Curtis' hand, folded it in half and
slid into her brazier teasing him like a call girl taking payment for services
rendered, opened the door closed it behind her and gave Vanessa a look
that let her know that she was the wife, in charge, and there was not a
damned thing she could do to change that.

Two seconds after Reneea's departure, Vanessa entered Curtis' office mad
as hell and the slamming of the door let him know just what she felt.

Would you like to explain that little bullshit visit? Vanessa…Don't
Vanessa me, what the hell was she doing here? Why in the hell wouldn't
you warn me that she was coming so I could at least have left for lunch so
I did not have to see my man involved or shall I say engaging his bitch ass
wife right in front of my damn….That will be enough out of you V,
especially when you brought that shit on yourself! What? Don't play
stupid with me woman, you know damn well that you are behind her
credit card being closed. How many times do I have to tell you to keep my
home life out of this? You don't fuck around in her territory and not
expect repercussions? What the hell do you mean her territory, the last
time I checked you belong to me…she is your wife on paper and in that
damned house, but this is my domain. Vanessa, I will only tell you once,
my son, my wife…the shit is not open for debate. Vanessa's feelings were
openly wounded and Curtis knew it he had cut her deep, but what else
could he do? He had to maintain order and Vanessa knew that she had
treaded in an area she could not win. She began to cry and Curtis knew
damage control was in order especially since he wasn't sure of what to
make of his sudden interest in Reneea and that the woman in the room
with him right now was the woman who made him feel so alive, sexy and
in charge. He knew that he was not ready to compromise his freak for his
good girl. No, he had to maintain his balance. "V" baby, come here, he
called to Vanessa the way he did whenever he wanted to make her feel
like she was the only one and would one day be and as always, it worked.
She slowly went to him as she really loved him and could not bare the fact

that she could possibly loose what time she had with him period. Curtis put his arms around her waist and began to wipe away the tears that she had shed. He pulled her close to him and fed her a line of garbage that melted every anxiety she was experiencing at that moment and time.

I love you and you know it, but sometimes you make me so angry with your jealousy…But Curtis…No, listen to me…I need you, no one makes me feel as good as you do baby. You believe me don't you? He looked at Vanessa waiting for her to validate him kissing her softly on her cheeks, nose and lips. She managed to pull herself together and respond. Yes, I do, I just get so mad at the thought of her with you, I hate it and I do little things that make me feel better when you're with her. I'm sorry baby how can I make it up to you? Curtis smiled as he knew he was back in control. Unfortunately, we have some work to do…but I think we could manage a little something right quick. Vanessa's eyes widen as she knew he had forgiven her and she would have the opportunity to be with him before the long agonizing weekend that he would be away from her and she wanted to make it good. Tell me what you want daddy and I'm here to please.

At that moment she saw the bulge in Curtis' pants and dropped to her knees to service him just the way he liked it. There he sat on the edge of his big massive desk allowing his mistress to suck him passionately and though it was feeling the way that only she made him feel, he could not shake the image of Reneea's face as he remembered her in his arms the night before and then just moments ago as she playfully excepted the money placing it away for safe keeping in her bra leaving him with the thought of later.

Vanessa completed her task and Curtis came with delight, watching her clean his genitals he decided at that moment to leave the office for the day knowing that this would be the last time that they would be together until Monday as this weekend he would be playing the role of the good family man. He had no intentions on letting her leave empty handed…He kissed her softly, thanked her for the favor and placed $500.00 dollars in her hand for her to treat herself to the spa while he was away. Happy with the small token of his appreciation, she kissed him softly, told him how much she loved him and left the office as if she were Queen of the world, satisfied with the thought that her man was well pleased with her and that no one, not even Mrs. Rae made him feel the way she did.

Chapter 7

Hey Hey The Gangs All Here

6 o'clock had rolled around and Reneea was ever so excited, Craig and Angel were coming home and she would be able to mother them and have company in that big old house. She smiled to herself when she reminisced over the wedding and rehearsal dinner, how she loved throwing parties and entertaining their friends, they hardly ever did that now especially since Bea had past. She was screwing Rick, Curtis was with his whore, and Michael and Tina were in the middle of all this nonsense. It would be good for everyone to be together again, however, hard it would be to be in the room with Rick knowing that he was just feet or inches away and she could not have him. The more she thought about it, it sort of turned her on to know that they had a secret that no one knew with the exception of Tina and she wasn't telling. Tina and Reneea were friends from childhood and there is no way they would sell one another out…no way in hell.

The phone rang and brought Reneea out of her thought, "Hello", Mom? Hey baby where are you? We are close just wanted to let you know we should be arriving very shortly and that Angel's mom and dad are looking forward to dinner tonight. Thanks for inviting them, Angel says. No problem dear, my pleasure. Listen, I just wanted to touch base with you, we should see you shortly, and did you cook all my favorites? You know I did boy! That's my girl. Listen, get off this phone and drive safe…I'll see you both when you get here. Okay mommy, see you. Love you. I love you too.

Reneea hung up the phone and decided she had better get dressed before company started to arrive. She turned down her pot to simmer everything was ready way ahead of schedule all that was left to do was slow cook the brandy wine sauce to her famous French Chicken, and took off to the master bath to shower. She did just what Curtis had instructed. The last thing she needed was more clothes but she thought since he was being so generous she might as well take him up on his offer. She did have impeccable taste. She knew how to be provocative and sexy without sluttish tactics, her body was toned for her age and she worked out to make sure that she maintained it that way, so it was easy to find apparel that would look as though it was wearing her. She slipped on the black laced thong with a black lacey satin bra that matched. It was trimmed in rhinestones that really made the ensemble. The thong had garter belts that held the smooth silky stocking in place, she slid on her black leather Prada Pumps but then decided that her Jimmy Choos would look much better with the sexy rhinestone back v cut Vera Wang Cocktail Dress that screamed sexy from the hanger to her shoulders. She was very impressed with her outfit and could not wait to see the looks on Rick's and to be honest Curtis' faces.

After carefully applying the right blend of make up, making sure her hair was flawless, she went downstairs and made herself a drink before dinner, she had to admit she was feeling awesome about her day. She had planned the perfect evening, shopped until her heart was content and made Curtis' mistress hate her more than she did the prior day. As she smiled about the dangerous office encounter, she thought about how good she was in playing the lover's game and quietly patted herself on the back for her accomplishments. Reneea heard the kitchen door open and knew it was Curtis arriving for the evening, but she wasn't expecting the other voices to accompany him. As luck would have it Rick, Tina and Michael had all arrived at the same time. Reneea? Where are you? I'm in the bar! Everyone headed in her direction, each with directives to poor them one too. Curtis was the first to enter the room looking as if he had never seen his wife before, and everyone else pretty much followed suit. Curtis was speechless gazing on the lovely vision that stood before him, Rick also stunned by how beautiful she was could only shake his head, Mike, who was not in the least attracted to his wife's best friend even had to take a second look. Leave it to Tina who would break the ice for them all. Damn! Girl what fucking fashion magazine threw up on you? Bitch, you are over dressed, but hoe you sharp! Everyone broke out in laughter even Reneea, herself. Shut up girl you so damn crazy what do you want to drink? Whatever's wet? After the laughter died down Curtis walked over to

Reneea and put his arm around her waist kissed her on her cheek smiled still taking inventory of her radiant beauty, softly whispered in her ear…*I can fuckin hardly wait to see what you purchased for private?* Knowing the inside joke, Reneea smiled and said *you shall get what you paid for.* Curtis took a sip of her drink from her glass patted her on her butt and walked off toward the kitchen to answer his ringing cell phone. Once in the clear, Rick made his way over to Reneea as Angels' parents the Coopers, had arrived and were in deep conversation with Tina and Mike.

Damn Ms. Rae, what are you trying to do to a brother? He asked as he candidly brushed up against her playfully stroking her hair out of her face, what… you wanna make him catch a case? Now why would you say that? You looking all good causing your husband to want to touch on my woman and I am having a hard time controlling my urge to keep from choking that nigga in front of everybody while at the same time refraining from grabbing you and fucking you in the room in front of everyone. Rick, your mouth is so dirty. She smiled and lovingly without being spotted, stroked his arm with her fingers and with her other hand rubbed the crotch of his pants. She teased him as if she were a professional licking her lips blowing him kisses that only he could see.

On the real, you look especially beautiful tonight; there is not a woman on earth at this moment that could compare to you. His eyes were so loving and filled with affection for her and she knew that he was sincere in what he said. Thank you Rick, I can't tell you how much your words mean to me, at least not for now. But I promise when this weekend is over with, you will know and experience all my gratitude. She felt herself longing to be touched by him and handled in just that way that only he knew how to handle her…the way she liked it. At that moment she was startled by the deep baritone voice she knew all to well…

Ma, she glanced across the room as she heard the commotion of everyone welcoming the long awaited guest of honor, and saw her son. Craigy, she sang out emotionally. Hey baby, Angel look at you aren't you a sight for sore eyes. She kissed her daughter-in-law before she turned her complete attention to her son and noticed that Angel looked particularly lovely almost as if she were glowing. Boy I swear you are getting more and more handsome everyday! Mom, I believe you are bias, as he smiled and hugged his mother that he had been much taller than since eighth grade.

Are you starving, you must be everything is ready. Reneea, let the boy get in and take his coat off, she heard Curtis say as he re-entered the room. Hey man! What's up dad? The two men exchanged masculine hugs and hand shakes. Reneea looked onward and was immediately reminded why she had never left Curtis, it was all for the sake of her son's stability and well being even into adulthood; she needed him to have that in his life and promised that she would never come between that. Looking at the two of them together made her feel that all was right with the world. Craig was the spitting image of his father and the beautiful factors of Curtis had been transferred to their son outwardly. They were both so handsome, she saw the younger version of Curtis when she looked at her son, the Curtis she fell in love with and understood Angel's attraction to her son as she herself had fallen captive once before to a man quite the same. If she were honest with herself, she knew deep down inside there were parts of her that would always belong to Curtis for that very reason.

Baby, maybe we had better sit down to dinner. Rick and Mike need to chase their alcohol with some food. Everyone laughed and agreed with Curtis' observation. Dinner was served and everyone was enjoying the wonderful food and conversation. Rick was catching up with his God son as Curtis and Bill Cooper traded conversation about business, Angel and Mike were dead locked in political conversation and Tina working her way through Vodka Martinis amused me and Rita about everything from her business deals to shopping. Everyone was really enjoying the evening. Periodically, Reneea would look over and catch Rick looking at her and she tried her best not to stare but she couldn't help but return the glances as she found herself imagining him inside of her earlier and thinking to herself that it would be a full three days before she would be able to lay with him and quench her desire to be pleased. Curtis continued to ignore the cell phone that vibrated in his pocket every hour on the hour as it was Vanessa and he knew that there would be no way to excuse himself to attend to her needs and desires as all eyes were on he and Reneea. Though he wanted to be with Vanessa, he could not get his mind off of how fabulous Reneea looked tonight. Though in a conversation with Angel's father, he periodically would glance over at her and remember making love to her the night before and her earlier visit to his office.

Hey Rick can you help me get more wine out of storage? Yeah man, excuse me Craig let me help your feeble daddy out…you know he's getting old? Nigga, whatever, I can still take your ass on the court… Put your money where your mouth is man that's all I'm saying. Everyone was amused by their rivalry. Imagine if Curtis only knew that they were both in competition for Reneea's heart.

You mean to tell me you couldn't carry two lousy bottles of wine upstairs? Naw man, I need to make a call and I need you to block for me…Man. Please nigga, I would do it for you. You wouldn't have too if I had that beautiful ass woman upstairs waiting for me. Curtis looked at Rick with disapproval…Don't start Father Rick… Man I am just stating the obvious. She is looking damn good tonight man you right about that. I know this. I didn't tell you earlier it slipped my mind actually. What? We fucked last night. Rick trying not to look pissed off but rather surprised as Reneea had already told him the sorry story once. What? Yeah man, it surprised me too. She came in from being with Tina, and her hair was down, she had been drinking and its no secret that she has a banging ass body, I had been with V and I guess I hadn't had my fill and she looked so hot that it got me excited and I started feeling her and one thing lead to another and we made love.
Rick thinking to himself that he would hardly call it making love, more like playing the part of a woman who had been condemned to a death sentence. Man you ain't right. What? She is my wife….At that moment his cell rang again for the tenth time. Hello. Baby, I can't do this I know I promised to behave for you this weekend, but I miss you daddy…the thought of her with you all weekend is killing me, don't be mad at me. I just needed to hear you say you love me before I go to sleep, the sultry voice demanded from the receiver. V, baby you know I love you. This will be over soon, I promise. We will go away next weekend I promise, just don't keep calling me, I wont be able to get away. Okay, I'll try but at least Curtis call to check on me. I will baby goodnight and I miss you. Miss you too babe. See you soon.

Rick looked at Curtis with pure contempt and knew that some how, some way he had to free Reneea from his grasp. The two men grabbed the wine and headed back upstairs to find that the Coopers were preparing to leave and Mike and Tina felt that they should follow them. Angel was looking a little tired after polishing off her third glass of Orange Juice which Reneea thought to be odd but never made mention of it. Craig noticing his wife's fatigue stated that they should also retire for the night as the drive had been a little long due to construction on virtually every Michigan major interstate. With Rick being solo, he felt that was his cue to depart. At that moment Reneea pulled a surprising move that Rick never expected.

Rick, I know you love my French Chicken and I know that if you don't take a plate you will stop and purchase fast food for your midnight snack so come in the kitchen with me and let me fix you a plate to go and I will not take no for an answer. Rick looking totally surprised threw up both hands with a smile broad and wide. Guilty, he said looking into Reneea's eyes, and followed Reneea to the kitchen as Curtis assisted Craig and Angel upstairs and had practically insisted that he follow his wife's instructions bid his friend goodnight and left him in the capable hands of his wife. I guess I will say my goodbyes now Uncle Rick until tomorrow? Craig, it was good to see you two and I will see you tomorrow for the game. Bet. Love ya man, love you too. He kissed Angel on the forehead as always, shook Curtis' hand and turned his attention to Reneea who was packing food into Tupperware containers.

After everyone had made their way upstairs, Reneea pulled Rick into the pantry where she kissed him and touched him intimately causing him to moan her name. Knowing that their time was limited and that they risked being caught at any second, they both got their composure and knew without words being said that it was time for Rick to make his departure. He looked back at her and mouthed the words I love you without sound; she in turn did the same. Rick picked up the bags of leftovers and proceeded to exit. She waved to him as she could see him getting into his Convertible Jaguar, chained and locked the door, shut off the lights and started upstairs. She thought of him going home and the fact that she would not be with him and decided that she would do whatever necessary to get through this weekend and keep her son's world safe.

As she entered the bedroom that she shared with Curtis, she noticed that the lights were dim and that mellow jazz was playing through the speakers in the master suite. As she continued to enter the room she noticed candles burning and Curtis waiting for her with a glass of wine extended toward her. She took notice of his smile which was beautiful since the first day they met and knew that he had not forgotten his request of earlier nor had he forgotten how she had cosigned his advances as well.

Is this for me? But, of course, who else? She accepted the glass took a sip and then in one sweeping motion decided to drink the whole glass without stopping only to extend her glass to request more. My, my thirsty are we? I figure that if you get me drunk and take advantage of me, I can't be held liable for what I do? Curtis filled the glass to the top and encouraged her to drink up as there was plenty more where that came from. God, Nea, I can't get over how beautiful you were tonight. Thank you. No, I mean it. I don't know when I have seen you lovelier. Feeling the effects of the wine, which also had the affect to make her horny, she noticed that there was candle light coming from the Jacuzzi area of the master bath.

Curtis, are you planning to seduce me in there? Baby I will seduce you anywhere you like. Reneea begin to undo the buttons on her dress and Curtis quickly came to her aid. Here baby, let me assist you with that. Curtis began to unbutton her dress slowly enjoying every minute of her surrender to him. Once each button had been handled with care, he unzipped her dress which fell immediately to the floor. Curtis could not believe his eyes when the sexy undergarments were revealed. He knew that tonight he would be pleased and that he and Reneea would make love even better than the night before. He knew that it would not be the hot steamy sex that he was accustomed to with Vanessa, but it would suffice for the time being until he could get to his bad girl and have her in everyway imaginable.

Reneea could feel the heat coming from Curtis' body. By this time, the wine had settled in causing her to desire him even though she truly wanted Rick. She was horny due to the amount of wine consumed and Curtis would due for now, she just needed to have an orgasm by any means necessary.

Reneea began to remove the remainder of her apparel, when she was interrupted by Curtis. Stop, I want to do that. Surprised, but intrigued, she did as he had commanded. Walking over to him seductively, sipping on the remaining wine in her glass, she noticed that he had removed all of his clothing and his penis was so erect that she found herself feeling desire for him. Yeah, come over here. Curtis removed everything she was wearing piece by piece and guided her to the Jacuzzi. Once safely inside, Curtis began to kiss her passionately, it was hard to believe that these were two people who were seeing other people outside of their marriage. She encouraged him to continue his barrage of kisses sweet and softly the water and steam was warm and comforting creating a relaxed atmosphere and Reneea found herself caught up in the moment. Don't stop Curtis; kiss me baby, that's just how I like it. You like it baby? Yeah…her breathing was staggered and slow. Her eyes rolled back in her head and Curtis feed off of every emotion she displayed his way.

Finally, Reneea had reached the point of where she needed love to be made to her and she wasn't shy about letting him know. Curtis take me to bed now, I need to feel you inside of me right now! Curtis was so turned on by Reneea's forcefulness; all he could do was comply with her wishes. Guiding her to the bed he noticed that Reneea appeared to be different than she was normally when they made love. She was focused and controlled and he found this to be a total turn on. It was almost as if she was some sort of bad girl herself. He did not recognize his wife at all.

Curtis laid Reneea back on the bed and began to kiss her tenderly. At that moment Reneea grabbed Curtis by the head and forced him down to her vagina and demanded that he kiss her there. Come on baby, I want to feel your tongue on my clit, make it wet baby, ooh make it wet, come on bitch, make me cum. Curtis was caught off guard by his wife's behavior, but he was so turned on by it that he did everything she demanded him to do. Curtis performed oral sex on her until she could hardly stand it. She thrashed back and forth in the bed damn near pushing herself off the bed. Curtis, who had been following instructions up to this point was totally into his wife's behavior, he decided that Mr. Nice Guy was out of the window and began to fuck her like a two dollar whore and to his surprise Reneea fell right in line with everything that he did to her.

The highlight of the evening came when Reneea made a request of him that he never thought would ever take place between he and his wife, this action was generally reserved just for his lover.

Reneea whispered softly…*Curtis, fuck me in my ass baby, I need it and I want it. I want to feel violated by you in everyway, come on baby give it to me damn it.* Curtis aiming to please grabbed Reneea forced her over onto her stomach, rubbed saliva on himself thoroughly and her rectum area, as there was no time for searching for lubricant in fear that he might break the mood, and began to force himself into her like a ravishing rapist. It was tight and it seemed as if it would not fit…Reneea moaned in agony and pleasure. When Curtis asked if he should stop, Reneea became belligerent. Damn it! I will tell you when to stop! Stop being a pussy! Fuck Me! Curtis was stunned but pleased with his instruction and did just what she said. One final forceful trust and he was inside her stroking her as if that was the way sex was intended to be. Reneea, could feel him inside of her, at one point she imagined him to be Rick who often entered her in this fashion, and she was pleased with the momentary fantasy. With every stroke she moaned and whimpered her cries for Curtis to stop fell on death ear as he was enjoying the tightness of her rectum, the panting of breath, and the moans that came rapidly from Reneea. With every stroke he felt himself becoming more forceful and at the peak of his penetration, he came violently inside her causing her to cry out. She loved what he had done to her and felt her body contract with each orgasm. Curtis was not sure as to what had just taken place, but he knew that he had just been introduced to a dark side of his wife that he had no clue existed and he knew that this was worth staying home for. They kissed a lay in each others arms exhausted and ready for sleep.

Chapter 8

Change is Coming

Curtis being the physical fitness fanatic that he was had risen early to perform his daily run and upon returning to the house he smelled fresh brewed coffee that alerted him to the fact that his sleeping beauty wife had awaken and began to start the days festivities. While removing his running shoes that he was never allowed to wear on Reneea's beautiful wood floor, he noticed that his wife was standing directly in front of him with a cup of hot coffee prepared just for him. He couldn't remember the last time this gesture had been performed at home by her, but then again a lot of things had taken place in the last two to three days that had him asking himself, who was this woman and what the hell had they done with the wife he had been so ready to leave if only circumstance and situations would present the opportunity.

For me?
Yes sir.
Thank you! Curtis smiled and removed the warm substance he craved every morning from her well manicure hands. Be careful, it's hot. Caught off guard by her concern and generosity, Curtis smiled and winked as he warmly thanked her and kissed her forehead. I really didn't expect you to be awake yet. Well, I thought with Angel's mom and dad coming for brunch, I had better get started in my preparation, not to mention the need for a hangover remedy had driven her out of bed. Although Reneea had called the caterers to provide this mornings meal she stilled needed to make sure that every detail down to the flatware on the table was perfect. She was very anal in this manner, she often wished that she could relax her standards but growing up in the household she was reared in it was just

47

something that had been imbedded in her that she knew would be apart of her for the rest of her life.

I guess…when I left this morning, you were sound asleep. Yeah, I was pretty exhausted from the whole day yesterday, looking at the date of the coffee creamer making a mental note that she would need to purchase more. The whole day huh, sounding skeptical as he knew full well that he and the wine played a major role in her sluggish mood. The marathon love making session was surely something to write home about and would definitely have all ears in a gym locker room where most men revealed the highlights of their sex life. Yeah, she answered smugly rolling her eyes. After last night's little performance I was worried that you may not want to get up for brunch much less anything else. Curtis had this terrible way of making Reneea blush where their love making was concerned and always had. She walked over to Curtis and placed her fingers over his lips as to quiet his conversation. They were close as he looked down into her eyes he could see that it was not a topic for discussion, kissed her fingers and backed away slowly. Curtis? Yes Nea? What happens in Vegas, stays in Vegas…let's just keep last night between lovers, not friends she said with a curt smile and a wink of an eye. Mimicking, a popular television commercial, she had just given direct instruction and Curtis read her loud and clear. But what had taken place between them last night was so sexy, stimulating, and satisfying that he thought he might die if he did not brag to Rick about the best night of sex he had shared with his wife in ages. He had to tell him what a freak his sweet innocent little wife had transformed into right before his very eyes. The problem with that was Rick was already very knowledgeable about the different styles of love making when it came to Reneea Rae, as he had been her instructor for years now and generally on the receiving end of her generosity. Reneea, knew she could always fall back on she was drunk, or that she had no choice in the matter as he is her husband and what else could she do? But deep down inside, she knew that everything that transpired did not have to and that she gave him more of herself than she would have any other time. She made love to him last night like a woman in love, but in love with whom? No, she couldn't let Rick know that she had given Curtis what was generally reserved for him, her wild side. Wife or no wife, he would not get past this as easily as he did before by her down playing what really took place. Besides she did not understand the change that was taking place between them and knew that Curtis had not changed over night and planned to stop seeing Vanessa and be the husband he should. No way! And with this in mind, she was not anywhere near ready to surrender her relationship with Rick all because a little wine brought out what she was really feeling for him.

Well I guess I had better take a shower before the kids get up and the Cooper's arrive. Besides I have one little business call to make, Charlotte is handling it for the most part, but I still need to be up to date with the projects progress, so if you will excuse me, I will see you in a bit. Sure, no problem, I have a few things still to attend to before everything is started. Curtis handed Reneea his coffee mug, patted her on her backside sweetly and walked away disappearing up the circular staircase to their bedroom. How she did still find him to be attractive, all the physical activity he performed definitely paid off…he still looked good like the days of college when he played ball. His walk had not changed much and the bowlegged stance still could cast a spell on any woman in her right mind. Yeah, he was still the Prom King in her eyes which made it harder for her to resist his new found interest in their relationship. Remembering work to be done, she placed the mug in the sink, freshened her coffee and proceeded to the dinning room to give it one last once over before the caterers arrived.

Craig and Angel were still in their room playfully enjoying one another's company. Craig! Stop! Do you want your parents to hear us? Girl, I am a grown man in bed with my beautiful wife, do you think that my parents think we are still virgins? Laughing together, No silly, it's just that they are right in the next room. I don't seem to remember you caring about that before we were married making love here on spring and winter breaks while we were in college? Angel struck Craig in the chest to make him hush. Craig that was different, we were kids that didn't know any better. Girl, do you expect me to wait for some loving all weekend, pulling her close to him in defiance. No, baby stop, you know I can't handle when you suck on my neck like that, that's why we are in the shape we are in now. Craig rubbed her belly gently that had slightly begun to show the evidence of their love and commitment to one another. Yeah, you're right about that and I can hardly wait to be the father to them that mine has been to me. You're going to be a wonderful father Craig; I am so blessed to have you as my husband and more importantly my friend. They kissed warmly and lay there looking into each other's eyes.

I am so nervous about telling our folks. Yeah, I know me too, but I'm excited man. I thought last night that my mother knew. Me too, she kept watching me drink the orange juice and each time she poured wine for everybody especially my favorite brand that I know she went out and got just for me and was trying to give me a glass and I would refuse…ooh I knew what she had to be thinking. Craig chuckled and shook his head, remembering the glowing comment she had made in reference to Angel. Yeah, my moms picks up on everything. But the best thing about her is that she has always been able to keep my secrets and let me make my own way, you know. Yeah. This is going to be quite an adjustment for everybody, Twins, can you believe it? They are going to be grandparents…how can somebody as sexy as your momma be called Granny? My mom maybe…but yours, hell no! Laughter erupts from both. I know did you see that dress she was wearing? My dad could not keep his eyes off of her. I don't think any man in the room could last night. I think I heard them getting it on when I went down stairs for your juice. Are you serious? Yeah man. Now that's nasty. Girl please… at least somebody in this house was getting some action. Angel pushed Craig back on the bed playfully, kissing him. I love you Angel Rae. I love you Craig Rae. The two kissed more intensely and within a matter of moments Craig found himself being pleased by his pregnant wife who had politely climbed on top of him inserting him inside her, relieving him of the love that had built up inside him during their conversation. Angel loved to please her husband and knew for him there was nothing she would not do as that was how he treated her. The two climaxed together, and as Craig was worried about hurting the babies when they made love now, he was gentle with her which made Angel desire him more, he had never been a selfish lover, he always made sure that she was being fulfilled and satisfied just as he was, and now he took precaution to a new level. He didn't hold back, but he was very conscious of the fact that his wife was carrying his precious cargo and there was nothing in his control that he would or would not do to make sure that both she and they were safe. They lay on the bed afterwards, feeling good about the news that they were going to share with their family and enjoyed the delight of the love they had just made.

After showering and getting dressed Angel and Craig joined his parents who were downstairs in the great room. Well look who finally made it up? Good morning. Morning. Craig leaned over to kiss his mother on the forehead, it was really endearing to her as he had done it since he was a small boy after seeing his father do it for years. She remembered the conversation they had with him about why daddy always kissed his mother and they explained that it was a sign of showing love for one another. They had to explain why the lips were reserved for the husband and wife. The whole conversation took half the day, but by the end he understood and had a lesson that he would one day pass along. Mom, ma…Reneea was brought out of her memory lane, by the sound of her son calling. I'm sorry baby, what did you say? Where is the grub? They are setting up now and Bill and Rita called and said that they were ten minutes away so it won't be long now. Cool, I'm starving. Angel? Ma'am? How are you feeling this morning dear? Did you rest well? Oh yes I always get a good nights sleep when I'm here that bed is so comfortable. I keep telling Craig we have got to get a mattress like that. What's wrong with the one we have? It's old and lumpy in spots. I like that bed it has all my grooves in it. Curtis looked up from his news paper with a puzzled look on his face, Boy, buy that girl a mattress! Dad, whose side are you on here? Normally yours, but a mattress makes a happy man trust me on that one. Really, Curtis is that the best you do? What? It's true. You don't see me complaining do you. You weren't last night, Craig slipped out before he could cut off his sentence. Both Reneea and Curtis looked at their son in shock? Excuse me? Angel tried to cover the smile on her face but she was too late. Ma, dad…stammering to get his words out without laughter, I was just making an observation, as I was on my way downstairs, for juice last night, I walked past your room and the both of you sounded very happy. Curtis looked at his wife, and then his son…put a smug look on his face, hunched his shoulders, and said…I rest my case. Embarrassed by the whole incident, Reneea tossed a throw pillow from the couch at Curtis for encouraging their son. Curtis ducked the attack and flashed his million dollar smile in Reneea's direction raising his eyebrows and remarked. Ah Ah Ahh, remember Vegas. At that moment the doorbell rang out and Angel was all too happy to excuse herself to answer the door. I'll get it and the two men continued to chuckle softly exchanging glances, Reneea being the butt of the joke, decided to check on the caterers.

Angel answered the door to her smiling parents and greeted them affectionately as now they had arrived and she and Craig could finally let go of their little secret. Walking into the great room with parents in tow allowing everyone to perform proper greetings they all adjourned to the dinning room where a spread fit for Kings and Queens had been prepared. Reneea, everything looks wonderful, girl how do you do it? Rita really, thank you, it's no problem at all. You guys know how much we love the kids. We feel that you and Bill are an extension of our family and nothing is too good for our family. Well girl thank you just the same. The two woman took seats next to one another, no doubt to start planning the days shopping trip that would take place while the guys attended the Piston's and Laker's game that they had been planning all week. Dad, would you mind if Angel and I took the lead positions today? Curtis stepped back from his usual chair and pulled it away from the table for his son. Not at all my man, it's your show, do your thing. Sliding down to sit next to Bill he glanced over at Reneea, who also had a puzzled look on her face flexing her eyebrows to signal her husband that she was also in the dark. Everyone took their seats and the servers began to serve the courses one by one.

Everyone was involved in conversation, food was being consumed and plans were being made, suddenly as it appeared that everyone had had their fill and the coffee was being served along with the Champaign Mimosas, Craig signaled Angel that it was time to make their announcement and as she nodded in agreement, Craig began to retrieve everyone's attention.

Excuse me everyone, if I could just have, I'm sorry baby, if we could have everyone's attention for a moment, putting his arm around his wife, we, would like to share a little information with you all. Go ahead son the floor is yours, his father-in-law stated. Thank you, sir. Everyone began to listen intently as Reneea looked at her son, she had a warm feeling overcome her as she listened she was always so in tune with her son that she had a feeling she knew what he was about to say. As you all know, I love this woman with everything inside of me. And you all know that I feel the same about Craig since the first day we met. Well as life would have it, in about seven more months, there will be two more reasons why we are so in love with one another. Everyone sat on the edge of their seats puzzled. I would like to inform all of you that my wife is carrying your grandchildren and we couldn't be happier about it. Rita jumped up from the table with her chair falling to the floor behind her. Curtis' mouth flew completely open with the widest smile anyone could have, Bill stood from his seat with his hands in the air, and Reneea simply sat in her chair looking up at the ceiling with tears in her eyes, her suspicions were correct though she did not expect twins, she knew that they were with child.

Rita hugged her daughter so tightly and then began making a fuss over her condition. Do you need anything, baby how do you feel, can I get you something? Mom, mommy really, I'm fine, mom don't cry. As Angel tried to console her mother Curtis and Bill were patting Craig on the back and discussing cigars that a client had given Curtis and that this was the perfect time to indulge. Craig made his way to his mother who was standing there with open arms. You knew didn't you? Well, to be honest, yes smiling broadly, I didn't expect twins though! Congrats baby you are going to be a wonderful father. Thanks ma, I love you. I love you to baby and I couldn't be happier. Reneea hugged her son so tightly, her baby was a man starting a family of his own and she was very proud. She kissed Angel and touched her on her tummy…Orange Juice huh? The two laughed affectionately. Thanks for not blowing my secret…Craig said he had a feeling you knew. Honey, I would not have said a word…his secrets have always been safe with me.

While all the commotion was still going on, Curtis realized that he had not addressed his wife. He caught her eye and smiled at her softly and walked toward her. As she noticed that he was headed in her direction, she decided to meet him. Well Mrs. Rae, it appears that our little bundle is going to have a little bundle of his own. It looks that way doesn't it? She put her arms around Curtis' neck as he wrapped his around her waist. They looked into each others eyes and they both knew that this changed everything, their family would be expanding and they now even more than before had a reason that tied them together. A single tear rolled down Reneea's cheek and Curtis wiped it away. To be honest, he felt as if he would shed a tear himself, but instead he kissed his wife tenderly which caught the attention of their son who loved to see his parents interact as that was all that he had been use to, he would never understand how the love had died and they both found solace in the arms of others outside of their relationship. He would never understand that theirs was a marriage of lies, so they choose to protect him at all cost and they always had, so they thought.

The phone rang and got the attention of all who heard. I got it guys; Craig darted for the phone before the caller was sent into voicemail. Hello?

What's up guy? Uncle Rick? Yeah dude. What up man, I thought you were coming by for brunch this morning? No, I thought I would let you guys catch up, besides we are supposed to hook up before the game, remember? Yeah, but Unck, you're family man! I was really expecting you here. Sorry guy, but there will be plenty of time for us to catch up this afternoon, I was actually calling to find out the driving arrangement for today? Both Curtis and Reneea observed Craig on the phone and knew it could only be one person, Rick. Reneea, knowing that he was the caller felt herself release and pull away from Curtis' embrace, which noticeably grabbed his attention. Nea, are you okay? Oh yeah, yeah…I thought you might need to take that call. Umh, I'm sure Craig has it. Dad, its Uncle Rick. I guess it is for me then. He walked over to the phone right as Craig began to share his announcement. Well since you were not here to hear it in person, I guess I have to tell you over the phone. What's up? Well your God Son is going to be a daddy. What? Man are you serious? Yes sir! Twins! Hell naw, my little guy is going to have twins under foot? Both men laughed loud and hardily. Congrats dude, how far off? Seven months, why didn't you guys say something last night? Tina is going to be pissed. I know, but we wanted to let the old folks hear it and adjust to fact that they are going to be grandparents without the jokes.

At that moment, Craig's news had caused pain to shoot through Rick's heart. This just signified that Reneea and Curtis had one more reason to stay married. They would spend time planning and preparing to be grandparents another thing that Curtis shared with the woman he loved, besides her bed. Listen man this is great news and I am very happy for both of you. I will buy you a congratulatory beer at the game. Sounds like a plan, here's my dad. What it is, Mr. Neal? Hey man from where I'm sitting you got the better hand. Man, I know can you believe this shit? My son will have a son or two even? This calls for real celebration today. After the game we are going to Mr. Nicks and get blew back. I'll set up a car service for us; fuck driving because I want to get completely inebriated. The two laughed and knew that this plan was a good one. Why don't you call Mike and tell him we will pick him up after the game so he can hang out with us. Cool, I can handle that. Bet.

Hey a Curt, is Reneea near by, I wanted to thank her for the food, but now I must congratulate her on becoming the worlds sexiest Granny, more laughter from the pair. Right man and you know this; she is one fine ass grandmother! Let me get her, she would be pissed if she knew **you** called and did not acknowledge her part in this. Babe, baby telephone, **Rick** could hear Curtis calling her affectionately and it made him sick to his stomach to imagine how he was there playing super husband, when just last night he had had him run interference just so he could call dial a hoe. Trying to grasp his composure, he heard the sexy voice of his desire on the other end of the receiver…

Hello?

Good Afternoon Ms. Rae. His voice had the power to drive chills through her whole body. She closed her eyes and slowly responded to him.

Hey you.

Congrats on the Twins…his voice though excited for his Godson was filled with disappointment and she knew it. She knew that he would be thinking the same thing that had been obvious to her earlier.

Thank you it's really wonderful news. I know they will be great parents. I wanted to thank you for the Chicken, but the truth is… I just needed…I had to hear your voice. The distance is…

Rick, I know baby, me too.

Are you sure?

Of course! Don't ever doubt it. He needed to hear that.

I love you so much, it really hurts and I have no one to blame for this but myself.

Don't say that Rick, please don't. She could see that everyone was still in the room so she was comfortable to speak freely as no one could possibly be on the other end.

Rick, she whispered, I love you and I am counting the days, hours, moments, down to minutes until I am with you, please believe that.

Suddenly, Rick's heart felt a little lighter and he hesitated before he could speak but finally was able to respond.

Get some rest Reneea; you are going to need it. Because, *when* I finally have the chance to be with you again…I'm going to tear your ass up! You will leave my bed knowing that you have been fucked and loved all in the same breath!

Reneea felt moisture appear between her legs and knew that she had to end the call before she gave herself away.

Well, Mr. Neal, I hope for your sake that that was a promise and not a threat.

I love you baby.

Ditto.

With that response, Rick smiled and hung up the receiver. Reneea followed suit.

Is everything good with Rick babe, Curtis inquired as he began to pay attention to Reneea's facial expression?

Yeah, he was just saying how he wished Bea was here to be with us for this wonderful news. She hated using her dead friend as a cover, but it was the only thing that would have justified the conversation at length with her husband's best friend without drawing suspicion.

Man, I wish he would try dating? Pain entered into Curtis face before he made his next statement. He has got to move on…Bea is dead and she is not coming back, I just hate to see my friend so unhappy.

He will be okay.

I am going to make it my mission to get that man laid! You know there is this waitress down at Mr. Nicks that would lay him at the drop of a hat. She wants him so bad she can taste it, but he want give her the time of day like he's in a committed relationship. This little bit of information pissed Reneea off but she did her best to conceal it, seeing that Curtis had let it be known that Rick had refused to share her love with anyone.

Curtis, don't push him, it could back fire on you. He will when he is ready.

He is so lucky to have you as an earpiece. Reneea smiled at Curtis, knowing that she was much more to him than that.

Everyone began making their individual plans for the day and like clock work Tina arrived for the afternoon shopping adventure and Curtis made preparation for the car service to drive him and the entourage around town like celebrities. Tina loved Craig and Angel, but more to the point, she loved her best friend, his mother, and was so excited to know that her Godchild would have children soon. Secretly there was once a time that she thought Craig and her daughter Mia, who grew up together and were the best of friends, would be a couple, but when they went away to different colleges, Craig started dating Angel and Mia, decided that Spence was the guy for her, however, short lived that was Craig and Mia had remained the best of friends throughout the years. Before they could leave the house, her credit cards had racked up double digits and Angel had been chosen their designated driver as the future granny's and auntie had plans to get drunker than the guys.

After a day of Shopping, the ladies hit the Martini Grille where they are regulars with the exception of Rita and Angel. The minute they hit the door, everyone from the wait staff to bartenders made a huge commotion about their appearance. Rita who was not much of a partier was extremely excited to be in the company of the two ladies who seem to be large and in charge. Angel was getting in the swing of things and enjoyed watching her mom who never really got out enjoy herself. They went over to their standard table and took a seat, before they could sit down good; their drinks were at the table as the waitresses made their apologies to the other women who were without drinks but were assured that this was only because they were new. After all orders were placed and drinks served the ladies began to discuss the actions that had taken place all day long.

Rita, who was not a drinker, was feeling the effects of her drinks and had decided to live a little, she became very gutsy and decided to order shots all around. The ladies began to follow her lead. Drink after drink, the conversation became louder, funnier, and raunchier. Angel could not remember when if ever she had seen her mother this intoxicated, and could not believe that she was discussing topics such as love making with her husband in front of her much less with anyone else. She was amused to see the spunk the ole girls still had. She was shocked, but only a little, to see the attention that men would try and pay to her mother-in-law. Several would stop by the table and offer to buy drinks and request a dance or two from Reneea, but always the class act would decline their advances as she really appeared not interested. She really was an attractive woman and was thankful for the genes her children would inherit. Tina, the bossy one of the crew was a little more matter-of-factly when it came to dismissing the unwanted attention of the gentlemen who could not take a soft hint. She was bold enough to let brothers know who stepped to the table they were out of their league and even a snowball stood a better chance in hell than they did when it came to pushing up on any one of the women at our table. Though a few would walk away with their feelings bruised and some not, the fact remains that they all just went away. For hours the ladies enjoyed their selves and she would have to admit learned a few tricks that the girls had up their sleeves when it came to their mates.

Tina, who was feeling very good from the Vodka Martini's she had consumed, took the conversation to a whole new level.

Ladies, in honor of Angel and Craig's new adventure, I feel that it is my duty to let you know our newest club member in on a little secret when it comes to children and marriage. Everyone sat back in their chairs and braced themselves for what she might say next.

Sweetheart, you are about to embark on a journey that women have taken since the beginning of time…You are going to get FAT as Hell! Everyone looked around as if to say is that it….
So what you want to do is eat like a pig every chance you can now, because after you pop those damn babies out, you shall be on a diet for the rest of your life. Puzzled by what she had just said, Angel just sat there clueless, while the other three women, burst out with uncontrollable laughter…failing to see the humor about becoming the Good Year Blimp, she decided to ask what the point was?

Very simple my daughter, her mother replied…Them there hips of yours have now become baby making hips with a mind of their own so you will have to watch your weight and plate if you want to continue to use your body as bait. More laughter arose.
Stop it guys, you're scaring the mother of my grandchildren, Reneea responded affectionately.
Thanks Ma Rae.
Don't mention it sweetheart, they are just having fun with you, besides my son is so in love with you…she paused before her next statement; everyone saw the emotion build up in her eyes.
He is so in love with you, that it reminds me of when his father and I first started out, we had nothing but dreams, hope and each other and a love that we felt could conquer anything; a tear rolled down her cheek and even though she was drunk, the pain that had suddenly attached itself to her was noticeable by Tina, who knew her best. Reneea managed to get her composure to continue speaking… Girl you could get as wide as the great outdoors and he would still come home to you and only you, just don't let the fires die out while you are pregnant, remember the love you made and the love you share help to create that little pair. So keep the intimacy that the two of you have and there will be no need to worry about whether or not your still the one.

Reneea knew she had taken the conversation deeper than she should have and immediately made and excuse removing herself from the group. Woe,

I think that last martini needs to come back, excuse me but I believe the restroom is calling. The ladies smiled noticing the awkward moment and Tina made it her business to follow her. Me too, Ladies I will be right back as well.

Baby girl, baby girl where are you?
I'm here, directing her to the last stall.
Honey you okay? Reneea opened the door looking devastated.
I really messed up our night, huh.
Naw babe. Everything is still salvageable. Its cool no one really knows; they probably think you are just emotional over everything that has taken place.
Tina, what in the hell is going on? This whole week has been one emotional roller coaster ride. I don't know what the hell is going on with me and Curtis from one day to the next; Rick and I are involved with feelings I can't just shut off and I'm not sure if I want to ever. My damn son and his wife are carrying the next generation of Rae's which has made it impossible to explain our affairs with other people? I just don't know what the hell is going on anymore. Last night, Curtis...I was so drunk. Tina looked on sympathetically trying to make sense of Reneea's ranting. He brought up a bottle of wine, he had this whole seduction scene going by the time I got upstairs, so I end up fucking him again which makes twice in one week, but I was really thinking about Rick and wanting him which caused me to do all kind of freaky shit with Curtis, who really got into it and to be honest so did I. Everything is all fucked up.

Reneea, girl, shaking her by the arms, Tina began to speak sternly. Nae-Nae, get a damn grip you have to pull yourself together. Now is not the time nor the place to discuss this shit sweetie we have company and you damn sure don't need Angel to go to Craig and hint that there could be a problem. Bitch, get your ass together now. We can talk in detail tomorrow, but right now we need to get back to the table and call it a night so we can get Rita home and your drunk ass in bed before you put your foot in your fucking mouth. Do you hear me?

Reneea, knew Tina was right. She stood up and shook off the effects of the emotional ride she had just taken, checked her makeup in the mirror and replenished her lipstick that she had smeared while wiping her tears. The two women hugged and gave each other a nod that they were ready to rejoin their party who awaited them patiently. She was not angry with Tina, because she knew that she was looking out for her best interest, she actually thought to herself that she would not know what to do if she was not the one thing in her life that remained constant.

Hell, I was about to come look for you two drunks, Angel and I thought you may have fallen in. Everyone laughed at Rita as Angel made the observation that it was time for her to take her band of hooligans home for the evening. And though they all campaigned for one for the road, she strongly suggested that they eighty-six that idea, got their coats and came along like good little girls as the hour was late. Playfully protesting the event, Tina and Reneea both were glad that she had put their exit plan in motion so that they didn't have to. Summoning the waitress over to clear their bill, they learned of a surprising discovery.

Ladies, can I get you another round or are you calling it a night? Darlin, as much as we would love to sit here and drink everything you have behind that bar, I'm afraid our designated driver is calling it a night for us girls, Tina said jokingly. No problem.
Reneea, attempting to hand her a credit card to settle their tab at that moment was rejected.
Not tonight Mrs. Rae, your money is no good here?
Excuse me?
Before you arrived, Mr. Rae called and told us to put every and anything that you ladies ordered on a running tab with a generous tip for whoever waited on your table tonight, so as you see your debt was paid before it was made and you are all free to leave.
The ladies looked at one another smiled broadly and agreed in unison to leave. In classic Tina style she mumbled. Wait until that Negro gets this bill! Everyone laughed uncontrollably and began to leave the bar.

On the ride home minimal conversation was made and all Reneea could do was think back on Curtis' unbelievably generous gesture. He was always a kind man where others were concerned but there had been so much this week to cause her to be perplexed where he was involved. She just sat there thinking why now, why was all of this happening now.

Man that's bullshit, there is no way that dude was in possession of the ball, it was a bad call and your ass is as blind as the ref's. Curtis and Rick were going back and forth about the game they had attended while the guys sat there laughing at the comical exchange between the two. Mr. Nicks was not as crowed tonight as most Saturday nights so the wait staff was free to attend to their table as often as need be and assure that everyone in attendance seemed to be having a good time.

Here you are fellows, just what the doctor ordered. Sherrie as always delivering drinks and massive doses of flirtation toward the guys was dressed in a tight black fitted mini skirt with a Mr. Nicks Bar T-shirt Tied in a knot with a little black apron tied around her waist and three inch heels that made her legs look sleek and sexy and she was in rare form tonight. Curtis, I didn't know you had such a handsome son? He looks just like you. Why thank you Sherrie baby, we are celebrating tonight he just announced today that he and his lovely wife are expecting twins!
Get out! Curt you're going to be a grandfather? You don't say? My loss huh another fine brother off the market. I guess there is just no action for me at this table with all of you married brothers, huh? Well except for Mr. Neal, who won't give me the time of day? All of the men took notice that she definitely wanted his attention; needless to say they all saw a reason why he should give her the time of day. Sherrie was very attractive and had the body to match. Rick doing everything shy of blushing at her response did the best he could to muster up a comeback as he knew he was surely going to catch hell from the guys either way it goes. Awe Sherrie, why are you doing me like that baby? You must feel the need to call a brother out tonight. Sherrie walked over to Rick provocatively making her way behind him putting her arms around his neck and spoke very frankly. No, I guess when you want something so badly and it won't give you a chance to show him how pleased he would be if he did more than window shop, it can make you say things you probably wouldn't ordinarily. She bent over and kissed Rick on his cheek, placed his Cognac in his hand which happen to be in his lap positioned on his genital area and grazing it as she moved her hand away, blew him a kiss as she moved on to serve the other customers.

While all of the other men had just witnessed the exchanged between the two and were practically salivating, there was only one of them that pulled themselves together enough to speak.
Excuse me Rick man, Bill Cooper said rather inquisitively.
Yeah man?

I have to ask… Are you gay, blind or seeing someone that we don't know about that would keep you from tapping that young ass every which way but loose?

Everyone at the table looked at Bill and laughed like hell, one agreeing with him right after the other even though his son-in-law was caught off guard by his remark. Curtis co-signed every word.

Didn't I tell yaw ass he was crazy? If anyone of us was free and she was throwing the pussy in our direction like she does to this brother, we would hit that shit so hard she would be unconscious. Even more surprised by his father's observation, Craig felt he should come to his Godfathers defense. Guys, guys, lay off the man.

Thank you Craig, Rick smiled feeling as if he at least had Craig on his side.

Besides Uncle Rick, we can understand you being a little apprehensive, it probably hasn't been unwrapped in a while, if you aren't sure what to do anymore, we will be more than happy to talk you through it.

Surprised by Craig's comments everyone started to laugh and give each other high fives; even Rick himself had to admit the joke was funny. Oh this nigga got jokes? Look! Fuck yaw married motherfuckers, just remember this, if I chose to, I could get it, hit it and quit it, while yaw haten on a brother. More drinks were past and more jokes were told. As they had been drinking earlier at the game, they all were good and drunk and the Limo idea made more and more sense as the night progressed. As time past, Sherrie's advances toward Rick became more and more relentless. She was definitely a woman with a mission. At one point she went as far as to sit in his lap and lean back against him as if they were dating. This move caught Rick off guard and caused a bit of arousal to occur. Seeing that she had awakened what was considered to be a sleeping giant, she took this opportunity to plant more of a seed of temptation. As some of the guys were engrossed in a dart game she decided to kick up her assault a notch. Sherrie slowly grind her backside against Rick's lap, pretending to be dancing to a hit record that was playing in the background, while turning to create face to face conversation with him.

So, surprise, surprise you're definitely not a Ken Doll?

Shocked by her statement and observation, Rick responded.

Not in the least, responding calm and calculating.

I would love to meet and greet it in person, and in private if you catch my drift?

Sherrie, are you sure you really want to go there?

As sure as shit stinks, I don't know why you won't go out with me? You are not married, I've never seen you in here with a date and unless you have someone totally devoted to you, there is really nothing wrong with two adults getting together to explore their options. Why don't you take my number and call me this time? I guarantee your personal satisfaction. She slid her phone number and address in his top shirt pocket, kissed him on his lips and slid off of what was now a full erection. Noticing what she was leaving behind, she smiled and turned to walk away as the mission was accomplished. He noticed that he was standing at attention and was slightly shocked. He felt bad that he had let her get him worked up and a little guilty as well, after all he had reserved himself for Reneea, no other woman had come close to making him feel what he felt for Bea besides her, sure there were women who came on to him, but he stayed focus because of his relationship with Reneea as in his heart she was all he wanted.

Damn it Rick, if you don't fuck her, I will, Curtis said with his son and Bill out of ear range. Rick looked over at Curtis who was watching her walk away from their table, at this time Mike chose to go over to Craig and Bill who were throwing darts. Curtis turned his attention back to Rick with a huge grin on his face, after her little performance, I just may have to go home and get some from Nae-Nae; damn um, um, um. Yes that is definitely a sweet piece of ass there. Rick was brought out of his train of thought by Curtis' remarks.

Who are you talking about man?

Reneea.

Reneea?

Yes Reneea, man, are you that drunk?

No, naw, I guess I'm just trying to figure out what you are talking about.

Are you still trippin on what took place the other night?

Naw man, I'm trippin on last night?

What…You were with her again? Rick was starting to become irritated by what he was hearing.

Well damn man, she is my wife, it is mine… when I want it; he stated matter-of-factly. You act as if, I'm doing something wrong?

Man you are fucking your secretary, and acting like Nae-Nae is some second rate hoe, you do when you have nothing else to turn to.
Man keep your voice down, do you want my son to hear your ass?
Both men were drunk and knew that this was not a five minute conversation.

Look man, Nae-Nae is my girl and …
And nigga, I'm your boy, why you got to bitch up on me like that? She is my wife, so why are you so shocked when I talk about fucking her?
Rick trying to regain some stability in the conversation, Sorry dude, I guess it's me, I miss being married that's all.
Man I know and I am sorry, but maybe its time for you to move on…I mean you can't stay in the past. Bea would want you to be happy. An as far as the married part, I understand. Last night while we were making love…it was like being with someone else; I mean she was totally brand new on my ass. It was like fucking a freak that I never knew I had. I promised that I would not discuss the details…Then don't man, Rick interjected trying to escape the fine details of Curtis' play by play. But damn Rick she was hot like fire. I was able to do things to her that I have never done before, nor did I think she would allow me to do, and it was good as hell. I mean she was like a woman possessed or some shit.

Rick sat there listening to him and grew angrier by the second. He knew exactly what he was talking about because he was the man that generally brought that out of her and could not believe that she would do this with his ass after the way he has treated her. He could hear what Curtis was saying and thought if he continued he would knock the shit out of him. Luckily the rest of the guys came back to the table causing the conversation to come to a direct halt. As he only would discuss details of intimacy with Rick he leaned in to him and told him he would complete the story later. They gave each other a pound and Curtis never noticed that his friend looked at him with contempt.
Well fellas, I need to return some of this rented ass beer, excuse me please. Rick got up and headed to the restroom with Curtis in tow. This made Rick pissed because he was trying to go clear his head for a moment and now his friend was high on his heels. The two entered the empty restroom and began to conduct their business, after washing hands Rick began to check himself out in the mirror.

Nigga, you still ugly ain't nothing changed. Rick chuckled at his friends attempted humor. Whatever man, I know somebody that likes it. Curtis assumed he was referring to Sherrie when really Rick was referring to Curtis' wife. No doubt about that man, I thought she just might fuck you on the table out there. Rick laughed and turned his head.

Man I envy you.

For what reason Curt? You got it all.

You can leave here with no strings attached, go to this chick's houses bang her brains out and there is no complications. When I leave here tonight, I have to go home to my wife with my son home…I can't make an excuse to leave and see V, so I am forced to stay at home make love to her like it's not a strain and everything with us is regular. But, I must be honest, if she continues to give it to me like last night; it will be less and less of an effort to have to make that choice…

She really put it on you huh?

Dude, you have no idea! To my surprise it was feeling so good, I think I said I love you in the heat of passion…no, I'm positive I did, hell man the shit was good…better than it has ever been in a real long time.

The very idea of what Curtis was saying was causing Rick great pain, for the first time since his affair with Reneea started, he felt hurt on a level that he was not able to cope with or understand.

He was angry, jealous and hurt all at once and someone, it did not matter who, had to pay for this pain he was feeling or at least make him forget it. The two men exited the restroom to find Sherrie standing near by. This time it would be Rick who made the advance, he would be the one on a mission.

Sherrie, can I holler at you for a second?

Sure baby what's up, you guys need some drinks or something?

Naw, nothing like that, I was wondering if you might be up for a little company tonight? Rick leaned up against her, while using his knee rubbing it up against her to signify what his interest were. Sherrie was totally caught off guard but was very pleasantly surprised to see that she may just finally get her wish.

If, you are serious about this, I get out of here tonight about 11:00, I'm home and showered by 11:30 and I would love some company in more ways than one.

Good deal. We're going to be leaving soon; I'll go home and get my car and meet you at your place no later than 12:00. And Sherrie, Rick bent down to whisper in her ear, *I hope that I can expect everything that you have been promising me for so long, it would be a great disappointment to find out that your a tease and not a please.* He kissed her on her neck softly, and heard her sigh with pleasure. He smiled and backed away feeling as if he had returned the pressure that she had been putting on him for months.

I'm looking forward to seeing you tonight, and you better not stand me up! No worries, sweetie, I will be there you had just better deliver what you've promised.

Rick rushed back over to the table where he was being viewed by all and they knew that he was ready to go. Gentlemen, it has been real but it is now time for us to be leaving as I have a little something, something to get into at about 12:00 sharp!

Now that's my boy! Curtis applauded his friend for getting back in the game. Everyone finished their last shot, grabbed their hats and jackets and headed for the door. It was on and poppin!

Chapter 9

The Games People Play

The Limo ride was long and sobering for Rick; all he could think of was what he was planning to do tonight and the reason for what it was he was going to do. The other men continued to drink in the car and talk garbage as a group of guys together usually do. As Bill Cooper was the first to be dropped off, Craig felt a little easier about joining the conversation as he knew his dad and Uncles Rick and Mike would keep their conversations private. He was proud to be a member of the boys club and enjoyed watching what he considered the older players at work. His dad and his friends had always been a source of entertainment for him for as long as he could remember, but tonight was different, he managed to see them in ways he had not before.

Craig managed to change his seating arrangement with the exit of his father-in-law and was now directly seated next to Rick. Uncle Rick, you sure you up to this tonight, you not doing this because everyone rode you so hard are you?

Craig, man, it's cool. I'm just going to hang out with the young lady and see what happens, and I appreciate your concern.

You my dude man and I don't want you to experience any hardship all because your boys have an opinion on how long, long enough to grieve should be for you, you know?

Thank you, and trust me I'm okay. Well this is my stop. He observed and smiled at Craig again looking into his eyes as the limo slowed down to a halt.

Fellas it's been real, but I've got a date that I need to get prepared for so if you will excuse me I will see you haters later.

A man, don't forget to get some rubbers, you don't need no little feet running around in this stage of the game, Mike had said very little about the subject matter all night partly because he knew slightly about Rick and Reneea. What he did know was that he did not want to be anywhere near this situation when hurricane Tina heard that this shit took place right up under her nose and he didn't mention anything about it to her. Rick laughed and gave Mike a pound as the others agreed to the fullest. Rick did give some thought to what he had said as he had not used rubbers in ages, there was no need with Reneea as she could not become pregnant anymore and he was not sleeping with any other women up until tonight.

Look man, get out tonight and enjoy yourself for a change, and you better tear that kitty up and tell me all about it tomorrow, Curtis whispered in his ear. Rick smiled gave his friend a pound and got out of the Limo. As they pulled away, Rick let out a sigh of relief that he was finally out of their midst. He walked into the house where his answering machine was flashing frantically. He noticed that he had ten messages. His mind told him not to listen, but his heart overruled; he just had to know if Reneea bothered to call. Rick laid his keys down on the table and pressed the play button to his answering machine.

You have ten messages.

The first seven messages where from business clients whom he chose to respond to in the morning, and the remaining three, where from Reneea. Rick braced himself to listen, still angry about the information that he had acquired tonight.

Beep, *Hey Rick we made it in and I am really tired and really drunk, I probably will be sleeping before long, but I wanted to call you and tell you that I miss you, yes I love you and I am counting down....*

Beep... Rick me again, I can't sleep, I've got to talk to you there is something I have to tell you...I'm sorry for all of this mess and problems... (Crying tape not audible) and Rick I promise...

Beep... Rick just know that no matter what my love for you was never a lie, if you saw me first, why didn't you tell Curtis...?

Tape end you have no new messages.

Rick put his face in his hands and sighed heavily, as mad as he was at her, Curtis, hell everybody he knew he loved her still and hearing her voice made him angrier than before. What if Curtis arrives tonight like he promised and makes love to her again, would she lie about that time as well or mention it at all? No time for this shit now, he had less than an half an hour to get to where he was expected and change. Tonight he was going to play the game too.

Rick took a quick hoe bath, freshened up his Cologne and made sure that everything he needed was at home. He got into his Jag, let the top down and proceeded out of his drive to make it to his destination. When he arrived at Sherrie's apartment, he put the condoms that he purchased into his pocket and took them out of the bag as he did not want to appear over confident that he was going to get a piece of action, but lets be honest, he knew why he had went there. He had a passing thought of Reneea and for a brief moment contemplated canceling the whole thing, but in the same moment imagined her in Curtis' arms making love and decided in that moment that she was not going to be the only one having fun. Here she was having her cake and eating it too while he sat back and waited to be tossed a bone. Not tonight.

Rick walked slowly up the walkway only to notice that the door was opened for his arrival, anxious for his visit, his hostess had been watching for him through the living room window.
Well hello.
Hey yourself, I started to wonder if you would really show up.
I told you that I was coming; I don't make it a habit to go back on my word especially when it's something that I'm interested in doing. Rick smiled at her and noticed that she was waving him in. Let me take your jacket, unless you prefer not? Remembering that he had placed the condoms in the jacket pocket he thought twice before surrendering the coat.
If you don't mind, I had the top down on the way over and it was a little chill in the midnight air so let me warm up a bit first.
Sure. When she turned her head or left the room he would be able to make the transfer to his jeans pocket and offer up the coat with no problem.
Suit yourself, however, I have just the thing to aid you in getting warmer faster; flirtatiously rubbing her hands across his shoulders.
You don't waste anytime do you? Why Mr. Neal what on earth do you mean? I was suggesting that I make you a glass of your favorite Brandy…What was it that you thought I was talking about; smiling as if she had no clue as to what he meant. Embarrassed by being so blunt he decided to do damage control and quick. Please pardon me, maybe it's just

all the excitement of me being alone with you that has me foreseeing a beautiful evening and hoping that we could continue our little meet and greet mission from earlier. He walked up to her smiling and hoping that she had bought his line of garbage and of course it worked like a charm. Hey no problem, I'm just glad to know that two consenting adults have come together with the same agenda in mine. When she turned to make the drinks he was able to place the package in his jean pocket and by the time she had completed her task she turned around to find that Rick was extending his Jacket in her direction which exposed the button up shirt that was opened just enough to show the sexy chest hair that laid on his chest. It was smooth like the texture of hair on his head that was a very decent grade, curly and soft. He always looked to be mixed culturally but she had never asked. This new found evidence both excited and intrigued her. Here you are, you take this and I'll take that, exchanging the drink for the coat. Please, won't you make yourself comfortable, pointing to a modest looking sofa, which went along with everything else in the apartment. It had the décor of earth tones, nothing flashy and exotic, but more of a mature feel type atmosphere. This pleased Rick because he knew that she may be a little more mature than he had first thought.

They set down next to one another and the conversation started to flow naturally. Rick thought about Reneea momentarily but as the evening progressed he was thinking of her less and less. The fact that this incredibly attractive female was in his presence and made no bones about the fact that she wanted him helped in this area. Feeling the effects of the alcohol, they started to become more and more enticed by one another with casual touching and soft kisses being shared between them.

So Rick, why don't we just get this out of the way? Sherrie sat straight up and looked him dead in his eyes to alert him to the fact that she was very serious.
What do you mean?
I mean the small talk has been nice and all, however, I think I am a pretty good judge of character and I know when someone has something on their mind that they just need to get off. Rick looked at her inquisitively, I'm listening. So with that being said, allow me to say this…I'm not looking for a commitment from you or a baby daddy; I'm not trying to get myself hitched, I really just think that you are a hell of a guy and it is no secret that I want to go to bed with you. From where I'm sitting, I know you

would like to go to bed with me as well or you, my love, would not be here, am I correct? Rick surprised by her extremely direct response nodded in agreement taking a sip of the amber colored substance in his glass and enjoying the taste. Well… with that being said we will note that we are both adults on the same page who want to enjoy one another tonight, and as I am feeling good and I have a throbbing in my panties that can't wait any longer to be introduced to all that manhood you have hidden in those jeans, what do you say we cut the bullshit, agree that it's just sex. Take these two bodies in that bedroom and fuck like there's no tomorrow; only tonight. She looked at him with wanting eyes and though just a little intoxicated, her actions were all her and she was not shy about it.

Rick sat his drink down on the coffee table along with his watch and cell phone stood up from the couch turned in her direction with a stern face and began to pull her up from the couch pulling her close to his body. He gazed in her eyes and started to speak slowly and sexy…Little girl, if you are not careful, that mouth of yours is going to write a check that that ass can't cash. You have been campaigning for this and now you have been elected, are you sure you are ready for me….looking at her seriously? Since you have been so direct, let me tell you a thing or two, if you can't hang, speak now because once we start there is no turning back, I like to fuck and if you are not willing to do what I want to do there is no need in trippin.

Boo, I can handle whatever you dish out. At that moment Rick untied her robe to expose her tender young body; he could see her nipples were hard and in need of serious attention. He began to kiss her on her neck making her moan working his way down to her breast, sucking her nipples faster and harder responding to pleas and cries for him not to stop. At that moment, he pulled away from her and she led him to a bedroom that was lit only by candle light with soft jazz playing in the background. Once inside the room he removed his shirt and allowed her to unzip his jeans. He couldn't help thinking of how beautiful her body was and he knew that he would have her in every way he wanted to.

Once all articles of clothing had been removed he began to command her like his sexual slave who was more than willing to participate in the game. He sat her down on the edge of the bed caressing her face and rubbing her hair and in one sweeping motion, he pulled her head to his penis and made her take him inside her mouth forcing her to give him head which he found felt absolutely wonderful and she knew it by the way he moaned and called her name softly. She was only too happy to please him. Once he had had his fill of this activity he laid her back on the bed kissing her and telling her how much he wanted to fuck her. This drove her wild with desire. She arched her back pushing her Vagina against him forcefully. With this little action he noticed that she liked it a little rough and he was more than happy to oblige her. He pushed her back forcefully kneeling over her kissing her while spreading her legs apart. He then proceeded to lick and kiss her clit causing her to lose total control.

Yeah baby, fuck me baby, give it to me…please give that shit to me. She begged and pleaded with him to enter her, but her cries were ignored. He was in control and it was his game to play and thus far he was winning. He knew it was good and had plans before he would put her out of her misery.

You want it don't you baby? He taunted her and teased her using his figures to open her up and draw out moisture. He then took his fingers and inserted them into her rectally. This move surprised her but pleased her as well. The more he worked them, the more she squirmed against him begging for him to make her cum. Rick was as hard as a brick and he knew that he would need to be relieved soon, but did not want to cum to fast as he was enjoying everything as well as she was. At that moment he reached back removed a condom from the wrapper applying it to his manhood and at that moment happy that he purchased the pre-lubricant type, began to insert it into her ass. Her moan grew intense and louder with each thrust.

Damn, baby, it's too big, I can't take it I…I…oh my…Rick no…
Do you want me to stop? He breathing heavily waiting for her to reply, but continued because he knew the game she was playing oh so well, I'm saying yes with my mouth but my body is saying no type shit. No, don't, but I can't… at that moment, he felt himself slide into her deeper and he knew that he had achieved success, as her cries became softer, turning into moans and whimpers of pure pleasure. He fucked her in an anal fashion for as long as he could stand it, and at the peak of his enjoyment he pulled back sliding underneath her and inserted himself into her vagina. He ordered her to ride him and she did exactly what he said.

Yeah baby ride it, ride it baby make me cum. Own that dick bitch. He was forceful and meant every word he ordered. She didn't even seem to mind that he called her out of her name, in fact the thought made her work that much harder as she knew she was now giving him what he needed, what he wanted and what she had promised. Besides, he had made her body feel so good that she was only to happy to do what he wanted and return the favor.

Finally, as she had rode him long and hard, Rick had proven that he was definitely worth the chase and wait, he came violently inside her groaning and gasping for air. He was glad that he was in good physical condition at this time in his life, he thought to himself, or that young piece of ass would have fucked him to death. His feet curled with sweet release and decided that he still had what it took to get the job done. With the thought he smiled and rolled over on top of her kissing her as a sign of being pleased with what had transpired between them. As he pulled away from her lying on his back he felt relieved and fulfilled all at once, but then it hit him that he had been with someone other than Reneea, thought of her phone messages and felt a little hurt and disappointed in himself. The fact still remained that she was Curtis's wife, but for the last three years she had been his life. He knew he loved her and that it was wrong but the fact remained that he had feelings for her that were indeed very strong. He looked over at Sherrie who had just performed for him so well and decided that for the night, he would let all other thoughts subside.

Well, well, well, Mr. Neal…you were even better than I imagined, thank you for one of best nights of love making that I have ever had. She smiled at him and kissed him on his chest. Rick turned in to face her kissing her on her lips…No, it is I who should be thanking you, and for the first time in a while I was free to just be with someone who just wanted me for me and I did not feel as if I was racing against the clock. She didn't quite understand his statement but figured it must be of some significance. You can stay the night; there is no need for you to leave before morning, if you like? Besides…I'm too exhausted to see you to the door. They both chuckled and decided that tonight would be alright. Before long she was sound asleep and so was he.

Chapter 10

Who's Cheating On Whom?

The door slammed and this immediately woke a sleeping Reneea, she glanced over at the clock to see that it was now 2:00 in the morning. She thought at first that maybe Rick was with the guys because surely by now he would have returned her calls. She could feel the throbbing in her head as much Vodka had been consumed by the ladies and she knew that her morning would not be pretty. As she found her way out of bed, she headed to the medicine cabinet for Tylenol to stop this pain that would not go away. She heard the two men climbing the stairs and realized that it was just Craig and Curtis, who both sounded like drunken sailors on leave for the night. They were in deep conversation and she decided to listen if she could.

Dad, this has been a great day, really man, from the game to the bar to the limo ride, you laid it out for us.
Don't mention it man, hey you are my son and I love you there is nothing to good for you or yours for that matter of fact. Man you are going to be a father, this is a big deal man…I hope that everyone had a good time.
Well I tell you who I know is having a good time tonight, and if he ain't it's a trick to it. Both men laughed hard. Who were they talking about, she was puzzled.
That waitress was fine as hell. Man I know…the killer part is that he has been blowing her off for the longest. Well why do you suppose he took her up on her offer tonight? Do you think it's because we were riding him? Naw man, it could have been a number of reasons for his change of heart. I was telling him earlier about me and your mother and how we sort of rekindled the fires last night and it probably just got him to thinking that he was tired of being alone. Reneea could not believe her ears. She was

furious with Curtis. She realized that they were talking about Rick and some woman being together, and she could hardly control her urge to open the door and go the hell off. I didn't know that he would get all worked up hearing about your mother and me, but I guess he did.

Ok dad, I'm starting to get the picture, and I think I have heard enough about you two. Craig made a face that let Curtis know that even though his son was a full grown man and expecting children of his own, he still did not want to envision him and his mother together.

Reneea heard the two saying goodnight and decided to back away from the door to make sure Craig was out of ear range for what was going to be one hell of a fight. Curtis entered the room completely unaware of what he was in store for. Curtis looked up and saw Reneea standing directly in his path.

Hey baby, did we wake you? I thought for sure that you would be asleep by now. Don't you fucking hey baby me! Curtis was caught off guard by his wife's demeanor.

What the hell is up? I know its late but is this necessary?

Curtis, I ask you not to discuss our love making with anyone deliberately and you do it anyway?

Reneea, whatever this shit is about its going to have to keep until morning, I'm tired and I want to go to bed. Curtis pushed past her as if to dismiss her from his presence.

The hell you say, we are going to get to the bottom of this shit tonight, my brother. Noticing the rage in her eyes, Curtis decided that he had better deal with her now rather than later.

Look Reneea, I am a grown ass man and I would like it if you would lower your damn voice before you wake up the whole house. Curtis how could you? How could you go behind my back and tell Rick about us, about what we did? Nea, what's the big deal about me talking about a little love making with my wife to my best friend? What is it suppose to be some big secret that you and I find ourselves fucking one another from time to time? What… do you have some special reason why Rick shouldn't know? What the fuck is up with that? Is it something that I need to know? Curtis was furious with Reneea for being so upset not to mention puzzled at that fact that she wanted to keep their love life a secret, he thought she would be happy for people to know that he had redeveloped an interest in their marriage.

For a brief moment, he began to think about how Rick had reacted earlier when he told him about his making love to Reneea and it resembled pretty much the same reaction that she was having right now.

Don't be stupid Curtis, of course there is no reason that Rick can't know, other than it was private things that we shared and I really didn't want my behavior with my husband being discussed as if I were a dime store whore! The things we did were for our eyes and ears only, how could you tell him what I did to you, what I let you do to me…not to mention I was drunk. Reneea began to cry and turn away from Curtis, when all of a sudden Curtis walked over to her and grabbed her by her wrist pulling her close to him. He was angry and she knew it, she never feared the fact that he would hit her, but the way he glared at her gave her cause to be alarmed. Curtis…let go of my wrist, your hurting me. She looked at him and noticed that he had a tear to well up in his eye.

Reneea Rae, I'm going to ask you only once…his voice was broken and scratchy and he spoke very slow. Is there something…, Is there something going on between…She interrupted him abruptly snatching herself free of his grasp before he could finish his sentence. You had better not be accusing me of what I think you are you bastard. All of your late night meetings and impromptu business trips, while I stay behind, now who's really cheating on who? You have the audacity to accuse me of something like this based on the fact that I'm a private person? You really got me twisted. He could see tears streaming down her face. She was crying partially because he had implied that she was sleeping around, but primarily because she realized that the reason that Rick had not responded to her and the fact that she heard Craig and Curtis discussing the fact that right now at this very moment, he was out making love to this woman all because Curtis had opened his damn mouth about the love they made because she could not get to him. She was going crazy inside with the fact that this woman was kissing him, touching and caressing him and God only knew what else. She thought that she might kill Curtis if she stayed in his presence a minute longer.

At that moment she put on her robe grabbed her cell phone and headed for the door. At that moment Curtis blocked her path to the door. Reneea, just where are going? We need to talk about this. Curtis Anthony Rae, right now we don't need to be in the same room together, yet alone talk about anything, I suggest you move the hell out of my way, or your son may really find out how his parents are living…She glared at Curtis in defiance, not backing down and Curtis did what any smart business man would do who knew that the stakes were to high to force his opponents hand. He backed away from Reneea and watched her exit their master suite entering a guest bedroom on the other side of the house, listening as the door locked behind her.

She walked over to the bed and slouched down on top of it sobbing quietly, she felt betrayed and hurt. She could not even remember feeling this hurt when she realized that Curtis was sleeping with Vanessa outside of their marriage. She was in agony over her lover and friend who had chosen to take comfort in the arms of another woman. What was she going to do now? How would she fix this massive problem, could she fix it? Would Rick return to her? Did he love this other woman? Did he love her anymore? Would he talk to her? Damn she thought to herself…who really was cheating on whom?

The night seemed endless and she tossed and turned until she had decided that it was futile to try and sleep. She sat up in the bed and stared out of the window feeling hopeless, wondering what her morning would have in store for her. She knew without a doubt, that she did not want to be alone with Curtis nor did she want to pretend that they were the picture of the perfect marriage another day. She prayed that some twist of fate would happen, maybe Craig and Angel could be encouraged to spend their final day with the Coopers, and this would give her time to make amends with Rick or at least see him and find out where his head was at. She had tried to phone him again only to have her calls directly intercepted by voicemail. This hurt her deeply as this had never happen before…even when he was in a session with a client he always managed to pick up the phone, explain his position and call her the moment he was available. This time, nothing no acknowledgement whatsoever, she laid there miserable and praying for day break to come.

Curtis was restless, but he managed to push the thought of his wife sleeping across the hall out of his mind. He was pissed at her behavior and for nothing he thought. He was not sure that he believed her where Rick was concerned but he wanted to. Maybe they had not been together sexually, but he felt in his heart of hearts that they may have had stronger feelings for one another than either of them had let on. Either way, he knew it was something that he would now pay closer attention to, especially since she had thrown up the fact that he himself could be called on the carpet for cheating. In any event he knew what his next move would be. He had done it before when he thought that Vanessa was not being exactly truthful with him and when he began working with clients that he needed background clearances on. Yes, Curtis was a shrewd business man and he always had contacts that could get the job done for him. Yeah, he knew what he had to do and who he had to call and would take care of it all in the morning. His bigger problem would be explaining why his fucking wife was clear across the hall with the door locked to his son who would definitely want to know if he was awake first.

Day break appeared and Reneea heard Curtis go down the stairs for his morning run and as soon as she was in the clear, she decided to go into her room to shower and dress before Craig could catch her coming out of the spare bedroom. Once safely inside her room she looked around and noticed that Curtis had made the bed to his ability and had left a note which read:

> *Reneea, we need to talk before this thing gets any further out of hand. I will start the coffee, hopefully, Craig and Angel will be visiting her parents and we can have a little time alone. I am sorry that you felt the need to retreat to another room and lock the door to keep me away, but I guess I should have not of grabbed your arm. I'm not certain what you are really upset over, but maybe we will find out together.*

This man must be on drugs if he thinks for one moment that I am going to sit around here with his lying ass, when my son leaves, so will I. She tossed the note on the dresser and gathered her clothing for the shower and prepared herself as fast as she could.

Downstairs, Reneea heard voices and knew that Curtis could not have returned from his jog so fast. She hurried down stairs to see what all the conversation was. When she entered the kitchen she saw suit cases and overnight bags by the door and saw Craig and Angel sipping on coffee and juice by the counter.

Well good morning you two! What gives that you are up so early? Hey mom. Morning mother, how are you this morning? I'm good, sounding and looking puzzled, she knew that she had hoped that they would go to her mothers but she did not think they would be packed and ready to go first thing in the morning. What's up with your bags? Oh yeah…while we were all out last night painting the town, my office called and I have got a major problem to deal with and I have got to get back to Grand Rapids today in order to deal with this mess, I was trying to wait on dad to get back so I could say so long. He shouldn't be much longer now…um speak of the devil, signaling to the drive, here he comes.

Curtis could see that his family was in the kitchen upon his approach and wondered if his son was discussing last nights events if he happened to go down for juice and by chance heard them arguing. He braced his self and went inside. Hey everybody, breathing staggered as he had just jogged six miles and as always in record time. Hey pops. Morning, dad. Curtis. Reneea's tone was dry and motionless, which caught her son's attention. He explained to his father what had happen and Curtis immediately agreed that he needed to get on the road and get back to Grand Rapids to handle this situation.

Craig and Curtis took the bags to the car and made casual small talks.
Dad?
Yeah?
Can I ask you question? Sure
Is everything okay with you and mom? Of course, why would you ask me that? I don't know, the two of you seem a little tense this morning? Nothing to worry about, we are often dry in the morning, its part of being married so long. Okay, fine…Is it a custom of you two to argue like cats and dogs and for your wife to leave the bedroom and sleep elsewhere? Curtis was surprised by his son's statement as he was shocked to know that he had that much information, had Reneea shared this information with him he wondered?
Craig that was nothing, we had a minor disagreement, and as we were both a little intoxicated last night we said a few choice words to one another that got a little out of hand. By the time you hit the end of the driveway, she and I will be in one another's arms trying to remember what we were ever fighting about.
Rick.

Excuse me? Rick, you were fighting about Rick. Craig, man you are concerned over nothing…nothing at all. Go get that beautiful wife of yours, kiss your mother goodbye and get on the road so that you can handle your business and leave all of this mess to me. Mom and I love each other and nothing can fade that.

Craig smiled at his father and felt assured that his father would smooth out whatever wrinkles there were between them that's what he did best. Okay, man I hear you. Thanks again for yesterday. Like I said, anytime. I love you man. Love you too dad.

They all stood outside saying their goodbyes and well wishes only to find Reneea extremely anxious for them to go so that she could get away from Curtis, and maybe, just maybe make heads or tails of this thing with her and Rick. She kissed her daughter-in-law, patted her belly and made her promise to take care of herself and her grandchildren. She received her forehead kiss from her son, and made him promise to call when they had arrived home. As their car left the long winding driveway Reneea retreated to the inside of the house with Curtis right behind her.

Did you get my note? Yeah. Well are you interested in talking now? Not really Curtis. I really don't know what I would say to you at this moment. Curtis looked at her and felt he had that and worse coming. Alright, then I won't push…
Fine…Reneea was dry and showed no signs of being agreeable.
I thought the kids were going to be here all day, but since they are not and you obviously don't want to be bothered, I will probably go into the office and do some paperwork or review the deal that Charlotte is covering to get up to speed on what's going on. I will more than likely be late…don't bother waiting up.
Curtis…did you forget or haven't you noticed, I gave up waiting up for you to arrive home long ago, as I was never sure when you were going to arrive yet alone come home. She was cold and direct, her eyes unforgiving and unyielding. Curtis went to the closet and grabbed his gym bag that always contained extra clothing inside.
I'll shower at the office, because right now I think distance from one another is just what the doctor ordered. Reneea rolled her eyes and place her hands on her hips waiting for Curtis' departure and thinking it would not be a minute to soon. Suit your self.

Curtis hopped into his BMW set his CD player on his favorite song and left without a second look in his wife's direction.

While the rest of the world was going insane, Rick found himself preparing to leave the young Goddess he had spent the night romancing and pleasing and was shocked that he actually had not allowed himself to return one call to Reneea Rae, who by now had to be out of her mind wondering where he could be, he thought to himself. Well love, thank you for a wonderful evening, I don't know the last time I've enjoyed myself to that magnitude. No, thank you for finally making my chase have meaning to it. He smiled at her and bent down to kiss her goodbye. Well I had better be on my way, I'm sure people are trying to contact me for some reason or another and I don't want them to think I have fallen off the face of the earth. I hope that you will look me up again Mr. Neal. Well, my love we will just have to wait and see now wont we? Rick got into his car proud of the way he had handled himself and the way his exit went off without a hitch…no strings.

Driving down Jefferson, he found himself wondering what he was going to say to Reneea when they came face to face, he knew he could not avoid her forever and that he would have to see her sooner or later, but how would he ever explain this or be able to listen to her explanation about her actions with Curtis. He also thought about his evening with the young beauty and thought though it felt good he would have rather been with the woman he loved, the one he had created…the one that knew him best. Damn Reneea…why damn it why! He was hurting and only time would heal him.

Curtis thought long and hard about the call he would make, he wondered if he cared enough to know…The thought of his wife tipping out on him had him crazy with jealousy and then he became just plain pissed off. As the phone rang, he knew what he had to do….
Hello?
Jamison? Yeah, who's calling? This is Mr. Rae. Hey my man, what it is? All you got it, I can't call it. What's on your mind? I need you to do another job for me. For sure man, whatever you need. This one is personal…I need you to trace my wife's every step, if she takes a piss in the middle of the day; I want to know about it. Yes sir. Names, places,

faces…whatever, Pictures…I need it all. When do you want me on it?
Yesterday! Say no more. Very good, you will receive payment the regular
way…you only report to me. Do not leave any messages with my
Secretary, got it? I'm ghost man. Later. Curtis felt bad for what he had just
ordered, but he needed to be sure. After his call to Jamison a private
investigator that worked for him before, he made a call to his loyal lover
who had nothing better to do than sit around and wait for Curtis to toss her
a bone, literally. Needless to say she was extremely excited about the news
that he would be spending the remainder of the day with her that she
sprung into action to make all the preparations ready for the man she loved
and loved to make love to. Curtis knew that he did not have to rush as she
would be ready to spring into action at whatever time he arrived.

Curtis pulled up in front of Rick's house at the same time that Rick
himself was returning home from his evening out and this excited Curtis'
curiosity as surely this brother hadn't been out all night with the hottie that
everybody wanted to be with. Rick saw his friend grinning from ear to ear
and knew that he was on an information expedition. He thought to himself
he had better get this over with if he wanted a chance in hell of taking a
shower and changing into fresh clothing.

To what do I owe this honor Mr. Rae? Nigga please, you pull up wearing
the same shit you had on last night and you think you ain't gone give a
brother details? They both laugh hardily as Curtis offers his friend the cup
of coffee that he had purchased for him. Thanks man, I can really use this
here. He took a sip of the coffee while unlocking the door and entered
while inviting Curtis to join him. Well? Well what? Man I don't have time
for the bullshit, what happen inquiring minds want to know? No, they
need to know! Hoe, please you mean dirty minds want to know. Whatever,
start talking. The two men entered the living room and both noticed that
Ricks answering machine was flashing uncontrollably. Rick trying not to
pay it any mind decided to walk past it as for all he knew it could have
been back to back messages from Reneea trying to find out his
whereabouts as he had turned his cell phone off in the middle of his date.
All he needed was to push that button and her voice ring out some crazy
sexy message of Love that he would not be able to explain and Curtis hear
it….For a moment he thought that that would be the end of his troubles for
Curtis to hear for himself how his wife wanted to be with him if it were
only possible…however, Rick also knew that it would really be the

beginning of his troubles and the end of Reneea's world as she knew it. Even angry at her, he couldn't do it. He loved her to much to cause her that much pain, not to mention the redecorating job that he and Curtis would do to his living room if he heard Reneea say some of the things she had said last night.

Hey man you must have a ton of messages here, aren't you going to get that? Curtis looked on inquisitively as if he himself suspected that he might hear something that would confirm his suspicion. Rick knew his friend, knew him all to well and judging by the way he had been acting lately where he and Reneea were concerned, he knew he had to think fast. Naw man, its probably just business clients or my sister trying to give me the week's forecast and projections for this weeks board meeting, not to mention if I stand there and take all of those messages in, you my brother would never get the dirt you so anxiously waited through last night to hear. He looked at Curtis dead in the eye and smiled as he knew he had won that round. True that, so start talking.

Curtis sat down and gave his friend the floor drinking his coffee listening intently as if he were going to recite the lines to a play. Well… Well since you must know ya nosey motherfucker…It was all that and then some, reaching to give his boy a pound. Man I knew that booty was gonna be right and tight. They both laugh. Yeah man, it's a good thing that I am as physically fit as I am or she would have killed my ass! Go on. Well…we agreed that there were no strings attached to the deal and that it was just sex and as consenting adults we would be able to handle that and walk away no problem and once that was out of the way, we fucked like rabbit dogs. Man the shit this girl did last night, made me remember why I got married in the first place! They both looked at one another and recited in unison *"All day all night sex alllllllllright"*. Yeah boy! That's for sure. But seriously I'm not looking to get married, it was just good to be with a woman, who wasn't hung up on trying to be a couple or who had inhibitions about getting it on. She was definitely not shy, if you get my drift. I have to know man…What? Did she give good head? Does a bear shit in the woods? I knew it man, why did she have to be stuck on *yo ass nigga?* I would have been given it to her… Rick looked at Curtis and shook his head as he knew full well that he was serious. Curtis Anthony Rae, this man had no limits, he felt that because of whom he was and what he had he could do anything he damned well pleased and generally did.

And this is the main reason he and Reneea had turned to one another. I know you did a little dinning out yourself, shit now days bitches make that a prerequisite, I'll do you only if you do me…Yeah I know, but really its part of the whole package, that shit makes a woman go crazy especially if you eat it right, man there is no limit as to what her ass will do in return for you. Curtis in agreement smiled at him and said …Rick my boy, you got a point there.

Speaking of married life, did you go home and have a good evening considering you are one of the lucky bastards that I refer to as the brother with the live in coochie. Man, hell no! What happened dude? Rick looked surprised and was surprised by Curtis' response, though relieved that he didn't have to hear about it, as he had braced himself to hear all about how he had to settle for Reneea, because he couldn't get to his tramp on the side and what he heard was the total opposite. Man what happen, I thought for sure with all the shit you were talking in the bathroom you were going to go…Curtis cut Rick off before he could finish his sentence. She must have been listening to me and Craig coming up the stairs talking about you and she heard me tell Craig that I had talked to you about me and her the other night and she was pissed. True she asked me not to go spreading her business but damn I mean come on, its you; Rick smirked as he knew full well why she did not want the story to be told…She has to know that I tell you everything? Go on, Rick encouraged him to speak…Well she got madder and madder and I couldn't understand all the attitude, she sort of reacted in the way you did when we were talking and I guest with all the alcohol I jumped to conclusions and said some shit I shouldn't have which really pissed her off and she started to cry.

What the hell did you say to her? Curtis hesitated before he spoke because he knew he would run the risk of insulting his friend as well, but he needed to see his reaction. Man I got pissed off and she tried to walk away from me and I wasn't having that disrespect…Man, man what the hell? I grabbed her okay? Rick looked as if he were going to knock the hell out of Curtis, he could literally feel his blood boiling his thoughts were racing a mile a minute and he kept waiting for Curtis to give him a sign that he was not going to have to beat his friends ass where they sat. Dude, did you…No! Hell no, I would never hit her…Rick felt a relief come over him because had Curtis said he had, all bets were off he was going to know right then and there that she had become his women, he was in love with her and there was no way in hell for any reason that he was going to put his hands on her.

Both men feeling the tension in the room began to settle down as emotions were running pretty high. Curtis continued slowly…I shouldn't have even grabbed her…I was so upset over the way she was acting as if she were some guardian angle appointed over you to watch out over you that I probably crossed sisterly love for attraction and I …. Yeah? I asked her if she had a thing for you, if there was something more going on here for her with you than she realized and the shit hit the fan. You Did What Nigga? Man I was drunk okay, I mean she went the hell off for nothing, because she heard us talking about you fucking Sherrie last night….Wait the fuck up, you told her this? No she overheard me and Craig in the hall. Rick thought about what he was saying and decided that the fact that Reneea already had a heads up regarding the situation just might work in his favor when it came time to explain. I mean you both had the same reaction. What happen then? She continued to cry, cursed me out a little more, threw up the fact that I had a lot of nerve accusing her when it was I that had all of the late meetings and overnight business trips yada yada yadaaa… grabbed her cell phone and took up residence in the guest bedroom down the hall locking the door behind her. The end…that's how my night went, while you were fucking Sherrie's brains out, I was getting mine cursed out.

Rick looked Curtis dead in his eyes smiled in his face and began to speak sarcastically…Nigga you got just what the hell you deserved. How the hell you gone come on her like that? You trippin. What else is new? Curtis, man, backing away from him and putting distance between them, Rick continued to enlighten Curtis on what time it really was; you are my boy we have been through a lot in our life time, but hear me and hear me loud and clear…if you so much as tap her in a way that makes her uncomfortable, I will kick your ass so bad that you would never know that we were once friends, our shit will cease to be especially over some bullshit like this with no evidence. Rick glared at Curtis in a way that let him know that all jokes were aside and that he meant every word that he had said.

Rick man, look, I know my shit was out of order, but put yourself in my shoes…She is the mother of my son the woman who's name is on everything that I own, I can't I wont loose all of that for nothing, and considering the way she loves you. A man could get a little leery especially when the feelings are so reciprocated. Curtis, you are a piece of work brother, you cheat on her daily, and have for years. You lie to her on a regular and have the audacity to sit there and try and justify the shit that you said to her that you said to me, are you serious nigga? You must be smoking to think that shit is going to fly. Look you are my boy and I try to understand, but from where I sit this shit is getting harder and harder to comprehend.

Look Rick, I know I have fucked up but I'm in too deep…There is a part of me that needs Vanessa as much as there is a part of me that needs to keep the appearance that Reneea and I are solid. Hell, in seven months our son will become a father…and I am not down with…No, I will not separate my family. They both stood there without words to say so Rick let him off the hook. Listen I know you have some place to be so why don't we just finish this at a later time, I need to perform the three S factor and get my day started anyway. Curtis looked up and smiled and they both repeated in unison "SHIT SHOWER AND SHAVE"! Bet, I do need to get out of here, I'm tense and after hearing about your little party last night, I'm in need of the right freak to set me off. I'm out man. Peace dude, don't worry, she will come around, she always does for you regardless to what you say or do. See ya man. Curtis picked up his keys and headed to the door; he never looked back and spoke quietly. Love ya man you really are the brother that I never had, take it easy…The door shut and Rick slumped down on the couch with passing thoughts of Reneea, where she was, how he could get to her and when he did, what would he say. The Skeletons in his closet were mounting as well.

Reneea had been a complete ball of confusion. She needed to see Rick, had to see him and with him not answering her phone calls, she did not know what to do. She dreaded the thought of showing up to his house unannounced, what if she had spent the night with him? What if she came to his door wearing one of his shirts which she often did after they made love? What if they were in love or something overnight after she has chased him so long and he was still angry about what Curtis had told him and he embarrassed her in front of this girl? No way in hell could she stand that! She could just see the 11 o'clock news filming the beat down of the century with her being carted off to jail. She had asked Tina to meet her for coffee and sat patiently at the Starbucks awaiting her arrival as she had to talk to someone, and she knew Tina would always be there for her.

When Tina arrived she was apologetic as she was held up by her husband who needed to be with her before he started his shift at the police station. It was always their rule that they made love before he went on duty in the event that God forbid he was killed in the line of duty, the last memory of her husband would be that they had made love and that she would carry that with her, even when they argued, the make up sex was off the chain because in his line of work as a Detroit Cop tomorrow was not promised.

Hey baby girl, sorry, I'm late, Mike had to work today…and you know, she smiled clinching her lips together.
Yeah, I know the rule.
That's right.
 Observing that her friend looked worn, out and no where near her radiant self; she took the approach of a concerned party. Ruff night sweetie?
The worst.
She began to tell Tina the whole sorted story by the end, Tina felt bad for her friend and wondered was this shit really worth it? She was sure that Craig, being a grown married man himself, would understand what his parents were going through? What was the alternative, stay miserable? During the conversation Reneea's cell phone rang. She glanced at the caller id and noticed that it was a caller from her past. Excuse me T, sure.

Reneea Rae, how may I help you? The caller on the other end simply said…You have been activated. Thank you for calling I will look for your progress report in the mail. She hung up the phone shaking her head back and forwards with a smile that made Tina question her friend about the call. Who was that sweetie? Was it Rick? No, not at all…let's just say that it was an old insurance policy that I took out in the event that trouble came my way. Trouble? What kind of trouble? Nothing to worry about T, and it is definitely nothing that I can't handle. She shook her head and was glad the she hand picked at lot of Curtis contacts over the years. She thought about it for a while and fanned it off as she had bigger fish to fry than what she was just made aware of. Tina, what would you do if you were me? Tina looked over the rim of her Cartier Glasses raised her eyebrows and stated…Boo; you don't want to know, simple as that.

Girl, stop it, really what would you do. At that moment the Starbucks employee came over to the table to bring Tina her special brew interrupting the conversation momentarily, after accepting and thanking the wait staff she returned her concentration to her friend's questions. Well, for starters, I would find out Curtis' net worth, figure out how much that was dead or alive, Reneea, began to smile as she knew she was in for a real comedic answer, then I would decide how to obtain his worth with as little hassle as possible, put that plan into action, call my grown ass son and his wife…let them know what time it really was, give their ass a holiday schedule as to who would go where on which days…after putting that house up for sale further expanding my cash flow, get a nice ass Condo on the Riverfront or the Shores. Find out how bad Rick really wanted to be my man, fuck his ass often as humanly possible and push the hell on with my life. Does that answer you question, my dear? Taking a sip of her coffee and looking as smug as someone who had come up with the cure for cancer.

You are stupid as hell, you know this right?

What? You asked.

The two broke into laughter that was uncontrollable for a while.

Seriously Nae-Nae, why are you continuing to do this to yourself? You can't shield Craig from the world for the rest of his life damn girl he is grown and about to be daddy, it's real admirable that you want to honor your marriage vows and all, but when you went to bed with Rick, you became as guilty as Curtis in violating the rules of engagement pertaining to MARRIAGE. Anyway you look at it it's all a lie, you deserve better. Maybe you didn't start the shit, but you are sure as hell keeping it going. I'm sure that once Craig and Angel got the whole picture the what's, why's and how to, would fall right into place. Tina, it is not that simple. Why the hell not? There are parts of you that love Curtis, and there are parts of you that love Rick…well what in the hell part of this shit loves you? Do you know anymore? Girl you were so wound up at the bar last night that I thought you were going to loose it in front of everybody. You can't keep going this way. Sure I wish if you had to fall in love with someone other than your husband that it wasn't his best friend, but now the deck is stacked and there is no way this can continue to play out without someone getting seriously hurt and as my best friend in the universe, the only bitch on the planet that understands me, I would prefer it not be you. Baby girl, I love you and would do anything for you, but I have to be honest this is not a win; win situation for anyone especially you.

Chapter 11

A Broken Heart Can Mend

Tina and Reneea spent a few more moments indulging in heart to heart conversations, but as the time passed, Reneea grew increasingly weary thinking about Rick. She had so much she needed to say to him, so much to ask him his thoughts on, but the bottom line was that she needed to hold him and have him hold her to be reassured that he still loved her in spite of everything that had taken place in the last 24 hours. She grabbed her purse and car keys and decided that if Mohammed would not come to the mountain, that the mountain shall go to Mohammed. She drove fast through the streets of Downtown and at one point it seemed as if the odds were in her favor, she made every light and as it was Sunday, not much traffic was flowing on Jefferson she made it to Ricks in record time. She always loved his neighborhood and the older homes that aligned the streets of Indian Village. It was a beautiful Victorian style home that had been refurbished beautifully and in the summer the flower garden was a wonderful place to spend hours outside just enjoying. She reminisced about the times she and Rick had spent evenings out there enjoying each other and the view with wine, she continued to think about how she had helped him plant flowers and weed through the lawn and how he would playfully wrestle with her in the grass occasionally kissing her and noting that many of their magical love making sessions started right there in that very spot. She had to make it right somehow, she couldn't risk them not being together in that way.

As she drove up to Ricks, she saw his car was in the back and that was a good sign, at least he was home as he drove his car everywhere and it was never put in the garage unless he was in for the night or had to go out of town. As she had not been receiving an answer when she called his cell phone, she decided that she would call the house and try her luck that route.

Rick heard the phone ringing and had thought twice about picking it up as
he was still dealing with his earlier conversation with Curtis, realizing that
he had failed to cut his cell phone volume back up and wanted to talk to
Reneea, he thought he had better answer it on the chance that maybe it
would be her. He darted across the room so that he would make it before
the caller either hung up or the voicemail decided to answer for him.
Hell…hello? Stammering, trying to respond as he was already three rings
in…
Rick?
Nae-Nae?
Yeah…umm, she let out a sigh of relief as his voice appeared to be softer
than before and the sheer fact that he answered period, not to mention
automatically assuming that the caller was her seemed to be a good sign
that a truce would not be far out of reach. Rick sighed himself as he had
sat there for hours trying to figure out just how he would call her and what
would he say once he connected to her.

Rick? Are you there?
Yeah babe, I'm here, where are you?
Well, believe it or not, I'm, I'm right outside your house. Rick smiled
inside and was relieved to be honest.
Are you?
Yeah… Rick looked at the security camera that scanned the entire
circumference of his front yard to see if he could see her and how she
looked. The cameras had been installed from when he used to see clients
at his home before deciding to move the business to the brownstone for
security purposes. He always needed to know who would enter his
residence.
I see you. Rick smiled at the thought of her just being there. You do, she
responded coyly as she knew about the cameras and how he always
checked them? Yeap. Are you planning on staying a while? Actually I am
if that's alright and if so I was wondering if I could put my car in your
garage. Rick was caught off guard by the request because normally when
she did that Curtis was out of town and she was planning to spend the
night without being detected. He wondered if that was her plan tonight on
a Sunday, it didn't add up. Of course, do you still have a remote opener in
your car?
Yes, and I will be right in. Nervously she pulled into the long drive which
lead to a massive yard she was very familiar with the territory and drove

right into the spot that appeared to be reserved for her. As she exited the vehicle, she wished that she had dressed more appropriately or at least sexy so that she could turn the head of her lover, however, at this time all she was working with was regular denim jeans and a MSU sweat shirt with a ball cap to match. Her long ponytail swung back and forth with the motion of her body making her appear so innocent. She was unaware but Rick was watching her walk toward the house and was pleased with what he saw. Yes, he did like it when she had all of her classy attire on or the sleek and sexy lingerie he loved to purchase for her, but most of all he loved her when he saw her dressed in the simple attire like the apparel of their Alma Mata or one of his dress shirts after they had made love. He rushed to open the door so that he could receive what he had been anxious to see all day. He favored when she made visits to his home as this was his territory and he felt comfortable there it seemed to him as though he had more of a right to her there, although the thrill of being with his beloved at her residence did spark of excitement as at anytime they could be found out by anyone.

Seeing her in person almost made him forget that they were experiencing a problem of mega proportions. As he was standing in the door way he stepped back to allow her entry. Why...he thought to himself, why is she with him and not me?
Smiling at him, she spoke with a feeling of relief and it was noticeable.
Hey you.
Hey yourself.
She was so excited to see him she became filled with emotion and her small little forced smile became and emotional gust of tears. All Rick could do was hold his arms open beckoning her to come inside.

Reneea had this way of rambling on when she was emotional trying to explain herself or her feelings that Rick adored and at the moment she began to speak he received a huge dose of it....*Rick I know your angry with me and I know that you probably don't understand...or that you don't want to see me, you are probably thinking to yourself right now, why am I wasting time with her when I can have a younger woman who is free and clear...or better yet you probably just want me to be on my way....but before you say any of those things please, please, please just try and let me explain but before I do...Could you? Would you just hold me for a while, I need you so bad Please Rick...* Before she could finish her sentence he

was holding her so tight he thought he might cut off her air supply if he
hadn't eased up. Reneea was sobbing uncontrollably not paying attention
to his directive to stop crying and that it was alright, he just began to kiss
her with force and passion in every place his lips would land. He moaned
that he loved her, that he was sorry for her pain, and that he wanted her to
stop crying and the more he did that, the more she cried. When she
realized that he was kissing her and caressing her, she in turn began to do
the same. She kissed him passionately and begged him not to stop. He
repeated the words I love you over and over again until she was returning
them to him. He was glad that he managed to shower as they dropped to
the kitchen floor stairwell and began to rip each others clothing off like
dogs in heat. Once free to pursue his body, she dropped her head in his lap
and began to give him head as if his life depended on being resuscitated.
He could not believe how incredible it felt. They had done this before, the
oral sex thing, but it never felt this way that he could ever remember.

Damn Nae, damn baby don't stop…oh its good um, um, um! Girl, yeah,
do that shit! Hearing him respond in that manner turned her on so much
that she felt herself have an orgasm before he even had the opportunity to
touch her. She needed him to love her still; she needed to know that she
was still his number one girl. When he could no longer take what she was
doing to him and needed to penetrate her walls, he pulled her up forcefully
pushing her flat on the ground mounting her with ease and familiarity and
thrust himself into her stroking her fast and furious, she moaned in delight,
scratching his back and screaming his name.
Yes, Baby Yes! I need it don't stop, don't stop! Harder, more give me
more, she screamed, more bay…Ahhhhh Shit, shit, shit, shit! Her breath
became ragged, I'm cuming Rick, baby I'm cum….ahhhhhh yeah her eyes
rolled back in her head and she flexed her legs around his waist and
pushed against his body with unbelievable force and at that very moment,
he knew he had pleased her and fucked her better than anyone ever could,
yes even Curtis…he knew that she belonged to him, married or not.

As they lay there in a puddle of their own sweat and bodily fluids, both to
afraid to move as they did not know the agenda of conversation that would
take place, the one thing for sure was that they were thoroughly happy
with what they had just done and that they were in love. There was no way
that this was infatuation or lust for either of them and what Tina had said
earlier was becoming more and more apparent to Reneea as her thought

process was that tonight going home and sleeping in the same house not to mention the same bed with Curtis was not an option.

Slowly Reneea turned to face Rick who had been looking at her the whole time they were trying to gather strength to get up. She smiled warmly and touched her finger to his lips. As he kissed them he began to speak. Nae-Nae?
Yes to weak to respond, but she did anyway.
You do realize that I have massive king size bed upstairs right?
Reneea looked around the kitchen stairwell and up at the ceiling, then back to Rick, who's eyebrows were raised in anticipation of her answer, and all the two of them could do was laugh at the place they had chosen for their ultimate make up sex.
Ah, about that…maybe we will get there for the second round. He kissed her on her nose and then her lips, stood up pulling up his trousers grabbed her clothing and picked her up in the same motion and began to carry her to his bedroom. She wrapped her arms around his neck and knew that this is what safe feels like.

As they made it to the bedroom, he sat her down gently on the bed leaning over her, to kiss her tenderly, he observed the fact that she might be thirsty after the love they had just made as he knew he was. Babe, would you like something to drink or food to eat? Have you eaten anything yet today? Lost in the thought that she really had not, she thought that food might be in order as they would have a long day ahead of them and if they were going to make love like that again; she was definitely going to need food for energy. She could not help thinking how in tune this man was to her, how thoughtful and considerate of her he was.

You know, come to think of it, I haven't eaten since yesterday, my stomach has been a little nervous; I suppose I could stand a light meal of some kind. Cool, I will order Thai and have it delivered, unless you want something different? No, Thai will be fine, just make my dish mild, she stroked her hair away from her face which had become loose after he removed her hat down stairs because the hair was only in pony tail form and held in place by the opening of the hat. Rick walked over to the nightstand to call ahead for the food as Reneea got up from the bed proceeding to his walk-in closet to select one of his shirts to relax in. As Rick knew what she was looking for, he just sat there wondering what color selection she would choose today with a smile on his face. Returning with the shirt, she went to the dresser and grabbed a pair of panties that were neatly folded on her side of the dresser that contained her initials embroidered on them. When he noticed that she was making a selection, still on hold to place his order he moved the receiver from his lips to speak to Reneea. Nae-Nae I don't know why you are wasting your time with those, you know they won't be on long, smiling at her as he knew without a doubt that most of their day would be consumed in passionate love making or raunchy sex, whichever came first. She just shook her head and continued to the bathroom to wash away some of the sticky feeling that was created by her lover.

After his call was completed he joined her in the bathroom as she was finishing her clean up and preparing the wash cloth to wipe her lover down, Rick came up behind her and put his arms around her admiring how they looked together in the large mirror over the bathroom sink. She smiled with approval of their reflection and wondered why it could not be like this all the time as this is when she was most happiest, she thought about the words Tina had spoke earlier *"well what in the hell part of this shit loves you?"* and they continued to roll over and over in her head. Rick must have noticed that she had drifted and called her name affectionately. *Nae-Nae, where are you babe?* She smiled at him and realized that she had drifted to deep in thought…I'm here, with you, where I want to be. This response made him happy and he turned her around to face him and kissed her long and hard. I Love you **Reneea Neal**! She loved it when he replaced her last name with his, though she knew it was not reality it was just something about how he spoke those words that solidify their relationship for her, it was as if that were her place and there was no other candidate for the position. Although today, which may not have been as true as it once was as there was someone who would like to have her spot and she was now painfully aware of this fact. Rick watching her reactions knew they needed to lay the last 24 hours to rest if there were ever going to be a hope that a broken heart could mend.

Pulling her by the hand from the bathroom, he began to speak softly, but firm. Listen, we have a minute before the food arrives, why don't we go down stairs, grab a drink, and talk while we wait for it? She was dreading this conversation but knew it had to take place. There were too many unanswered questions and she knew that this would have to be resolved. Ok, lead the way, jumping on his back for him to carry her down playfully. Once in the living room, he went over to the bar station and poured two glasses of white wine, re-corked the bottle and took a seat on the chase lounge chair which seated two comfortably. He sat the wine on the table and opened the floor for conversation.

Shall I start Reneea, or would you like to go first? I may as well since this whole thing may have been avoided by me Reneea said matter-of-factly. Rick looked at her lovingly as she had taken it upon herself to take the blame for what had happen. Rick, I am so sorry, I don't really have a way to explain myself except for the fact that I was drunk, missing you and in need of physical and sexual relations after you left. That brief moment in my pantry with you had me so wound up that I could have ran right out of that door behind you, and when you mouthed the words I love you, I was so….I wont lie, the fact that I had seen Curtis earlier that day in his office, I knew he was going to pull something as he was stuck at home with me because of Craig's visit, and just wanted to satisfy his manhood, the fact that he was paying me attention as a women for the first time in God knows how long….maybe I should have been more careful not to allude to the fact that we would be together, as really all I wanted to do was get under Vanessa skin by showing up there in the first place! Because of the flower incident and the Bitch had the nerve to cut off my company credit card. It was nice for a change that he was remembering the fact that I was his wife and should be reverenced as such. Rick looked on with urgency in his eyes, fishing for any sign that would point to her lying or not being completely honest about the situation.

She paused as if to hesitate. Go on, he persuaded her, I'm listening. He had brought the wine upstairs and proceeded to give me glass after glass, I needed it in order to stay in character and I drank it faster and faster I was well passed the point of buzzing, damn I was just plain drunk, hell at one point, I really thought he was you as my mind and body wanted to be with you so desperately. As you know, he is my husband and there had been some sexual history between us he was familiar with me and emotions were running on high I was bound to react to things he did. I am human and my body will respond sexually to sexual advances. I told myself to think of you and in the moment I did, I allowed him to share areas of love

making in which you taught me and explored with me, but it became
clearly evident that he was not you as I did not reap the same thrills from
him that you give me. It became more like playing a part or having an out
of body…Rick I don't know, I just knew that it was happening and I could
not tell you this again because there was no real way to explain it except
that it had happened and we had been intimate again on a fucking fluke
and you would not possibly understand that and think that in someway I
really wanted to be with Curtis, I could not see that look in your eyes.

I asked him to keep this between us because one, yes, I just did not want
you to know about this or have to hear it again and two, because I did not
want him making it seem as if it were this whole romantic encounter
where I was so in to him, at one point I had to muffle my screams as I was
calling out your name, not his. She stopped speaking and Rick noticed that
she began to cry. He hated putting her through this and himself as well,
but he had to know how this could have taken place? And as he sat there
listening he knew that he also had some explaining to do. Just then a
knock on the door startled them both out of their conversation and Rick
checked the cameras to make sure that it was the delivery man. He
excused himself, stood up taking money from his wallet and preceded to
the door to pay for their food. Once back inside he sat the contents of the
bag on the coffee table that smelled delicious but for the moment would
have to keep. They were on the road to healing and it needed to be
completed.

You were saying, encouraging her to continue. Anyway, Curtis and I had
this big fight because I overheard him talking to Craig about what he had
told you, and I heard them joking about that damn waitress, which Curtis
has mentioned before about you, as I had said before he was going to
make his mission to get you laid it made me angry. I just couldn't take the
fact of what they were saying. I couldn't famine the fact that you would
turn to another. I was out with the girls we had drank unbelievable
amounts of Vodka and Tequila and I just lost it. Curtis grabbed me and I
almost blurted out that we were in love and that I was leaving him. Rick
looking shocked at her statement, but wishing she had of as he
remembered the conversation of earlier when he learned that his friend
had handled her in a way that he was truly not please with. Continuing to
speak, Reneea became uncertain of her next choice of words. I couldn't do
that, because….well it wasn't so much because of the thought of my son at

that moment, but because I was afraid that you now had found someone else and that you too would be leaving me and all because I am married to this man that values me as one of his possessions, not his life or wife…Her voice broke off and she could no longer speak. At that moment, Rick felt worse about what he had allowed Curtis to do. He knew now that Curtis purposely told him the story so that he would force him to sleep with Sherrie in the event that he needed this as leverage somehow but he could not figure out just what he would do with it. Rick watched the woman he love cry and knew that whatever he said now would only make her feel worse. He could not tell her that he enjoyed this woman or that she made him feel pleasure, he would run the risk of hurting an already damaged Reneea to the core, but he had to be honest with her. Regardless whatever he said the fact still remained that he loved Reneea not Sherrie, no matter what he had done to or with her.

He pulled her close to him and calmed her tears and fears, stroking her hair away from her tired and sad face, he noticed that the gleam in her eyes was dull and he knew it was because of what he would say to her next. Rick sat up and looked directly at Reneea and began to speak calmly while looking into her eyes.

Baby, I will not lie to you, I can't…I was hurt when I heard that you had made love to Curtis again, but I was more hurt because of the way you made love to him. The things he was saying to me had me so angry I couldn't see straight. I too, was drunk, we had drank at the game, in the limo and by the time we got to Mr. Nicks one more was all that was needed to put a brother over the edge. I was so wasted; that I keep looking at Craig and the more I looked at him, my mind began to see a resemblance of me…his eyes seemed as if they were mine. This should give you some indication of how drunk I was… In any event, they began to egg me on about Sherrie, as she was relentless in her pursuit of me and though this was nothing different than before and I have resisted, I had the factors of all the alcohol so I can understand about doing something while you are drunk…but the worst part of it all was the fact the Curtis told me you let him in my door, the back door and this made me furious. Reneea cringed at his words and she knew that he was right. This had only been something that she allowed him to do to her and now that sacred spot with the reserved for "Rick Neal Only" sign had be desecrated. Rick continued to speak slowly; Hearing this made me want to hurt you back, and though it was wrong because after all he is your husband and he has a right to you in everyway…That belonged to me as far as I was and am concerned. Seeing that since we have been together I haven't been with another woman, I felt betrayed by you and decided that I could do it too.

It was just sex…I know you don't believe that, but for me that's all it was. I didn't want her before he opened his mouth. I will not lie and say that she isn't desirable or beautiful she is, but Nae-Nae she's not you. I also, had been suffering your absence on the phone and in my bed…I was lonely and I needed to be held especially after hearing about the Twins coming and watching him play the role of the perfect husband…it pissed me off. Then to top it off, I bet you guys think that Curtis is the one who picked up the tab for your little party at the Martini Grill didn't you? Reneea looked shocked and responded. Why, yes, because the waitress said Curtis had taken care of the bill? Yeah, he called because he knew you guys would go there and that they knew you by name and would recognized Rae before Neal he said he wanted to make sure that they allocated the funds correctly, but he did not bother to say that it was from the guys just him… But the credit card receipt bares my name. She was out done after she had given Curtis so much credit which belonged to the one who really loved her.

Rick I had no idea, Thank…he kissed her interrupting her appreciation, and she kissed him in return. Reneea, I love you and the more I think about this shit, I guess I always have. She saw a single tear roll down his cheek and the thought of it all became so overwhelming for her to take in.

Rick…I need to know something…do you have feelings for her? Do you plan to see her again? He looked at her puzzled, slightly laughed shaking his head from side to side. Woman do you understand what I am telling you? I guess not. Let me put it to you like this…If they could resurrect Bea and bring her back now, it would be no way that I could leave you. I'm in LOVE WITH YOU, and baby there is no changing that for me.

She smiled at him and grabbed his hands, she was on top of the world as he had compared her to his wife she knew it was wrong but she could not help feeling victorious that he would choose her…Rick, I know this is going to sound so high school, but, curiosity is killing me…Was she bet…was she…Hell I can't I don't want to know pulling back from him.

He leaned into her and finished her statement. *"Was she good or better than you?"* Is this what you want to know? He knew the way he answered this had to be handled with the utmost care. His mine replayed inserts from the evening and he answered her as truthful as he could. I won't lie to you baby, I am a man and when we are in bed with a woman our mission can be one sided depending on whom we are with. Yes, it felt good because I needed to release. But that was it. So in that respect it was good...noticing her face which looked like that was not the answer she needed to hear, he continued lifting her chin up with his finger so that her eyes once again met his, but a bowl of wet Jello would probably do the trick as well. As for it being better than you...This was a 27 year old who has yet to live, she does not know my body like you do, she was no where near you and I don't have feelings for her or love her like I do you so there was no way in hell that she was better than you, there was just no comparison in the two what-so-ever. This was true and he knew it and she felt it as he had already tried to explain how much he loved her by comparing her to his deceased wife. They begin to kiss each other tenderly, stroking each others hair and back as he caressed the frame of her face.

I love you girl.

I love you boy.

They held each other in silence for a moment as she laid her head on his chest listening to his heartbeat at times it seemed to be in rhythm with her own she thought. Silence fell upon the room with the faint sounds of Luther playing in the background.

Rick?

Yes baby?

She paused and looked up at him...In the event that you are feeling lonely or you are missing me...

Uh huh?

Do you have any Jello that you can make?

They were quiet for all of two seconds and they busted out laughing.

Only you girl, I swear. Getting up from the chair and bringing her behind him, Come on lets go microwave this food up so we can eat and I can get your butt back up stairs as I wont need Jell-O today. She smiled and agreed, "That's for damn sure."

They spent the rest of the day together enjoying one another's company in different ways whether it was conversation, love making or working cross word puzzles together which they often did as a past time even from their days in college. Curtis was not on the minds of either of them and Reneea made no mention of the hour growing late and/or her having to leave. They lay together as if they were the ones married to each other and believed in their heart of hearts that they had a right to. Reneea, excused herself to make a call to Tina, he could hear her talking in the other room and he could not believe his ears. She was making preparations to have Tina run interference for her, you know cock block. She had no intentions on going home tonight and he could not have been happier. At that moment, he called his assistant and asked her to begin calling clients that were scheduled for the morning to push their appointments to a later time slot or reschedule altogether. Megan had, no problem doing whatever Rick ask as he had always been a generous boss and would definitely compensate her for working on a Sunday afternoon. He quickly made the call and returned his cell phone to the same position it was before she left the room. He hoped he wasn't jumping the gun, but even if he had he knew he would be exhausted after they were done tonight. Returning to the bedroom where she had left Rick she noticed that he was smiling wide and broad which let her know that he had probably heard her conversation with Tina, so in classic Reneea, form she took advantage of the situation.
And what might you be smiling about so?
Me? Nothing, I'm just glad that you are back in my view.
Is that right?
Yeap, my story, and I'm sticking to it.
Uh huh…well I guess I had better get dressed and get out of here. Rick's eyes nearly popped right out of his head. Tina and I are going to catch a movie and have a bite to eat before Curtis, gets home. It's been a wonderful afternoon. Not cracking a smile anywhere. Instantly, Rick's smile turned into just the opposite, he was blatantly confused about what she was saying and as serious as she appeared he felt that maybe he may have misunderstood the whole conversation. Reneea, notice that he had become a little troubled and slightly annoyed, as she went into the bathroom to act as if she were getting her things in order. She peeked out of the bathroom door and saw a noticeably irritated man slouched on the bed completely disappointed looking down. She continued her task in the bathroom for a few seconds longer and decided that he had had enough. She walked out of the bathroom with her hair freshly brushed, her lipstick

freshly applied, and completely nude with the exception of the Candi Apple Red Pumps that she kept there for times such as these, to stand before him.

Well, I guess I'll be going. Trying desperately to conceal his disappointment, he looked up slowly to respond to find her there in front of him as naked as the day she was born smiling seductively. This pleased him so much that he rose up from the bed taking her all in his sight, walked toward her wrapped his arms around her and just looked at her. He could have choked her shitless for making him suffer needlessly.

You know that shit was foul right?
Reneea smiling and licking her lips laughed quietly rubbed her hand across his face grabbing his ears and responded.
Now! That's what you get for eavesdropping on my conversation big head! They kissed passionately with him backing up toward the bed and falling backwards with Reneea coming down on top of him laughing at the entire scheme. How she did love him and yes this was quite a risk that she was taking but he was worth it. They made love again and all was right with their world.

Chapter 12

Friend or Foe?

Tina laid her cell phone on the table and looked at the clock on the wall and decided that the day was going by slow, she glanced over at the television and realized that she was watching something that had been on for a while and she could not make heads or tails of what the show was supposed to be about. In her irritation she shut off the television with the remote, tossed it on the couch and walked over to look out of her balcony window, which stretched the entire span of her living room which was massive. She had a spectacular view of the water and Canada. She liked living on the Riverfront as yards and picket fences had never been her thing. She always said that her green thumb stood for making money as plants were not her by any means. She thought about the conversation that she had had with Reneea just moments ago and wished that her friend did not have to go to such lengths to be happy. She felt guilty sometimes because she was happy and content with her marriage and in her career. She also knew that it was largely due to the support that her friend had given her over the years as she had had family troubles early on and Reneea was always there for her. She wished that she would come to her senses and see that she deserved better than what she had been given. True, she had plenty of wealth and fine things that she purchased and a lovely home that Curtis had built for her from the ground up but none of those things could make up for the love and respect she lacked when it came to Curtis. He had cheated on her for years and everyone knew it. Little did Reneea know, but Craig knew it as well. Craig and Mia were still close and they discussed a lot over the years and this had often been a topic of discussion between the two of them, as he did not want his wife to worry and fear that he was the same or would turn out like his father was or would end up cheating on her, he did not let on to her about his fathers short comings, he valued her way to much, instead he would make out as if Curtis was a great husband who had weathered many storms in his marriage and managed to remain a husband. Truth be told when it was something about his marriage that he needed direction on, he went to Rick. Tina did not have the heart to tell her friend that Craig was in the know and aware of his father's antics. It often surprised Tina that Reneea did not suspect that he knew as she was so close to Craig and generally in tune to his feelings. Nevertheless her friend asked her to cover for her and she would walk through hell fire to make sure that she was safe and protected. Besides Curtis was a smart man and knew all to well that performing any type of violence on or toward Reneea would find her a widow as Tina's family was one of the largest well known families in Detroit, who were known for their drug dealings and homicide activity in the past. Until this day, people still suggested that though he was locked up, Dutch still ran much of the cities drug activity and being the daughter of a notorious Drug King Pin had its advantages as well as disadvantages. Tina's identity had to be changed on more occasions than she cared to remember for various reasons throughout her life. She still remembers how difficult it was dating Mike who majored in Criminal Justice in college and had nothing but contempt for the criminal element and the corruption that was so apparent in the major police departments. She was so head over hills for him that she never told him who she was until she was sure that he was equally in love with her, if not more. By then it was too late and turning back for him at this point would be like cutting open a vain to end his own life. She thought back to how she broke the news to him about who she really was and how he just stood there in a paralyzed state trying to figure out what he was going to do about the problem he had just inherited, and how it was Reneea that went to Mike and brought him to his senses. The little lie she fabricated about Tina being pregnant helped as well Mike came from a broken home and was definitely not going to let his child feel for a moment that it was not loved or wanted. Growing up in an orphanage can do that to a child. Luckily that night Mike returned to make up with Tina and let her know that her past was not what mattered but the future that she was building with him would be everything, they made love and really did conceive Mia that night and have been in love ever since and he was always the adequate man she needed to be honest, he was more than enough. He went through hell when it came time for promotion on the force to be a plain clothes detective in the drug division as they performed background check after check mainly because of Tina's ties to Dutch.

Curtis would think long and hard about hurting Reneea as Tina was still owed favors in the city and beyond and she had warned him years ago that if he ever thought that Baby Girl resembled a punching bag that a telephone call would be the beginning of his end and he knew she meant it. In the middle of her thought she heard the elevator and keys began to jingle in the lock. Bay, she heard Mike call out to her and was surprised as she was not expecting him home until late.

Hey Babe what are you doing back here?

We were over staffed and a double was not required as I had officers that wanted to pick up shifts. I see. Well I'm not complaining I'm always willing to have my husband home with me especially on a Sunday afternoon.

Is that right, pleased by his wife's statement walking over to her to hug and kiss her? I thought by now you and Nae-Nae would be knee deep in Nordstrom's somewhere. No. Not today, baby girl has other plans. You're blocking, no doubt?

What else can I do, but? She really needs to cut her losses and be about her business. I'm not certain but I think Rick went out with that waitress from Nicks? Curtis all but paid her to fuck

with him all night. Well, you are right and Reneea knows. What? Yeah, he told her all about it today. Damn…She's cool. They apparently had a long talk about everything and they know that Curtis is behind all this shit; besides she can't really fought him, she's is married to his friend.

Mike I want her out of that marriage. Baby there is nothing you can do if she is hell bent on staying with him for appearances. I know, but I just want her to be as happy as we are, kissing her husband softly and caressing his arms. Everybody isn't us, and keep in mind this will not be a smooth transition for anyone, Rick and Curt go back a long way. Craig will be mixed up in this shit; don't forget the babies are coming. No this will not be a fairytale come true…Hell I might even have to take a nigga to jail when this shit comes out. Let's hope not. Curtis grabbed Reneea last night but he did not hit her. Mike looked concerned as he knew the promise his wife had made several years ago as well. Is she alright? Are you being notified of a homicide? Don't say shit like that babe, you will make me a co-conspirator. Don't ask! Mike laughed but knew full well that she was as serious as the day was long.

You know you are a hell of a friend…Tina smiled at her husband and said…Well it sure as hell beats being a foe, she has enough of those in her life. Mike walked up behind his wife who was still admiring her view, put his arms around her waist and kissed her softly. Tell me. Hum? Do you have plans for the rest of the afternoon, or might I interest you in a little mattress mambo? You get the oil and I'll get the wine. Bet! They headed off in the direction of their bedroom and Tina thought to herself that she had to be the luckiest woman in the world. To be loved by such a terrific guy.

Curtis lay on the bed looking at Vanessa, how she was a sight for sore eyes. He was thankful that he had her as she was the only one who truly knew how to satisfy his appetite for pampering and catering to his major size ego. She catered to him hand and foot, she reminded him of the movie "The Stepford Wives", where the plot consisted of men turning educated woman into servants of the men who worked and they stayed home and prepared everything and prepared their homes like the woman you hear of in the 50's. He could hardly call what she did at the office work anymore, considering she spent most of her time going down on him under the desk and fetching his whims, wants and needs. In any event she made him feel like the man he wanted to be. Tonight he was having a hard time getting use to her again as he had spent two whole days making love and spending time with Reneea, who had surprisingly become someone so different. He thought about how she had let him perform anal sex on her and how she had spoke to him like an S&M porno star who knew exactly how she wanted to be pleased and how she wanted to please. He smiled when he thought of her lying on her belly demanding that he stroke her harder and harder and remembering how she came so violently that he became aroused, which was identified by his lover who thought she was the source of his erect penis. Either way, his dick was hard and she was there to relieve him.

Ooh baby, is that for me? She asked touching him gently.

Who else bitch? Don't you want to make daddy feel good? He played up to her like she knew he would…it really turned her on when he talk dirty to her and called her names that were far beneath her.

She saw the longing in his eyes to be satisfied and she was more than willing to give him any and everything he desired. She stood directly in front of him and began to remove her clothing like a trained stripper; she had missed him so much and was so glad that he had come to her. She straddled him like she was mounting a horse and rode him until he came inside her like a volcano. Watching him ejaculate, she wondered why she allowed him to treat her the way he did but because she needed him so much, loved what his money did for her, and had no desire to be poor ever again…she had made it up in her mind that if he told her to stand on one leg and bark like a dog in order to prove her love and loyalty to him…she would.

After they made love for what appeared to be the 5th or 6th time, he decided that he should probably call Reneea and let her know that he would be in the office overnight as the deal Charlotte was working on was going south and he needed to salvage it. Of course this wasn't the case; Charlotte was a shark when it came to business, no one got off the hook without signing and deposits were rendered in cashier check form if not cash. But he needed a reason not to go home tonight as he needed to be with Vanessa who stroked his ego by any means necessary and he was long overdue for stroking. Little did he know that Reneea would see right through this as she had known Charlotte's tactics and knew that if there was a buck to be made she would find it, not forgetting she had been on staff for years and Reneea was the one she was really loyal to and that she was the one who kept her informed about the business dealings of Rae Enterprises as the Foundation of the business was built on Arthur/Craig the majority share holders of the corporation in which was founded by the MAC Foundation, Matthew Arthur Craig, Reneea's, father who had left her a considerable share of the business. Poor Curtis never knew that at anytime Reneea could snatch the ranks right out from under him and his little whore if she so chose. See, what Curtis forgot or never gave much thought to was the fact that Reneea not only majored in Beauty and Cheerleading in college, but she graduated with a Master's in Finance. All the while Curtis thought that Charlotte was loyal to him and Rae; she was just protecting the family jewel.

Reneea's phone rang and she noticed that it was Curtis calling, she rolled over off of Rick as he had just made her feel so incredible she felt she could take on the world. She answered and her voice was short, direct and to the point.
Hello?
Nea?

Yes? Hey um it looks like I will be in the City for a while the deal doesn't look like it is going to close and I need to make sure it does as this is a considerable amount of money at stake. I thought I might be home later but it looks like an all nighter. Vanessa was thrilled to know that her man was making plans to be with her until morning and smiled as if she had won the Nobel Peace Prize. Reneea, knew he was lying and was relieved…

Oh no, that can't happen, she said frantically and sarcastically.

No…it can't, so you will understand my urgency to be here tonight? Of course Curtis, after all this is our financial stability you are speaking of correct? Exactly dear, our future depends on it. Reneea rolled her eyes up in the sky as she knew this was just another lie. Rae was financially sound and she had the portfolio to prove it. Well, I was still out with Tina and I thought I might spend the night with her as Mike is on a double anyway so I guess I will see you at five tomorrow. Yeah, that's my plan…did you set the alarm on the house by any chance? Yeah the house is secure, don't worry. Ok, I will try and call you before I turn in on this old sofa, if I turn in, I can't imagine what could have gone wrong? He gave Vanessa a signal that it was all clear and she smiled as if she had won the lottery.

Ok Curtis, I will see you in the afternoon. Good night.

Reneea?

Yes?

I love you. This little additive always pissed Vanessa off; however, she knew it was necessary so that he would not blow his cover, so she thought. Ok dear thanks. Her response caught Curtis off guard as she did not bother to return his sentiment. Did you hear me, he retorted?

Yeah, I said ok?

Bet, he said and hung up the phone. Her little reaction let him know that she was still angry. He heard the click of the phone and then the dial tone and decided that Jamison needed to be contacted. He dialed the number and waited for the response.

Jamison?

Rae here.

Hey guy, how's it going?

What do you have for me man? Curtis was not interested in any small talk just the facts, irritated that his wife had not stated that she loved him as they departed the phone call.

Are you sure of the target?

Yes, I'm sure why?

I was just wondering why you wanted to pay me all this money to tail a housewife that spends the day cleaning your house, inventorying your cabinets and lunching with her best friend. Oh yeah picking up dry cleaning? And don't forget watching old movies at what looks to be a slumber party for the night?
Is that it?
Ah…yeah!
What about my boy Rick?
What about him?
Was he with her at all today?
Jamison laughed as if Curtis had told a joke; unless that nigga was disguised as a bottle of fabric softer…he was no where around.

Curtis could not believe his ears he thought for sure he would know what was up today. Jamison always got the details he needed. It was obvious that Curtis was puzzled.
Jamison, you are sure there is nothing else?
That's it my brother….Curtis was baffled he just knew there would be some mention of Rick in the mix. Well, stay on it until you hear otherwise.
Yes Sir your dime, your time.
Bet.
Curtis hung up the phone and decided that he would now place a call to his boy, to see if he would slip up and say that he had seen her or heard from her.

Rick's cell phone rang and he knew beyond the shadow of a doubt that it was Curtis. He looked at Reneea who was busy in text mode with some sort of business, and decided to answer after she looked up and saw him put his finger to his lips to silence her alluding to the fact that it was Curtis.

What up Curt?
What up man?
Shit, I'm just laying here trying to get my energy up from last night that was a lot of drinking we did.
Yeah I know… and nigga you ain't foolin nobody… yo ass is trying to recuperate from that young girl who put it on you last night. Rick laughed as Curtis had no clue…yeah he was recovering, but it was from the good sex that he had just performed on and with his wife.

You home?

Naw man? I was wondering if you had seen Reneea or talked to her today. Naw dude, not all day. I just told your ass I been home trying to get myself together, I have an early shoot and I need to be on point. This client right here is the money shot, and I have got to be on my game in the A.M. What, you haven't talk to her? Not in a minute, I called the house and she didn't answer…I thought maybe she would have contacted you. Now you know if she is going to be with anybody on a Sunday afternoon, and you're not home it has to be T. Yeah I thought about that. It's just that when the two of us have a little disagreement she calls and talks to you…Not all the time. You think she still mad about last night between you two? Probably. Well don't matter, I'm not going home tonight no how. I just was wondering if you had heard from her. I don't need that mental anguish bullshit, when I can stay in the arms of woman who is willing to treat me like a king and reverence the blessing that I am in her life, you know?

I guess so man…Rick answered him with disgust as Curtis really did see himself as some kind of real catch. He had always thought a little too highly of himself than he ought to. Well a if, and that is a big if as I am going to turn off my cell after I get a little food in my stomach; if I hear from her I will tell her to call you as you are worried about her. Man don't bother because as soon as I get my energy back from what my boo just did to me, I will be tapping that ass again and won't want to be disturbed once I get in the groove if you know what I mean? I hear ya brother. Well take it easy. I will see you at the court tomorrow. For sure.

Rick turned off his cell phone as he had the woman he loved lying next to him and did not have to worry about her calling and missing him, not to mention that he just did not want to hear from Curtis again tonight. Rick rolled over on his back and looked at Reneea who had put on his shirt and had sat back against the head board looking at the television and all of sudden felt him watching her. She noticed that he was smiling and looking at her with love and adoration, something she loved about him because she never had to guess what was on his mine or in his heart.

Hey you?

Hey you?

Penny for your thoughts?

How about I just give them to you for free?

If you prefer. Rick sat up on the bed next to her and began to caress her face, smiling while looking lovingly into her eyes. I was just thinking about how much I love you and wish that it could be this way always. I was thinking about how important our time together is to me and when you finally come to the crossroads and decide that this is the turn you want to take, how much more happier I will be. Reneea kissed him tenderly and felt that there were no words left that needed to be said.

As they slept the night away, periodically waking up through the night to make love and please one another intimately, morning would find both Rick and Reneea struggling to get their day started. She was beautiful to him no matter what the morning held and as there was no hair rolling or wrapping she awoke to find that a comb was definitely in order. Noticing that she was laying alone, she quickly sat up to see that breakfast in bed had been prepared for her and this thrilled her so much. Rick was so considerate; there was nothing that he would not do to assure her of happiness. Craig reminded her of him in this matter as she thought about how her son fussed over his bride so much this weekend and really anytime that they visited. She thought this to be an admirable quality of her son and could not remember it being that present in Curtis.

Good Morning! Good morning baby. Is this for me? I'm guessing yeah since there is no other beautiful woman that I love in my bed waking up to greet me. Reneea smiled because surely she must look like hell. She proceeded to enjoy the coffee that he had kept warm for her as he ate a piece of toast that he had taken from her tray. Suddenly Reneea sat back against the headboard and sighed heavily. Noticing her discomfort he began to enquire about what was troubling her.

Babe, what's wrong? Nothing, I'm just thinking about my night of pleasure being over and my day of what the hell do I do next and where in the hell do I go from here starting. What, no plans today? Rick do I really ever have plans, think about it? Well…he paused as if he were searching for an answer.

Tina has her company to run. She can go to an office and do something meaningful. You have the studio and your clients and when you feel like it, you can go play CEO of a company you don't even want to run as Rachel does it for you. And Curtis, well, he has Rae Enterprises, while I the socialite wife, get to lunch with friends if they are available, putter around a house that I have rearranged and decorated more times than I care to mention and shop as if that is the only thing I was meant to do.

Boo, if this bothers you so much? Why don't you take a more active roll in the company? Come on Rick be for real as if Curtis is going to let me hang around his little hoe haven all day? Besides it is because of his ass that I don't have a real job. He wanted me to stay home and raise Craig, be there for him washing, cleaning and pretending to be the *hostess with the mostess* that I forget about all of my plans and dreams. Then baby...take them back. Reneea just looked at Rick and shook her head. She knew all to well it was just that simple for him as he had never asked Bea to defer her dreams and goals when they got married. She was a doctor and it never threatened him that she was successful in what she did. He was always supportive of her and her plans. She envied that about him and Beatrice as a couple. Rick had played pro-ball right after college and this was his passion as he suffered the knee injury and was never a 100 percent after that he retired and went into his major in college, photography and videograhpy. He was damn good at what he did and photographed many top rank stars not to mention the video shoots he had worked on. His father was upset when he did not join the family business after the ball career fell through as Rick had a head for business and he was his father's only son, but in his passing he still left the business to Rick even thought it was his sister Rachel who had the passion to follow in their father's footsteps. She never blamed Rick for this as they were close and she understood that her father was a bit of a chauvinist especially since Rick only ran the company in name only and was perfectly fine with Rachel being at the helm of the company. She knew he was an advocate of following ones heart.

Nae-Nae, you do realize that those four years in college, and the graduate school business sent you on your way with a Master's Degree don't you? And you have always wanted to be an event planner, so why not start your own thing baby you have more than enough resources to do it and I will help you in any way that I can. You are so talented, yes I think that you are being wasted in more ways than one, but only you can change that. I know that if you were my wife I would definitely be pushing you to do you! Boo, I would never hold you back from anything you wanted to try or do. Reneea, looked at Rick in disbelief, would you really support me to go off on my own endeavors without interference? Baby, you are a bird that was meant to be free, I could never clip your wings. They kissed and embraced each other almost causing the breakfast tray to tip over. Seeing this Rick jumped up to catch the tray and prevent the mess setting it on the breakfast nook table that adorned the bay window of the master bedroom. As he turned to face Reneea, he saw that she had removed the shirt she had slept in over night and was motioning for him to come to her. He had said such loving and endearing things to her that the only way she could think of making him feel as good as he had just made her feel was physical. Ricks eyes rolled up in his head smiling, knowing exactly what treat he was about to be in store for and did exactly what she demanded of him.

Lord, give me strength, he said as if he were exhausted from what he anticipated that she was going to do. She pulled him in close to her touching him to make sure that he was ready and noticing that he was, he moaned....*Be gentle with me.*

They would make love prompting her exit to return to her world of anguish, Rick's world of silence, and Curtis' world of self indulgence, with all of their excess baggage on the side.

Chapter 13

Running On Empty

As time passed, the months and days grew shorter, summer had come to a close and another year would soon be coming to an end, Reneea grew increasingly weary married to Curtis, but managed to keep her wits about her. There was no doubt in her mind that the love she felt for him was just remnants of what once was. She managed to deal with it the best she could, however, his constant need to be away from the house helped and the frequent business trips made it easier for her to put plans and ideas into perspective more clearly when it came to her life. She had begun to work on her business interest and decided that she would pay more attention to Rae Enterprises from a distance. She had a plan and putting it in action the right way was most important but concealed at the moment.

The holidays were approaching fast and were always a good time. The kids came down and now with the anticipation of the twins, everyone was excited with shopping and preparation. December would bring the arrival of two special little people; it sort of gave a whole new meaning to Christmas. Since Tina and Reneea were kids, they had grown up together and spent most of their holidays together, because Tina was being stashed away for safety with her. Reneea's family was gone with the exceptions of a few aunts and a brother who lived in Anchorage who was from her mother's first marriage so they were not particularly close but kept in touch like polite strangers as they were still blood. Tina was estranged from her family by choice due to their unspoken criminal activity but she still managed to keep in touch especially if it became necessary. She often sent her father cards in prison all from different post marks with different names and surrounding cities throughout Michigan and Ohio sometimes she would have them sent to him as far away as California, whatever she

117

needed to do to keep her family safe and her father's involvement in her life minimal. Mike, who grew up in the Sister's of Mercy Orphanage had no family outside of his wife and daughter and a few of the guys in the department so it was natural that Tina's friends and family would be his. He often wished that Mia would marry and have grandchildren that would create a clan all his own, but he was still waiting as Mia had no intentions of settling down until she found the man that would come partially close to filling her father's shoes. He loved his daughter more than life itself and to be honest no man would really ever be good enough for his princess. Rick had Rachel and his mother as his father had past some years back but he had always been close to Curtis' family and the rest of the gang especially after Bea died. He just did not find it necessary or comfortable to be around her family as he felt out of place; sort of like the sore thumb sticking out. He always felt as if they were trying to overcompensate for her absence, they would avoid saying her name or talking about their life together. All of this forced behavior made Rick uncomfortable not to mention that Bea and Reneea's families were close as their mother's use to belong to some kind of charitable organization group together. Considering that Rick and Reneea had this unspoken love affair going on now just made it more difficult for him to be around them also? Curtis had no siblings and Rick had always been the closest thing to a brother there was, and the majority of his family spent time at his home as it was the largest and it was always assumed that he would foot the bill for the family gatherings because he had the most money. This irritated Reneea somewhat as she had always thought his family to be moochers; they came around when it was a benefit for them or if financial gain was their motive. However, it was only twice a year that she would have to really deal with them and then they would crawl back under their rocks until the next event or somebody somewhere had baby momma drama and needed a loan or a problem fixed. Besides, Curtis liked it when he got to play big man on campus and everyone flock to him, it appeared to feed his ego as if he were a king and his loyal subjects stood about and talked about how great he was. This is why Reneea was glad that her inner core group would be there to balance off the tension that so easily arose when they all came together. She didn't know when the change had taken place in Curtis all she knew is that it had and she hated the person he had become. When they were dating he was so different back then. She loved him even if he were not her first she always felt that he should have been, but at a time when she needed him most, he was no where around. She often wondered if that should have been her first clue to warn her of what was to come.

Last year it was decided that he would only have the whole family in for Thanksgiving and that Christmas would be just a private setting with their close friends and family along with a few Rae Employees who were considered top executives. So Reneea was really much more excited about that. Nothing much had changed in their mundane life together, they were still pretty much just going through the motions of a married couple who lead totally separate and different lives under one roof. If and when Curtis desired his wife, it would be nothing like the passionate and exciting times that he had encountered over the summer with her. No, it was more like the Reneea who was there when he could not be with Vanessa and because he had gotten a hard on and needed to release, she was better than his hand he thought. Reneea was still beautiful and had a wonderful body, but her responses to Curtis' touch were so cold and ridged. She did not enjoy making love to him anymore because the more she stayed with him and realized just what type of man he really was or had become, she continued to fall further and further out of love with even the memory of once loving him. Curtis had given up months ago having her tailed by Jamison who offered him nothing substantial and could not bring him the proof he needed that she was sleeping with Rick or anyone for that matter and because he had always trusted Jamison's information he had no reason to keep him spying on her. He was relieved that he had not reported evidence of her sleeping with Rick because this would cause him to loose his wife and best friend all at once, he didn't care too much that he would loose the wife, but he needed to have the partnership he had with Rick.

Reneea had remained in their bedroom with Curtis because she knew she had to for appearance sake. She thought about the night before his business trip while he was packing that she had decided to turn in early and would shower while he had the luggage on the bed as this would give him time to complete his task and be out of her way by the time she was done. But suddenly she saw him come into the bathroom disrobing, the pure thought of this sickened her and she wished she could disappear before he had a chance to touch her. He entered the shower where she was and told her that he was in need of a little quality time with his wife before he left town. She couldn't help thinking to herself that he was providing her a pity fuck as he knew that he would spend the entire trip with his tramp and needed to make it seem as if he would be missing her. Curtis, removed the bath gel from Reneea's possession as she managed a forced smile, and began to apply it on her with his bare hands, caressing her body and lathering her in areas that would ordinarily spark excitement for a couple who were going to engage in love making. He rubbed her nipples which responded as it was natural and began to kiss her. Her natural reaction as a woman being aroused kicked in so that he would just do what he needed to do and get away from her. He inserted his penis into her from behind turning Reneea away from his face so that he could not see her looking at him with contempt. He stroked her rapidly and then gently, hoping for some sign of affection that never appeared at this point it really did not matter to him; he just needed to get off. She could feel him inside of her and she allowed him to make her cum just so that he would stop and hopefully, let her alone. After faking that the orgasm was good, Reneea pulled away from Curtis who had just climaxed himself as she felt used and empty inside where he was concerned and continued to wash his juices away from her thanking God that she was already bathing and would not have to smell his scent on her a moment longer than she had to. Curtis who was noticeably disappointed in her performance turned toward the other showerhead, cleaned himself and exited the shower just as cold as he had entered it. She thought about how this could not continue, but realized that she had to be smart about what she did and when she would do it.

Curtis was headed on a business trip, some type of Marketing Convention in New York, where members of his staff would be required to accompany him on the trip, some for business and the secretary for pleasure of course, his. The thing about all of this was that Curtis grew more and more daring where Vanessa was concerned. It was almost as if he did not care if people in the office knew about their office romance as there was not one person who wanted to be unemployed because their boss could not keep his dick in his pants or at home with his wife where it belonged so they made it their business not to mind his business. Charlotte, on the other hand, could care less about whether or not he knew of her disapproval and often locked horns with Vanessa on occasions that it became necessary. Considering the fact that Charlotte was far too important to the company structure, he tried his best to keep the peace between the two, when he could. Vanessa knew that sexually Curtis belonged to her and she did not hesitate to use it to get what she wanted. She also felt as if he cared for her more than he let on and to some degree she was correct. He always made it a point to let her know how good the love making was especially when he had to be away from her for extended periods and times. Vanessa fed every desire that Curtis had no matter how belittling it was for her. During the business trip, she was flaunted and paraded around like a show pony in front of Curtis' clients and business connections. He was not above allowing them to cop cheap feels off of her if it would seal the deal he needed to accomplish, the skimpier she dressed the better the finesse, he always said as most of the time the men were to busy looking at her breast to concentrate on the business that Curtis spoke of. Before they knew it, they had been captured by the lovely Vanessa and were signing on the Dotted Line for Curtis. At one point during the trip, he sent her to the hotel room of the president of a company that Curtis wanted as a client with contracts to sign and herself as a bargaining tool. Needless to say the deal was cinched as giving head was not considered intercourse in Curtis eyes, more like a favor for a favor type service. He rewarded her handsomely when she returned to their suite with contracts signed in hand.

Proud of her accomplishments, she returned to the room with anticipation of how her lover would reward her for what she had managed to do. It never even crossed her mind that she had allow a man that she had no feelings for put his penis in her mouth for his pleasure while she made her bosses pockets fatter as she knew that it would ultimately trickle down to her. Entering the room she saw Curtis waiting for her with cocktails in hand.

Here you are Daddy.
Baby, is that what I hope it is?
Have I ever let you down Curtis?
Not that I can remember, now bring them to me you sexy bitch. Vanessa loved the effect that she had on him. She was such a turn on for him and she knew it. She moved slowly and seductively toward Curtis with the contracts extended in his direction, she saw him become hard as a rock as she walked toward him, she could feel the desire for her as she grew closer and closer. He snatched the contracts out of her hand glanced at them to make sure that the signature was correct, tossed them on the bed and pulled Vanessa to him tightly kissing her and congratulating her on a job well done. This excited Curtis so much that he was hard and wanted her right then and there. He ripped open her blouse, not concerned over the

damage that was caused as buttons flew everywhere from the $600 Vera Wang blouse he had just purchased for her last week, exposing her firm breast and hard nipples while hiking her skirt up to her waist, which revealed that she was not wearing panties. He saw that she was moist between her legs which meant that she was excited with the anticipation of what was to come. Curtis began to kiss her breast making her moan with pleasure sliding down to sit on the edge of the bed where he began to lick her clit going into a full oral sex maneuver that pleased her so much as she began to moan and thrash about digging her nails into his shoulders. She loved how he made her feel and ordered him not to stop. She begged him to give her what she needed. Suddenly, he stopped looked her in her eyes kissed her and pulled her down on top of him putting himself inside her stroking her slowly kissing her with every thrust inside of her. He picked her up still stroking her as she screamed and moaned his name. "Give it to me Curt, don't stop baby, I need it, I want it don't….Faster and faster he stroked her until he exploded calling out her name and telling her he loved her. Curtis laid Vanessa on her back, pulling himself out of her and off of her. She looked up at him puzzled as to why he was stopping. How she loved his body, he moved like a cat on the prowl and when he was totally nude it turned her on so much. Curtis walked over to his Jacket and retrieved something from the pocket and returned to the bed where his lover waited in anticipation of explanation. He lay down next to her and began to speak softly to her.

You know that I love you, don't you V?
Yeah…well I pray you do, because I love you so much. Daddy, I would do anything for you, kissing him softly.
I know, you proved that tonight; I know you are tired of being my woman on the side, but to tell you the truth, everyone knows that you are the one I love and want to be with, you believe that don't you baby?
Yes…Curtis…
Let me finish love. I know that I promised you that you will be the only woman in my life one day, so I am asking you to have a little more patience. This thing with Reneea and I will be over soon, I can feel it in my bones. You know with the company and all, I just have to be careful to protect what I have worked so hard…what we have worked so hard to achieve…This was the first time that Curtis had said this to her directly and he almost convinced himself. One thing he was certain of was that things were definitely different between them and he wasn't sure how or

when but he was certain that the marriage of lies was coming to an end, if he was not careful. Blowing off the thought, Curtis kissed Vanessa and continued to shower her with sentiments of love.

V, give me your hand. Vanessa, who was excited and nervous did as she was instructed as she did not know what to expect. She extended her hands as she knew a gift of some kind was coming. At that moment Curtis placed a three carat diamond ring on her finger, it was no where near the size that he had upgraded Reneea's to just this past August for their anniversary, but it was beautiful and a diamond just the same. Regardless of the size, to Vanessa it said "I love you and I will marry you one day." She was so excited, that she jumped to her feet nearly in tears.

Curtis! Baby is this what I think….Wait, wait, wait baby, I still have some issues to resolve, but yes it is a commitment to you, smiling as he knew he had just bought himself time and pacified her needs all at once.
Curtis its beautiful baby and I love you so much for this.
I'm pleased you like it. They kissed and embraced. Vanessa knew it was just a matter of time before she became the first lady in his life and that Reneea would be sent packing and this empty shell of a marriage that he had with her would be over. I mean think about it, she reasoned with herself, he is hardly ever at home, she accompanied him on most trips and company parties that Reneea did not care to attend, she was the woman who ruled his bed and now this show of affection literally just solidified his promises to her. She loved him so much at that moment all she could do was give him the fuck of his life. This time she took charge and made him the one pleased as only she knew how. They fucked for hours that night each time became more and more vulgar then the first, and Curtis loved it. He couldn't help but to lay back and think of how his plan had worked even better than he expected it to work.

The trip had been profitable in more ways than one; Curtis walked away with three new large corporate accounts, made sure the business he already acquired stayed in tack and was making money hand over fist. He also managed to make his secretary happier than ever by lavishing her with gift after gift while using her for favor after favor for business purposes of course as he put it sealing their future. On the plane ride home he watched her sleeping next to him on the plane, as he thought about how he did desire her. He knew that she would never be his wife, as his wife, would not possibly ever be a woman that would let another man enter her in any fashion, only his whore would. Even he knew that you could not turn a whore into a housewife. However, he was content with the thought that his little diamond bonus would keep her in line for the time being. He could deal with the thought of her parading around as the queen of England as he knew there was only one, even if their life together was running on empty. Curtis glanced up from his gaze and noticed that Charlotte was watching him. She was beautiful and he wondered why there was no real relationship in her life besides Rae Enterprises. He had never thought of her as a woman he would pursue, but the sheer thought that he could not have her, made him wonder how much it would take to conquer her Mount Everest. He smiled at her knowing that she was probably thinking how much she hated Vanessa due to her fondness of Reneea. He could not help thinking to himself that if she had ever taken a ride on the Curtis Express, she would understand why Vanessa loved him so. Charlotte who saw him smiling at her politely without fear smiled sarcastically back at him while shaking her head in disapproval. She extended her arm up showing him the middle finger of her right hand pointed in the direction of the sleeping Vanessa. This humored Curtis, it also intrigued him. Why would a woman with no sexual interest in him be so upset over another woman who had interest in him, unless secretly down inside her she had her own arterial motives or an agenda of her own…He blew her a silent kiss raised his eyebrows at her and closed his eyes. Laughing to himself he thought about the uproar that would be caused at work when the people got a look of the ring that Vanessa would surely be brandishing around the office and was tickled at the thought of the office placing bets about whether or not a wedding or divorce would come to pass. How arrogant he was but he was Curtis Anthony Rae, and nobody stood in his way.

As Curtis had been out of town on business Reneea continued to make plans for the holiday festivities that would be approaching soon, not to mention, kept company with the sexy incomparable Mr. Rick Neal. He had a way of making her forget all of her troubles and misery that came attached to being Mrs. C. A. Rae. They spent quality time together when it could not be quantity time. They even managed to make the best out of the time they spent together when they were in a group setting. They had code body language that no one understood but each other or would bother to catch if they tried. He did things with her that a husband would and should which made it easy for Reneea to love and desire him. He was not only helping her with the holidays but he had also begun to help her put her consulting business plan in motion. She had not discussed her plans with Curtis as he would just shoot them down as he always had as he felt there was no need for the wife of a prominent business man who made loads of money to work. She should be content living the life of a socialite, spending time on charities and attending parties of the rich and well connected as work did not have to be in her future. But this type of activity had left her feeling empty inside and without a purpose. She saw no reason as to why she should not be able to work and be a wife, mother and grandmother now as so many women that she knew, did it for years and were much happier than she was. She knew that a major source of her unhappiness came from the fact that she had surrender her life to Curtis without a fight and had allowed him to make a fool of her practically in front of everyone they had known and caused her to be the laughing stock at Rae, Enterprises. No more, she thought to herself, she was literally tired of running on empty and knew it was time that she do something about it.

As Thanksgiving and Christmas was fast approaching, she had the decorators come in under her direct scrutiny, and began to get the house in festive order. She ordered tables and chairs and the perfect linen and place settings for the season. As Christmas was a more private setting she would decorate the table herself. She shopped with Rick in tow as he carried her packages and waited patiently for her to complete each task and mission. They shopped for one another in lingerie departments especially Ricks favorite store to shop for her, Victoria Secrets, he loved the sexy apparel they offered and could hardly wait to see her in them. They ate lunch and had real meaningful conversations together, something that she had not done with Curtis in years. She loved this man so much and knew that he loved her too. There was no guessing game with him. She did however, receive a scare as the waitress, at first, did not want to take no for an answer and continued to pursue him even after he point blank told her that his sleeping with her was a mistake and that he did not want to see her in that manner anymore. She would call him and pressure him to come over or press up on him at the bar when he was there and as Reneea could not be with him all the time, she was afraid that she just may worm her way back into his bed or he in hers as the case may be. But Rick was strong and proved to her that she was the woman that he loved, adored and wanted. He put her fears to rest and decided that little time with her was better than no time at all.

The time that Curtis was away on business, Rick would spend the night with her and slept in Curtis' bed making love to Curtis' wife and dined on Curtis' dime. Sometimes he felt bad about it but when his friend would call him from different cities and hear about the things he was doing with and to this other woman, his guilt went away all to quickly as he felt that Curtis deserved everything that he and Reneea dished out.

During this last trip Rick surprised Reneea by making her dinner while she worked in the office on her plan. She could smell the food which tempted her in the directions from where it came. She went to the kitchen and noticed that a private candlelight dinner for two had been prepared and that Rick putting the finishing touches was just about to retrieve her to join him.

Well, well, Mr. Neal, what do we have here?

Awe…Baby! I was on my way to come and get you; I thought you could use a little break and some food the way you have been at it all day.

Isn't this so thoughtful? I love you so much Rick. Reneea was genuinely pleased with all of Rick's efforts as she knew they were from his heart.

I know and I love you too. He walked over to her, put his arm around her waist and kissed her tenderly. Come on a sit down Nae, because if you don't the food will get cold because we will have to make love immediately if you don't stop touching me like that. Alright, alright, I guess I will just have to wait for my desert; she smiled as she sat in the chair that he had pulled out. Rick was quite the chief as he had been on his own for a while and he loved to watch cooking shows and try to imitate what he saw them prepare. He had created a feast of lamb chops and petite shrimp with seasoned wild rice and steamed vegetables with a delectable salad on a bed of greens. They enjoyed the meal and each other along with the chilled wine that he keep replenishing for the both of them as he knew the affect that wine had on Reneea.

Here baby, let me pour you another glass.

Rick, are you trying to get me drunk, so that you can have your way with me?

Is it working?

Yeah, but I'm sure that you know you don't have to get me drunk to do that…just ask for what you want and it's yours…its all yours. Reneea was feeling the wine and Rick as well. She stood up from the table grabbed the bottle of wine signaled for Rick to get the glasses and led him upstairs to her bedroom where she took off her clothing and waited for him to join her. Right as they began to make love, Rick's phone rang and he saw it was Curtis, he stopped in motion against Reneea's wishes and answered. Yeah, Curt?

Hey man, are you busy?

Well I was about…

Dog I've got to tell you about this shit, cutting Rick off before he could respond. He began to tell Rick about Vanessa going down on a dude for him to get the contracts he wanted and how he had given her a ring to make it all possible. Rick trying to shield Reneea from what he was saying quickly turned the phone volume down but was too late. She had heard him speaking. Pissed off by this, and continuing to fondle Rick, who himself was turned on by the fact that he was doing his wife while he was on the other end of the phone, Reneea let out a moan of pleasure, directly into the receiver loud enough for Curtis to know that Rick was not alone…Damn, man I caught you at a bad time, why didn't you say so? Nigga, you didn't give me a chance before you started running off at the mouth his words were being muffled as Reneea was forcefully kissing him and sticking her tongue into his mouth to arouse him…My bad brother, go ahead, get your freak on with that fine ass Sherrie, but call me back, hit it for me too dog. Rick just smiled and said, naw man all this loving right here, is reserved for me, he hung up the phone and looked into Reneea eyes, who was so focused on him and could have cared less what Curtis might have said. At that moment they both had no shame or guilt about what they did with one another in Curtis' bed or his house…he deserved all of Reneea's infidelity, Rick's disloyalty and to be the financier of it all.

After a while of making love, Rick felt his body craving her in that way that let him know he was the only one. He pulled out of her and looked her in the eyes. Nae-Nae, give it to me baby, you know what I need…at that moment she rolled over onto her hands and knees and arched her back against him and allowed him to fuck her anally for as long as he desired, with her talking dirty to him the whole time he made love to her. She taunted him and drove him wild with the way she moved her body and commanded him to cum and to fuck her, as there was only pleasure in the pain of what he was doing to her she came causing him to do the same. Rick let out a groan that pleased her as she knew she had just pleased him. They lay together listening to each other breath knowing that this was meant to be. She had to free herself from Curtis, she did not know how and she did not know when, but she knew that for her; running on empty would come to an end.

Chapter 14

The Way We Were

Thanksgiving had come and all of the friends and family had arrived.
Music played throughout the house and everyone admired how wonderful
Reneea and Curtis' home looked. Craig and Angel were home and Angel
looked radiant with the glow of expectancy all over her. She had done a
remarkable job of watching her weight, however, heavier than she had
been before the pregnancy she still looked beautiful and Craig still looked
at her as if she were the only woman on earth. Mia, was home and brought
in some new guy that Tina was less than thrilled about as she felt he had
no future and saw her daughter as a new meal ticket. This caused Mike to
have a background check performed on him only to find out that he was
the son of a well known politician who considered himself to be a rebel
that buck the administration at all cost. He decided that he was in touch
with his afro-centric side that gave off the presence of a bum. In reality
was well educated and saw marriage as legalized fucking. It was no
surprise that they were not in any hurry to send out the announcements
that their daughter would soon be wed. Rachel arrived with her and Rick's
mother who just enjoyed being with the group as she did not get out much
since the passing of Mr. Neal and her beloved daughter-in-law, who made
it her mission to keep her busy. Rachel ran the company full time and did
not have as much time to spend with her mother as it was a lot of work
being the one in charge. Rick made it clear he had no interest in being tied
to a desk except when necessary. Rick was happy to have his mom out and
enjoyed his interaction with his sister. Tina and Rita had a field day with
Martini's as the drunker they became the less irritating Curtis' family was.
Rick, Mike and Bill were enjoying the Sports on television while Curtis
paraded around like the greatest host there ever was. He often would come

up behind Reneea hugging her to give off the facade that they were still the happy couple the way they were years ago.

This irritated her and often her son caught the grimaces that came across her face. He knew something was different between them but knew this was not the time or the place to question her about it. She continued to serve her guest and make out like she was having the greatest time of her life when inside she just wanted everyone to get out and go home. They dined sufficiently and more drinking was done directly after dinner. As she had such a hard time mingling with Curtis' family she found herself helping the wait staff that she had hired for the night. When Curtis saw this he became upset as he was paying these people top dollar to serve and his wife should just be mixing with the guest not cleaning.

Reneea, may I see you for a moment?
Curtis, just a second let me clear this table and I will be right with you. Upset by her defiance, he raised his voice slightly to gain her attention. Reneea! I want to see you now, not later. Reneea looked up at Curtis who was noticeably pissed and began to following him into his study.
Yes Curtis, what is it that was so important that you could not wait one second? I am paying these people to serve and clean, you are my wife and should be in the room with everyone else entertaining our guest, not cleaning behind them. Excuse me Mr. Rae, I thought this was my home and I was free to do as I pleased in it. I did not know that I had a post that I needed to be in at all times for the sake of your fucking ego! Lower your damn voice Reneea. No Curtis, I certainly will not you are the one that called this little meeting now lets talk damn it! Reneea… Reneea my ass, you are so concerned with appearances, that it doesn't even matter to you that people have been laughing behind our back all night thanks to your relatives who were having a nice little conversation about you and your whore at our expense. Curtis was shocked, he had no idea that this was taking place, nor did he know that anyone in the house would be privy to such information.

What the hell are you talking about Reneea?
Oh come on Curtis, This isn't the way we were, your getting careless brother or maybe you just don't give a damn about who knows your screwing around. Reneea proceeds to walk away from Curtis when he grabs her arm, snatching her back to him.

Let me go you bastard.

Stop it Damn it! You will not walk away from me in my house another damn time, tightening his grip.

You are hurting my wrist Curtis…Let me fucking go right now….

Out of the darkness he heard a voice calm and collective chime in…Yes, my brother, you had better fucking let her go this minute if your ass wants to live to see day break…walking slowly in the room, it was Tina, who had witness the whole display that lead up to him calling her in the room.

Curtis released Reneea, cleared his throat and began to speak.

Tina, this is between me and my wife I would appreciate if you…if you would excuse us.

Tina laughed sarcastically…Baby girl, come over here now. Reneea began to walk past Curtis glaring at him with each step.

Are you alright?

I'm fine, just mad as hell.

Okay, rightfully so.

I want you to go up the back stairs, wash your face and replenish your make up; my brother Curtis and I are going to have a little talk, okay?

T… Nae-Nae it will be alright…just do as I said ok. Reneea never gave Tina hassle, especially when she got into mode of gangster daughter as she knew her bite was entirely worse than her bark. Reneea left the room not bothering to look back at Curtis.

Tina clicked on the light switch on the wall so that Curtis would have full view of her and see her facial expressions. Without raising her voice or batting and eye she began to speak in what appeared to be a most threatening tone.

Motherfucker, have you lost your damn mind, or are you trying to see if fat meat is greasy? I told you that if you ever felt the need to put your hands on her, your ass was as good as dead. Do you not remember that?

Look Tina, you got it twisted...

No nigga, you got it twisted. All night she has had to endure bullshit from your stank ass family, listen to people laugh behind her back as they drink her liquor about you and your little whore secretary that you parade around town like shit don't get back and because she is trying to keep up appearances for your punk ass, you get pissed because she picks up a serving tray? If you had any balls about yourself you would stop pretending this shit is the way it use to be and get the fuck on so that she can have a life.

Curtis was visibly pissed, but knew all to well she was not the one to fuck with as she truly was her father's daughter and had seen enough people killed in her life time to get the job done herself as well.

Look Tina, I would never hit Reneea, I was just angry and I wanted her to stay and talk, trying to smooth the situation over. Curtis, tell that shit to somebody buying, because I ain't interested. What I do know is this…She stays with you because of her son and children his wife carries, but if she ever feels as if her life is in danger and I am made aware of it, I will personally see to it that you are sorry that you ever laid eyes on Reneea Rae. Oh… and Curtis, this is not a threat, but a promise. Tina made a hand gesture of someone pulling the trigger on a gun and backed out of the room as she never turned her back on a man or anyone for the matter especially after she had just threaten them, adjusting the back holster, he knew she wore.

Curtis was shaken and knew that every word she spoke was the gospel according to Tina Jones Vaughn. He walked over to the mini bar that he kept in his study and poured himself a stiff drink. He drank it and felt the need to contact Vanessa, who was in Aspen skiing as he could not be with her over the holiday. He dialed her cell phone and she answered on the first ring.
Hey Daddy, miss me yet?
Yeah, change in plans; you need to get your ass back here tomorrow on the first thing smoking I can't wait two whole days to see you. But I thought that…You heard me, change in plans I need you home. Ok, whatever you want, I will make the arrangements tonight. Curt? Yeah? Do you plan on spending time with me when I get home? What do you think? Now get your ass back here. He hung up the phone feeling empowered, this was the one place that he was the boss and when he talked people listened.

Returning to the gathering, he could see that the crowd had thinned out some. Rachel and Rick's mom were gone as it was late and Mrs. Neal needed to be in doors by a certain hour. This disappointed him as he always liked to flirt with Rachel as if he would ever get a chance again. He was married and she was no longer an idealistic teen who thought that her brother's friends being taboo was code for please proceed. He often wondered if Rick ever found out that he was Rachel's first, but considering that Rick was so protective of his baby sister, this may have very well been the thing that ended their relationship long before now. He noticed that the majority of his relatives had left with the exception of his mother and her sisters who were enjoying their time with Craig and Angel. Reneea had tried over the years to get along with the majority of Curtis' family, but it did not always work. They thought that Reneea was uppity as she was college educated and came from a family with old money she never really fit in with them. Curtis' mother always felt that she was a good wife for Curtis but wished he had of married a woman less beautiful as she would have had more children for Curtis and the Rae name would live on longer and would not have been so concerned with her flashy life style. He also notices that Rita and Bill Cooper were preparing to leave as he had and early morning meeting. He walked over to them to say good night and noticed that Mia and her mother were locked into a tight discussion turning his attention away he noticed that Rick and Reneea were conversing about something that looked serious and wanted to get over there and see if they were discussing the incident that took place in his study. As Craig and Angel showed her parents to the door, Curtis made haste getting over to Rick and Reneea.

Noticing his approach, they switched the subject to be about his morning shoot. What are you guys looking so serious over? Is there something wrong? No, Rick was just telling me that he was going to shoot Detroit's First Family in the morning and how he needed everything to run smoothly, I was trying to see if there was anything I could assist him with? Yeah, the good Mayor and his wife have decided that it is time to update the photos that they use. Oh wow. You didn't mention that earlier. I guess it slipped my mind with all the excitement of everyone getting together tonight. I guess. Your mom looks good. Yeah she does Rick. Thanks guys, she doesn't get out as much any more and wont travel without one of us with her so I'm glad she is doing as well as she is. They exchanged a little more conversation on the same lines and Curtis decided to go on a fishing expedition.
So Rick, where is Sherrie tonight? I thought that surely you would have invited her as I called you from New York and the two of you were getting your groove on? What happened man? Really Curtis, do you have to put this man's business in the streets like this, Reneea asked being embarrassed by his statement as she knew full well it was not Sherrie that

he heard in the background making love to Rick? Rick smiled shaking his head back and forth in amazement. Man, you are a piece of work....
What? Man come on Nea, know you getting busy with the hottie. I thought it was weird because when I tried to apologize for my untimely call while I was at Mr. Nicks for lunch, she had no idea as to, or what I was talking about?
Maybe, because she didn't?
What?
I never told you I was with Sherrie...you assumed.
Nigga What! You holding out your boy? You mean to tell me that you are seeing someone else and I don't know about it?
Where is it written that I have to tell you all my business?
Nigga whatever. They laughed and even Reneea laughed as Curtis was clearly the joke here.
Man you better tell me something.
Alright, alright, because you are clearly not going to drop it are you?
Hell naw....
Just what I thought?
Reneea stood back and braced herself for what she would possibly hear. Well, she is beautiful, I met her when I least expected it and I have been in love with her every since turning to look at Reneea, with his beautiful smile. She is sexy beyond belief and in bed she is definitely something worth writing home about. To be honest, not even my wife took me to places that this woman does every time I'm with her and in her. Sherrie could not even be in the same league as this woman. She is my fantasy in everyway. Hell, just talking about her right here and now, makes me want to be with her. I respect her and I am closer to her than I ever thought any woman possible. She is definitely wife material and I hope that one day I get to show the world and all my friends just what she means to me. That's all I can tell you for now. Curtis smiled and sipped his drink.
Rick, if I didn't know any better, I would think that you had just described my wife as there can't possibly be two of the same women on this planet; he put his arm around Reneea's waist. Reneea was so full of emotion at that moment as she heard her lover describing her to her husband and how he felt; and he had no clue that she was it. She heard his polite comment and was glad that he had given her an excuse to let a tear roll down her cheek. But Rick knew that the tears she shed were for him and how he could hardly wait to catch her alone and thank her for showing that display

of emotion. At that moment, Tina and Mike walked over and decided to join the group.

What? Is this a private party, Mike asked bringing over the cognac to refresh everyone's glass. No way, baby; especially since you and your lovely wife are baring gifts, Curtis welcomed the couple in their circle holding out his glass for a refill. Tina smiled at Curtis, never letting on that she had just threatened this man's life or that there had been an issue between the three of them. Tina raised her glass and began to speak.

I would like to propose a toast…

To the way we were, and the way we are now…. let us remember those who have gone on before us, everyone began to look on emotional as Tina had a way with words that could stop a person and make them think especially in emotional settings… *as they are gone but not forgotten and would want us to pursue happiness and fulfill dreams that we are so deserving of. Let us remember the days at State…Our very first dates, and now let us drink up niggas cause it's getting late….*

Everyone paused and looked at her…and Reneea began to speak…

Bitch that's it…, that's how you're going to end this beautiful ass toast you started, clearly puzzled?

Tina looked her square in the eye and responded…

Yeah, hoe I'm thirsty….

Everyone broke out in full hardy laughter as others in the room looked on to see what they had missed.

Only Tina could get away with assonating a moment like this, Rick spoke out…Girl I swear you need your damn head examined. Maybe so but yaw are the fools that keep hanging around me. I have not changed in twenty some odd years so don't expect me to now, glancing over at Curtis as she spoke. It was sad to say that he really did fear this woman in his midst. He did not fear her physically, because as a man, he could physically kick the shit out of her and not give it a second thought. However, she had a deadly past there was no denying this and her family was still powerful, and dangerous and Reneea was well connected to her and very much protected due to the favors that Attorney Craig had done for Tina's father to keep Tina safe. Not to mention that Mike was a cop with a gun who would not hesitate to defend his wife's honor and the chance of an investigation thoroughly being conducted he highly doubted, so he played it safe and kept his cool.

Many other family members started to clear out and Craig and Angel who had decided that this visit they would stay with Rita and Bill said their good nights and departed. Angel clearly needed to put her swollen feet up as the day had been long and could no longer stand the conversations that they were being forced to have with his father's side of the family. He never really had much in common with them, nor did he spend a lot of time with them when he was growing up as Reneea just preferred that he did not as some of their rearing was less than appropriate for children. Mia and her new guy friend decided that they had taken all of the concerned stares that anyone could take for the evening and decided to call it a night. Tina made her daughter promise to be at the house early for Black Friday shopping and after getting what she wanted let her depart with the Bob Marley want-to-be who clearly showed his less than impressed attitude with the entire gang. This by the way caught Mia's attention whom was very fond of her mom and dads friends as they were considered her family and her parents whom she adored, and Tina knew that it would only be a matter of time before she sent dude packing for that little incident. Not to mention she was sure that Craig had given her a, what for and a how to where this man was concerned. Tina smiled inwardly and felt that by morning brother would not be singing *"This is love, this love, this love that, I'm feeling"* No, no one disrespected her parents. And Craig's opinion would always matter.

As it was just the inner circle that remained, Rick put on some music and as always, this got them to dancing around to the oldies and reminiscing on who were the better dancers out of the group. They were talking loud and enjoying each others company and there was still plenty of drinking going on. Rachel had decided that the evening was still young after dropping her mother off and returned with her two friends Davis and Tasha who were no strangers to this group. They were a younger version of Rick and his friends. Reneea noticing they had begun to consume way to much liquor made it her business to go into the kitchen for finger foods to coat her friend's stomachs and was joined by Rick. Once into the kitchen, they laughed and joked about the evening, but then Rick, who had fought his temptation to touch her all evening, had a sudden desire to feel his body up against hers. She also wanted him as he was dressed in her favorite color to see him in, all black from head to toe. There was something so sexy about a man in black especially this man and his height and skin complexion topped it off beautifully. His cologne smelled wonderful and called to her body like a hypnotic spell.. She attempted to reach a platter that was above her head and of course seeing that she couldn't he rushed to her aid. Standing directly behind her which caused his penis to brush against her backside, that instantly caused her nipples to respond and a tingling in her stomach set off alarms within her that caused her to arch her back pressing her but cheeks up against him, that pleased him and though keeping his eyes on the entrance of the kitchen he bent down an whispered in her ear.

Damn girl…you make it real hard on a brother to keep his cool, nibbling on her ear as he spoke.
Well hell, with what you're doing to me, I'm not exactly having a picnic here, the shear thought of them being exposed at any minute turned her completely on.
Nae-Nae, I want you so bad…
Rick don't…I…being interrupted as she felt his hand sliding up her leg and around to the front of her slightly caressing her crotch.
I've got to kiss you baby…
I know, me too
When we take the food back in the room, meet me in the hall bathroom.
No that is too risky meet me in the wine cellar it will be more believable.
Okay.

They straighten their self up and began to take the food into the recreation area where everyone was having a good time. Curtis was talking with Tasha, which looked more like he was trying to get her phone number while everyone still danced around and proceeded to attack the food. Reneea gave Tina a look that let her know she needed her to have her back and Tina nodded in agreement. Reneea told Rick to help her get more wine from the basement and he followed her directly. Curtis never looked up as Tasha's doubled D's appeared to have his attention for the moment and after all it was just Rick being big brother who helped out as there was no woman there for him to focus his attention on and with him assisting Reneea, it was one less thing he would have to do and could continue his flirtatious assault on Tasha.

Once downstairs out of view, Rick and Reneea kissed each other passionately being carefully not to make to much noise as they were by the ventilation units in which sound could travel. Reneea felt as if a ton of weight had been removed from her shoulders and Rick did as well. After a few more quick feels and kisses which appeared to satisfy their urgent need for one another, they returned upstairs with no one even knowing they had just pacified their desires right under their noses and the party continued not missing a beat.

Rachel saw her brother standing alone by the CD's looking for more music to put on and took this as an opportunity to talk to her brother one on one as they had not spent much time in each others company. So, BB, she affectionately referred to him as BB which was the acronym for big brother, tell me about this mystery woman Curtis has enlightened me about that you claim you are seeing…looking at her brother matter-of-factly. Rick smiled and taped her on top of her head with a CD that he had chosen, trying to change the subject…Rachel, come on girl, you know Curtis, always the shit talker.
No, not this time? He was adamant in his description of her, even said that you had real feelings to show when you spoke of her. It was clear that his sister had no intention of dropping the subject.
Well, as a matter of fact there is someone, but I am not ready to introduce her yet, there are some complicated issues involved and I just need to make sure that everything is worked out before I…
Yeah, yeah, yeah complicated, I'm sure.
Listen girl, you of all people know I would introduce you first, Curtis is just on a fishing expedition to see if you know more than he does.
Now that, I can believe, agreeing with Rick's statement she sipped her drink smiling.
See?
But what I can't believe BB…as smart as he is that he hasn't put two and two together yet smiling sarcastically?
Rick obviously concerned by her last statement spoke slow and sternly, Excuse me little sis?
I mean come on, he said that you have been in love with her from the first day you met her…he's so stupid street wise, that he can't see what the rest of us have known for years…
Rach, are you drunk?
No, by no means, I am just smarter than your average business person, male or female. Tell me BB…when do you think he will realize that you are seeing his wife?

Rick was stunned at her accusation choking on the sip of his drink he had just taken, and began to pull her into the sun room. Startled by her brother's forceful behavior, Rachel thought it best to go along with him without drawing the attention of others. Okay, Rachel Neal what the hell is up? Why would you come in here with some shit like this?

Relax Rick…

No, you don't come off saying some shit like that and expect me to relax; do you realize what you are accusing me of? Do you have any idea the shit that could be caused by what you have just said?

Boy! Slow your roll, damn it, snatching her arm from Rick's grasp and getting control of the situation. She spoke softly but in a tone that let her brother know she meant business.

Negro, FYI, for years I have stood back and watched you roll over for Curtis Rae. I have watched you put his happiness before your own, have the things you should have acquired and receive the accolades that were designed for you. I watched how you set your best friend up with the girl you wanted all because of a guilt trip he put you through…hell that sneaky bastard has always managed to get what should be and what is rightfully yours. Not that it ain't fucked up, because it is…in my opinion, you have just taken back what was yours in the first place. You have to be Ray Charles and Stevie Wonder rolled up together not to notice the chemistry between the two of you…I know that when Bea was alive you steered completely clear of her and she of you…but Rick you can't help who you love….

Rachel, this shit is not that simple…

Oh yeah? Well how simple was it that when you and Tina were trying to help Reneea over the grief of her dying father, that Mr. Big Shot over there was fucking your girlfriend, who said they missed their flight down from Florida…Yeah,… that's right Bea and Curtis were fucking the weekend of Spring Break when the rest of you decided to hang around and help Reneea. You look stunned BB, see I managed to overhear the two of them talking at the wake about how awful they felt, not being here to support Nea, but wasn't sorry that they got each other out of their systems once and for all…they promised that it would not happen again and that it would just be between old friends and lovers….that's right they dated prior to Curtis and Reneea and you and Bea. Bea wanted to tell Reneea, but did not have the heart to do so.

Rick looked sick and felt even sicker and angry all at once…Rachel, why are you telling me this now? After all of these years… why now? I guess…Rick I guess, I'm just tired of seeing the good guy come in last, not to mention that Curtis is and will always be the same sneaky motherfucker that he has always been. He likes to take things that don't belong to him and he has to be stopped, wife or no wife. Rick pulled her into his chest and hugged his sister as if his life depended on it. Rachel in returned hugged her brother, she never wanted to hurt him but she had had it with Mr. Rae and decided it was now her brothers turn to come in first.

We better get back inside, huh?
Yeah, we probably should.
Rick, your secret is safe with me it always has been, I just thought, I needed to level the playing field a little.
Rick?
Yeah Rach?
It was good seeing Craig and Angel tonight.
Rick smiled as Craig held a special place in his heart; yeah it was. He has really turned out to be a handsome man, didn't he?
Yes, he did…I was thinking that he looks more and more like his father the older he gets, I wonder if anyone else notices that? With that being said Rachel picked up her glass from and end table and exited the room in party fashion singing along to Knee Deep that played in the other room and joined the others who were dancing.

Rick, who was trying to rebound from the conversation that had just taken place with his sister, walked immediately over to the bar and poured himself a drink and drank it down without hesitation and repeated these steps twice more. Reneea noticed that Rick was hitting the bottle pretty hard and walked over to him and begin to interrupt his process. Woe, cowboy, that will be enough don't you think? Rick beginning to feel the effect of the alcohol smiled and with slurring speech began to speak.

Hey baby, have you come to join me?
No, I don't think I could keep up or catch up for that matter. Why don't you come, sit with me and talk?
No, no, no! See this is a party and there is drinking to be done and dancing to be done…
Rick come on baby let's get some food, huh?

Uh uh, not hungry for that…and what I want I can't have, touching her playfully on her butt.

Reneea shocked by his actions, concealed his hand and spoke secretly, Rick, are you trying to get us caught whispering?

CAUGHT! HA HA HA CAUGHT! My boy can tell you about getting caught, right Curt now hollering at the top of his lungs? Suddenly, everyone stop dancing and talking and started paying attention to Rick and Reneea as Ricks little outburst put everyone off guard.

Awe shit, Nae-Nae what's up; Tina, ran over to assist her…

Teeeee - na BABY BIG BABY! This motherfucking…Curtis

Curtis was visibly confused by everything that was going on sat down his drink and rushed over to his friend to assist the girls who were trying to calm him down.

Nigga, what's up baby? You drunk dude…Trying to grab Rick by the arm causing him to struggle away from him pushing him backwards by the chest. This instantly made Mike go into police mode stepping in between the two men. Alright everybody be cool, Curtis back up...

Back up? Fuck that this is my house, nigga what's up with you? Rachel looked on knowing that her little information had fueled the anger her brother was displaying…BB come on lets go, lets get out of here let me take you home.

Naw baby sis, you right, this bastard has taken everything from me…and still taking. You fuck Bea? Everyone looked on horrified in what Curtis' answer would be…

Negro, what the hell are you talking about? Nigga please, punk you know, you know what the fuck I'm talking bout, I'm talking bout Bea Bitch MY WIFE! YOU HOE! You dated her? Curtis knew that this was something he was not going to talk his way out of … Rick man your drunk, let me take you home. Oh yeah you'd like that wouldn't you? Get me out of her life for good? Fuck you I don't need you…RACHEL, GET ME THE HELL out of here…Rick rubbed his hands over his wavy hair put on his Jacket that Reneea was holding and a single tear rolled down his face when he noticed the horrified look in her eyes? He reached out his hand and caressed her face, now in a full blown cry.

Nae-Nae, I'm sorry honey, that I ruined your party, I would never hurt you ever, you can't hurt what you love…Reneea began to cry as she did not know what sparked this behavior and was truly puzzled. Rachel, take care of him. I got him Nae-Nae, I'll spend the night with him Tasha can take my car home. She put her arm around her brother with Mike and proceeded to take him to the door. In passing Rachel glared at Curtis on the way out as he continued to look shocked that this came out tonight, but how and why. Passing Curtis, Rick looked up at him and spoke quietly, from now on, if its mine, I'm coming for it and if it was meant to be, I will know…I will find out. Mike continued to take him to the car as everyone looked on in disbelief; this was so not like Rick.

This had pretty much put a damper on the festivities and everyone thought it best they should leave. Tina offered to stay and help pick up but she told her not to as she had contracted a cleaner to come in the morning and take care of the cleaning. The two women hugged and made promises to call first thing in the morning. Reneea made her apologies about black Friday shopping but Tina understood and said that she would explain her absence to girls in the morning.

Everyone left and Reneea made her way upstairs to her bedroom…she was clueless as to why the outburst had happened and wondered if it had anything to do with the conversation that she notice Rick and Rachel having prior to the whole display. She showered and prayed that Curtis did not attempt to join her as she was clearly not in the mode for his presence or his attempt at being a husband as she was still pissed at what he did to her in his study. She also could not get past the words Rick yelled about him dating Bea…this bothered her as she thought that she knew of every guy that both Tina and Beatrice dated and Curtis never was made mention of. Her mind did venture off to one guy this jock that no one had been introduced to but had heard her speak of by the name of Tony whom her father did not care for. He called him slick as goose grease and dumb as dirt she remembered. This couldn't possibly be Curtis, especially since she had introduced him and she acted as if she had never met him before in her life, however, they did become fast friends where as Tina, never really did care for Curtis right off. Bea did and she always thought it was because of Rick who she was now dating and wanted the six of them to remain good friends, the other couple being Mike and Tina of course.

She finished her shower and dressed by the time Curtis came upstairs. She really had no words for him but knew they could not be avoided. Seated at her vanity table brushing her hair before going to bed, she noticed that Curtis had a long somber look on his face and that he was staring at Reneea's reflection the mirror.

How much do you know?

Excuse me?

How much of this mess do you know?

Reneea turned around to face Curtis and waited for him to continue. You are of course, talking about what Rick said tonight?

Come on Nea, it's late and I just want to get through tonight and get some sleep.

Well, why don't you; preparing to turn her chair back around to continue her task?

Oh hell no, so you can hold this shit over my head tomorrow, uh uh, we will get it over with tonight. So I will ask you again, how much do you know?

Irritated that he was pressing the issue and trying to make her the villain in this sorted mess, her voice elevated as she began to speak; *apparently not enough Curtis so why don't you start from the beginning, shall we?*

Alright, I met Bea in our freshman year at State. We went out a couple of times and that was that. I would periodically date her on and off throughout our sophomore and junior years but by the time we were seniors it was done. Her father did not care for me, thought that I was not good enough to date his debutant doctor to be daughter so she ended it for good when she found out that I was interested in you. She never met Rick because I was not sure if Bea and I would ever be a couple outside of fuck buddies okay. There you have it. Curtis unbuttoned his shirt and tossed it into the laundry basket marked dry cleaning. Reneea stunned by his confession could not believe the cockiness he displayed when talking about her diseased friend as if she meant nothing at all.

Curtis you are a real piece of work. You act as if you have a license to shit on people and nothing is wrong with that? You lied to everyone, you hurt your best friend and you have the nerve to sit here and play the victim. I am amazed at your nerve. Reneea what do you want me to do, it's done and over with, I can't re-write the past, I can't return us to the way we were and Bea is not here to explain her side, though if she were, I'm sure she would explain as she wanted to before, but our wedding was scheduled, your father was dying and I thought it best that she didn't,

Baby I didn't want anything to keep you from becoming Mr. Curtis Anthony Rae, especially because then you loved me, you were the only person who saw the good in me and when we made love before the wedding, and that test came back positive, there was no way, I was going to let you go through that alone. I know that our being in Florida when your father took that turn for the worst, did not help but I knew that I could eventually love you through everything you were feeling and make everything right with us. There was no need to rock the boat. Rick was dating her now and it was getting serious, he finally stopped wishing that he had...Curtis stopped short of completing his sentence and Reneea knew that it had to do with Rick's interest in her. She and I got drunk because we missed our flight and found ourselves in bed together and knew it was a mistake, but never touched each other again and this I swear. Reneea looked at Curtis with unbridled hatred and could not stand to listen to him anymore, the whole thing was so painful she could not make heads or tails of what was true and what was a lie.

Just stop Curtis; I really can't take anymore of this tonight. I'm just glad that Craig and Angel were not here for this and that your family had left as well. I've got to lye down; I need time to sort all of this shit out. When my father was handing you the MAC Foundation on a silver platter you were making plans to make his daughter your prisoner of lies for the rest of her life congratulations on a job well done.

Nea, it was not like that at all....I love...
Curtis please spare me the bullshit...I can't, not tonight I am all out of cheeks to turn tonight.

Chapter 15

The Truth Hurts

The sun light that plowed through Rick's bedroom window was enough to make Dracula die instantly, which is completely how Rick felt when he opened his eyes, rolling over slowly he grabbed his head which felt as if a wrecking ball had collided with him and he lost.

Oh, my God…he mumbled trying to get his composure.

You can say that shit again. He heard his sisters voice coming from directly above him as he barely made out her facial features.

Rach?

Yeah BB it's me, come on sit up so you can take these aspirin and drink a little of this coffee so you can chase them both with an Alka-Seltzer.

Oh God, what the hell happened? How much did I drink?

Well lets start with Martell which you chased with Crown Royal and topped it all off with Patrone.

You have got to be kidding me? My car? Where is my car?

It's in the garage thanks to Mike…

Mike?

Uh huh, Mike. He knows you hate to leave it out overnight so he followed me here to help get you inside and then he put your car in the garage while Tina helped me get you in the bed. All of a sudden Rick had a flash of the night before and sat straight up in his bed…

Oh dear Lord, Nae-Nae, did I hurt….What the fuck did I say?

Relax Rick, Curtis was the target of your attack and you left Nae-Nae's honor in tact. She's safe; in fact she just called a moment ago to see how you were.

How did she sound? Was she alright?

Rick she's fine, just worried about you.

BB, I'm sorry, I had no idea you were that drunk or that you would go the hell off like that. I was buzzing myself and a little angry that Curtis had pushed up on me last night with his wife in the next room. I just snapped and told you all that shit I should have said at another time if not at all. I'm so sorry, man I never meant to hurt you, I just can't stand Curtis' ass for so many reasons.

Don't sweat it Rachel, hell the truth hurts and it was bound to come out sooner or later. I just can't believe that I have carried this guilt inside me all these years and I find out that this man has been making a fool out of me for as long as we have been friends. He begged me not to pursue Reneea even when I saw her first. He kept using Rashonda Mayham as his basis and I fell for that shit. How much he liked her and wanted to get with her and found out that the two of us were kicking it…Now that I think about it, this nigga has never really loved anyone but himself. I can't even remember seeing Bea with him prior to all of us meeting up at school together. Well, don't try and rack your brain about it now? What's done is done dude, and you have to move on. Now, if you ask me, what you need to do is decide how long you and Reneea are going to play this cat and mouse game? It's complicated, Rachel. Craig, the babies, he adores his parents. Yeah maybe he does, but he loves you Rick and I am sure that once he knows about his father and what he has done to his mother all these years, he will eventually understand.

Rachel, I love Craig like he was mine and I understand her when she says she can't see hurting him. Rick, unless Craig is mentally retarded, he has to have some idea that his father is unfaithful. You could hear all the talk around the room over there at Thanksgiving dinner that was one of the real reasons mother was in such a hurry to leave! She idolizes that boy and the fact that his cold hearted relatives were carrying on so, made her sick to her stomach. I can't tell you what to do BB, but you guys can't go on like this. The truth hurts, but it can also set you free, the choice is yours boy. Besides, I'm not so sure he isn't yours. Come on Rachel, don't talk like that, that is Curtis' son, if there were anyway that he was mine, Nae-Nae would have told me. She would not have let Curtis think anything different.

So you are not denying that you slept with her before the wedding? Rachel man, come on moving quickly to turn away from his sister's glare! No

Rick, you come on. Is there a possibility that Craig is yours and you don't know, hell that Reneea doesn't know? That damn boy has our genes, look at him…you have to see your eyes, daddy's eyes…I've heard of people who hang out together starting to look alike, but not their kids? I'm just saying is there a possibility that the both of you made love to Reneea but you are the fertilizer of that seed. Okay Rach enough my head is killing me and I can't deal with this right now. It's just too much to process.

Alright Rick, I'll drop it right now, but there is another generation of Neal's coming and you owe it to yourself to know the truth. Rick stood up and took his sister by the hand and began to speak softly and calmly…Rachel, Reneea's father was dying, Curtis was away, and she was hurting. She turned to me for comfort and I let things get carried away, we have not spoken of this night ever since it happened except maybe once as I felt guilty as hell that I made love to my best friends girl, not to mention I was dating her friend. It was innocent, and needed. Yes, I did sleep with her, but she was already promised to Curt and I could never let her be embarrassed or hurt because she was weak with grief and I was weak with love and I knew that I could not have her, but, for that one night, she was mine. She was not out whoring around on him; please know it wasn't that way. I believe you BB…it's just ironic that your mates were…think about it. I need to get out of here Tasha is outside with my car and I have to change my clothes, hell I have already missed most of the black Friday sales screwing around with you! She smiled at her brother and kissed him on the cheek. Okay kiddo, I'll see you Thursday for the board meeting? You bet. Love You. Love you more.

Rachel took off down the stairs and upon exiting, she ran into Reneea who was coming up on the porch who was shocked to run directly into Rachel she wasn't sure just how much she knew about their relationship but pretty much figured that the cat had to be out of the bag. Hey Nae-Nae! Rachel, good morning, I wasn't sure if you were still here? I was just going to check on Rick before I headed off to shop and…I… Rachel interrupted her in her statement as she could see that she had startled her by seeing her there without calling.
Nae-Nae, its cool you don't owe me any explanation as to why you are here to see my brother, she smiled an easy smile to let her know it was alright and Reneea let out a sigh ease accompanied by a smile. I know about the two of you and I have for some time now…there is no judgment

here, but I will offer you some advice... Life is short, live it happy. She hugged Reneea and proceeded to walk off the porch.
Rachell?
Turning to look back at Reneea she answered softly, yes?
I do love him, I just want you to know he is not just a passing fling of a scorned spouse...I love him with everything inside of me. Reneea felt relieved as she had never spoken those words to another soul out side of Tina and admitting that somehow made her feel liberated.
I know honey....trust me, I know. Rachel returned her smile and turned her attention to her friend who was waiting patiently for her. Reneea proceeded into the house where she saw Rick standing directly in front of her. He had this look of unbelief on his face blended with a smile. Reneea entered the house and closed the door behind her.
Good Morning! Caught off guard by his gaze she inquired about his look. Why are you looking at me like that?
Rick walked closer to her and put his arms around her waist and drew her near to him and spoke slowly in his response.
Good morning yourself, and...I am looking at you because I've never heard you tell anyone other than me outwardly and openly that you love me, imagine that, you love me and it felt good to hear that, so very good. Before she could respond she noticed that Rick was crying and everything in her wanted to make his world safe and all the pain that she knew he had to be feeling based on the information he had just learned the night before and what she had heard Curtis confess to she wanted to make it disappear from both of their worlds. She wanted to make Bea the Saint that he always thought her to be and to make Curtis' involvement in their life instantly disappear, but this was not a magic show and nothing could turn back what they now knew.

Continuing to caress his back softly she spoke with gentleness in her voice that let him know his tears did not have to be tears of shame, but that it was alright to let his guard down as there was nothing artificial about their relationship; she knew that real men cried as they were human and also hurt. I do love you Rick, and at this point, I'm starting to care less and less who knows it. Nae-Nae, we still have to be careful there is so much at stake here where you are concerned. I know baby. But I also know that I can't stay with him, I can't do it. Rick looked surprised and happy at her statement and without trying to show too much emotion, he uttered the only words that would come out, Are you sure? She looked at him with conviction and sincerity and spoke, I am positive. After the holidays are over and the Twins come, I have got to…I have got to be free of the man, this foul ass, loveless marriage, and any ties that bind business and or otherwise. I can't do this shit anymore, No…No…I WONT DO THIS anymore! Where is he now, probably with Vanessa? I don't know and I really don't care as long as he is away from me. The kids are supposed to meet us for dinner and I am just praying that I can make it through that. You can baby, you have been strong thus far you will make it. After what he confessed to me last night, I'm not sure if I can. She shared the entire story with Rick which left him speechless more so than last night. He could not believe his ears, however, things were starting to make more sense to him now than they did before, like how Beatrice always seem to get his jokes when no one else had, or during the times they would be out as couples she would always know what foods he liked or how they danced together as if they had always danced together, how she knew his moves without being talk through them. And last but not least, how he cried at her funeral as hard as Rick had and how he bent over her at the hospital and kissed her once she was pronounced dead like he had lost an old girlfriend…all this time Rick thought that it was just support from his friend, when all the while he had been grieving the loss as his own. Reneea brought Rick out of his train of thought as she began to speak.

You have so much faith in my ability. I don't know how I would have lasted so long if it had not been for you in my life as my friend, my confidant, and certainly my lover, smiling at him devilishly attempting to get a rise out of him and change his focus of attention. Believe me baby, all of that has been my pleasure, he kissed her on her lips and then her forehead. You know Mr. Neal…I just might be able to get through dinner tonight if you were to provide me with a little energy or incentive. Oh yeah? Yeah. Well, what did you have in mind, what is it that I could possibly do for you standing back away from her so that he could take her body in his whole sight. Well for starters, we could go up and take a shower together looks like you are in need of some warm water hitting you in all the right places, or perhaps I could just bathe you? Rick raised his eyebrows in pleasure at the proposition. She continued in her same sexy and sultry manner as she noticed she had his interest peaked; maybe a little massaging and afterwards you could make love to me and workout some of this tension that has built up overnight? Uh huh, I see…let me get this straight, watching Reneea as she begin to unbutton his Pajama shirt, you think that by me making love to you that perhaps you will be strong enough to get through dinner with your husband and son? Oh definitely, without a doubt. By this time Reneea had managed to drop his pants to the floor letting him stand there in just a pair of sexy briefs that she no doubt had purchased for him as she saw the Calvin Klein Logo on the front. Well it has always been my character to help a friend in need Ms. Rae, and you are my friend in deed so it would only be right for me to *cum* to your need, making a jabbing motion up against her crotch with his very erect manhood she understood the metaphor of cum. Yeah baby, now you're talking. By the time it took Rick to finish his statement, Reneea had removed the first layer of her clothing and was working on the undergarments as she proceeded toward the upstairs. When she came to the top of the landing he was behind her assisting her in removing her bra as the panty he always like to save for last. He removed the hair clip from her hair and watched as it fell freely onto and past her shoulders, how he loved her beautiful hair he thought to himself, he clutched a hand full and gently tugged at it making her kiss him and as their tongues explored one another they entered the shower allowing the steam and heat to captivate their bodies as they pleasured each other with touching and rubbing and finally as the foreplay grew extremely intense and neither of them could hold back any longer, Rick lifted her up as a delicate flower hoisting her onto to penis and begin to stroke her with force as if he were trying to implant himself into her body. She loved what he did to her as her moans and whimpers of enjoyment rang out letting him know that he was definitely hitting the spot.

Yes baby ooh, keep it right there, don't stop, please, don't stop.

You want it, is it good to you Ma?

Fuck me Rick, Fu…

They went back and forth for what seemed to be hours though they knew it had not been and at the pinnacle of his performance as he was ready to release inside of her, she pulled herself off of him sliding down to her knees taking him orally, sucking him until he cried out while she swallowed his love juices tasting him, desiring him, pleasuring him and knowing this was where she belonged. Watching him climax she rose slowly to meet his eyes as he lay back against the shower wall trying to regain his strength and composure she knew that she had just pleased him thoroughly when he was able to open his eyes, she could read them and they let her know that she was definitely good to him, no one could make him feel this way, and she was exactly what he needed to start his day. Coming into himself he began to speak.

You don't play fair Ms. Rae.

No, I play to win love; you must know that by now?

Well, baby you won this round hands down. At that moment, he remembered replacing the water tank and going for the larger sized and being thankful that he now had as the water was still warm and he decided that since she had given him the release he so needed, the least he could do to thank her for her love and care would be to bathe and massage her, treating her like the queen she was.

Curtis had the worst night's sleep he had had in a very long time, he couldn't for the life of him figure out how the information of he and Bea became common knowledge? Who would have known this information and want to hurt Rick by letting it out, or were they trying to get at him secretly? He remembered the comment that Reneea had made about his family discussing them behind their back, and thought some of them may have common knowledge of his relationship with Vanessa Winters, none of them could have known about Beatrice Neal, it just didn't add up. He continued to drive over to Vanessa's apartment as he needed her more than ever right now; she was the only one that could take away his pain and humiliation by treating him with the respect he deserved. She would know just what to do for his ego. Upon arriving he noticed that her luggage was still in the living room and he could hear her on the phone in the bedroom so he waited before calling out to her as he was unsure of whom she could be conversing with. He walked into the kitchen and grabbed an energy drink she always kept on hand and cold for him. She was so well trained and thoughtful in that area, Reneea would purchase them from the Grocer but never managed to put them in the icebox so they would be cold and ready for him. Finally, she emerged from her bedroom to see Curtis waiting for her.

Well what's so urgent that you cut my trip short sweetheart?

I just needed you here with me; can't a man miss his woman? Curtis snapped at her as she had the audacity to question his motives.

Yeah, sure baby, why so tense? You told me to leave town and enjoy myself when you booked the trip because you were going to be tide up with that fake ass family tradition, remember. Noticeably pissed off by his irritation with her she walked over and sat on the sofa waiting for his response. V, I'm sorry baby, I missed you, I needed you and can you blame a man for wanting his future Mrs. by his side, hump? Well since you put it that way, I guess not leaning over to kiss him as he had sat next to her.

Curtis if this is the case you wanting to be near your future Mrs. and all, tell me why your wife is throwing a little party for some of the office staff on Christmas Day for all of their hard work and you are not making provisions for me to be in attendance? Yelling at the top of her lungs and standing up to her feet directly over Curtis waiting for his response. As this information has totally taken him by surprise and considering he was already drained from no sleep and the confrontation with Rick, he tries to recover control as he has no clue who would have possibly leaked this information and how she heard about it so fast. Then it struck him…Charlotte. This was a planned attack and he never saw it coming. Charlotte must have told someone in the secretarial pool and she knew that it would make its way back to Vanessa before the ink had a chance to dry on the invitations. It was true Reneea was always thoughtful to the employees at Christmas time, but he never expected her to invite those in the inner circle to the house for a party with their family and friends in attendance? There would be no way in hell that he would be able to bring his side piece of ass into his main lady's stable, no way in hell.

Well Curtis, explain…I mean I am a valued employee of Rae aren't I? I do a great deal for the company or have you forgotten? I mean I can think of a cool 2.5 million reasons as to why I should be there, not to mention that I should be the leading lady at the head of your table considering I am wearing this ring and that I have more involvement with you than she has in years? She was furious and there would be no calming her down with anything less than an invitation.

Curtis had to think fast, he sprung to his feet setting his beverage on the coffee table and began to reason with her. V, have you lost your mind talking to me like that? In case you haven't noticed, I pay the lease on this damn condo, I pay your bills, I am the man flying you all around the world, I am very aware of who you are and what you are to me…No damn dinner invitation can validate you, baby I validate you. I keep Vanessa Winters soon to be Vanessa Rae in excellent living conditions and fashion don't you ever forget that! Anything you have ever done for the company, me and/or otherwise has been to secure our future together, how dare you have the nerve to come at me like that. Vanessa was not giving in that easily, she really took that ring on her finger as a commitment from Curtis to her, not to mention she was getting tired of waiting. She began to cry and pull away from his grasp.

Curtis! This is bullshit! I don't give a damn about your things and what you buy, damn it baby I want you! I want you to myself…I'm so damn tired of sharing you with a bitch that doesn't even know your favorite color, or what you like to drink…she doesn't share your interest in the business, she sure as hell would not go the extra mile that I have to help you maintain or retain your business. I will walk the fuck away from this apartment in a heartbeat. You don't get it Curtis; I walk the halls of that building and hear the conversations about how I will never be your wife and how you are only using me for personal gain and sex. I hear those jealous bitches making fun of me all the time and most of them want to be me. You are not the subject of ridicule because they know you will fire their ass…Baby, all I'm asking for is a little recognition, for you to show me the respect I deserve and how truly important I am to your world; this wont happen if you continue to put me to the side when your "*family*" has to be front and center. How do you think I feel when the holidays roll around and everyone else is with the ones they love and are enjoying their mates? I sit here alone night after night, I sleep alone except for the occasions that you throw me an overnight stay. I have to think of her laying next to you touching you sleeping in a bed meant for me, that shit tears me up inside Curtis, sure, she gets you I get a fur coat to roll around in, but that damn coat can't hold me back. I am giving you the best years of my life and I can't have you for a holiday meal, I'm not welcomed in your home?

As far as I am concerned Curtis this is just one more straw breaking the camels back and I can't promise you that I can hold on for much longer with fragments of a relationship here and there. I love you and I have proved it over and over again. Now, I'm asking you to show me that same love in return…I went into this with my eyes wide open in the beginning I knew we were just fooling around on the side, but it was you that changed the stakes. It was you that made me exclusive to only you, you who decided to take things further by telling me you wanted me to be your wife, you are the one who changed my world from the way it was before and now you can't just change it back or keep me in a box while everyone else lives free! You can't do this shit to me Curtis; you just can't let me be treated this way.

Vanessa at this point crying inconsolably pulled away from Curtis' grasp and began to walk toward the door. Curtis was shocked as she had never displayed this type of behavior in the past and clearly knew this was not a good sign and that he would have to act fast because Vanessa was clearly not going to give in to him just that easily the one thing in his world that was constant. The one thing he knew he could always run to and take charge of was seriously in jeopardy of being destroyed. He did have feelings for her he loved her his way; he loved what she did to him on so many levels and though he knew he never would marry her, he was not ready to loose what they had together especially over some stupid ass party invitation that he preferred they would not host in the first place.

Vanessa walked to the door as Curtis stood behind looking at her not quite sure of what her display was going to be knew that he would do whatever it took to calm her down. Vanessa looked up at Curtis with tears in her eyes as she opened the door and begin to speak. Curtis, you need to leave, I need time to get myself together, and right now I don't have the energy or the strength to cater to your needs; please…just go. Vanessa, don't do this girl, you know that I love you and I want to be with you more than anything. Baby, please I'm begging you, and you know Curtis begs no one, sweetheart calm down so we can talk about your feelings about this thing…we love each other so much that we can get through anything. He walked over to her trying to remove her hand from the door handle while trying to embrace her as she struggled against his advances and attempts of trying to smooth everything over with a kiss. While resisting him she couldn't help but be drawn to him as she was so attracted to him and did love him so. He managed to move her hand and close the door, as he pushed her backwards up against the wall pinning her down with his body's weight. He continued to kiss on her and rub himself against her while she protested his advances and cried wanting to be able resist him but finding it increasing impossible to do so.
Curtis, please, plea…please stop don't do this to me.
V, baby I love you, please let me just love on you, let me make it feel good to you baby. You want to feel good, don't you?
Ooh Curt, baby… please stop.

Don't stop me, you know you like when daddy licks on you like that. He was in control of the situation once more and he knew it by the way her body responded to his touching her. As he pushed up against her, she could feel his penis swell up against her and though she tried to fight it, she could feel herself grinding against him in the rhythm that their bodies were accustomed to. She wanted him badly and he knew it but today it could not just be sex alone he knew that he would have to make a promise in order to keep his planets aligned. He knew that to save one he would ultimately sacrifice another but the kind of man he was spoke volumes as he was used to having things his way and was not going to be denied of what he felt was his.

Noticing that she was falling in line with what he was doing to her he decided to take it up a notch. Yeah baby, that's it give it to daddy I know you want this, you want me to love you and I know you do…Curtis caressed her face rubbing the tears away from her eyes, taking his hands down rubbing them across her partially exposed breast to remove them so that he could suck them while using his knee to stimulate her between her legs he heard moans of pleasure and approval with each touch he provided to her. She felt herself become weak in her knees and allowed her body to go lifeless.

Curtis, please baby I need more of you. Curtis…

As he heard her speaking and he felt her body surrender he picked her up and took her into the bedroom laying her down on the bed he began to remove articles of clothing slowly as not to be to anxious to make love to her as she was still in a fragile state.

Vanessa, baby you have to know that you are my every desire and there is nothing I would not do to make you feel loved. Don't ever doubt that. It kills me to be apart from you knowing that you are lying in this bed alone wanting me as badly as I lay in my bed wishing she was you. His words were so believable that Vanessa began to loose sight of her original anger she had towards him she felt his touch and embrace his flesh against hers and she wanted him more than she had before. Wounded from the previous night, he had to make sure that he wasn't loosing his grip on Vanessa as well so he made it his mission to make sure that she was the focus of this love making session. As she began to bend her head toward him to give him oral satisfaction, she was stopped by Curtis who had other plans.

No baby, this is not about me right now, its all about you. Vanessa was shocked as it had always been written in stone regarding their relationship that she pleased him in this manner to get the party started. As she was lying on her back she closed her eyes and prepared herself for what was to come. Curtis kissed her from head to toe stopping dead center to lick her vaginal area and tease it causing her complete arousal. She moaned with total delight. He knew he was good to her by her body's reaction to him the entire time they made love he concentrated on making her feel satisfied and letting her know she was the focus. After he dined sufficiently performing oral sex like a pro, he penetrated her gently making sure that she climax while denying himself the pleasure of releasing to soon to make sure that she was good and satisfied with his performance.

After he completed his mission he laid with her making sure that she felt whole inside. Once he was sure that it was safe to converse he decided to do what he felt would keep his world safe. Vanessa?
Yes?
You're absolutely right, you are very important to Rae Enterprises and you are extremely important to me. You are without a doubt a member of the staff that should be recognized for everything you have done to support me and if attending this simple little dinner party will show you how much I love, want, and need you, than by all means you shall be in attendance with everyone else it is high time for me to treat you as special as you are. So if you need this, it is what I want for you. His voice was calm, kind and gentle and this made her so happy. Once again he had managed to pull off the impossible and made Vanessa feel number one again. Of course by doing so he knew that he would definitely be opening the flood gates for trouble at home, however, he was Curtis Anthony Rae ruler of his domain; and just as he had managed to control the situation with Vanessa, he was completely sure that he would be able to do the same with Reneea as well. Maybe the rest of the world needed a wake up call as to who he was, but he was certain of his power and it mattered not to him how others would be affected as long as he was able to get what he wanted.

By 6:30, Reneea had returned home and was dressed and ready for dinner. Craig and Angel were meeting them at the restaurant and she was sure that she would be able to make a good showing at dinner for their sakes. She thought that it would be best not to mention to Craig and Angel what had happen after they left the house. She paced back and forth waiting for Curtis to come down from their bedroom she thought about having a cocktail before they departed but she thought that she had better not in order to keep her attitude in check. She was wearing a simple black sweater with perfectly pressed wool slacks and had decided that her black mink jacket would top of the outfit just right it was unseasonably cold in November even for Detroit and as they were going to dine near the waterfront she thought that it would be best to wrap up warm.

She heard Curtis coming down the stairs and mustered up what was left of her energy to make it through the evening. Looking upon him she noticed that he was dressed casual but nice he too had chosen to wear black and though it looked good on him, it did not thrill her in the same manner as it did when she saw Rick in the color. He was taller than Curtis and the height made all the difference. Curtis, however, was a very attractive man and was often looked at by other women when they were out. This use to make Reneea proud as she knew she was the envy of a lot of woman, but now it only made her wish that one of them would take him off her hands for good.

Reneea, are you ready to leave?
Yeah… we should get going our reservations are for 7:00 and though there may not be any traffic on the way down, we shouldn't push it. I agree; which car would you like to take yours or mine? I haven't driven the Benz in a while, let's take yours. Very well then, I'm ready. Reneea picked up her jacket and attempted to put it on. As Curtis walked over to her to assist her with her coat, they caught a reflection of themselves in the oversized mirror that hung over the huge brick built fire place. They both just stood there looking when Curtis broke their silence with a question that was to impossible for either of them to answer.
What happen to us Nea? When did we fall off?
Reneea looked at him with a cold gaze, smirked and answered…Somewhere between I do and love, cherish and honor and the other woman you needed more than me. She put her purse on her shoulder and walked away from Curtis and his reflection and the obvious fuck you bitch he had plastered across his forehead, and headed for the garage calling out for him to come along as she did not want to make Angel wait for to long as eating was important when you were eating for more than

two. They drove down the Lodge expressway in thick silence until it became unbearable.

Reneea, if it is all the same to you, I don't think that we need to share what has come into play from last night with Craig and Angel. I really see no sense in them knowing about Rick and how upset he was last night. Besides, he and I will get around to discussing this and we will be fine in a matter of days so there is really no reason to burden Craig with the woes of his father and friend. Sure Curtis, after all, isn't this what are marriage is about... protecting Craig? Continuing to look out of the passenger door window as she did not want to make eye contact with him period, she thought of what Rick must be doing right now and wished that it was he next to her and not this man who obviously had no clue. She continued to look dead ahead. Did you speak with Rick today anyway? Annoyed by his investigation she answered but wondered why he was bothering to ask such stupid questions as he knew full well something like this is not dropped in your lap and you don't call the other parties involved to see if they were feeling as horrible as you may have been or thought they were. Yes, I talked with him just to make sure he got home okay and to see if he was hung over, he was fine but understandably upset. Nea...I... Curtis if you don't mind, I would rather not rehash this whole thing right before dinner, to be honest with you, it has me quite dazed and confused as I really can't put it all together and to be honest right now, I don't think I want to.

Sure Reneea, no problem, lets just get through dinner, with our fake ass display of emotions and retreat to our mutual corners in the end shall we? Sounds like a plan to me. They approached the Renaissance Center where they pulled up to the Vallet who knew Curtis extremely well and was genuinely happy to see him.

Good evening Mr. Rae, nice to see you this evening, recognizing Reneea, he nodded and spoke to her as well looking at her as if he were surprised to see her in Curtis' company. Good Evening Ma'am.

Evening, poor man, Reneea thought to himself, she knew he had to be puzzled that Curtis did not have his regular dinner mate with him this evening and was not quite sure if he was addressing the wife or the trick. She decided to let him off the hook by extending her hand and introducing herself. Good evening, I'm sorry where on earth are my manners? I am Reneea Rae, his wife.

And a lovely one I might add if you don't mind me saying so? Not at all and thank you so very much. Curtis aware of what Reneea was doing

decided that he had seen enough of her display decided to get the man's
attention in order to enter the restaurant before something was said that
shouldn't be. Bill if you don't mind, please keep it parked close so that we
can leave right out after dinner without the wait. He handed the man a
$100.00 tip which caught the attention of the other patrons placed his hand
on the small of Reneea's back and guided her inside. He loved to make an
entrance and an exit he liked the attention he gained as people took notice
speculating on who he might be.

Poor people if they only knew the snake he really was they would run for
the hills in fear that he might slither his way into their paths, Reneea
thought privately as they entered to be greeted by the hostess who had
previously seated Craig and Angel. Noticing his parents, he immediately
stood recognizing his mother's presence at the table pulling out her chair
as Curtis took their Coats to be checked.

Hello, Hello Everyone.

Hey Mom.

How are you both this evening? I'm sorry sweetheart I take that
back…how are the two of you and the three of you, smiling at her
daughter-in-law who looked as if after Christmas could not come soon
enough. They both laughed at the humor his mother displayed. Mom, to be
honest with you…if I did not love this man so much…may I be frank? Of
course sweetheart, Reneea encouraged? Very well, there is no way in hell
that I would be going through this right now for anything. Reneea
understood her discomfort and let her know that she was entitled to feel
however, she wanted to feel. As small framed as Angel was prior to the
pregnancy, she knew that this experience had taken a toll on her.

Baby it will all be over soon and you will be back to your old self in no
time and I am going to take care of you every step of the way. Craig loved
her so much and it made his mother so happy to know that she had raised a
son who had turned out to be a wonderful caring man. Mom, did I tell you
that I took the twelve week FMLA Leave so that I could be there with her
through the early stages when she really needs help?

No, Craig that is a wonderful idea, I think you guys ought to consider
staying down here for a while after she has the babies so that you can have
all of the help you need.

Well, we don't want to inconvenience anyone…Nonsense, both your
mother and I would kill to have you here with our little ones. By this time
they noticed that Curtis was headed to the table and Reneea was pretty

sure she knew what had taken him so long. Her whole demeanor had changed and Craig spotted it right away.

Mom?

Hum?

Are you okay?

Yeah, fine, I could use a cocktail or a glass of wine if our waitress would ever bother to stop by. They had chosen to dine at Seldom Blues an extremely popular Jazz Supper Club and Friday night was a hot night. Finally the waitress made her way to the table but she already had drinks in hand. Puzzled by this Reneea looked at Curtis who sat there smugly as if he had done something so right. The young lady sat the glasses in front of the correct person and begans to take their orders; she had to admit it was pretty nice of him to take care of that up front. Reneea was impressed that Curtis had only excused himself twice to attend to business calls each time his phone rang.

After dinner, they listened to the band that was the headliner for the evening. They watched their son and his wife enjoy the music and each other and Reneea silently prayed for them that the love they were experiencing right now, though it would be tested throughout time, that it would last and renew its commitment to each other as they looked so happy together and she knew all to well first hand what could happen if the fire and desire died. Her life was not one that she wished on anyone, definitely not her son that she tried so desperately to protect.

After dinner, Reneea and Curtis returned to the house where she found herself dreading the thought of being alone with him as she had managed to lighten up her assault towards him, she did not want him to misinterpret this as a sign of a truce and think that she wanted to be bothered with him as this was not the case. She merely wanted her son who had been paying attention to her all evening to stop thinking that there was something wrong. Once inside she hung up her jacket and proceeded upstairs to change. Curtis followed her without saying a word. He was thinking to himself how he had promised his lover that she would be able to attend a party at the home of his wife and imagine the fireworks that house would see if it turned ugly. He must have laughed out loud because she turned around to address him.

What's so funny?

Excuse me?

You were laughing; I just asked what was funny? As lying came easy to Curtis he was able to respond quickly on his feet.

Oh, oh I was just thinking about Craig trying to dance close with Angel and after noticing that the babies were in his way, how he turned her around just to be close to her. She smiled at the memory that he spoke of herself.

He really loves her.

Yes, you might be right there Mrs. Rae.

Who says you can't have it all? Love, family and a career...it will be a juggling act but they will manage. She reminds me of you when you were pregnant with Craig, you were so pretty pregnant.

Negro please...I was fat.

No, not really, you were all belly and boobs. He walked over to her assisting her in releasing the clamp to her necklace, looking at her in the mirror he noticed that she had tears forming in her eyes.

Reneea, what is it?

Nothing.

I know, I've hurt you so badly with this thing with Bea and all, I never meant for either of you...at that moment, he stopped talking and put his arms around her waist from behind holding her tightly. She was quiet and hoped he wouldn't try to kiss her or anything she really didn't want him to think he was going to sleep with her and make it all go away. At that moment, he turned her around to face him. Nea, I wish I could turn back the hands of time. I would do a lot of things differently. If I only knew how much I was going to hurt you, I would have....I would have just told Rick not to get your attention. You deserve so much more than what I have offered you throughout the years. I don't blame you for being angry with me, but when I think it over I would rather you be here and angry with me than to have you leave and destroy my world. The only world I know is with you and Craig. Please Nea, don't leave me I know I can make you love me again. I'll try harder than before. He kissed her on her lips as tears continued to roll down her cheeks, and as he wiped them away he kissed her on her neck begging her not to go.

Nea, just tell me the truth...do you still love me? He looked at her hoping for any sign of something positive, and as so much time lapsed between his questions and her answer, he knew that it couldn't be anything good. She just looked at him with tears in her eyes and slowly she spoke pulling herself away from his grasp; Curtis hasn't anyone ever told you, the truth hurts? She picked up her robe and went into the master bathroom locking the door behind her. Curtis sat on the bed knowing that short of a miracle, his life as the husband of Reneea Rae was fading fast.

Chapter 16

Breaking All the Rules

As time marches on, Rick knew that in order to maintain his constant unnoticeable connections with Reneea, he would have to maintain his friendship with Curtis in order to do so. As hard as it was, he met with Curtis and actually managed to pull off the act that bygones would be bygones and that they would continue their friendship as Bea was deceased and no one could change the past. She was not there to tell her side of this sorted tale, but in no certain terms did he think his sister would ever lie to him about what she bare witness to or what she knew. Besides he was reaping his own silent revenge that no one was the wiser about except for him and the love of his life who would be the one who would ultimately avenge his dignity for him when it was all said and done. He continued to indulge Curtis in his man about town stories and even manage to pull off a cover or two for him during the holiday season when he wanted to be with Vanessa. After all he was only too happy to do it. Curtis would pay for Rick to wine and dine his wife while he got the opportunity to be with his mistress. Not that Rick needed to use Curtis' money at all, he had his own of course, it just made the deal that much sweeter that Curtis would be out of pocket for the expense as Reneea definitely deserved that and more. The whole set up was perfect and Curtis was clueless to the advantage he had given his best friend where his wife was concern. It was like taking candy from a baby and Rick could have cared less about Curtis' feelings anymore. In his opinion, Reneea belong to him, should have been with him and there was no changing that in his mind now or ever!

Craig and Angel had moved back to Detroit with Angel's parents as she was becoming closer and closer to her due date and Craig needed her to be near the family. To be honest, his first time becoming a father, he also wanted to be near the family as he had no clue what he would do to assist with one baby not to mention two. He decided that he would work from home until she actually delivered and this would give him more time with her. Curtis offered to put them in one of the Company Condo's for more privacy, but they declined as they thought it would be best just to stay with the Coopers who had gone through so much trouble preparing for their arrival. Though Angel's father made a good living for his family, he did not have the money that the Rae's had and she did not want her parents to feel as if what they were offering wasn't as good as what Curtis could provide. Angel who discussed everything with her husband opened and honestly was relieved that he shared her sentiments in this area, not to mention that Craig enjoyed his in-laws as they were always good to him from the beginning of his relationship with Angel.

Tina and Michael, who had been vacationing in Jamaica for their wedding anniversary which fell on the Saturday after Thanksgiving, had recently returned; as they made it a point to never be away from home on Christmas as their daughter, though grown and on her own, was simply not having that. It was a tradition that the Vaughn's, Neal's and Rae's were always together during this season and now with the anticipation of the babies, there was no way that this tradition was about to change now. This was the time of year that Tina and Reneea, enjoyed having money as they spent it as if it grew on trees. Nothing was too good for their family and friends not to mention that they volunteered at the shelters for battered women and children and had gotten Mia involved by the age of 16 so that she could see that her life could have been much different and that it was only the grace of God that she was not in their shoes. She was taught a lesson to never look down on or judge another as you really had no idea what hand had been dealt to another and it was not up to you as a person to say what should be the fate of another. Mia always said that the time she spent with the women on that day as she was growing up made her stronger and more in tuned to others feelings. By Mike being on the police force, they were able to reach out and touch many families in need and they had always enjoyed doing so, it truly made them as women in good positions thankful for what they had. It often made Tina think about the safe houses that she would be housed in from time to time until Attorney Craig, Reneea's deceased father, came into her life. She was eternally grateful to the Craig family for so many things and because of this, Reneea and whomever she loved would always have a friend in her.

Curtis used this time of year as a reason to be away from home as often as he could get away with as he had to divide his time between home and his lover. He often spent the night away claiming to be on business trips that could not wait while he was really shopping with his woman who would not be ignored during this time of year. This year would be a little different, with Angel expecting any minute and Reneea preparing the house for the small business Christmas Party he was not able to get away as much as Vanessa would have liked, but this time she did not care because she was finally going to be recognized for her important role in Curtis' life. She did much preparation for this as she shopped for the perfect outfit and shoes to wear as she knew Reneea Rae had a flair for dressing she would not be underdressed for her own coming out party you might call it. She wasn't sure what to expect, but she knew all the rules would be broken this holiday as Curtis had invited her to Reneea's domain and surely this would cause her to come unglued and show everyone she wasn't as classy as they thought she was.

Meanwhile, back at the Rae residence, plans were developing at a steady pace while Rick and Curtis had been appointed assistants to Reneea as she was very meticulous about functions that would take place at her home. All day she had the two men rearranging furnishings, hanging decorations and assembling model trains that ran throughout the house making it classy and festive and a sight that would be enjoyed by all in attendance. As this was all well and fine, Curtis had had enough of family togetherness as his body yearned to be pleased by the one he loved. Curtis decided to make a break from the house while all the decorators were there and Rick was there so it would be easy for him to slip away as Reneea would have someone to focus her attention on.

Returning from his study completing his phone conversation as he was in ear range of his wife, he made sure that she had taken notice of what he was saying. *"Thank you very much, I do appreciate your diligence in tracking me down this is a very important client and if I had missed this there would have been hell to pay. Thank you again I will take it from here."* Curtis protesting his mistake under his breath appearing to be upset with the news he had just heard walked over to his wife and began to explain his situation. Hey Reneea, uh, I have got to meet a client for a late dinner this evening; the whole thing slipped my mind as I was really getting into helping with these lights and all. She knew this was a lie as all he did was made phone call after phone call the entire time they were decorating. The answering service just called and said that they had been waiting for my arrival. Do you think that you can manage without me? I'm sure Rick will be here to give you the assistance that you need, I mean if he doesn't have to go be with that special lady of his and all...*THAT WE STILL HAVE YET TO MEET*...being loud and sarcastic enough causing Rick to look up from his task with a smirking expression.

Whatever Negro...responding to his friend, we will be fine and no, I'm not going to see her until later this evening smart ass!

Yeah...right...this evening smiling at Rick as if he did not believe a word he was saying as Rick thought to himself. *Yep, the minute you walk your ass out that door.*

Reneea never bothering to look away from her task of hanging lights over the massive fire place responded in a tone that let Curtis and anyone else listening know that she could have cared less about what he was saying...No problem Curtis, I'm sure that Rick will be able to give me whatever I need, and then some, after her statement she smiled at Curtis giving him assurance that his absence would be excused while thinking to herself, *how soon can you get the hell out.*

Are you sure baby? I really hate to go like this; I know this is family time. No, go on, business is business right? You don't have to keep Va,...stammering to catch her statement, THE, the, client waiting any longer than I'm sure she, he, he's already waited for you.

Rick's eyebrows rose as he heard her speaking aloud obviously what she intended to keep inside.

Curtis noticing that his wife was having some difficulty getting her statement straight began to complete the statement so that he could be on his way. Okayyyyy.... fine and it is a he, Marshall Johnson of the Kirmark Division Group, wants me to meet some young hot shot executive he has brought on board to run his marketing division Donica or Monica Price something or other before we take on his project, Curtis said as he leaned in smiling to kiss her on her lips, however, only managing to catch her cheek as she had already began to extend her cheek in his path.

Right, noticeably pissed about the cheek business responding dry, well I better go.

Hey, Rick, be a dear if you don't mind and lock the door behind Curtis please?
Rick who was stunned by Reneea's lack of interest in her husbands departure spoke up quickly to ease the obvious tension in the room, sure no problem, wouldn't want you to get off that ladder and see your husband out, and he really did mean that, though Curtis thought that Rick was being facetious letting her know that her not doing so was noticed. Rick walked behind Curtis as he protested all the way.

See man, that shit right there, right there is what pushes me into the arms of another woman every night. Even you noticed that bullshit about not seeing me to the door, looking for some sign of reinforcement? This shit is not a marriage, it's a fucking joke. That's exactly why I'm on my way to get me a piece of ass that knows how to treat a man, you dig?
Curtis, keep your voice down man if you want to get back in here tonight. Man whatever, sometimes dog…Some days, I wish I didn't have to come back to this motherfucker. The harder I try the worst her ass gets. I'm telling you man this shit is a joke. Curt, man, who made it that way, Rick said directly looking at Curtis as though he had been some innocent bystander or victim to say the least?

You telling me you didn't see her ass give me her cheek when I was aiming for her lips and you gone stand there and tell me this shit is right? I'm not saying shit about right or wrong, I'm merely stating that it took two to get to this point, don't forget your part in this shit. I have been covering your ass for a long time now, and your shit stank too.
Man, true that, and maybe so, but, man…I just wish that sometimes, her ass would push on if she is so unhappy with me.
Rick could see the sincerity in Curtis' eyes and he knew that his friend was starting to weaken in his position and simply proceeded to caution him once more. You know what they say Curtis, be careful what you ask for, you just might get your wish…Rick looked at his friend with cautioning eyes.

Whatever man, I'm out of here I've already kept her waiting long enough as it is…I will probably be late getting back, it's cool if you want to stay in the guest bedroom and keep her company, maybe it will take her mind off of me being gone and I won't have to rush my baby while she is trying to please me and do her *thang, you know what I mean?*

Whatever's clever dude, if you don't mind it is getting late and all, I can chill in the guest suite tonight. My baby will understand why I'm here…Rick thought to himself *this was too easy.*
Cool, I'll hit your hip when I'm on my way back.
Bet. The two men gave each other a pound and Rick watched Curtis pull out of the circular drive onto the road as fast as his car could carry him.

Laughing inward to himself, he couldn't help but remember the words of his sister, *"To be such a smart businessman, he has no street smarts; when will he put two and two together and realize that you are seeing his wife"* no one could be this damn dumb, he thought. Turning around to rejoin Reneea in the living room where he had left her, to his surprised he turned right into her as she was standing directly behind him after he had shut the door. She was smiling biting her lips together and they both exploded with laughter, shaking their heads at their unbelievable luck they both thought that they would just have to settle for being in the same room together tonight and this man made their dreams come true by leaving.

Guest Suite my ass, nothing but the Master for my boo, glaring at Rick as she spoke as though he were a million dollar lottery ticket and she was extremely ready to cash in!
Come here you, reaching for her arm to pull her near him, how long had you been standing there?
Long enough.
Long enough what?
To hear him say he would be out late and that you could sleep in the guest suite…oh and to say he wishes that I would push on if I'm so unhappy.
In other words you heard it all?
Yes, I did and I am not the least bit phased by any of it. Although, I'm glad I had the good since to have the guy from the Spy Shop stop by while the decorators were here earlier. You mean the place that did my house surveillance? Yep, he managed to find the hidden camera in the guest suite just today. Curtis told me that there was a problem with the cable in that room and he had this guy here looking at it this morning, imagine that shit? A whole house full of cable television and the only one not working is a room we hardly ever use? So, while he was out…I called my guy. You are fucking kidding me, surprised that Curtis could even think that far? Nope! This, my dear is a set up, a sloppy one but never-the-less a set up. He just broke the rules. What rules? The Rules of Engagement…you

know…don't ask, don't tell? Were there anymore cameras? No; just in there where he offered you to sleep tonight as if we creep in that style. Well I guess he left us no other choice but to make love in his bed. But baby, that's where we always make love? Oh that's right, well I guess it will be even better tonight. Rick looked at her unbuttoning his shirt with wanting eyes that desired her so badly, send the decorators home. She walked over to him placing her hand on the crotch of his pants that had already started to swell rubbing him seductively, Sweetheart… I'm already ahead of you they left out the back door through the service entrance of the house while you were still conversing with Curtis. If you wanted to, you could take me right here and now.

Uh, uhh…naw…I want you in that motherfucker bed so that I can leave him a present.

And what might that be?

My NUT, now get up them steps with your fine ass he ordered as he patted her on her butt as she backed away from his advances. Rick and Reneea made a mad dash for the bedroom preparing for what was sure to be a marathon fuck session. He went down on Reneea as if he was sure to find gold between her legs. He was so forceful that she moaned uncontrollably. Not knowing whether or not tonight was the night that they would be caught while in the throws of passion made her more excited than ever before. She actually hoped that Curtis would come in and fine Rick inside of her and enjoying being thoroughly fucked by a man who was commanding as much attention from her as he was rendering. She called out his name loudly begging him to do her telling him where she wanted to feel him inside of her next. Damn she thought to herself, how this man could fuck her. She rolled over on stomach and waited patiently for him to re-enter her when she looked back to see what was taking him so long she noticed that he had stood back and was smiling at her wickedly licking his lips…What's wrong baby? Why are you stopping barely with breath in her to speak? He wouldn't answer her and he knew that this was pushing her buttons. Damn it Rick what are you doing? Are you soft, you can't go on, what?

I'm fine baby, nothing like that at all.

Then fuck me would you? I need it baby. She was like an addict craving that fix she could not manage to get her hands on.

You want me to make you cum, he taunted her?

Yes…please oh God yes!

Then lay back and spread your legs for daddy like a good girl.

Okay baby whatever you say.

He walked slowly back up to the bed where he had some sort of gadget in his hand she could not make out, but soon heard the sound of buzzing coming from his direction. He slid down on the bed next to her kissing her and rubbing her breast placing his hand between her legs as he bent his head down and kissed and licked her clit making her wet with each moment of anticipation and when she thought she could no longer take it, she felt the vibration between her clit which stimulated her so much that she began to cry out in pleasure. Damn it BABY that feels sooooo good! As she trashed around the bed under the weight of his body she cried with tears streaming down her face as it was feeling so good to her she thought she might pass out. Rick had introduced toys, a powerful little vibrator if you will, into the love making and it was wonderful in her mind, he loved to watch her body jerk against his hand knowing that he was only taking her to higher levels to achieve greater ecstasy it was erotic for the both of them and right at the moment where she thought she couldn't take anymore, Rick forced himself into her stroking her until they both climaxed strong and hard the friction between them created a warm sensual heat. They both gasped for air as if they might die from lack of oxygen. She repeated his name over and over again saying how much she loved him as did he. He had cum and snatched out of her to allow it to run onto the sheets just as he promised forbidding her to change them but little did he know she never had anymore after making love to Rick in Curtis' bed, why bother after all laundry day was Saturday and it gave her extra time to enjoy his sent. After they got themselves together she lay in his arms watching him and he her. Rick broke their silence as he could not get over the way her body responded to the extra curricular activity that had taken place.

You know baby?

What?

Looking down on her with playful eyes he simply stated…You a freak… Reneea looked up at him laughing and softly responded, yeah…maybe, but you made me this way.

And I never want you to change; he said smiling lovingly staring into her eyes.

I love you, she kissed him tenderly and he kissed her back.

I know and I love you more.

They both showered together and changed after which decided to go into the recreation area and watch a movie as they fell asleep on the sofa not

Breaking All the Rules   171

caring who would or would not find them, they were well pleased in the arms of one another and had broken several rules of their own tonight.

The sound of the kitchen door closed and Rick woke up to find that Reneea was still fast asleep on the opposite end of the sofa. Rick heard Curtis in the kitchen and decided to head him off. Hey man. Oh sorry man, did I slam the door to loud? No, you know me I'm still a light sleeper. Right, I forgot about that. Reneea still up? Naw, she feel asleep on the couch shortly after the movie we were watching went off, I think all the decorating must have tired her out. Probably so. Now that your back, I can head upstairs and get some sleep, I'm a little tired myself. Should we wake her or let her stay asleep? At that moment, Reneea, made her way into the kitchen as she heard the sound of voices…No need look behind you, Curtis was pointing to a sleep broken Reneea.
Hey guys what time is it?
Half past 1:00.
In the morning; Curtis are you just getting in?
Yeah, the meeting ran longer than expected. Oh, I see…well I guess I will go to bed and you can tell Rick all about it. She turned to go up the stairs as both men watched her disappear into the darkness of the halls.
Dude, there is no way I can change in front of her tonight.
Why? What's up? V got a little drunk and put passion marks all over me? Are you serious? Man that shit is so high school. You do realize that you have a wife upstairs right? Dog, thank you for all of your wonderful observation work but that shit is not going to help me tonight. Man you are on your own, on this note I'm going to fucking bed. No, you are going to go in my bedroom get my robe and meet me in the downstairs bathroom. Man what if she is getting undressed or something? Knock first? Man, quit bull shitting and go get my robe, whispering desperately for his friend to help him.
Alright man stay put, I'll be back in a sec. Damn…Thank you.

Rick walked away from Curtis laughing in his face to something obviously Curtis did not find humorous. Approaching the master suite, he thought about his unbelievable luck that he was having tonight and wondered if fate would allow him a second chance with his beloved but decided that he would just play it safe. He knocked on the door and found that Reneea seemed to be expecting him. She opened the door slowly smiling as she was dressed in only her bra and panty. Rick could not believe his eyes and dropped his head immediately as he could not look upon her for to long as he knew her husband was just downstairs and he did not want to respond in a fashion that could get them both killed.

Ooh damn, sorry Nae-Nae, I was wondering if I could…
In a soft sweet whisper she responded, yes baby, you can anytime, any place…
Girl, you had better quit fucking with me with that nigga downstairs, I'd hate for him to come up here and see me up in you, looking at her as serious as anyone could be.

I'm sorry baby, I couldn't resist, and I heard the two of you and knew you were coming to help that fool. Rick was amazed at her restraint to keep from running downstairs and killing him with her bare hands it only meant one thing to him and one thing only. She was really through with Curtis and any love that she had had for him was a distant memory. She really did not care that this man had just confessed to being with another woman. Take this damn robe downstairs…and if you really want to do me a favor? Keep his ass down there too. She did not crack a smile. She opened the door just enough to kiss Rick on his lips and backed away shutting it tight as he stood there praying that the erection he had just developed would go the hell away before he got down stairs to face his boy. Returning to the kitchen he saw Curtis peeking around the corner waiting for him to return with the goods.
Boy you look like a nigga hiding from an ass whooping, extending the robe to Curtis.
Dude whatever; just give me that shit before she decides to come down for a drink or something. I don't think you have to worry about that, after you left, we got really busy and I think she's a little wore out and just wants to go to sleep. Rick said smiling at Curtis.
A little busy, Curtis said looking at him inquisitively, doing what?
Rick looked at Curtis with a fuck you expression. Fucking! Nigga what the hell were we doing when you left? Honestly sometimes your ass can be so stupid. Man calm down, I'm just fucking with you. You guys did a great job, the house looks great. Rick thought to himself… his dumb ass was so engrossed in trying to get to his woman he hadn't noticed that all of this shit was done before he left. Rick laughed and shook his head. What?

Nothing man, nothing at all. Look um, I notice some James Bond was about to come on I think I'm gonna check it out before I turn in, care to join me? Yeah in a minute, I want to check something out upstairs first. Cool, I'll be in the back when you finish. Alright.

Curtis walked up the back stairs looking back to see if Rick had bothered to follow him and slipped into the guest suite. He walked over to the television cable box and flipped the switch in the back and while waiting for the picture to show. When it came on he was shocked at what he saw to the point of disgust, his own. He had video taped his son and daughter-in-law making love on their last visit home as there was something so terribly wrong with seeing his children nude and together in that way he tried to react quickly to make it go away in his shocked state fumbling with the remote to fast forward he dropped the remote and quickly picked it up to continue his fact finding mission to only see Reneea hanging clothes and changing linen, while signing along to Mary J off key which he thought was adorable. No sign of his friend except for when he changed in there tonight and that was obvious because he was wearing the clothes of Curtis that he had just seen him in. He was pissed but relieved all at once by what he saw as there was no trace of his wife and his best friend together making love. He almost felt bad for what he had done but hell…he was Curtis Anthony Rae and he had a right to know if his Classic Caddy had another mechanic under the hood. He shut the T.V. off and exited the room quietly stopping by the master suite looking in on his sleeping beauty who had no crimes to be accused of tonight as surely she would not ever let another man touch her in his bed…he walked in and stood over her looking at her hair tossed about the pillows and in her face she was so sexy and so beautiful he thought to himself, why? Why couldn't he just let himself behave? Why couldn't she be the women he needed her to be? He bent down and kissed her on her lips and smiled as she turned over sweetly. He suddenly remembered his boy was downstairs watching Bond and decided that he would join him as that was probably the only action he was going to see in that house tonight.

Chapter 17

Who's Fooling Who?

With Christmas around the corner, everyone's mind at Rae Enterprise was on the wonderful party that had been planned for the top executives and V.I.P staff members that had been invited to attend, and those who hadn't would receive a special luncheon that Reneea would have catered by Delectable Delights a wonderful eatery the upscale clientele frequented all the time. She was very thoughtful and had not planned on leaving anyone out. She always worked with Curtis at this time because bonus time was something she enjoyed as she knew if it were not for the men and women who came to work on a daily basis and made the wheels turn in that place, there would be no fortune five hundred company for either of them. She always felt the need to remind him of that. This was something that her father drummed into her as a college student at MSU. He treated the employees and clients of Arthur/Craig Attorneys at Law like family. This, she never forgot neither did those who either worked for him or had family members that worked for him. During this time was year end and Curtis needed to make sure that as much business was on the books at years end that could be was; this was needed to keep them in good financial standing with their creditors, banks and vendors. He was an asshole, but he was a good business man and what he couldn't manage to get done as CEO, his CFO, Charlotte could. She was well connected in the business sector and her name carried an awful amount of clout. They were solid from her stand point.

The one thing Curtis had not lied about the night he interrupted the family decorating evening, was the name of the client that he and Charlotte had been courting so intensely and that was Mr. Marshall Johnson, owner of Kirmark Division Group. This would be an account of mega sized

proportion and would set the company over the top financially for 2008
even when Detroit was experiencing its worst economic year of all times.
Johnson was a sharp businessman and made his selections based on gut
instinct or his top advisors. As luck would have it, his top advisor was Ms.
Donica Price, a well educated sister with an Ivy League education who
knew Marketing like the Pope knew Catholic. She was a beautiful woman
who had a great deal going for her and she carried herself in that manner.
She intimidated most men who did not have their shit together and did not
hesitate to let them know that she knew it. She was single and many
thought that this may be the reason why. Few had bets that she was
bedding Mr. Johnson, but if she was her game was so tight that you would
have never known unlike Vanessa Winter's who allowed all of her cards
to be laid out on the table, office nicknames, such as Curtis' Hot Twot,
and Mattress Mabel never seemed to knock her off her square.

Curtis had been working all morning on gathering projections and data
with regards to the company he would soon be entertaining. He had not
had time to attend to his long legged beauty who had been rather pissed by
his absence between her legs during the work day and pretty much the
pass week. But Vanessa was a professional and she knew that Rae
Enterprises came first where Curtis was concerned so she actually had
days where she was required to be more than just beautiful to him she
actually had to work in those cases. It didn't bother her much because after
a day like this, Curtis would need to unwind and she was generally the one
doing the unwinding with the love making he craved especially after he
had signed a big deal such as this. She knew that the meeting would take
place and knew that she would also have to play errand girl and that
Charlotte would be on Curtis' right side guiding the deal and being a
major factor in the project so she would have to be on her best behavior
where she was concerned, but once it was done, the gloves were off back
to battling that bitch for her station and position in the company when
visitors were not around.

Vanessa? She entered the office as she knew this was not a respond from
her desk type day. Would you get the coffee ready for the guest, make
copies of the last folder I put in your basket in triplicate, and make sure
that *all call's even Reneea's* are held once the meeting starts…I don't need
any distractions where this man is concerned. Yes sir, Mr. Rae…Oh and
uh V…making the tone of his voice a little softer and more endearing.

Yes, answering as if she were completely annoyed, turning to look at him with much attitude inside? *You look beautiful today sweetheart*, smiling at the secretary he had realized he had not bothered to reverence outside of business. Vanessa smiled at him, licked her lips winked her eye and responded softly; Thanks for noticing finally. As she walked out of his office she put a little more spin in her hips as she knew he was watching. Curtis couldn't help but watch her as she did things to him no other woman, not even his wife, was capable of doing. He knew tonight he would definitely have first, second, and third helpings of her, just for his little compliment that he had made to her in the midst of all his preparation. Right at that moment, Charlotte entered his office like a hurricane. She was dressed in a sexy two piece Coco Channel with three inch alligator pumps. Her hair was flawless and she smelled of Jadore and the reason he knew this was it was the fragrance that his wife wore daily and he loved what it did for him as she walked by. Looking at her outfit he thought to himself he had to review what her salary was to see what she was being paid as she looked like a million bucks, the shoes alone had to hit for at least five bills. She really was a beautiful woman and he could not understand why she was always working or home alone, he thought. He also had the thought of what it would be like to make love to her but the moment it entered his thought process, it vanished as she was far to valuable to the company to fuck it up for a roll in the hay. She wore make up but it wasn't over powering and did not take away from the features of her face.

Damn Char!
What? What's wrong? What are we missing? She was like a cat on a hot tin roof and more edgy than he had ever seen her before, but he understood, this would be the deal of the year and its importance was made known to the whole team that worked on pulling it together. Nothing boo, smiling and laughing as she was noticeably over the top about the upcoming meeting. I was just observing how incredible you look for today's meeting, that's all. Oh, thanks, sorry, I just need everything to go as planned…the company needs this contract and I don't want anything to be out of place. Speaking of which…did you talk to your girl out there? Don't worry about Vanessa she knows how important this is for everyone, she will behave.
She had better, walking over to Curtis, which, appeared to be seductively in Curtis' mind, with her fist clinched tight, or it will be her ass in the

parking lot, and not the way you like it either, she glared at Curtis to let him know she meant what she said. Charlotte had such a gangster girl flavor about her but also a sweet mix of class and sophistication she never hesitated to let you know that she came up on the East Side Bewick and Mack and if she had to she would definitely set it off.

Calm down smiling at her licking his lips...daddy got this.

Um hum, he had better if he wants this, waving the Kirmark Contracts back in forth. Curtis smiled thinking that those contracts were not looking half as good as she was, and unfortunately as bad as he wanted the contracts...he was starting to want her too. Is that Jadore you're wearing Char? Why yes it is, it was gift from your wife, I remember remarking about how lovely her fragrance was and the next day, there was a gift bag from Nordstrom's Department Store on my Desk with a card from Reneea...she really is so thoughtful. Curtis thought to himself that this was true or was it her sweet little way of letting him know that she was always present in one form or another. He just closed his eyes and smiled as Charlotte had continued spreading the information materials on the conference room table in Curtis' office.

The clock on the wall read 1:00 p.m. straight up and Curtis' cell phone went off, he noticed it was Reneea and he deliberated over whether to answer it. Flipping the top back he decided that he would answer quickly in case she was calling to say that Angel was delivering early.

Rae here?

Curtis?

Yeah...Reneea?

Sorry to bother you, I just wanted to wish you luck on the meeting today, I know you'll get it, and believe it or not...it's your fate. You will get exactly what's coming to you, I can't think of anyone more deserving than you.

Curtis did not know what to make of the conversation, she sent so many mixed signals, but he knew for sure that she was sincere about RAE being a success.

Damn he said softly...*Thank you Nea*, I'm sorry, I don't mean to rush you but my appointment is about to get underway and I've got to go, but I will call the moment I'm done here tonight, this could be a long one.

Oh, I'm sure, don't worry Tina and I have plans tonight. You just do you, alright?

Cool babe, I'll talk with you soon and thank you for calling; it means a lot. Curtis hung up the phone not knowing what to make of her call. She had been so cold lately and all of sudden this? He managed to shake it off as he heard Vanessa's voice over the intercom announcing their awaited appointment and saw that Charlotte had taken notice to his distraction and stood there as she always did with disapproving look on her faces as to how he dealt with his wife.
Please, Vanessa, show them inside.

The door opened and to Curtis' surprise there stood a young beautiful woman dressed in a black two piece suit that accented every curve she had she also reeked of Jadore with a tiny frame and breast that said hello before she had a chance to speak. She had a diamond on her right hand that damn near blinded his ass and her ruby read lips looked as if a man would want to die with them wrapped around him anywhere on his body. All he could say inside was DAMN, DAMN, DAMN, and pray that his dick had not noticed her presence as there would be no way he could explain his salute. Charlotte, whom expected his reaction, swung into action with greetings and salutations and Curtis could not have been happier that she had.

Good Afternoon Ms. Price, so glad you could make it, extending an invitation for her to sit down, and shaking her hand. Will Mr. Johnson not be joining us this afternoon? Curtis managed to rebound after his trusted side kick had stalled for him long enough to gather his composure.
No, I'm sorry, he was called away to New York, just this morning. He sends his regrets but rest assure, if and that is if, I see fit that there is no reason for us not to proceed, than we shall, no problem. Mr. Rae will that be alright with you, or do you prefer to meet once he returns? No, not at all…I am a business man and if I had to be called away, I am more than confident that my second in command, turning to acknowledge Charlotte, could handle business on behalf of the company and myself as well or she would not hold the position that she does and I trust he feels the same way about you, or you would not be here to carry on.
Very well, I'm glad that you feel that way; I see no reason why we can't proceed? Charlotte noticed that everything was under control and saw no reason that Curtis should not take the lead and sat back as if she were expecting to be dismissed at any time.

Now let's see, what would you like to discuss first Ms. Price?

Please, call me Donica.

Alright, Donica, is there a certain interest of business that you would like to attend to first turning on that Rae charm as if it were attached to an automatic mechanism that knew when it should engage?

I'm interested in the McMillen Account, I noticed that you did some really state of the art cutting edge type things for them that worked and I am really interested in seeing how that might be interacted with what we have going already. Rae stands out as an innovative company and I would like that sort of attention given to Kirmark.

Sure, no problem.

Clearing her throat, as she had just been thrown a curve ball and she knew it, interrupted in a quick manner. Slight problem, Charlotte interrupted; Mr. Johnson did not request that projection so it is not amongst what I have for you here at the moment, however, if you would excuse me for twenty minutes or so I can return with a full presentation for your viewing or perhaps an overnight study.

That would be fine, and trust me I understand it not being here as my boss is a meat and potatoes guy who likes to see the basics; he leaves the creativity up to me so it would not have been one of his selections, and me on the other hand…well you understand.

No problem, I'm on it, Curtis, I trust that you being the boss can take it until I return looking at him as to tell him to be a good boy?

No problem Char, I've got us this far, smiling that million dollar smile that no woman has been able to resist. On that note Charlotte excused herself and left the room right smack dead into a fuming Vanessa.

And just where the hell are you going? Excuse me bitch? Why are you leaving him in there with her…ALONE? What? Are you worried; Charlotte looked at her as if she could laugh at any second? No, not at all I just want to know why you would leave an important meeting such as this. Not that I answer to you…but if you must know there is documentation that I have that they need and I am going to retrieve it. Further more if you want to know what's going on between your little fuck buddy and that fine bitch that he's in there with, alone? Just do what you always do…put your ear against the door and listen if you can. Charlotte stuck her tongue out gave her the middle finger and proceeded down the hall laughing all the way. Vanessa was hot like fire and knew that an outburst at this time would be the wrong thing for her to do with them just on the other side of the door. As they still must have been a little louder than expected, Curtis came out and pulled the door closed behind him.

Trying to whisper without raising his voice, you could tell he was agitated by the interruption. What the hell is going on out here? Nothing, sorry, it's just Charlotte, being her bitchy self. Well keep it down, we have company I thought I made that clear? Yes Sir Mr. Rae. He mouthed the words thank you and blew her an air kiss winking at her which made her feel at ease for the moment.

Curtis returned to his office where he noticed that Donica was looking at his photos on the credenza. I apologize for that, my assistant and my CFO have quite a dislike for one another but they are both extremely important to the company structure.
I see.
No problem though they are harmless to everyone else, your safe they are just a detriment to each other's health. Donica laughed and returned her focus to the photos.
Is this your family?
Yes it is.
This is your wife.
Yes, Reneea Rae.
What a beautiful woman, and a beautiful name too, Reneea she said it and it rolled off her lips as if she were doing a study of it.
Thank you. My son and his wife are expecting their first children this month.
Children? Twins?
You got it, we are excited about it.
Imagine that, you a grandfather…not possible as sexy and young looking as you are? What are you about four, five miles daily? To be honest six miles every morning rain, sleet, or snow?
I can tell.
Why thank you and grandfather is correct. And since you started with the compliments, may I be as bold to tell you, that you are gorgeous and I now know why Marshall is so happy everyday.
Oh yeah and why is that Mr. Rae?
Uh uh, if I'm calling you Donica, you must call me Curtis…and I would think that with all of this beauty surrounding him everyday, he can't help but smile.

Thank you very much.

Noticing the time and that she were checking her Rolex, he figured he had to do something to distract her. I don't know what might be taking Char so long. Well in all due fairness I did throw her a curve ball, she was prepared for steak and I requested lobster you might say. And, as time is passing us by, I'm afraid that we will not be able to conclude our meeting today as I do have another appointment soon.

Please, if you would just allow me the opportunity to go and assist her I'm sure we can get you what you need and sign the contracts before you leave. I don't know, I have to get all the way across town and back; that might be cutting it close. Charlotte and I have done business before so I'm sure she can get what I need to my secretary and it won't be a problem. No, not acceptable. At least, meet me for dinner tonight and I will bring them with me and before day break we will have a deal. You are a hard sale aren't you? Is there any other kind? Just let me check my schedule. Curtis walked over to the desk not taking his eyes off of hers and buzzed Vanessa's desk.

Ms. Winter's?

Vanessa heard her last name called and thought to herself instantly, what the hell type shit is he pulling? Yes Mr. Rae?

Can you log my calendar for dinner tonight?

Clearing her throat and speaking rather frank…You have a dinner scheduled already sir? Yeah, I know but I'm certain that I can reschedule that appointment. At that moment, the door to his office flung open and Vanessa stood in the entrance with a look on her face that let Curtis know that this was a problem.

Sir, it would be in your best interest not to cancel this dinner tonight, you have been trying all week for this appointment. Vanessa, I think we can as this is for the good of Rae. He excused himself and escorted Vanessa to her desk closing the door behind him.

Have you lost your damn mind V?

Curtis you are not going to put me on hold for this bitch.

Lower your damn voice, and if you want there to be a Rae Enterprises for any of us, you had better get your shit in check and see that we need this account. There is always tomorrow and I will see to it unless you continue to act like a jealous ass school girl. Curtis, damn you; is it not enough that I have to compete with your family for your time, now this. Pulling her in closely as he could see that this was not going to be as simple as he hoped…Baby, I'm doing this for us, for you. Do you think I would jeopardize what I have with you for her? Kissing her on the lips where anyone could have seen. Now be a good girl and understand this is business, *you are my pleasure* touching her between her legs to reference his remark. With those words she gave in to him as she always did. Ok, but no excuses tomorrow. You bet. He opened the door and continued making plans for tonight. As they had arranged to meet at Andiomo's downtown Charlotte, reappeared with the documents that they had waited for.

Donica, I'm sorry, when I got back to my office there was a problem with one of our clients out West and I had to take care of it myself.
No apologies needed I know what it's like, trust me.
I have what you need and the contracts ready for signature.
Why don't you have all of that packaged and send them with Mr. Rae as we are going to meet for dinner tonight, would you like to join us. Curtis could feel the hairs on the back of his neck as he had other plans that did not include Charlotte.
Ooh no, I can't tonight, I have a prior engagement and I can't get out of it? If you would like to reschedule I can…
No, that won't be necessary, Curtis spoke up quickly, with the holidays right here and we obviously want to put us to bed, I'm sorry this deal to bed, both women looked at him as if his Freudian slip had not gone unnoticed, there is no better time than tonight, beside once we are all signed and Marshall is back we will all go out and celebrate in good fashion, what do you say?
Okay, since you are adamant about this, Donica said looking at Charlotte, I guess your right.
Of course. Great that's settled.
Charlotte walked over and laid the documents on Curtis' desk, Well Donica, allow me to walk you out and make sure everything is set for this evening.
Alright. I'm sorry but is that Jadore, your wearing Charlotte asked inquisitively? Yes it is I noticed it on you also, it is such a lovely fragrance. I agree Charlotte said as Curtis listened on. I received it as a gift from Mrs. Rae because I remarked about how lovely it was on her. Donica looked up and responded, well wasn't that thoughtful? Funny you should say a gift, as mine was a gift from my Soror. Really, the two woman found

that to be comical, the only thing Curtis was doing at this time was thinking to himself how great the two of them looked from behind, two tight asses that he would love to be in between. As he noticed that they had concluded their conversation and were reverencing him he returned his attention to their faces. Mr. Rae it was wonderful meeting you and I look forward to seeing you this evening, contracts in hand?
I will be there with bells on 7:00 sharp.
Charlotte opened the door and turned to face her boss so that he might see the urgency in her eyes, Curtis if you would afford me twenty minutes once I come back.
No problem Char.

Well, that was quick. Did you doubt that it wouldn't happen? No, I can't say that I did. Mark, would you get Ms. Price's car and bring it around front please? Yes ma'am. It's the Red Lexus. No problem back in a flash. Thank you. Well be careful and thank you for the meeting. Don't mention it I have a feeling it's going to be *my pleasure*. The two women shook hands and departed with Charlotte headed to Curtis on a mission.

Charlotte marched into Curtis' office with a chip on her shoulder as wide as the great lakes. Vanessa excuse us please we need to conclude our meeting.
Oh hell no! You don't dismiss me, looking at her with eyes of fire as she had taken all that she was going to take at this moment; as Curtis set back and enjoyed the fireworks.
Very well, Curtis, tell your bitch to go fetch your lunch! As Charlotte was not backing down from her adversary, Curtis decided that he might want to step in as the last comment was bound to draw blood.
Oh Fuck that! Alright, alright that will be enough, V; I need to talk with Char and lunch does sound good, why don't you go get us some, please?
Vanessa looked at Charlotte with eyes that could kill. Yeah alright you won this one but changes are coming, enjoy this shit while you can.
Fuck you… And I say again, your ring may look like hers…but it's just a cheap replica and so are you. Go Vanessa, I will handle this. Vanessa all but pushed out of the office grabbed her keys and stomped out of the office damn near taking the entry door off its hinges.

Damn Char, I get it ok? You don't like her, but do you have to cut so deep all the time?

You know me Curt, I don't half step shit.

You know I don't get you, walking towards Charlotte who was now leaning against the door. I don't understand this loyalty you have to a woman that you hardly see. What is it with you, huh? You are damn good at what you do, but I can't let the two of you continue to go at it like this. Curt this shit here between us, not important, I want to talk to you about this little dinner date that you have arranged with Donica, just what the hell do you think you're doing? We can not afford to loose this account and if you go sniffing around Marshall Johnson's private stock, that's exactly what's going to happen. Damn, how many women do you need exactly you are only one fucking man? Relax Char, I got this shit, I am just doing what I do best, business. Why are you so worked up about this shit anyway? He moved closer to her and noticed that she had not moved. Come on Char, level with me. Why are you so upset about other women finding me attractive or sleeping with me, hum? Do you secretly want the experience for yourself? You can tell me, your secret is safe with me? His voice had softened and his eyes were hazy and sexy there was no denying this man had skills. At this time he had managed to insert his knee between her legs just inches away from her vaginal area as he was pressed against her. He was smiling at her and she could feel his body heat against her the smell of his Calvin Klein cologne was titillating her senses. You really are a beautiful woman Char. For the life of me I can't figure out why there is no other relationship in your life outside of Rae Enterprises? With his body pressed against her, and his hand caressing her waist, you could have any man you want, hell you're just as beautiful as Donica, hell, my wife even don't you want a man? Char continued to listen to him and looking up at him as he was doing his best to seduce her, and for someone who wanted him she could imagine that it would talk them right out of their panties every time. Please, Char the only other conclusion that I have come to is that you are…you know, Lesbian?

Obviously shocked at his statement and somewhat amused, Charlotte took her hand and rubbed it against Curtis' chest touching his nipples that were now apparent through his shirt and it was definitely to his liking as she felt the bulge in his pants make its way closer to her. Curtis don't flatter yourself and don't go there…Baby there is nothing Lesbian about me as I am strictly dickly, however, back in college there was that trios incident but only because my man wanted to fulfill a fantasy that I was only to happy to provide for him. So don't get it twisted. You my brother are just a little to light bread for me and me, I like'em a little thicker with a bad boy feel, you know rough neck…not slut. So don't worry about whether I'm being fulfilled because I am on a daily basis, and the shit is good, not like this empty ass shit you chase around here because you don't have sense enough to know the good thing you have tucked away in that baby mansion of yours. I get pissed because I pride myself on being incapable of bullshit. I'm a woman and a good one at that and we recognized when our sisters are being treated like dirt and that baby, is the only reason for my anger with you. Now, back the hell up as you are in territory that's not down with OPP. Curtis frowned as if he was puzzled by her remark and upon noticing she clarified her statement. OPP, OTHER, PEOPLE'S PROPERTY, as she pushed him backwards. Remember Curtis, this deal with Kirmark is bigger than you and a lot of money is riding on this don't blow it because you can't see past your dick. She opened the door and walked out shutting it behind her. Some would think that Charlotte's interaction with him would have shut him down, but instead it was just the opposite, he now wanted her all the more and was sure that he would have her…so much so that he called Rick Neal to give him the 411 on what had taken place today and with whom. I mean after all who was fooling who? You can't beat a player at his own game and he was not accustomed to not having what he wanted and he saw no reason to start now.

As the day progressed the tension at Rae was so thick you could cut it with a knife. Curtis concentrated primarily on his meeting he scheduled for tonight, and Vanessa walked around pissed off at the world as she felt that her space had been invaded and Curtis was doing very little to reassure her that her place was safe. As he was such a self-centered human being it really never occurred to him that his secretary and lover had spent the afternoon glaring at him as though she could kill him with her bare hands. Curtis? Curtis!
Yeah babe?
I have a tremendous headache and I'm leaving for the day, so if there is something you need leave me a note and I will attend to it tomorrow or whenever.
Awe baby, I'm sorry that you aren't feeling well, come over here and let daddy kiss it for you. No, that won't be necessary, it wouldn't help today. Curtis finally noticed that she was no where near herself, decided that he had better get up and approach her as there could be hell to pay if he had not. V, are you still angry with me for canceling tonight? Curtis it doesn't matter, you are going to do what you want anyway so just let me go, I'm

tired and a bottle of wine is calling me from a far. Vanessa, you know I love you, you are wearing my ring and it is your bed that I want to be in…there is nothing that that woman has that I want besides a signature that will make us a whole lot of money, please believe me. I love you and I am not going to loose you for someone who looks as though she has been around the block a time or two. Curtis kissed her and touched her on her face. Trust me I will call you the moment I get home.
Promise?
I promise.
With that she left the office content that she was the one he wanted and there was no changing that.

Reneea and Tina had spent much of the day together as Tina had done something that she had threatened to do for years. She hired and office manager that would free up a lot of her time. She was the Christian type woman who came highly recommended by Rachael Neal. Her name was Faye and she had impeccable clerical and customer service skills she had been with her for a while she and trusted her to do pretty much what it took to get the job done. She was a mother of two beautiful children and recently separated from her husband who decided that marriage was not really his thing. In any event it was great having her although she found that she had to watch her mouth in her presence as she easily embarrassed her with her colorful less tactful words. This didn't even matter because she was a good worker and served the purpose.

T, I don't know the last time we have hung out this much? Girl me neither, between the office and trying to get in when Mr. Neal didn't have you hemmed up has been quite a task. Bitch whatever, between all your honeymooning and vacationing with Mike you mean. Girl please. What's the agenda tonight? Well Curtis has a meeting so if you want or you are free we can catch a movie or go by the Coopers and see Angel. No offense but please don't make me go over there…Rita is fine to be around in spurts but I can't sit over there and listen to any of her wholesome housewife tales from the dark side today…both women chuckle about Tina's observation and agreed. Let's just kick it like old times. A movie sounds cool or we can go to the crib and have a few drinks whatever's cleaver…or… they looked at each other and chimed out The Martini Grill has a booth with our name on it. Well you're the driver and you know the way. Are you sure Rick's not going to call and you have to shoot out of there like a loose cannon? Bitch, be quite as if you wouldn't for Mike. True that. Besides, Rick has a late shoot and because neither of us is sure of Curtis' schedule tonight we have decided to forego each other's flavor, not to mention that I am waiting for a business call a little later tonight. Oh yeah, how is that plan shaping up anyway? Tina I have to tell you at first I wasn't sure if I would be able to pull it off but now it looks like things are finally coming together just the way it should. Cool! I always knew that you would come around to your natural calling. I guess. I have so much to fill you in on hurry up and get to the Grill so we can let it all out. Hoe please, your ass ain't fooling nobody you want that Martini! The two women laughed hardily and continued to talk amongst themselves as if they had not had a moment's separation from their regular ritual.

7:00 rolled around and Curtis found himself at Andiomo's wondering if he had brought his A game and whether or not Donica Price would notice. He had taken the time to go home to shower and change and as Reneea was not home to reinforce whether or not he was irresistible he would have to rely on the attention that he was commanding from just about every woman that came across his path and made eye contact with him. Some even went so far as to wink at him or wave. He was wearing a three piece Tailored suite that was cut precisely to accent his body and show off the broad shoulders that were a major attraction about him with a pair of $750.00 gators that screamed at any man who wished they could but knew that they couldn't walk in his shoes. Yeah he was hot and had always been as long as he could remember he never had a problem getting a woman to be with him or give up the panties and this one would be no different than all the rest and no matter what Charlotte had said earlier today he knew that she was feeling him and the only thing stopping her was that his wife had some type of magic about her that made people instantly love her and protect her. As he approached the greeter who knew him there as well as he often wined and dined client's downtown and this was one of the better Italian eateries in the city it was not a problem to get service.

Good evening Mr. Rae. Antoinio, do you ever go home from this place? Not when it is my life and my wife is awake. They laughed and enjoyed a few more pleasantries. I understand that you will be joining Ms. Price this evening. Shocked that he was aware of who he was meeting he found himself stammering while answering. Auh, uh, Yes Donica Price, asking as if he were checking to make sure that it was his Ms. Price? But of course, is there another? He smiled and escorted Curtis to where she was seated. When he arrived at the table he knew he had to display a tad bit more cool than he did earlier in their meeting, he did not want to give off the air of a man that lack confidence or cool for that matter of fact. Upon his approach he could see her sitting there looking sexy as hell. She wore her hair short and sassy which framed her face beautifully. She had chosen to wear a little black dress that gave mini a new meaning with a pair of stilettos that were dainty on her small foot and again with that lipstick that stood out and said these lips were made for kissing.

Good Evening Mr. Rae.
Are we starting from square one?
Excuse Me?
Mr. Rae? I thought it was perfectly clear that we were on a first name basis?
I do apologize, Hello Curtis smiling at him which appeared to be an invitation.
Hello Donica.
Please won't you sit down? Don't mine if I do, and thank you. He placed his briefcase on the floor and unbuttoned his jacket to look a little more comfortable. You know, I thought you were beautiful in the office this afternoon, but tonight you are just radiant. Why thank you and allow me to say how handsome you are as well. Tailor Cut? I'm sorry? The suit. Is it tailored cut? Why, actually it is, how did you know? By the way it hung on you as you walked through the door, off the Rack doesn't quite fit the body the way a fine tailored suit does. I agree, how did you become so astute when it comes to men's clothing? Let's just say I spend a lot of time with men who have to dress to impress, and if I might say so, it's wearing you.

At that moment, the waiter came over to take their drink order. Curtis I hope you don't mind, but I took the liberty of ordering our appetizers, as I did not know how pressed for time, you might be. No, that's not a problem at all and as far as being pressed for time, tonight, you are my only agenda. Is that right? Yes it is, I believe in giving a client 100% of me when I am in their presence so the best way to do this is to lay other business aside and any other distractions that might take place to keep you from reaching your appointed destination. And what destination might that be tonight, Curtis? Success, what else? Two companies coming together to gain a common goal, more success. I like the way you think. Good. Donica.

Yes?

No, I was just saying your name it is quite interesting. Well, my father wanted boys and on the second attempt when he did not get it, he decided that he would combine his name with my mothers and he came up with Donica.

Do you have a nickname? Yes, but it's reserved for friends.

Oh really?

Uh huh.

Well what is it?

I have not determined whether or not I'm going to allow you to be my friend yet.

You should, I am an awesome friend.

I'll be the judge of that. Well why don't you tell me anyway I wont use it until were friends and we will be friends.

You think so?

I know so.

Doni, my nickname is Doni with and I. That's cute just like you.

Seriously, cute?

More like adorable but I didn't want to push my luck. They smiled at one another as the waiter reappeared with their drinks. He uncorked the wine and poured a glass offering it to Curtis for approval; once he received it he poured them both a glass and left the table. Tell me Doni with an, I...are you in the market for new friends? Um, the jury is still out on that. Why is that? Well I can't be your friend as you are already over extended. How so? Well there is your wife, whom is supposed to be your best friend and then there is Vanessa, who wants to be your only friend. What do you mean? Oh come on Curtis, I saw the way she was insistent on you not breaking your dinner appointment that you had previously made, obviously it was with her and she was trying to protect her investment. I actually understand why after seeing you in that suite. It sort of makes me wonder what is going on under it. Curtis raised his eyebrows at the possibility of satisfying her curiosity. At that moment her cell went off with a text message. I apologize with Marshall out of town I have to take this. By all means please. After reading it she placed it in her hand bag. I'm sorry where were we? Look Doni, I find you extremely attractive, why don't we get business out of the way and go somewhere and talk.

Donica laughed out loud which puzzled Curtis. Curtis really, do you want to go and talk? Sure. Baby, I don't mix business with pleasure, it's just bad, and shit happens, judgment is clouded, so if you are remotely interested in pleasuring me as I am you, business will not take place between us. Curtis heard her loud and clear and knew that whatever the outcome he had to get the contracts signed or risk loosing his life by morning if he returned to Charlotte empty handed. Fine then…I won't lie to you as that is not my style. I want the pleasure, but, I want the business also, so can we find a happy medium? How so? Well we can conclude our business and commence with the pleasure later. Donica smiled and shook her head…Babe I don't think you understand, with me; it's one or the other. If and that is if we do business and pleasure in the same night, all business contacts between us, are off.

I can live with that.

Can you?

Sure, why not business, pleasure, and you can deal with Charlotte from this point on. I have the contracts you have yours we sign and I spend the rest of the night making you feel better than you have ever felt in your life. Win, win situation. He glared at her looking into her eyes letting her know he was not backing down from her challenge and was more than ready to go the extra mile.

Curtis, you do drive a hard bargain.

Sweetheart, you have no idea how hard, reaching over to caress her finger tips which lay on the table especially the middle finger.

Donica smiled as she was now ready to proceed to the next level.

How hungry are you?

For food, not really.

Why don't we move this to a more private venue?

Name the place, I will meet you anywhere.

I have a room upstairs in the Westin, actually a suite as she took her card key from her purse and slid it across the table in his direction. My room number is 1735. Why don't you go up, make yourself comfortable and wait for me, I'm sure you will find the accommodations suitable for a man of your caliber. Curtis slid the card key off the table placing it in his top pocket grabbing for his briefcase. Aren't you coming with me? Yes, most definitely if you don't cum first, smiling at him. I just need to handle the bill and I will be right up.

No, no need I invited you; allow Rae... interrupted before he could complete his statement. Oh sweetheart I intend to allow Rae all night, however, Kirmark will pick up tonight's tab they insist; I just want to have a few things sent up to the room, don't worry I'm right behind you go upstairs and enjoy the view I will be there before you have your suit on a hanger. Curtis kissed her hand winked at her grabbed his brief case and headed for the lobby elevators on cloud nine.

Donica watched as he exited the restaurant while motioning for the waiter. As she proceeded to exit a voice from behind a menu startled her.

Just what the hell do you think you're doing?
Donica almost jumped clean out of her shoes as a voice came from behind a menu she was not expecting, though she knew to be there.
Damn girl, where there hell do you get off scaring a bitch like that?
Just keep in mind that you have a job to do, tonight.
Sis, have I ever failed you or not come through with what you needed?
No, and tonight... is not the time to get sloppy, I told your ass he can be charming I need to know that you are on your game tonight, these Detroit Niggas are not the sweet southern guys from the ATL, the dirty South. They play to win especially that one, do you hear me?
Yes, I here you Chucky, I heard you earlier...
Good, as the menu was removed there sat Charlotte looking at Donica as though she was looking in a mirror, how on earth had he not detected their resemblance? Though they did not have the same mother, their father's genes were so dominant that they were dead ringers for relation. I see you still got it. Girl, please as long as a bitch has breast and ass and a treadmill she will have it. Good girl. You know how high the stakes are tonight, don't let me down. Total domination, nothing less, he must sign without reading. I got you and your girl too.
I just wish you didn't have to fuck him, she's family. Yeah, yours, Soror to me ...girl please I'm getting a piece of that tonight, got my motor running and shit, yeah I'm fucking him for my pleasure, she'll understand, by any mean necessary, right?
Do what you must, but signatures first, you hear me? Yeah, yeah, Doni is a pro; don't forget that, after all how many companies strong are we bay, we paper chasers or did you forget?

Doni, do you need a pen, all signatures in blue ink nothing less? Right, got it. Charlotte held up her signature gold Cross pen. Daddy's Pen. That's right and bitch I wont it back afterwards you hear? Maybe.

Maybe will get that ass tapped. I want my pen back after he signs by morning. Alright, damn it Donica starts to walk off but has a second thought and turns around.

Chuck?

Yeah?

Do you think daddy would be proud of what we're doing tonight?

Are you serious? Daddy was a shark remember two wives, two babies, two households at the same time and it's for uncle Matt's honor… what the hell do you think? We would be recipients of the Player's Award 2009. Now, go get our shit back, tonight. Doni, Charlotte who was calling out to her sister with concern in her voice.

Yeah Chuck?

Be careful, he will be good. No more hurt for you can't make this stray dog a house pet, he's just not trainable.

Love You.

Love you back and tell her don't worry, we got this.

After, Charlotte watched Donica exit the restaurant, knowing that her sister would succeed at her mission she removed her cell phone from her purse pressed her contact button seeking who she sought and waited for the phone to be answered.

Hello? The voice answered as if they were expecting the call.

Hey.

Hey you.

It's a rap, tonight.

Very well, I will see you tomorrow,

For sure. With that being done, she motioned for the waiter. Yes ma'am,? I would like to settle for Ms. Price's table and mine and whatever she ordered to be delivered upstairs can be attached to my tab as well.

Yes ma'am. That will be $482.75. Without batting an eye, Charlotte removed $600.00 dollars from her purse and hand it to the waiter. Keep the change and could you have my car brought around front. Right away Ms. Price. Sergio? I'm sorry Ms. Williams. Thank you.

Charlotte Price Williams, she thought to herself. She finished the contents of her wine glass and left as undetectable as she had arrived.

Curtis had entered the suite and could not believe his eyes. The view of the Riverfront was spectacular and the fireplace going with soft music playing and candles blazing…he had the attitude that he was definitely on top.

Well, I'll be damned; she planned to be alone with me all along? Go figure. I thought I was going to have to work for this shit. And it looks like its being handed to me on a silver platter. Curtis removed his jacket and laid it on the back of the sofa while removing his shoes. Suddenly, he heard the door open and turned to see the vision of loveliness he desired walking through the door.

Well, well, when I said make yourself at home you took me literal didn't you? Well I figured with all that you had going on here tonight; it was obvious that I was going to be a friend sooner than I thought. Woe cowboy, the valets have specific instructions as to how I like to retire for the evening as I am a regular here. I have a place off the River however I am having some renovations done and since I am a five star customer they do what I need done without asking. So if you had the idea that I was planning to seduce you here tonight? You would be surprised to find had you been here the night before, you would have found it in the same exact state. She looked at Curtis as if his plot and plan had been foiled.

Well doesn't matter because I'm here now. True that, so tell me…Curtis… what do you plan to do with me. Um, a woman of your caliber surely has to have some idea of what is expected?
Humor me.
Well, as I am a man who has no inhibitions, nor am I timid in the area of fulfillment and pleasure, I plan to do to you whatever you like. How does that sound?

Sounds like a plan. Donica walked over to him and turned her back to him, right away he noticed that the zipper would need to be released and he did it just as she thought…slowly and thought provoking. As the zipper was released, the dress cautiously fell to the floor exposing the sexiest bra, panty and garter belt combination he had ever seen. She stood in front of him with crotch-less panties and noticed that his penis was about to make its own exit had she not unzipped his trousers. Once completed she saw that she would not be disappointed and that all the reports she had received with regards to his manhood were true.

Ooh wee, Mr. Rae that looks inviting, gazing at his dick as if it were diamonds or gold.
Yeah, you think so and it has your name written all over it, come over here.
At that moment she dropped to her knees remove it from its restriction, which totally threw him off his square. She cupped it with both hands, looked into his eyes and went down on him like she had not been fed in years. Curtis damn near lost his mind standing there being taken by this lovely woman who purely had no hang ups about what she wanted nor who she wanted it from. He could not believe how she was making him feel, only Vanessa had taken him to these heights and it was unconceivable that another could do to him what he thought only one other woman knew to do and right when she had him, when she knew the thrust was not far behind. She stopped stood up and backed away from him while he longed for her to complete her task.

Baby, what…what are you doing?
I almost forgot…Business first or I can't please you.
What is it what do you need from me?
Signatures, please hurry, I need you inside me now!

She extended the golden pen toward him with the papers she managed to get into his hands. He was so fucking excited by what she had began he could have cared less if he was the signer to the declaration of independence he just needed to get his penis back in her somewhere. He grabbed the pen and begins to sign frantically. Seeing this turned Donica on more than she was in the beginning as she was excited with her ability to make a man completely forget his mission only to be drawn into her advances. After signing both documents he threw them to the floor and went to her almost zombie like he needed to release and fuck her with no holds barred. After receiving what she needed, she knew she was free to do whatever came natural to her and that she did. They fucked for hours on end. He road her from behind, and from any other angle, that she would allow him to. He ate what he considered to be the sweetest pussy this side of the Mississippi and she enjoyed it as a virgin knowing that she had been around the block before with this treatment being nothing new but it felt so damn good. Damn, he was as good as her sister had cautioned and the thought of this man not inside her ever again had to be a joke. They fucked until they both erupted in sweet, sweet ecstasy. Afterwards he knew that he would definitely make the friend list and wanted her on his as well. He laid there trying to get his breath and thought of Reneea slowly switching his thoughts to Vanessa, who he thought no other women could possibly compare to, but did and then some, and then to the one who got away…Charlotte and wondered how awesome it would be to have them all in the bed together at first embarrassed by the thought but knew it was natural for a man to think of all his lovers and wished that God would grant him the satisfaction to be serviced by them all. Suddenly, the silence was broken and he could not believe his ears.

What did you say?
I said, I have to get up early tomorrow, you should probably go as its getting late and I need a little rest, huh baby? Curtis could only shake his head because in his mind he had just been chopped and screwed and he was generally the one on the issuing end not receiving. As he knew he had met his match tonight, he laughed to himself and got out of bed knowing that he always had another alternative as Vanessa would always be willing to take him no matter what hour day or night that he called. To be perfectly honest, the contracts were signed and his objective had truly been achieved…business was conducted and he had received a good piece of ass that only sweetened the deal.

Well since you put it that way, would you mind if I showered first as I have another stop to make and I need to freshen up before I go. No, not at all you should find everything you need in the bathroom looking at him seductively still nude and lying on the bed where she had just had one of the best sexual experiences that she could remember in a long, long time. Care to join me? Oh no baby, if I join you we run the risk of never getting you out here and I think that would be detrimental to both of us lover. Curtis smiled as he picked up his clothing and briefcase and proceeded to the bathroom. He took his briefcase because he was always prepared for a pit stop he never knew when the occasion would arise that he would need his own colognes and shower gels to rid himself of the passion that he might have encounter with another and needed to make sure that there was nothing out of the ordinary detected on his body sent wise. As he showered he thought about what had happened tonight, knew he had signed contracts without reading them, but trusted that Charlotte had dotted all I's and crossed all T's prior to doing so. He now knew how Vanessa was able to make a man submit to her will when he sent her on a mission and thought to himself that he could not believe he had fallen for his own game. Never-the-less the dollar signs would be worth it.

Upon returning to the room, he noticed that Donica was up and dressed in her black satin robe and had picked the contracts and the golden pen off the floor and had placed them on the table. I trust that once you have allowed Marshall to review and sign on the dotted line that my office shall receive a copy? Without a doubt, Charlotte will have them by morning. Curtis looked at the pen and made an observation…
The two of you have so much in common.
I'm sorry?
The pen, Charlotte has a pen either just like that or something similar.
Well it is your standard Cross Pen, the tool of Champion Executives everywhere, not to mention she looks like a woman who enjoys the finer things in life I would imagine that the Cross would be her style.
I guess. Well sweetheart, as I have been given my walking papers I should go.
Don't say it, like that Curtis, I really do have to get up early and there is no sense in me entertaining the thought of keeping something that's not available to be kept smiling at him with warm thoughts. There is the matter of a wife, or have you forgotten? Not at all and no I don't need reminding. We have an unusual circumstance between us and I believe we are both in mutual agreement here lately that we are together in name only for the good of our family. Does she know this or you are doing what most men tend to do, assume, therefore, making an ass of both you and she?
Curtis looked at her wondering why a woman who had just fucked his brains out and wanted more of him would be concerned over a woman whose husband she had just boned. To answer your question, I'm pretty sure she knows and on that note, I think I will head for the hills as I feel an Oprah moment coming on. He laughed picked up his briefcase and headed for the door with Donica in tow.
Well Doni, I can call you Doni can't I?
But of course, after what took place between us I certainly can't see why not?
Allow me to thank you for a wonderful evening, and I trust that this will not be our last encounter.

Remember, Curtis, there can only be pleasure, as business is now off limits. You crossed that boundary and there is no going back.

Very well, I think that has been established and to be honest, though you are a wonderful business woman…I think I prefer your skill as a lover much better. With that being said, Curtis kissed her as he rubbed his hand across her butt giving it a playful squeeze and left watching her close the door behind him.

Curtis reached his car and could not believe what he had just experienced. He dialed Rick who would be expecting his call as he told him earlier that he would call him once he completed his mission.

Hello?

Rick?

Yeah man.

I am a motherfuckin PIMP! Proud of his accomplishments.

Rick who was annoyed, but glad at the same time who figured at the rate he was going he would drive Reneea right into his waiting arms for good. You got the booty no doubt?

No digitty, no doubt, and shit was off the hook. She made V look like an amateur man! Damn and the body, oh wee, most def, something to write home about.

Well did you get your contracts signed?

Now nigga you know business first, hell yeah. I feel like celebrating, why don't we hit Mr. Nicks for a brew or two?

Man as good as that sounds, I'm still working on this layout and I have to have it finished by morning, no can do brother.

Damn man, don't bitch up, as good as you are with that shit, you can do it with your eyes closed.

Naw, I really do have to pass, but why don't we hook up tomorrow, I will even buy to toast everything you've got coming your way. Bet, it's a deal. Besides, Vanessa wouldn't mind seeing a brother anyway.

They hung up the phone and he dialed his faithful companion and as always she answered.

Curtis?

Hey baby.

Hey baby, I was just thinking about you.

You were? Uh hum, I was so sure we would be together tonight that I had planned this elaborate supper for us and everything and I was just putting it all away as it wasn't as fun eating alone. Remembering that he hadn't eaten as he was more concerned with getting into Donica's bed and was a little hungry, he thought this was perfect. Well, sweetheart, why don't you make daddy a plate get him a nice cold beer out, take off whatever you are wearing and be prepared to be in my arms all night.

Really, Curtis! Are you playing with me boy?

Not at all, I'm just ten minutes away. Cool baby, I will have your dinner on the table when you get here.

Curtis?

Yes?

I love you.

I love you too baby, see you in second.

He drove down the road and could not believe how incredibly good it was to be him. He had a passing thought of Reneea and her earlier call to him and wished that it could be her that did the things to him that these other women did for his ego and his body, but he knew that that was all a pipe dream. He knew that she was just the woman that shared his life on the surface as they had fallen to far apart to mend whatever road that was left between them. He wished that he could be what she needed and since he obviously had no clue as to what that was; he had long since stopped trying to be. Maybe Craig would understand? Maybe a divorce could be amicable; maybe she would just be satisfied with getting the home and furnishing and a generous alimony settlement in exchange for her freedom…Maybe, but in the event that she was not, he could not risk a messy divorce or her departing with half of what he considered to be all his.

Sorry baby, it looks like it is us for life. Who was really fooling who?

Chapter 18

Blood Is Thicker Than Water

Business was going well and everything had gone according to plan. Charlotte had prepared her financial reports for the year's end board meeting and all was right with the world. Rae Enterprises had a record breaking year for revenue and all of their ducks were in a row. The Christmas luncheon had been a success, however was interrupted as Angel gave birth 17 days earlier than her original due date on the 21st which was just 4 days away from Christmas causing Curtis, Reneea, Rick, Tina, and Mike to make a run for it, almost trampling everything in their path.

Curtis got the call while speeches were being made to honor the employees by all department heads and executive staff. Upon receiving the call he rushed over to his wife who was enjoying a bite with Rick, who was always invited to these events as he photographed most of it for the company's brochures and other keep sake memorabilia. Charlotte could remember the look on Vanessa's face who was less than impressed by the show of emotion between the two who were about to become grandparents together who took a second to embrace one another as their son would soon welcome his children into the world. She also noticed that Mr. Neal was less than pleased with the kiss that Curtis planted on Reneea in front of everyone as if he were the husband that he ought to be, she remembered his expression as he looked at hers and he knew that she had seen him and smiled at her to let her know that he was aware. Charlotte had encountered many conversations with Rick Neal as he was Curtis' best friend and could be found in the building from time to time, not to mention the occasion that he had tried to fix his friend up with his trusted side kick only to have them both tell him thanks but no thanks. December had proven to be a month full of surprises and with any luck would surely go out with a bang.

The sounds of Donny Hathaway rang out in the background as Reneea danced around the house preparing for the guest to arrive. She had never been a singer by any mean's but it did not detour her from belting out her favorite Christmas song, This Christmas, Curtis often referred to it as cat calling but enjoyed to see her do it just the same as she was quite comical and enjoyed it even if no one else did. She checked on the nursery and made sure that the intercom system was working as surely the babies would not need to be in the room with so many people as they were literally born just days ago. The house had had a steady stream of well wishers and people who brought gifts. Even though she had had a wonderful baby shower thrown by her mother, Reneea, Tina and Mia, people were still bringing presents as Angel was quite popular and with such a lovely personality never met a person she didn't like. Not to mention Craig's crew and the neighbors who had watched Craig grow into a man over the years. Though they had been staying with the Cooper's it was decided that as Christmas would be at the Rae's and their home was much larger to receive all the well wisher's that they would leave the hospital and stay there until new year's. The babies were beautiful Rita Rene Rae and Craig Richard Rae, Richard was actually Rick's birth name and Rick was thrilled that his Godson loved him so much as to make his first born son his name sake. Needless to say, Curtis was not too thrilled with it but as this was his son's choice what more could he do. He was jealous and did mention the fact to Reneea about it, but managed to play it off as if it were just something that he was going through as a man and would be fine with it as he said after all; they are my grandchildren no matter what their names may be Rae is at the end. She couldn't help thinking of how beautiful they were as babies they had so many of Craig's features as a newborn. She was not surprised that they were such cute babies as Craig and Angel looked as though they could have been models themselves it was obvious that they would have a handsome family.

As a knock came at the door, her thought process was interrupted as she did not know who would be arriving at this hour and all deliveries generally went to the back she thought it would be wise to hurry. I'm coming just a moment... She peeked out of the window to find to her surprise it was Rachel Neal, who had come barring gifts.

Rachel, hello, Merry Christmas, come in.

Merry Christmas, sorry Nae-Nae that I did not call first, but I knew the later it got the harder it would be for me to get by.

No, no, no problem at all. Of course you will be here for Christmas dinner tonight right? Actually no, mother's sister is in town and we are scheduled to go by our cousins, you know the whole driving Ms. Daisy Thing. The two laughed. But I imagine Rick will, so I wanted to drop off his gift my gifts to you and your family and possibly get a peek at the two newest arrivals. You are in luck as they just arrived not long ago and Angel is just in back in the Nursery attending to them come on, give me your coat. At that moment Curtis and Craig entered the room deep in conversations male bonding type stuff. Merry Christmas Rachel, Curtis said as he noticed that she was standing along side Reneea and extended his arms out to hug her. Hey Curt, Merry Christmas to you; as she hugged him she felt him rubbing against her and she felt sick to her stomach knowing that he was touching her and thinking of how he could casually cop a feel and it not be detected. Don't you look lovely? Thank you. Hey Aunt Rach! Hey boo, you are really the man of the hour I came to see until I get my hands those babies. She hugged Craig smiling at him; she was so fond of him and in heart she knew she had a reason to be he was her brother's Godson and had spent much time with him over the years but she always had felt a deeper connection.

Rachel you're a little early for dinner, aren't you? No, I won't be here for dinner, mom's sister is in so I will be dining with the family tonight and then Davis and I have something going this evening with some shot callers and ballers we have been trying to snag, so I won't make it. At that moment, Reneea and Craig went to make sure that Angel was prepared to receive visitors. Curtis who never allowed an opportunity to flirt with his once young protégé to go by and he saw no reason for this to be a first. Once he was sure that they were out of ear range he did what always came natural to him.

Damn Rach, you get sexier every time I see you, is that a deliberate attempt to make a brother want to reminisce about the past?

Obviously disgusted by his approach, she spoke to him with contempt that should have let him know where he stood. Don't flatter yourself Curtis, you may have had it like that once before when I was young and foolish, but it ain't hardly laying like that no more.

Walking up to her getting closer to look in her eyes, he began to speak frank and direct. Yeah, you talking that shit now, but it was once a time that all I had to do was give you the nod and those panties were off before quick could get ready, no matter where we were, remember that night in your parent's bedroom?

True, but, I also use to make mud pies and play in dirt, and as I have out grown that, I also outgrew lying down with dogs.

You sure are funny little girl…but I remember how you use to like the fact that I was a dog, especially when I hit it from the back, I can still hear you moaning my name.

You ain't shit and one day all your shit is going to catch up with you…mark my words this day, Curtis Anthony Rae, you shall reap what you sew, it all comes back. I just hope I have a front row seat when it all blows up in your face…Nigga! At that moment Curtis was unable to respond as he heard Reneea returning to retrieve Rachel for a visit…

Rach, this ain't over boo, I will see you again.

I count on it.

Reneea returned happy and proud as any new grandparent could be to get Rachel without even noticing the tension in the room, probably as none would have been expected. Come on back Rach and get a look at, the most beautiful babies in the entire world, if I may say so myself. Reneea was beaming as if she had just given birth.

Lead the way, Curtis you coming, looking at him as she knew she had pissed him off royally. No, you guys go ahead, I have a call to make. Okay, suit yourself as she laughed wickedly walking away from a bruised ego and was proud to be the one who had delivered the knock out punch.

With all the excitement buzzing about, he had realized that he had not spoken with Vanessa to wish her a Merry Christmas this morning as there were presents to open and they had to retrieve the babies from one area of the house to the next and that had certainly been chaotic, not to mention that the time he had to spend with her this week had been so minimal as he had been dividing his time between her and the lovely Ms. Donica Price when her need for him arose. He knew it would not be a problem though, as she was going to be at the house for dinner along with other staff members of Rae, who he had still not let Reneea in on nor was he planning to. He was the King of his Castle and he had a right to do whatever he wanted and to whomever he wanted.

Rachel entered the room and saw Angel with the most beautiful smile sitting in the midst of her two beautiful children and her adoring husband and all she could do was smile herself.

Well aren't you all a sight for sore eyes.

How are you feeling?

I'm fine really, I'm actually doing better than I expected I would. When I look at my little wonders every inch of soreness, or restless night without sleep all seems worth it.

Rachel smiled at her statement, I don't know from first hand experience, but I can understand how you could feel this way.

Would you like to hold your niece or nephew first Aunt Rach, Craig inquired and his questions did something to her heart that no one would understand.

Well Craigy, why don't you give me little Craig Richard, so I can see those beautiful eyes. Alright…Craig picked up his son and cradled him in his arms with such love and happiness on his face and a pride that could have squeezed everyone else out of the room, and right at that moment before he handed the baby to Rachel, Rick walked in much to the liking of everyone in the room.

Hey Unc!

What up man.

Hey BB you're just in time. Craig turned the baby over to Rachel who actually had a tear in her eye and a smile on her face as wide as the great outdoors.

Guys, he is just beautiful, Craigy, he looks just like you when you were born, doesn't he Rick? Yeah, he does, look at those beautiful eyes, Rick responded as he looked onward.

You see them, Rachel inquired?

Rick hesitated and smiled before he responded. Yes, I do.

No one really understood Rick and Rachel's emotions but like everyone else that was there it was no questions that they were feeling everything that all the others were. Reneea looked on at the sister and brother enjoying her grandson and for a moment allowed herself to imagine that it were she and Rick who were the proud grandparents and the family were there to support them, but it was just a fantasy in which she was brought out of abruptly when she heard the sound of Curtis' voice…

He's gorgeous isn't he guys, just like his ole man, who looks like his ole man. Rick looked up at Curtis and spoke slowly, yeah dude, I finally agree. Rachel looked at her brother and then at Curtis and said…Blood really is thicker than water, which made Rick laugh, but no one else understood why he was laughing as he left the room in search of a drink…Anyone up for a cocktail? We really have to celebrate this new generation, he winked at his sister slapped Craig on the back and made an exit with Curtis behind him seconding his motion.

Rachael visited with babies and the mother a little while longer before she had to depart and Reneea was busy making sure that all details were in place for the party. Tina and her family had arrived with Mia and her new companion that appeared to be more to her parents liking. Even Craig gave her a sign that she had apparently chosen better this time around. Those two would always be thick as thieves and at times had a language all their own. Though it is customary for the mother of the Children to choose the Godmother of her children which would obviously be one of her close friends or a sister, Angel pulled a surprise move that not only shocked the whole house but pleased her husband and mother-in-law as well. As they were all gathered around the babies as Mia was seeing them for the first time and expressing her happiness for the couple which really was genuine, Angel spoke up and said she had an announcement to make. Tina who was great with one liners stopped her in her tracks. Damn, boy didn't that doctor say don't touch her for six weeks? Everyone died laughing. Oh hell naw G-ma you did not go there. Angel I'm sorry G-ma could not resist that.
It's cool, and please, believe, I just had two babies, count em one, two, come out of me he had better of heard that doctor. More laughter arose.

Angel resumed her composure and began speaking once more with everyone paying attention. On a serious note, since we are all together and I can't think of a more perfect time to do this… I have a Christmas present that I would like to give Ms. Mia. Mia was shocked as she had just opened a present from her and Craig moments ago. Mia, you are so important to my husband that at times before I knew better, it was scary to think that another woman other than his mother could be so important to him and as I grew to know you and see that Craig's happiness meant the world to you and that you understood that I made him happy I started to see exactly why it was so important for you two to remain friends and why he had

your back so tough. Anybody that loves my husband as much as you do
and it is proven strictly in a family capacity would do no less in loving my
children, and I was wondering if by chance you would be the Godmother
of our son and our daughter because if God called me home today, I would
go at ease knowing that you had his back and theirs.
By the time she finished speaking there was not a dry eye in the room.
Reneea and Tina were clutching each other by the waist with tears
streaming down their faces in total shock as they knew it had been
difficult for Angel to except Craig and Mia's friendship at first. Mike,
Rick and Curtis were blown completely away at her move…while Mia
could not get her composure still hugging Angel who was crying herself,
and Craig just stood there looking at the two of them in disbelief as he had
no idea that his wife was planning to do what she had done. Once Mia
stopped crying long enough to except she turned to her friend to see if he
knew and he could not respond. Craig walked over to his wife and took
her by the hand and gently pulled her up and close to him wiping her tears
away, he kissed her and began to speak.
Baby, the fact that you love me so much and trust me so much blows my
mind and I want you to know that I will never hurt you and if I could, if, if
I could, I would re-marry you every day of our lives together. You have
given me the most wonderful gift a woman can give a man, a child in his
image and you are so incredible that you have given me two, you have
validated me in front of our family and friends and I love you so damn
much for all of it. They kissed each other and wiped away one another's
tears and he placed a beautiful two Stone Diamond mothers Rings on her
finger for a Christmas present that she would never forget.

Curtis was proud of his son, and knew more than ever that he would not
understand his actions as he had previously thought. Rick looked at Craig
and Angel and knew that they were meant to be, he was amazed as that
was the love he held secretly inside for Craig's mother and knew that
somehow he had to convey it to him he just had to he could not go another
year with this secret locked up inside. Everyone else just looked on in
amazement.

At that moment, Troy, the companion with Mia for the evening stood up.
Wow, uh, I don't know anybody here except Mia, so if yaw don't stop
with all this happiness, and love passing, I'm going to look like a real
punk standing here crying over a bunch a people I don't even know, or

worse I might break out into song like at the ending of a Tyler Perry Musical,…Please, for the love of God and all that is humane, don't put a brother through that, I am seriously trying to date this girl so I would really like to keep my masculinity going here, can anybody feel a brother? Craig noticing that they had sort of put ole boy in a tight spot and was truly amused by what he had said…decided to help him out. Our bad dude, please whatever you do, don't break out in song, cause we will talk about yo ass. The mood became lighter and everyone realized that a party was about to start.

Baby girl, did you know about this?
No idea what-so-ever, but I am extremely happy about it.
Bay, you and me both. This has made Mia so happy look at her.
What do you think about Mr. Man over there?
The jury has not completely rendered a verdict, but, he did impress her father with the car door opening and closing along with the umbrella over her head as he came to the door to get her and while walking her up all of those damn steps you got out there.
Whatever hoe!
You know I'm right about that shit, hell somebody could slip and fall down them damn things and live off yaw for life, smiling.
He was pretty funny bringing us out of our, we are the world moment though.
Don't look half bad either.
Craig gave her the nod about ten minutes ago, so dude might get a chance.
I really wish she would settle down.
Don't rush her; you know what hell she can go through if she marries Mr. Wrong, just look at how her Godmother is suffering, as they both look over at Curtis who was playing man about town as guest had started to arrive from the company. Tina put her arm around her friend and smiled warmly as she knew that her statement was all to true.

Most everyone had arrived and everyone was enjoying the hospitality and festivities. Angel and Craig had retired the children with the nanny that had been brought in by Tina as a gift for the evening so that they could enjoy a little of the party even though Craig and Angel took shifts going back and forth to check on the situation. Rick kept looking at Reneea as he was drawn to her like a moth to a flame. Everyone in the room noticed her too as she was dressed impeccably in Cream Winter White with rhinestone adorned **pumps,** no doubt Jimmy Choo, her hair was flowing and fabulous even as it **was** pinned up partially and her five carat diamond wedding ring was beaming, but had competitions on the left hand as she wore a six carat diamond with an inscription inside that read,

You were and always will be the one, Love You More RN,

that she had received from Rick as a Christmas Present in Private. There was nothing gaudy or tacky about it or she, the sad part is that Curtis had not even noticed the new ring. His pompous ass probably thought that he had given it to her.

Reneea went down stairs to retrieve a special bottle of wine that she had purchased for Angel who now had her body back as her own and had chosen not to breast feed, and knew she would enjoy it. And to her surprise, when she turned around, there he was, Mr. Good Bar himself.
I was wondering if you would follow me.
Come here baby, you know what I need.
Reneea smiled, sat the bottle of wine down and walked over to him with her arms extended and kissed him so passionately that it made them both long for time to be together so that they could make love.
Nae-Nae, I can't keep going like this, I have to be with you permanently baby.
Rick, I know it's killing me too. I know what I have to do. I'm almost ready, please just be patient a little while longer. Please stay strong, for me, for us. He kissed her and they decided to get back as they heard the doorbell and Reneea was unsure as to who it could be as everyone invited had already arrived.

When they emerged from the basement wine cellar, Reneea saw Charlotte standing in the kitchen with a less than please look on her face. Reneea not wanting to read too much into her expression, thought it best that she inquire.
Chuc, Charlotte, is everything okay?
No ma'am Mrs. Rae at that moment she motioned to the dining area, where she saw Vanessa Winters standing next to Curtis wearing the exact same outfit as she had on down to the shoes and the faces of the other guest in attendance that looked absolutely mortified, with the exception of Curtis, who had obviously been expecting her, Troy, Mia's date who did not know any better, and Tina who looked as if the Devil himself had

transformed into her body, and of course Vanessa Winters, who stood there looking at her with a Take This Bitch In Your Face attitude. Craig was furious and embarrassed for his mother and if looks could kill his father would be dead. Rick stood behind Reneea looking at Curtis in disbelief, he knew his friend was capable of some real shit, but this was going too far even for him. The awkward silence was deafening and Reneea, who was blown away by what she saw, knew that she had to draw first blood. She mustered every ounce of strength and courage that she had left and entered the room in elegance and sophistication as only she could.

Why Vanessa, I was not expecting you tonight, and obviously the other women did not get the memo to wear our matching outfits this evening, huh? Reneea smiled and broke out into uncontrollable laughter as the whole thing really had become funny to her. This is hilarious, you know when I bought this on sale, explaining to her guest in stand up comedy form, I told my personal shopper that I was running the risk of running into someone with the same exact outfit as I would be wearing, and yaw know I hate that getting a laugh from her daughter-in-law who had become her amen corner, I just didn't know that it would be in my own home at my own party, and that's what I get for wearing half off. Everyone, who knew what she had just done, damned near died laughing, especially Charlotte who was floored by the class of Reneea Rae. Tina looked at her and did not see a damn thing funny as this bitch had no business in her home and she knew it.

Oh hell no Reneea, this shit has gone too far, Tina was pissed and not even Mike could gather his wife under control grabbing his wife's arm only to have her snatch it back. No Mike, let me go. T, T, Tina baby, Reneea managed to get her friend settled down and focused on her. I need you to come up stairs and help me change, okay, com' mon being playful beckoning her friend to leave the room as they were all about appearances for Craig's sake. Tina walked out of the dinning room reluctantly and gave Curtis a look that let him know that he had fucked up this time in the worst way. If you will all excuse me, I really should change it will only take me a second, please have some more to drink the bartenders are here for your enjoyment and we will not hesitate to have chauffeurs take you home if you are in fear of consuming to much alcohol this evening. When I return it will be time to serve, and again thank all of you so much for you patience. At that moment, Reneea noticed the diamond ring on Vanessa's left hand it was exactly like the upgrade Curtis had given her for their anniversary this past August, only smaller. Craig also took notice at the same time his mother had and became even more upset at his father for the pain his mother was obviously feeling.

Vanessa, that is a lovely ring you're wearing, it looks like mine only smaller, tell me, are you promised to someone?
Vanessa looked at her and simply responded…You could say that, yes, yes I am.
Good, I'm sure you deserve each other.
Funny you should say that Mrs. Rae, I have been telling him that for years. What can I say, us girls know best. With that said Reneea looked at Curtis, smiled politely, and proceeded up the stairs behind Tina whom she was literally pushing after that last engagement of words.

Baby Girl…this here is some bullshit! He's got her here on Christmas, why don't you just let him shit on you in public, it would be less humiliating!
Calm down Tina, I can't explain everything, but this shit will be over soon…don't worry okay, I've really got this.
That's all well and fine, but you have a house full of people right now down there putting two and two together, if they didn't know he was screwing her, they damn well know now. Whatever your next move is, make it soon. If you don't I can't promise you that I will allow him to continue living on this same planet with us, you heard?
Reneea still not allowing her voice to go above a whisper, Patience T, he is shooting his own foot off. Now hand me that bag marked Versace. Tina grabbed the bag and tossed it to her friend whom she could not believe was not even breaking a sweat over the fact that her husband's hoe was right downstairs in her own home, wearing her exact outfit down to the shoes and a ring that looked as though it was birthed from the one she was wearing.
Reneea completed removing her outfit and tossed it in the trash can laughing openly. She was dressed sharp as hell before but the dress she changed into was dropped dead gorgeous it was a gold beaded form fitting number with a jagged bottom with fringe that moved with her body with a high neck in the front and backless that ran from the nape of her neck in v stopping short just above her buttocks. She slid on her matching pumps and removed the pins that were holding the sides of her hair up allowing it

to fall down freely. She touched up her make up looked at friend through the mirror who was looking at her as if she had just stepped out of a fashion magazine. Damn bitch, if I did not love you so much, in that outfit, I would be hating your ass and watching my man closely. It is definitely on now. Reneea smiled at her best friend grabbed her by the hand and said. Let's go party!

Upon returning downstairs the atmosphere was thick, no one was really enjoying themselves except for Curtis and Vanessa. There were casual conversations taking place between most in groups and several of the other executives and Rick was dead locked in a conversation with Charlotte that looked very serious. Tina entered the room causing everyone to notice that they had made their way back but once she moved out of the way Reneea made an entrance that would have definitely been a show stopper. She was fucking gorgeous and everyone in the room knew it. Her smile alone commanded attention and from everyone. Curtis could not believe his eyes, she looked like an angel she was beautiful and he was almost sorry that he had invited Vanessa as this would surely be one of the nights he would play the husband card to get inside her. Rick literally dropped his drink where he stood and could care less who had noticed his reaction. A few of the executives also looked as if they needed someone to manually put their tongues back into their mouths before they were stepped on. Vanessa looked as if she had been out done and knew it. Craig and Angel were so pleased to see her enter the room looking as if she had not a care in the world, and Charlotte looked at her as if her hero had come back like Superman after he had been given a dose of Kryptonite and was the first to speak as the maids were trying to clean up the drink Rick spilt and he was just trying to regain his composure. Mrs. Rae, if I might say so, you are sharp as HELL!

Thank you sweetie, see no worries, I have a closet full of something to throw on in a pinch. Curtis, would you do the honors of calling everyone together for dinner?

Curtis could hardly respond as he was mesmerized by his wife's unbelievable rebound...Ah, uh yeah sure thing Nea. Vanessa noticed her stammering fellow and was aware that he only did that when something caught him off guard or had taken his breath away, and as that was generally her she did not like it. He did as he was asked and just as he was about to show Vanessa to the dinning room to be seated, Craig came up to his father and demanded a word with him.

Ah, excuse me Vanessa pushing past her to step to Curtis, dad, could I have a minute? Craig you heard your mother, she's ready to serve. DAD, this won't keep I need to see you now. Vanessa looking on and slightly worried as Craig's tones was harsh and undeniably angry. Rick also noticed that the two men were less than happy with one another also tuned in to listen and make his way to intervene in what he feared may be and altercation and so did Mike.

Alright son, why don't we go into the study? Vanessa, make yourself at home and follow the others. Sure Curtis. They walked into the study with Rick and Mike not far behind.

What is it that could not wait until dinner; your mother is going to be pissed if we take much longer...

Fuck what you're talking about right now Okay. Curtis was stunned that his son was using such foul language in his presence not to mention that it was being directed to him.

Craig, you had better slow your roll dude.

Slow my roll, dad...have you lost your mind with that woman in my mother's house, with her ass seated at her table? You must be crazy to pull some shit like this?

Curtis was not sure why he was reacting in this manner unless he knew more than they assumed. Craig, lower your voice and I will not tell you again to watch your language when speaking to me. In case you hadn't noticed my name is on the deed to this fucking house and I have the right to have guest in my home without your approval.

Oh, I'm sorry dad; I didn't know that your guest list included your whore. At that minute Curtis grabbed Craig who was not backing down from his father which now at this time prompted Rick and Mike to enter without haste.

Rick pissed by seeing Curtis in Craig's face, threw himself right into their path...Guys, Guys uh uh, not now, this is not the time for this shit to happen. Curtis, take your hands off of him.

Nigga, contrary to your belief, this is my son, my blood bitch, and you or nobody else will tell me what to do where his ass is concerned. Rick was furiously pissed by his audacity to have Vanessa there and was really ready to whoop Curtis' ass especially after that last statement. At that moment Mike came in between them to break it up.

Fellas, think about what you are doing right now. Nae-Nae is dealing with enough shit out there, and Curtis if you don't want this shit throughout the halls of Rae, of your ass catching a beat down in your own home, you had better remember that you have employees out there and settle the fuck down.

All three men backed away from one another with anger in their hearts and minds and noticeably on their faces.

Dad, I will not eat here with that woman at my mother's table. Either you make her leave right now, or I am getting my family and getting the hell out your house tonight.

Craigy, come on man, he can't just throw her out.

Why not Uncle Mike? Isn't that what he did to my mother...that bitch come in her wearing her outfit and a copy of her wedding ring, no doubt that he gave to her ass and we are suppose to sit back and take this shit?

Craig, your mother's tough, she is handling this shit like a pro, she can deal.

Naw Rick, this is bull?

Listen to Rick, Craig, he seems to know all about what your mother likes, wish I could be as sure that my best friend wasn't boning my mate as your good wife seems to be...

Rick pushed Curtis by his chest into the bookcase as he had pushed Rick's buttons to far, Motherfucker, what you saying?

You tell me, Vanessa's being here ain't no different than you?

Rick, this shit ain't worth it, Mike cautioned gabbing Rick by the arm.

Think of Angel, the babies and Nae. Don't do it man.

There is no way, that I can be your son, cause I never would do this shit to my wife, no way I can be your blood man. I'm out of here.

Craig, don't, Rick reaching to grab him but unsuccessful.

Naw Rick, I'm out, talk to your boy over there?

Merry Christmas, you asshole. Both Mike and Rick left the room trying to persuade Craig not to leave, with Curtis following slowly behind.

Upon entering the room they saw Reneea who was full in her glory leading the conversation who had just handed out the bonus envelopes to the staff as Curtis had not returned and they were on a schedule. Oh there you guys are, I was about to send out a search party for you all...Mom, Craig cutting her short, something has come up and I have to go...

Go? Go where, it's Christmas? Angel was confused and could not get her husband to settle down.
Mommy, I will not eat here with this…with these…Mom, I'm Sorry…
Craig looked at his wife and then Mia who were both concerned Angel slightly in the dark but knew that it had something to do with her father-in-law's secretary and Mia who knew exactly what the problem was. Both of them followed behind him, as everyone else looked on in sadness and disbelief as what started out to be such a good night had gone to hell in a hand basket quick. All because Curtis thought he was larger than God Almighty himself and chose to play with everyone's life, not considering the affect that it would have on everyone else or the toll it would take. Craig flung open the door and jumped into his car driving like a bat out of hell down the road with his wife screaming for him to come back. Mia went out after her retrieving her to return to the house as she had just had the twins and did not want her to end up back in the hospital.

Vanessa sat there looking smug and proud of the mess that had been created in her honor. Charlotte glared at her and now more than ever was determined to destroy the woman who had been the center of this controversy and most certainly the man behind the scenes of everything that had unfolded. Reneea looked at Rick for some sign of what had happened and he just shook his head letting her know that it was bad she put her hands up to her mouth and he noticed that his ring was now the ring on her wedding finger and Curtis' ring was nowhere to be found. He knew more than ever that he was going to take her away from all of this shit leaving it and Curtis behind.

Suddenly Curtis stood up from his seat and gathered everyone's attention. Excuse me everyone, I want to thank you all for coming out tonight and though the night did not go as my wife and I had planned due to unfortunate circumstances, we appreciate your being with us in any event. I see that my wife has given you your year end bonus and I trust that it was to your liking. All employees with the exception of Vanessa and Charlotte began to look at one another smiling and nodding their heads in agreement of appreciation. As we are experiencing some family difficulties, I do apologize that we need to cut the evening short. The wait staff is in the process of preparing dinners to go and we hope that you will understand our position at this time. We do apologize and will definitely make it up to you at a later date.

No Problem Mr. Rae, Bob Jones, District Manager of Distribution, began to speak. I think I can speak for all Rae employees represented here tonight that we are very grateful to you and your wife for your hospitality and your generous gifts we have received as well as your treatment of us throughout the year and we more than understand that the evening must come to an end and we will take our leave with the utmost respect for you both, your home and your family and friends. With that being said the wait staff began to issue beautifully packaged dinners and desert boxes for their departures while the others assisted with coats and hats. Vanessa walked directly over to Reneea, smiled in her face and spoke as if she had been vindicated, Mrs. Rae, again I do apologize for the outfit mix up and thank you for welcoming me into your home I hope everything will be ok tonight with Craig and all. Tina looked on in disgust while imagining shooting her where she stood as did Charlotte.

Reneea walked up to her and smiled. Vanessa, do you read the bible?
What an odd question she thought while replying, From time to time, but not regularly, no, answering as if puzzled by her question.
Do you believe that we are our brother's keeper?
In some cases, yes.
Do you know how Judas betrayed Christ?
Now more that ever confused along with everyone else that stood by, was it with a kiss, for money or something?
Precisely…at that moment she kissed Vanessa on the cheek tilted her head and smiled at her. Vanessa was totally confused by her behavior, but did not know how she should react.
Again, Ms. Winters, congratulations on your engagement; I'm sure you are getting a wonderful husband that no one deserves better than you. She turned and looked at Curtis and walked away turning her back to the both of them as Charlotte and Tina looked on and something about their stares made Vanessa a little nervous and Curtis as well.

Come on Vanessa, I will show you out. Curtis placed his hand on the small of her back and guided her through the hall. Out of ear range, Curtis began to speak candidly…Well sweetheart, do you believe me now that it is you that I love? Yes baby I do, why else would you risk your relationship with your son if I were not important to you. Exactly, I will see you tomorrow afternoon. Drive safe and call me when you get home.

She left and Curtis dreaded going back to face the others as he knew that it would not be pretty.

Reneea went upstairs and had changed and was beginning to worry about Craig as he had been drinking and had now been gone a while. Everyone that was not a part of the inner circle of friends had left with the exception of Troy who was beginning to realize that some major shit had taken place there tonight and he was sure that when the smoked cleared there would be a body count by morning. Angel was noticeably worried as Craig would not have gone off and left for this long especially now. He was not answering his cell phone as it was going directly into voice mail and though she had left several terrified messages he had not bothered to respond.

Curtis' cell phone went off and he answered noticing it was Vanessa. Hey what took so long for you to get home? There was some kind of horrible accident on Telegraph that had traffic all tied up leaving your direction, whatever it was someone had to be really hurt bad the car was upside down and they had fire trucks and cop cars everywhere. Okay, get some rest and I will talk with you tomorrow. He hung up the phone and felt in the pit of his stomach that something wasn't right? His son had been drinking and was quite angry when he pulled off. His mind began to wonder if the accident could be tied to his son's long period of absence.

Not wanting to cause any alarm, he walked back in to join the others who were now worried as well. Has Craig called anyone lately? Everyone just looked in his direction shaking their heads but no words were spoken.

Mike, could you come here for a second?

Yeah Curtis what's up?

I don't want to alarm anyone but is there anyway you can call some cop folks or something and see if Craig has been in a wreck, Vanessa called and said that there was some sort of accident leaving from here that had traffic tied up for a while.

Yeah, no problem. As he prepared to dial, his cell phone rang and it was his Captin. Vaughn? Hey listen man this is Shelton, don't you have a nephew or family member by the name Rae, C. R - A - E?

Craig Rae?

Yeah that's the name I just got across the scan.

What up?

Man it seems that he has been in some sort of wreck and they are transporting him to Providence man from the sounds of it, it's pretty bad. Mike, looked like he had seen a ghost.

Man what, Curtis inquired as he knew something was?

Its Craig…he's been in an accident, and it's bad.

Where is…

Rick noticed that Curtis and Mike were dead locked and entered the room where they were.

What's going on?

Craig's been in an accident, they have him at providence and from what they say it's pretty bad.

All hell naw Rick felt himself become weak in the knees!

Look pull it together we have got to get there now. I will get the girls have the cars brought around front and lets go the nanny is here with the babies. Curtis you call the Coopers and let them know where we are headed.

Upon entering the room Angel just started crying as she knew all along that something was wrong with Craig.

Listen Craig has been in an accident and we need to get to the hospital right away the nanny will stay with the twins. But we have to go now. Everyone grabbed coats and just left the house. Reneea just tore out the house without anything other than the clothes on her back demanding that they go now. Troy put Mia in the car and followed out one car behind another.

Upon reaching providence, they tore into the hospital and it was good that Mike was with them and he had his badge as he was able to get service that ordinarily people would not have been given. As they were a large group someone from triage took them to the back to be placed in a private consultation room so that they could be briefed on Craig's condition. By this time Rachel and Davis had made it to the hospital as well because Rick phoned his sister who would want to know the outcome. Even Charlotte, somehow appeared at the hospital too who walked in with the Coopers who had been called by Curtis. Angel laid in her mothers arms and cried inconsolably. As Reneea held on to Tina with everything she had and Rick was right there at her side.

Shortly a team of doctors came in and asked for the wife and parents they offered to take them somewhere to talk but Angel ordered that they say whatever they needed to say in front of everyone there as they were all family. They explained that Craig had been hit by a drunk driver and that he had considerable internal organ damage and major blood loss and was being prepped for emergency surgery. They suggested that as many members of the family that could give blood would and almost everyone volunteered except they declined Angel as she had just given birth and was already trying to regenerate her own blood levels as it was. They asked the parents go as they would be automatic matches and all other's go to test to see if they were compatible donors should the need arise. After testing Mike went to make phone calls to see if he could find out more information about what had taken place.

Everyone was on pins and needles as they waited for what seemed to be hours on end. Curtis sat staring into space as he knew that it was his action that had put his son in the awful position. He should have been at home right now with his children and his wife enjoying his first Christmas as a father, but no his need for this woman and his major ego had destroy this for his son. He could die and this would be on him for the rest of his life. Reneea could not even talk to him she was so grief stricken and scared. That was her baby in there hooked up to all of those machines and she was powerless to make him alright. Mia was sick with worry as she held Angel's hand and rocked her back and forth trying to support her and keep her comfortable, she should have been lying down, they made a makeshift bed for her on the waiting room furniture. At that moment, the doctor came in to the waiting room and called for Reneea Rae and Rick Neal. They both stood up and Curtis did as well. Oh no sir, I will just need these two, the parents. But I'm his father, Curtis Rae; I just gave a pint of blood. The doctor was thrown off, Right you did, however, his mother is a universal donor and so is Mr. Neal here they can give more. His statement caught Rachel off guard as she knew her brothers blood type as he had given blood during the time of there father's surgery in the event he needed blood and made it a point to remember their types but she set back and said nothing. Oh, okay. I'll give more that's my son. I understand sir but I need you to keep your strength as we just tested Mr. Neal and we can now retrieve a pint from him allowing everyone who gave time to rejuvenate, in the event we need more. We will get you if we need more after this, I promise.
Alright.
Reneea, Curtis called out to her hoping she would give him a sign that she forgave him, would you like me to come with you? No! No, Curtis, you've done quite enough tonight for me, for all of us. She looked at him and her

eyes told him everything her words could not say. They proceeded down
the hall and Rick put his arms around Reneea who just dropped her head
on his chest as he walked her down the hall in tears. Curtis looking
through the window, felt lost and knew that he was really now the source
of her misery and had no idea as to how he was going to change that ever
again.

While Rick was giving his second pint of blood, the doctor told Reneea he
had forms for her to fill out and requested that she follow him into the
consultation office. Once inside he shut the door and made introductions.

Mrs. Rae, I am Dr. Lewis Sams and I have called you in here because,
well, I think you know why I've called you aside. Reneea's face grew
weary, and she spoke in a shaking voice trying to get her courage
together…Is my son going to die? No, No, Mrs. Rae he is stable at the
moment…that's not it at all…At that moment he looked at her and felt
compassion as he knew she was clueless and what he would say would
change her whole life. Oh my God… you don't know do you?
What? Your blood…You are Craig's birth mother?
Yes.
And Mr. Rae is your husband?
Yes…
Who is Mr. Neal? He's my sons Godfather, a long time family friend.
I see. I'm sorry this isn't easy for me to ask you…Mrs. Rae is there a
possibility at all that Mr. Neal could be Craig's father?
She was shocked at his question and thought it to be a bit obserd…No, I'm
married to Craig's father, Curtis.
Ah huh, is there a possibility that another man could be his father?
No, slightly embarrassed as a woman of her years, I have only…I've only
been with two men in my entire life and…at that moment her face went
pale and she started to panic. Oh my God, oh no, what are you saying.
Mrs. Rae your blood type is O positive, Craig is A positive, Mr. Rae is AB
Negative. There is no way possible that he is Craig's biological father. Mr.
Neal on the other hand is AB Positive and their DNA is identical. Reneea
sat there thinking that she was going to faint at any minute she could not
believe her ears and had no clue as to what she was going to do. Mrs. Rae,
this is a family matter an I will not say anything, its our job to get Craig
well you have enough to worry about right now, there is no need for me to
add fuel to the fire. So when you are ready you can be the judge of what

you tell your son and his father. I thought you needed to know this information so that you can act accordingly. At that moment the door opened and Rick stood there as he had finished giving blood and wanted to let Reneea know that they could return to the family.

Nae-Nae, is everything okay, did you fill out all the forms you needed to fill out?
Forcing her self to answer, she could only say *Yes...*
I will give the two of you some time, you can return to the waiting area when you're done. Thank you, Dr. Sams, for everything. He smiled at her and left.
Nae, baby what is it. She looked at Rick and all of a sudden she felt free and scared all in the same wave of emotions. A single tear rolled down her face. Everything is okay, or it will be. Are you sure?
Yeah. Still trying to come to grips with what was just told to her she continued to speak in strange patterns uttering words that did no make sense to Rick.
What the hell have I done? This can't be true? Dear Lord how...
Baby your scaring me, what is it.
Rick?
Yes? Holding her close to try and make out what she was saying lead him to believe that whatever it was would be either mind blowing or altering if not both.
Beginning to cry and ramble as she did from time to time, I'm sorry, I'm sorry...I didn't know?
Know what Reneea, becoming more and more concerned by her reactions. Baby is there something wrong with your blood, boo you can tell me. The way she was acting, he thought that the doctor had to have told her that she had and STD or something. She put her hands over her mouth and took a deep breath.
I don't know how..., I don't know this could have happened, we were careful...you had pro...
Just say it, what is it becoming for forceful with her?
Slowly she took a breath, looked into his longing eyes and blurted out what he never thought he would hear in a millions years, He's yours... pushing away from Rick in fear of how he would react.
What dazed and confused and not certain he had heard her correctly?
Craig...he's your son, he is yours. Rick was at a loss for words. He did not know what to say, how to say it, he had mixed emotions and though he

was elated, he knew that this was going to cause major problems for Reneea and Craig who would have to adjust to the whole idea.

Say something Rick? Do you hate me? *Please*? Now sobbing uncontrollably.

Rick looked at her with tears in his eyes and walked over to her caressing her face.

Did you know all these years?

No I swear I didn't I had no idea until just now when he showed me proof that Curtis could not be his biological father and since I've only been with one other man, he being you and your DNA is identical and your blood is AB positive there is no other solution. Craig Allen Rae is your son, not his.

He held her so tight that she wished they could just run as far away from the world as possible. While holding her, Rick thought back to that night that he allowed himself to hold Reneea and care for her on the living room floor of her parents home as they had been at the hospital all day having doctor after doctor paint a grim picture for her father's chances of recovery that she loved so much, he remembered how she cried and pleaded with Curtis to get home by any means necessary and how he made excuse after excuse. He remembers smelling her perfume and wishing there was something he could do to take away her pain, he thought about the anger he had for both Bea and Curtis for being gone at a time when she needed them both so badly. He remembered how good it felt just holding her and having her need him which turned into him wanting her knowing all the while that she was promised to another, his best friend for God's sake, and had they been home there would not be the opportunity for him to be this close to her or needed by her. He thought back to how she looked up at him and asked him to stay with her through the night and while agreeing not to leave her side, how she kissed him innocently enough at first, but how that the second kissed was filled with passion turning into desire and need on both their behalf's and how he laid her back and began to kiss her in ways only reserved for lovers and when she had not resisted his advances how it turned into combustible fire between them, her shedding clothing and giving herself to him with he doing likewise even as she cautioned that she had never been with a man before his promises of being gentle and safe when he remembered trying to apply the rubber that had a slight tear at the top with no other replacement or time to retrieve one, which had to have broken all the way through once penetration was engage. He closed his eyes at that thought and before he could catch himself, he uttered the word ***damn***, causing Reneea to look at him with concern over his last remark.

What?

Nothing, I was just thinking, Nae-Nae, I love you and I believe you when you say you didn't know and this is just as....I am just as much to blame here if not more so than you, it took two of us to create that seed I was a willing participant if not more than you to make love to you that night wrong or right, I knew what I was doing and the possibility of what could happen.

I'm glad because I never would have let you think other wise all these years, not even for a second.

They kissed and promised that they would discuss this later but for now they would pray for their son and wait for him to pull through this mess before saying anything to anyone. He was glad to know that the eyes he saw were his and that he was not just seeing what he wanted to see, anymore.

Chapter 19

Diva's Out Cold

Day break came only to find a room full of people dressed in Party Attire that looked less than pressed with some whose ties had been ripped from their very necks and lie on the floor waiting for their owners to come and claim them. There were high heeled shoes that were long abandoned and hair do's that looked more like don'ts. Mia and Troy had returned to the Rae's Residence to check on the babies as Angel was not leaving the side of the man she loved until he opened his eyes and knew who she was and as Mia's first assignment as Godmother, she would not let her friends down and Angel had no fear that she had chosen the right woman for the job. Mia, was surprisingly impressed by Troy's level of commitment to see her and her family through this thing as they had only been dating a while and she took note that any other guy that she had dated in the past would have well been past the point of their level of commitment after the fight broke out, but in her eyes Troy appeared to have staying power. Mike had left to retrieve a change of clothing for his wife as he knew that short of God coming down and taking her away she was glued to Reneea's hip like conjoined twins, and also to check in at the station about the arraignment of the guy who had caused the accident that badly injured Craig and as they learned last night, killed the passenger who was in his car. The Coopers, who were not leaving their daughter, did manage to go and get food and coffee for everyone who had been waiting for results.

Curtis sat across from Reneea and Rick who had been quiet for most of the night, but appeared to have something in common on their minds as they were not even making small talk with one another anymore, and Charlotte was busy working on her lap top computer, which didn't surprise Curtis as he knew that if you cut open her veins, she would probably bleed droplets of blood that formed letters that spelled RAE Enterprise. He did find it comforting to know that in his time of grief and hardship, he had someone in charge that would not let the business fall by the wayside. His cell phone went off it appeared every hour on the hour, if it were not Donica it was Vanessa and he answered when he could trying to be discreet, while wishing he could be between the legs of either one of them right now having the stress he felt relieved rather than to be in a hospital room waiting for his son to show some sign of recovery. Rachel sat on the opposite side of her brother knowing that when this was all said and done, Curtis would pay for what he had done in a major way, as surely Reneea would not stay around after the pain he had caused her only son. She could taste the victory just around the corner for her brother who had for so many years come in second to a man that not only was a lesser man than he but to someone who had been undeserving of her brother's loyalty for years.

Angel....Angel, bay bab-e... Angel who was sleeping with her head on Craig's bed noticed that he was trying to speak jumped up from the chair causing it fall to ground startling everyone to their feet.
Craig, baby, I'm here...
What happen?
Baby don't talk, somebody get the doctor, she screamed as Rick tore out of the room to retrieve medical personnel.
I'm sorry sweetie; I guess I ruined Chris- Christmas huh?
No, Craig, you did no such thing, Reneea rushing to her son's side.
Mommy, I'm sorry mommy, do what you have to do okay...?
Craigy save your strength, I need you to fight baby. Excuse me I need everyone to clear out so we can check him out, please, clear the room, the voice of the doctor who had entered cautioned.
Baby I'll be right outside okay, I love you, Angel hollered as they pull the curtain blocking her access. She collapsed in Reneea's arms who consoled her and did her best to believe her own words. Angel, listen to mom, Craig is a fighter and he is going to be alright, do you hear me? Yes, I love him so much Ma, I need him, the babies need him, God please don't let him die. Everyone feeling her pain could not help but cry as she had been through hell and back it seemed.

Just then the doctor came out and asked if there was a Curtis Rae amongst the group. Ah, doctor, I'm Curtis, I'm his father...Rick sighed at the sound of that, causing Rachael to take notice. Is he asking for me? Just the opposite sir, he is requesting that you leave and not be allowed access into his room. Curtis hearing this was shocked and protested…What the hell do you mean, surely it's the medication…or something… let me talk to my, Curtis becoming combative and agitated was detained by the doctor and Rick. Sir, I don't know what's going on but for the sake of your son's recovery I am asking that you leave, please sir…You want your son to get better, do this, we can't risk elevated blood pressures of any kind as the body is trying to mend itself and we do not want him to bleed out…please sir…

At that moment, Reneea, who had had all she could stand from Curtis, approached the men and began to speak strong and stern…Curtis, I have had all the shit that I am going to take from you to last me a life time, you have fucked over me for so long that it has become common practice, but where my son is concern? I'm drawing the line. My damn son is in there because of you and he is fighting for his life…I am telling you the second man to leave my life will not be my son by way of death, but it will be yours if you don't get the hell out here right now, as I will kill you myself. Now take your ass to wherever you need it to be as long as it is as far away from My SON AS POSSIBLE! Have I made myself clear you bastard? Rick, see your friend to the door.
Sure Nae-Nae…just calm down. Rick was pleased at what he had just witnessed as the fact of the matter was, Craig was a Rae in name only just as Reneea was and he knew that there was no turning back now. Rick turned to Curtis and motioned for him to follow him. Curtis, who was obviously shocked and pissed by Reneea's actions just backed away from her as he knew the odds were stacked highly against him and today, he could not win. At that moment, Reneea turned her focus to Charlotte who had been observing everything.

Charlotte?
Yes Mrs. Rae?
Responding in a voice that appeared to be strong and direct, Do it now, there is no further reason to wait.
Charlotte placed her lap top in the carrying case stood to her feet putting on her coat, looked at Reneea, smiled politely, nodded…Very well, consider it done. Reneea nodded and backed away to attend to her daughter-in-law. Everyone looked at the two of them strangely as no one

knew what Reneea, could have been talking to her about. Tina thought to herself…Do what now? She was confused but inwardly pleased by her friends new kick ass and take names demeanor but puzzled all at the same time? It was generally she, who fought Reneea's battles, what was she doing. She had no clue, but she knew that the Diva was definitely out cold.

Several hours had past since Craig regained consciousness and it appeared that he was out of the woods and would make a recovery in no time as he was young, in good physical condition prior to the accident and was responding well to every form of treatment. He had become stronger in his speech and convinced his wife to go home and tend to the babies and get a nap in for herself. Tina had long since called the agency and had the nanny dispatched back to the Rae's for a longer period of time and Curtis was no where to be found, however, everyone had and idea of his whereabouts but it mattered not to anyone. Reneea went home and showered but returned to the hospital as soon as she made sure the house was in order Angel was cared for and the twins were okay. Mia, who had left before here friend opened her eyes had managed to change clothes with the assistance of Troy going to the apartment and grabbing a few things for her, changing clothes himself, had managed to come back and take her to the hospital for a visit with her friend who was now in better spirits though sore and able to stay awake long enough to hold conversations. Rachel made her exit after making sure that her brother was okay and retrieving a promise from him that he would call her as soon as he was able as she had gone to the house to get a change of clothing for him as he was not leaving the hospital in case Curtis decided that he was going to have things done his way and try and see Craig. If he had it was not going to be good for his ass. He had cause Craig enough damage. Rick sat at the side of Craig's hospital bed watching television and assisting Craig when he would either wake up thirsty or need the nurse for pain management. Still reeling from the information he received on last night and though he had always loved Craig, just knowing that he was his son, made him that much more in tune with his feelings for him. How could he not have known all these years that this man who grew from a boy that displayed so much of his characteristics and resemblance was his son? God how would they tell him what would he say? How would he react? Would he hate his mother? Or worse would he hate him and ban him from his life as he had done Curtis?

He sat there continuing to think when he looked at the door and saw
Reneea smiling sweetly at them and he returned her smile. She came in
quietly as she noticed that Craig was sleeping, she thought. Shutting the
door behind her, she made her way to Rick.
Hey you.
Hey yourself.
How's our patient?
Just beautiful as the day he was born, he smiled at her lovingly.
Is everything okay at home? Yes, Angel is sleeping and the twins are
wonderful. She misses Craig, she was talking in her sleep and she was
talking to him. Noticing that Reneea was breaking down at the thought of
him not returning home as she started to cry, he rubbed her arm and back
softly as to pat away her worries. Don't Nae, he will be home to her soon,
to all of us.
You need a hug, he asked soft and sweet?
You know I do. They knew it was risky, but no longer cared, she went to
him hugging him and caressing his back as he held her and kissed the top
of head endearingly. She whispered I Love You, and he in returned
whispered I Love You More, always, thinking they had been undetected,
they both turned to see that Craig had been awake and was watching their
every move. Reneea was startled at the fact that his eyes were opened
focused on the two of them and she tried to make light of what had just
taken place between she and Rick.
Straightening her sweater, she walked to the bed…Hey sweet pea you're
awake.
Um hum …smiling at his mother loving, and you're busted?
What? Honey what? Craig looked at his mother with loving eyes.
Why don't I let you two visit and I'll go grab coffee and I will be back in
second.
Rick, I would prefer you stay, Craig requested, motioning for him to let
his bed up.
Alright dude, anything for my favorite nephew.
Stop…just stop.
Is the bed to high?
No, stop with the nephew shit… he paused as both Rick and Reneea
looked on in confusion as they did not know where he could be going with
his statements. He was obviously pissed by what he had just witness take
place between he and Reneea.
I know…

Reneea was obviously rattled, you know what honey?
Mom… I know that you two are involved. Rick looked at Reneea and
sighed covering his mouth with both his hands.
Hey man lets just get you better okay we can talk la…
No, we will talk right now.
Craig, please…you don't understand…
Mom, don't.
I'm not a baby and I haven't been for a while now, smiling at his mother,
and I know this because I just recently made two babies of my own. I saw
you together at Uncle Rick's laughing to himself, now look who doing the
nephew stuff; I went there to pick up my gym bag that I had left after we
had a game, and when I got there, I saw the two of you together. You were
crying and complaining about dad, hump, Curtis and Vanessa and you
were telling mom to tell me so this could come out. You kept telling her
how much you loved her and she kept telling you back and the two of you
started…you started to make love and I knew it was because Curtis was
cheating and had been for years…Mia and I caught him with her at the
house once, and he told me it wasn't what I thought but I knew better, I
was still in high school. Reneea began to cry as she had no idea that her
son had witnessed his father's infidelities or hers for that matter.

Reaching out to take her hand, Mom don't cry, you have cried
enough…Rick, what I don't understand is how you couldn't know?
Know what Craig?
Craig paused and took a deep breath…
Are you in pain? Do you need the Nurse?
No, no meds, I got to finish. How could you look at me everyday of my
life and not know I'm your son?
Oh My God Rick did you…?
No I swear…Nae I…
No mommy, he hasn't said a word. I overheard the nurses in here earlier
taking about us and what the blood proved when the donations were taking
place last night for me. They thought I was asleep…they said that Curtis
could not be my biological father as our types did not match and we were
not compatible, but my Godfather was my identical match and they
laughed saying that somebody was in for a surprise meaning me, but you
can't surprise a person who has always known in his heart that the wrong
man raised him for whatever reasons and the father that should have,
never knew. Again dad, just him calling Rick dad sent his emotions into

overdrive, I ask you how you could not know, by looking into my eyes. I always thought it was funny how much I looked like you; I even have your height?

Both Rick and Reneea stood there with tears in their eyes, full of emotion, not knowing what to say or what to do. Finally Rick gathered enough courage to walk over to Craig and speak.

Craig, you have got to know this first and foremost, neither your mother nor I had a clue that you were my son. We had not been sleeping around together behind Curtis' back it was something that happened one time prior to them getting married the night your grandfather Craig died. I was the first man your mother had been with and your father being the second was engaged to her. I wanted so badly to be with your mother, but Curtis was my friend and he ask me to take a back seat on this one, and foolishly, I did. I can't lie I have always loved your mother and I have always wished that you were mine. But I could not change the hand that God had dealt me, so I decided a long time ago to be content with the fact that you were in my life and that you loved me and for me I tried to make it enough. Craig you have to believe me…had I known you were my son; the hounds of hell, could not have kept you from me, friend or no friend, this I swear.

Rick looked in Craig's eyes and saw tears and wanted with everything in him to take the pain away and erase the past. Reneea looked on just hoping that her son would not hate her as she so loved him. Suddenly she broke her silence. Craigy, can you ever…will you please forgive me; everything that I have ever done, endured or suffered through has been to keep you safe. You are the most important thing to me…the money, that house, the business though it belongs to me…I will walk away from all of it to keep you in my life. And…and, sorrowfully looking at Rick somberly, if you can not except my love for Rick, I will walk away from that too…please…Rick looked horrified, but understood…Craig turned to his mother and tried to smile…
Mom…, mom…why would I want my parents apart…

Rick looked up at the sky as to thank God…and Reneea dropped her head into Craig's chest weeping softly as he had given her the answer she needed to hear; and she knew that she was set to live, to love, and to just be. Rick walked over to Reneea grabbed her by her face with both hands looked in her eyes and kissed her until he couldn't anymore. Did you hear him baby? Did you? He wants his parent's together; they smiled and held each other as he had just given them a new lease on life.

Do you know how good it felt to kiss you like that in front of *Our Son*? Reneea smiled and simply said *yeah.*
Excuse me, hello; trying to regain the attention of them both...does anyone care to know how I feel over here? They broke their embrace and turned their attention to Craig apologizing for their over indulgence. This is going to be difficult to explain to Angel, that she has to change her name and the babies' names and that we will probably not have the nest egg as we once thought, so if you don't mind, I need to tell my wife in private? They both agreed in unison, of course Craig, we wouldn't dream of saying a word, Reneea completed. Rick turned to Craig touching his shoulder and began to speak...Son; I just want you well, please. Damn...What? They both inquired. Son...I never thought I would ever...Craig noticed Rick's emotion and softly said. Rick I have always thought of you as a father...remember Lil Craig, bares your name for a reason before this. Rick bent over and kissed his forehead as no one knew what that meant to him. Just think he went from being a widower without the possibility of children to a man with a grown son and two grandchildren in one day...

And, Craig, about the nest egg parts...don't worry, your birth father and his sister have a lucrative construction business and Rae...well, you shall see. The only real difference will be the change of your name. Listen, we need to let you get some sleep, so we should probably get out of here. Anyway they say if you continue doing what you're doing we can possibly take you home with a private duty nurse you shall be fine, and that wont be a problem. That would be great; I need to be with Angel and my babies. Please take care of them for me guys.
No doubt, it's handled. Is there any word on my car? Rick laughed and said yeah...Totaled that's a word. Reneea chimed in and said don't worry a car is the least of your worries, I took the liberty of ordering you a brand new Mercedes Sedan fully loaded on Rae Enterprises, by the time your home it will be in the driveway. Mom, you didn't have to do that? No, I did you deserve it considering what you have been through for so long. Rick laughed and shook his head.

What? He's my baby?
No, it's not that at all... Rachel and Davis...also ordered him a car
courtesy of Neal/Davis Construction.
Craig smiled at the risk of sounding spoiled...Can I keep'em both? Get
some rest Craigy, Angel will be back this afternoon.
They both gathered their things and began to make their departure. Hey
guys, Craig called out as they were leaving. Yeah, they looked on
questioning his stopping them...I love you both and thank you for your
honesty.
We love you Craig.

As they departed the hospital room they walked hand and hand which was
not something that they had been able to do so freely before and it caught
Rick off guard but made him happy just the same. Damn Ms. Rae, pretty
gutsy of you in broad daylight and out in public and all? She looked at
Rick stopped him cold turned him to face her and kissed him right in open
view for all to see. This brought a smile to Ricks face and a sexual
sensation to Reneea. Ms. Diva, you had better watch yourself. No Rick, I
have been watching myself...Now...this Diva is out cold. They continued
down the hall to the parking lot. Think we can make a pit stop, Rick
asked? Where to? Well there are too many people at your place and my
place is all the way down town...Reneea put on her shades removing her
car keys from her Prada bag...No problem, I do believe the Embassy has a
suite with our name on it...Then lead the way *Ms. Thang.* She grabbed his
hand and pulled him behind her smiling all the way. Rick could not
believe the boldness that Reneea had about her...from telling Curtis to
leave with threatening overtones to the open show of affection with him in
public places, but he knew that he liked it and could not wait to see what
else was in store in the days to come.

As Reneea left the parking lot of Providence Hospital she made several
phone calls from her cell phone, most of which appeared to be in code and
a lot of it sounded like business, as Rick knew she had been working on
her business plan he had not allowed himself to be to consumed unless she
asked questions of him. He was actually proud of her as it appeared she
had taken his advice and she was taking control of her life and destiny
once again. This was the Diva from State...she had vision and knew what
she wanted before she had surrendered her all to Curtis. He thought to
himself that he would have never asked her to be a puppet as she was a

woman with her own direction and she had to operate in it. He did, however, know that one of the calls was to Reservations and that she had reserved a Suite in her full name and dining accommodations and preparations had been made as well. She called Tina and gave her a brief update but told her that as she was pressed for time that she would have to give her more details at a later date.

Damn, look at my baby go he thought as he just sat there smiling at her, completely in love. Reneea took notice of Rick's attention to her. She was curious as to what he was looking at and inquired why the stare.
What?
Hum baby?
What are you smiling at?
The thought of how much I love you.
I like that thought, and I didn't even have to offer you a penny.
Don't ever worry about that, you will always know what's on my mine because nine times out of ten, it will generally be you. Reneea looked at Rick in a hungry manner smiled and responded rather matter-of-factly…Boy keep talking like that when we get to the Embassy, I am going to tear that ass up like never before. Rick liking the sound of what he heard issued a few threats of his own and ordered her to drive faster. I've been meaning to ask you, what's in the bag Doc? Rachel the, thoughtful little sister that she is, went by my place and grabbed me a change of clothes as she knew that I was not leaving the hospital and as my car is in your driveway from last night, she thought that I could use a fresh change. Oh, that was thoughtful…I thought it might have contained your little bag of tricks and toys. Girl you so nasty, I don't happen to walk around with them, but if you have made that a prerequisite, I suppose I shall have to as I do aim to please. Well sweetheart in a matter of days after everything goes as planned, you my love will have to go no further than *our nightstand* to retrieve your little goodies. Rick looked at Reneea strangely…Do you know something that I don't because the last time I checked, we lived at different residences and unless you are planning to change addresses, I don't think Curtis is going to be willing to share his nightstand with a brother, much less anything else after last night. Reneea glanced over at Rick and said you let me worry about that. Well, are you planning to change your address?
No, Curtis is, he just doesn't know it yet.

That last remark sent Rick over the moon, he turned to face his desired licking his lips…Dropping his voice a deeper octave, *Nae-Nae…baby please drive faster, I need to be inside you now, baby right damn now.* Rick, patience is a virtue, haven't you heard? Yeah, I got your virtue right here, making reference to the bulge in his pants.

Upon arriving at the Embassy she found a spot right out front. Rick gathered his belongings and as the temperatures had dropped and it was Michigan in December, they walked hand and hand briskly into the hotel lobby right up to the front desk.
Good afternoon, welcome to the Embassy, I'm Shannon, how may I help you?
Yes, Shannon, good afternoon, I believe you should have a Reservation for Reneea Rae?
Yes ma'am I have it right here. The lady looked at the Card and repeated *Rae are you by any chance related to a Curtis Rae?*
Why yes I am, not even surprised that the woman knew who he was.
Wow, that's deep he has this same suite on a standing reservation weekly. I know, imagine how upset he will be to find out that he can't have it today? The young lady was puzzled as surely he was standing right next to her?
Rick looked on as he, knowing the relation could not believe she was taking this in all so well.
Is he your brother? The young lady asked innocently enough, as they had now caught the attention of the other staff members standing behind the desk as they thought what a coincidence?
No…he's my Husband, she completed signing the guest card put her sun glasses back on, picked up her key card turning to Rick, Ready baby? She asked as she motioned for him to kiss her on the lips and he did and responded, lead the way *Mrs. Rae.* Everyone behind the counter stood there in disbelief as this woman was out cold. The manager who was on a first name basis with Mr. Rae as he saw him so frequently spit out all of his coffee as he was laughing so hard and the others knew that they were in for some juicy gossip the moment she walked away. Spill it Tony the other employees demand! Well, I don't know who that is but I know who he ain't and that would be Curtis Rae, this dude is about 3 feet taller than ole boy and obviously doing something Mr. Rae ain't? And what's that, they looked on…*Mr. Rae's wife.* Laughter broke out from everyone standing there. Reneea and Rick entered the glass elevator's showering

one another with kisses and hugs all the way to the ninth floor not caring who would or could see them.

Upon entering the suite, Reneea saw that everything she had requested was done. The atmosphere was perfect, and she had only one thing on her mind, making love to the farther of her child. Come here baby, she called for Rick in such a way that he couldn't resist if he wanted to. Girl do you know how much I love you right now at this moment. I think I have a good idea, but I would not mind hearing it over and over again, especially with you lying on top of me giving me every ounce and every inch, making reference to his penis, of you. No worries, it's on and it is all yours. I thought that you might like to take a nice hot bath with me first, so let me fill up the Jacuzzi while you uncork that Champagne over there because we have an awful lot to celebrate. I second that. Reneea, are you really ready to close the door on this chapter of your life with Curtis or are you just angry enough to? Richard Neal, I have never been so sure about anything in my entire life, except for loving you, than I am about wanting this man out of my bed, house and most certainly my life. Rick you have always been all of the man I needed and I knew it from the day you made love to me at my parent's home. As I stood at the alter looking at Curtis, knowing that Beatrice was behind me…I prayed that when the Minister asked the question is there anyone that objects, that you would have spoke up grabbed my hand and drug me right out of that church. Rick laughed to himself as he could not believe his ears. Nae-Nae you won't believe this but I kept looking for a signal from you saying that you wanted me to stop you. Damn, so much time has been wasted between us. I don't know if we will be afforded time to make up all of it, but I sure as hell plan on spending the rest of my life trying to find out. Reneea allowed her clothes to fall to the floor while backing away to enter the Jacuzzi holding her hand out to invite him to join her and she had said nothing but a word as far as he was concerned. They spent the afternoon making love, sharing emotions, and making plans. It was truly the perfect end to the day no matter how tragic it began.

Curtis sat on the sofa at Vanessa's waiting for her to provide him with food as he realized that he had not eaten and was feeling a little out of sorts, he had not exercised and knew that he was rebounding from that as well. His thoughts were a world wind especially after filling Vanessa in on all the details. He couldn't believe that his ego and need to show who was in charge had caused all of this. Who knew that his son would become as angry as he was and how did he even know that Vanessa was his mistress in the first place, damn his talking ass relatives he was sure that he had to hear them at the house over the Thanksgiving holiday? How could he talk to him in such a manner? Why would he be asked to leave the hospital like that and where in the hell did Reneea get off talking to him like she was running shit and in front of everybody like that? Who the fuck did Rick think his ass was in the first place…This motherfucker would surely be in for a rude ass awakening when the shit was over. He had free reign over Curtis' family were he was concerned, long enough and he was going to put this Negro in his place once and for all. He was also going to put and end to all his time he was spending with Reneea too…if nothing was going on he was definitely going to put a stop to this shit before it started he thought to himself. She was his wife and was going to deal with her as soon as Craig got out of the woods.

He was glad he had a change of clothes that he always kept at V's as the Tuxedo had long since needed to come off and relaxation was just what he needed after all of the stress everyone had put him through. He thought that he would steer clear from the house for a while as he knew that everyone would return there after leaving the hospital and really just needed to get his thought process together and he was in desperate need of the company of those who recognized his importance. Of course there was waiting by the way side Vanessa who did just about anything that this man wanted her to do, but today he was restless with her flavor and really wanted to be in the company of the sexy Ms. Donica Price…she too knew how to make a man forget his troubles and feel so damn good inside and out. He was glad that he had a date with her that he was looking forward to later that day. He would just simply tell his adoring Vanessa that he had to go home and deal with his family issues and would be back later. Yeah, he had it all figured out how good it was to be Curtis Rae, even on a day like today. You bring a man with options down, he just simply moves on to the next best thing. While Vanessa was in the kitchen trying her attempt at being Susie Homemaker, and was far enough out of ear hustle range he decided to make sure everything was set for his little private meeting he was looking forward to this evening.

As he dialed the number he was glad that she was not in attendance last night as he had contemplated inviting her to the function but thought that it would be best for Vanessa and she not to be in the same room together, he hadn't even given any thought to the fact that his wife was a factor in this.

Hello Curtis.

Hey baby, you sound as if you were expecting me to call.

Well to be truthful sweetheart I was.

Good, I like that. I was just calling to make sure that everything was set for the Embassy tonight?

Funny you should ask?

Why's that?

Well I called there as you instructed me to and I was informed that the suite had been taken for the night, I thought maybe you had a change of plans and neglected to tell me or something.

No, Not at all and what the hell do you mean the suite is unavailable and has been booked by someone else? I have a standing reservation there in suite 900.

Lover, don't get testy with me, Come on Caesar don't kill the messenger, I am simply stating what they told me.

Bullshit, I will get to the bottom of this and straighten everything out.

Don't bother…to be honest, tonight would not really work for me anyway Marshall has plans this evening and he has requested my presence to be in attendance, so it's probably best that this happened as I would have cancelled anyway. Maybe some other time, huh.

Awe babe I was really looking forward to seeing you tonight, can you get out of it? I promise to make it worth your hassle.

Curtis that all sounds lovely, however, I want to be with him, its important to him, you understand baby, right?

Yeah ah, sure…

Well a man like you, with so many options, why don't you call up little Ms. Cancellation Prize behind door number two, I'm sure she will be waiting and willing to take you on, an if that doesn't work, there is always your lovely wife. Goodbye Curtis. CLICK.

Donica hung up the phone without so much as allowing him to say one word in rebuttal. What the hell was going on, with these bitches today? It has to be full moon somewhere; this is the second woman to get out of order with him in a single day he thought. Well she was right about one thing he thought to himself as he looked up to see Vanessa buzzing around the dinning room table making a feast for her King. She looked at Curtis and smiled lovingly motioning for him to come and join her as she was ready for him. He thought, what the hell, why not stay with old reliable over there at least he knew she would suck him until he was content and stress free, with no questions asked.

Donica closed her cell phone and picked up her drink and took a long sip and exhaled long and hard turning to look at her dining companions. You know you bitches owe for that right?

Doni chill, you aren't really missing anything tonight anyway! Rumor has it he is more like a little lamb than the roaring lion everyone is use to after Ms. Thang ripped him a new ass earlier anyway! They all giggled with two of them giving each other a high five.

Girl please, that nigga is good in bed, I will give him that… he eat a coochie like a two piece and a biscuit, finger lick'en good, more laughing and agreeing to this statement!

You are so stupid Doni…, laughing at her humorous analogy.

No, just horney as hell…Marshall's ass will not be back until the end of the week and when he does he will be so busy counting all of our money to make love properly, shit, I am a sister that needs proper tending to, that rush job shit ain't gone do…

D, when this is over with you can fuck him until the cows come home for all I care, but right now we need you to focus. Chucky, fuck what the two of you are talking about, love you as you know I do, this Diva needs to excuse her self, go get her black book and dial a hoe tonight, so be a dear get the bill, hum? I always get the bill or hadn't you noticed? Whatever, it's been real big sis, you too cutie addressing their other companion, taking the final sip of her drink while picking up her Coach Bag, but, I've got to fly, and maybe Rose can hook a sister up with a brother at the Station if I catch her right after she gets off the air. How is Ms. Rose these days's, still making men buy her, The Hoe of Channel Four? That's rude…she's fine and yes, they both laughed. You know you definitely got daddy's genes…What, the business gene? No, the slut gene…That's Cold Chucky, even for you…Cold as hell…Well, sluts got to run love you. Love you back…Doni? *Yes Chuck!* Obviously annoyed, No Curtis tonight you hear me? I know, I know...focus.

After watching Donica exit, Charlotte made a couple of calls as she was in the process of setting up a series of meetings at Rae and everything had to go according to plan with perfection there would be no margin for error, nothing less that complete success was the goal for the next move. After she was finished and still joined by her dinner companion, everything was right with their world in both their eyes. Tomorrow would prove to be both very exciting and lucrative, providing that all players came to the ball and with the invitation they would all receive, no one in their right mine would dare miss it. Charlotte raised her glass and said a toast, To Daddy, Uncle Matt and them OUT COLD Diva's the Ladies of Detroit Society! Her companion simply lifted their glass, nodded and smiled as if they had just conquered the world. Taking a sip of the $340.00 bottle of bubbly they both agreed that Charlotte had chosen a fine selection of Champagne once again. Upon looking at her guest, she could not help noticing how relaxed she looked.

I don't know the last time I've seen you so relaxed.

Maybe that's because you haven't in a while, agreeing.

I thought it might have something to do with your, how I shall I put it…Breakout performance.

Her companioned took another sip of their drink, winked their eye and replied, *it's possible… it's possible.*

Now drink up, I only have a little time and we have much to discuss.

Okay, you're the Boss!

Chapter 20

Who's on 1ˢᵗ? What's on 2ⁿᵈ? It's All Over Now

The weekend proved to do wonders for everyone pretty much as Craig was making a wonderful recovery and had been released to the care of his wife and mother with the assistance of a private duty nurse. The doctor had given a forecast of complete recovery and saw no reason why he could not rehabilitate in his own home with his family and friends attending to his needs. Everyone thought that the idea of him being home with the babies gave him even more of a drive to get better as this was supposed to be a time when he was assisting his wife with their care, not the other way around and in his mind he was more determined than ever to bounce back from his unfortunate episode. He began to remember more and more details about the accident and was able to be extremely helpful to the Oakland County Prosecutors Office in bring charges against the person who had brought these unfortunate circumstance into their lives as well as to the family of the young woman who had perished at the scene.

In the days ahead, Craig and Curtis were still not dealing with one another the way they had in the past despite Curtis' attempts to do all he could to get back in his son's good graces, it was still pretty much falling on death ears, one would say there was an invisible agreement to be polite but there was definite love loss there and everyone knew it. As the Rae's home was large it was easy for them to put space between themselves to keep down confrontation as Reneea had asked Craig for his silence and assistance until she was able to fill him in on all the details that he play along with Curtis not mentioning even to Angel yet of what he had learned about his true birth identity and by no means let on to Curtis that he had planned to sever all ties with him period. In all honesty Craig was happy and slightly relieved that she had ask him to delay telling Angel as he was still not sure how he would come up with the words to tell his wife, Oh yeah babe, by the way, we will be changing our last name to Neal and Rick's my dad? No matter how he rehearsed it, it still sounded a little weird coming out even though he had expected it and in all actuality, accepted it. Curtis and Reneea were only dealing with each other in passing as she had made it perfectly clear that she did not want anything further to do with him as a husband. With this being known, Curtis had consulted his personal attorney who was advising him to stay as amicable as possible so that he would not be asked to leave the residence, even thought this had not yet been a requirement of Reneea as surely she needed him close by until the end. Besides his attorney needed him there so that they could build a good case against Reneea should they have to go after her for her abandoning the marital bed and the relationship as a whole? He had assured Curtis that he was in pretty good standing with what a judge would think and that the monies they were planning to offer should the need arise, Reneea would be more than happy to except, and that all he had to do now was to wait for Reneea to file as surely she would not be able to put up with his behavior much more nor him hers. He was pretty much coming and going as he always did but at times a little more than usual as he now had two hens in the roaster house to attend to. He was not lacking in the department of sex and could care less if Reneea was, as he felt it was her choice to go without as there was plenty of him to go around so she could suit herself if she didn't want him, even if secretly he still could not help desire her from time to time, she was beautiful with a natural sexy quality about her that was not forced. To be honest her, *no don't touch me attitude,* was turning him own as she had now really become a conquest. It was sort of like with his attitude with Charlotte, who he had still not given completely up on the idea of making love too eventually as he felt it was just a matter of time before he wore her down, her defenses dropped and *Bam! Panty Removal Engaged!* Changing his thoughts back to Reneea, yes even after she had spoke to him the way she had in public, he still wanted to have her as she was his wife and she belonged to him and in all fairness she had a little right to be angry she was scared for her son's life and naturally would blame who she thought to be at fault even though Craig acted like a spoiled child, in his opinion, an ran off half cocked, causing all this.

Rick and Curtis had discontinued any further communication and though Curtis attempted to contact Rick in an attempt to put all of this behind them, Rick made it very clear that he was not remotely interested in maintaining a friendship with him as he could not get past what he had allowed to take place on Christmas as the outcome for Craig could have been much worse and Curtis was chalking it all up as a "Shit Happens" moment in their lives. He decided that in order for him to keep quiet about his new found real relationship with Craig, it would be best to stay clear of Curtis as he knew that should the opportunity present itself, that he would surely tell Curtis in the worse way possible with papers to prove it that would be accompanied by an ass kicking that was long overdue. By this being the case, Rick was relying on Curtis being out of the house before stopping by or his beloved coming to him and this had been rare lately as Reneea had been extremely busy cooking up some big business venture that he too would have to wait for complete details. So when he saw her he made the best of each visit no matter how long or how short their time was together. When you are a man in love who has waited this long for the woman he loved, what would a few more days, weeks, or months matter, especially when you knew the outcome was completely in your favor.

Tina by now had an understanding that Reneea had reached her breaking point and would soon be delivering a fatal blow to this imposturous shit called a *Marriage* and felt that the decision had not come a minute to soon, she also trusted her friend was in complete control and though she did not know what she was up to, she knew that it would be big and that they would go into 2009 with a blast! She had managed to talk to her daily even if she could not get by the house as often as she did have a business to run it was year end for her as well and as it was the holidays and her Office Manager, Faye, had small children she had given her the opportunity to take some time off to spend with the them. She did stay abreast of Craig's progress and the newest little Rae's in town because it seemed that Mia had a different roll of film for the twins every time she walked in the house as she and Angel had manage to become even closer since all of the madness with Craig and as Mia and Craig took best friends to a whole new level, there was no way in hell that she was not going to see to it that her friend was alright on a daily basis.

As time was marching on, Tina and Mike were also noticing that they may soon have something of their own to celebrate as Mia and Troy were becoming quite an item. They could not be happier about it as he was really a guy after Mike's own heart, considering he just about had Mia's and her mother's heart in the bag. He was respectful, responsible and most of all employed with his own place of residence, meaning that he was not shacking up with his daughter or in his momma's basement. But, the best thing about this guy was that he had not made children and left his responsibilities on some young lady to be a mother and a father which was very important to Mike. He also noticed that Troy knew a thing or two about cars which was a passion of Mike's and was able to hold conversations for hours about carburetors, engine's and cars with muscle which never made sense to Tina or Mia, in their opinion you take a key stick it in the ignition turn it on and go, enough said, so they often declined invitations to car shows and conversations concerning them, as they enjoyed seeing the two men enjoy each other's company; as the both of them had hinted that this could be love and wanted to see the young man stick around for a while. He had also gained the respect of Craig, which said a lot as he was very protective of Mia and knew just anybody would not due.

Tina loved to see her daughter happy and was always finding ways to have the two over for this or that, but she really didn't have to try to hard as Troy was very family orientated and was pleased to know that Mia was the same. She was not afraid to be with a man whom respected and loved his mother, nor did she classify him as a momma's boy as this had gotten in the way of his previous relationships which he told her right from the beginning. Troy had made a promise to his father to take care of his mother so that she did not have to depend on the kindness of strangers as she grew older in the event that he wasn't around. As his father had died many years ago, he held true to his promise and nothing or no one could change that for him. He was just glad that she understood as he found himself looking at rings thinking to himself that she could be the one and her feisty attitude was just a bonus. The apple had definitely not fallen to far from the tree where Mia and her mother were concerned. If you closed your eyes and were in another part of the house, you would have to decipher which of the women where which.

With New Years Eve fast approaching, Reneea knew that it was now time to put her plan into action as the clock was ticking and it was time for Curtis' Carriage Ride to turn into a Pumpkin once again as he had really over extended his welcome in all of their lives. As they normally would spend the holidays together and so much had happen, it was safe to say that a party of the magnitude that they were accustom to throwing on New Year's Eve would not take place this year at all. As luck would have it no one would be let down even if the Rae's had decided not to throw a party as they all learned that they all received another invite that was sparking controversy everywhere. They would all be in store for a treat that no one in attendance would soon be able to forget.

By the close of business Monday, everyone had received a beautiful engraved invitation on the most exquisite stationary money could buy. It was delivered by messenger so that it would be known that all invited would be notified in order to attend what was going to be the party to stop all parties. Yes, there would be plenty of other parties to attend around Detroit on the last day of the year as it was known as the party capital of the world especially after hosting the Super Bowl a few years back. There would be celebrities performing in different venues and concerts that people would not dare miss. But to those who were invited to this little shindig, you could best believe it would be worth all that and more.

One by one they would all received their invitations and open them and as they read the suspense would be killing everyone involved. It was sort of like a parity of a comedy skit of many years ago, Who's on 1st, What's on 2nd; and no matter the outcome there was an air about the invitation that let some know, *it's all over now*.

The invitation read

Come One, Come All and Watch Us Nail that Ass to the Wall
The honor of your presence is Requested by the
Diva's of Detroit Society
To join us in our celebration of
Living Fine in 09
As we get rid of the Old and bring in the New
It is extremely important that we have the attendance of you!

You won't want to miss it as it is long over due and a celebration
Of the this magnitude wont be a party without you, you and you!
We know that we'll see you there, as you can't possibly resist.

As it is yourself you'll be kicking if this event you miss.
Bring a date and don't be late.
Please R.S.V.P no later that 9:00 p.m. tonight
at 1(304) 317- 07734 ↑ ↓
You will receive the address and directions
from the recording when you call.
Your Access code to enter when responding is 304 - #1
Attire, Dress to Impress!
Can't Wait to See You, Happy New Year
Your Host of the evening will be
"Diva's of Detroit Society"
With a Special Presentation by Big Sister Got Cha Ass!
Don't Miss This One!

One by one, everyone who received an invitation either discussed it with whomever they were with or called another to see if they had received one for themselves. As Curtis, had to sign for his personally, Vanessa looked on with an inquiring mind wanting to know who would have sent an invitation to them both as they, as a rule publicly did not travel in the same circles with one another with regards to parties and social settings unless he deliberately requested her presence there. Surely it had to be someone from their office throwing a party and with some type of masquerade flair. What else could it be? As Charlotte had received one as well and made her way to Curtis' office to see what his thoughts were. She could see other's walking around with them in hand from Management and Department Heads alike? Perhaps some client that they did not want to offend had sent them Charlotte suggested as Curtis inquired about her opinion to what she thought it was. He, generally trusted her instincts and decided that if anyone at the company received an invitation that they should definitely R.S.V.P. and attend as they needed 2009 to start out strong as the future forecast for Rae looked extremely bright and Curtis could not afford running the risk of alienating anyone else, especially were business was concerned. So they all did as he had requested, more like ordered that they do. Plans or not, their jobs were on the line and to be honest by the way the invitation read it sounded as if it were going to be a kick ass event. Yeah, Charlotte responded as the observation was made, *but whose was surely the question?*

Vanessa put the phone on speaker and dialed the number and while waiting for it to answer she made the observations that if you turned the invitation upside down and read the number, backwards it read HELLO LIE HOE. Charlotte could not resist responding after she had. Well I'll be damned, funny it would be you that would notice…Curtis finding her statement humorous had to stop the two of them as they were more than ever like oil and water ever since the Christmas Party at the Rae's, they just didn't mix. Shush, listen.

Hello, and thank you for calling. You must be in receipt of your invitation to what promises to be the Party of your life. Please listen closely as we would not want you to miss a thing. The Diva's of Detroit Society Welcome you to the Beautiful Grand Ball Room of the Westin Hotel in The General Motors Building and Renaissance Center Located on Jefferson in Beautiful Downtown Detroit. And as I am not program to except regrets and/or group responses, please enter your very own personalized access code so that your host will be aware of which very important guest you are that they are thrilled to be expecting, now ;Beep_____

Vanessa entered her pin in slowly for fear of messing up and Charlotte could not believe that she had not paid any attention that her pin appeared to be calling her the #1 hoe and laughed to herself inside.

Thank You, Ms. Winter's, Remember Dress to Impress and prepare to be blown away in 2009 Goodbye!

Oh my God can you believe the expense these people have gone through for a simple New Years Eve Party? Vanessa stated as she was clearly impressed that a machine recording knew her name. Yeah, I was just thinking the same thing Curtis replied. Now I really have to see what this is all about. If this is some new marketing strategy and my competitor has beat me to it, man I am going to be pissed, slamming his hand on the desk. Relax Curtis, Charlotte said rubbing him on his back to calm his fears and moving in dangerously close behind him, so close that he could feel her breast touching up against him and he liked it…You have had the most talented people working right here, or with you right under your nose and surely this is something that we would have given you. Liking the fact that she was touching him in that manner he dropped his guard and softened his voice. Your right Char, I guess I'm just on edge with everything going on these days looking at her as if he wanted more than his backed rubbed. Vanessa who was less than thrilled about Charlotte's attention to Curtis and figured that that was her place that Charlotte was messing around in, cleared her throat bringing their attention to her presence in the room, Why Charlotte, don't you have somewhere to be before this little break I was taking dictation and we probably need to complete it. Curtis noticing that she was possibly stopping what he had been wanting for so long spoke out quickly… No we don't dear, Curtis interrupted and as Charlotte still had not removed her hand from his back which now appeared to be at waist level, he was now more adamant about getting Vanessa out and on her way any where but there, in fact I was ready to call it a day, why don't you go and get something to wear to this affair before traffic gets really thick and I will see you later.

Curtis I…

No, *I- insist…leave*, it's getting late, you don't want the boutique to close or your shopper to leave do you, as he had purchased her, her own personal shopper too after the Christmas party disaster when Reneea came down in a second outfit that made her really look like sloppy seconds. Since you put it that way, *no*, how much should I spend? Whatever you like, charge it to me. Goodnight. The nerve of this motherfucker dismissing me like that, Vanessa thought, I'll show his ass. Charge, oh that's nothing but a word.

Once Vanessa left the office he closed the door and turned his attention back to Charlotte. Now where were we? Charlotte looked at him as she already knew what he was thinking and to her it was working just liked they all planned. She just needed to make sure, she practiced this time what she preached.

Well Curtis, I was telling you not to worry as surely you shall get everything you deserve, you had good people in your life who have loved you unconditionally an with a new year rolling around there is bound to be changes for you. She smiled at him and it looked warm and inviting.

I hope so, as the end of this year finds me questioning that.

How are you and Craig really? Not good, and his mother and I even worse, Rick and I non-existent. Awe, as she extended her hand to cup his face softly rubbing his chin with her thumb and forefinger, I'm sorry. She couldn't help thinking that he brought all of this on himself. I appear to be running a little short in the friend department, well at least I still have you, even if you aren't down with OPP, smiling as he had referred to an analogy that she once used to tell him that he would never have a chance in hell with her. Charlotte allowed him to come extremely close to her as she was sitting on his desk. He straddled her legs which she did not bother to move and put his arms around her waist looking into her eyes.

And what is it that you think you're doing, Mr. Rae?

Well I thought you might give a friend a hug as he is desperately in need of one. Charlotte stood to her feet which brought her even closer to him. I will do you one better Curtis...

Oh yeah, smiling as he liked that sound of that, what might that be? At that moment she put her arms around his neck and drew his head down close to hers while closing her eyes and kissed him passionately with her tongue moving along in motion with his while moaning his name softly and sucking his lower lip causing certain arousal for the both of them allowing him to rub her backside and squeeze her buttocks which gave him and instant hard on causing her to back away but slowly as she was enjoying the kiss as she had been told she would.

Clearing her throat and straightening her blouse, while wiping away what had to be smeared lipstick. Curtis appeared to be frustrated with her discontinuance.

Char why do you insist on fighting this?

Curtis, I've told you before...

Yeah, yeah OPP, but that's bullshit baby, you want me and I have made no buts about wanting you. Why can't we just let this happen? Huh baby? I promise you it will be so good to you, I have no doubt that it will be good to me? I'm so sure that you will want it, that I am willing to go down on you right here and now and lick that sweet little kitty cat to give you a preview of what you would be in store for and what you have been missing out on all this time. Baby, just say yes, Reneea will never have to know, keeping you in good standing with her. Please, just let me make love to you once it will be nothing like you have ever had before.

She could not believe the balls this man had, or his insatiable appetite for women. No Curtis, this ain't in the cards for us, no sir, no way, and no deal.

She picked up her invitation and started walking to the door. Stopping short, she turned around and said, but I need you to remember, remember that I did it with a kiss….
Char?
Yeah Curt?
Save me a dance?
She just looked at him thinking you arrogant bastard…You Bet, You will be the King of the Ball…She smiled and walked out. Curtis watched her leave and was now more than ever sure that he would take her to bed. He had her and it was all over now! Curtis, Curtis, Curtis, you are indeed the man. He only wished that he could call and tell Rick about it all.

As Curtis had been sleeping in the Guest Suite from time to time and Craig and Angel had their bedroom moved to the lower level of the house as it was easier for Craig and she both when he returned from the hospital it was pretty easy for Reneea to come and go without being detected and the same went for Curtis. The night before the New Years Eve bash that by now everyone in their circle was now talking about as they had been requested to attend in some form or another, Curtis decided that he would retire to his master bedroom as it had been a while since he last enjoyed the luxuries of the master bathroom that he had designed for the comfort of the King he thought he was and the Queen he thought she should be. While letting the oversized Jacuzzi fill with water, he thought of the night that he and Reneea had made love in there during Craig's visit earlier in the year that now seemed like an eternity away. He thought about how he enjoyed his wife's company as she had transformed into a Love Goddess before his very eyes and he found himself wondering why he could not be content with just nurturing what was beginning to be a promising relationship between the two of them. Surely if she had gotten as far as to allow him to do what he did to her that night, he could love her past her inhibitions and/or hang ups to be the lady in the streets and his freak between the sheets that he needed. Instead he was still enticed by the sexual demands his body put him through which made Vanessa a requirement and Doni just a pure damn sexual desire. He now found himself running basis back and forth between Doni and V and prayerfully, he was now getting Char up to pitch hit for the team if he could only get past first base so he could see what was on second, it didn't matter to him who was already on third.

As the tub was filled and the steam was inviting him to enter the tub and allow the water to soak away every thought that ran through his mind, he saw a shadow of the reflection inside the master sweet bouncing off the wall from the candle light that flickered through the cracked door. He could now make out that is was Reneea and called to her as not to startle her should she enter the bathroom as he was sure that she would not be expecting to see him there.

Nea?

Yes Curtis?

Oh, you know it's me?

Who else would be in our bedroom Curtis? He paused before answering as her observation made him look completely foolish. I just wanted to let you know that I was here so you wouldn't be startled.

Thanks. She responded as dry as she had been talking on the other side of the wall, but what happened next was so totally unexpected.

Are you going to be long, I guess we both had the same idea, and with her last statement she was standing directly in his view completely nude?

Curtis sat up as he took notice and was completely caught off guard. I'm sorry, excuse me what did you say? I ask you if you were going to be long…I thought about this myself all the way home, still standing before him without clothing on. She had an amazing body and always had, her skin tone was beautiful and even as if she had been dipped in a vat of mocha and cream and dried to perfection and he could not take his eyes off her she noticed his stare and shifted her stance as if she were posing purposely for him. Well Curtis?

Oh shit um sorry, no, I just got in, I'm still hot, I mean the water, the water is hot, if you would like to join me, I'll keep my distance, I was just about to turn on the jets.

Sure, I don't see why not. She laid her towel at the base of the tub and cautiously entered sliding down seductively as to purposely tease him with the package she knew she had together. She sat straight across from him looking at his eyes as she spread her arms out across the back of the tub moving sensually in the tub allowing her hair to hang down becoming wet transforming it into a wavy texture. Suddenly she closed her eyes and laid her head back against the built in head rest.

Um, this is just what I needed at that moment she turned on the surround sound with Jill Scott singing smooth and mellow, it was a tune from the latest CD that told the story of a wife whose husband left her feeling lonely even in his presence which had her contemplating what another man had began to say sweetly to her, as she listened she swayed softly against the head rest which caused Curtis to take notice to her actions as he listened to her sing the words of the song.

Reneea?

Hum, not opening her eyes trying to lose herself in the music?

Is that what happen to us?

What Curtis?

The song is that what happen to us? I left you feeling lonely?

Curtis…let's just soak in silence, I don't really think either of us has the heart for this right now? As the song came to an end she got up with his eyes upon her with her every movement. She wrapped her towel around her body denying him access to the view and walked out of the bathroom leaving him in agony as he wanted her and knew after that, and the hidden message in the song that she and he were not an option and he had no idea when they would be again.

Reneea removed a gown from her dresser looking in the mirror and spoke the words, Consider that your last supper here, put on the gown and exited the bedroom so if he hadn't got the picture upon entering an empty room he would have by then.

Chapter 21

Let's Just Kiss and Say Goodbye

Rick looked at himself in the mirror and was impressed with what he saw. He had allowed Reneea to send over a Tailor that created the tuxedo that he thought was way too expensive. He was a guy who was comfortable in a pair of jeans or sweats most of the time and did not see where the need for him to have a $1,500.00 tux, that he probably wouldn't wear again until he was invited to a wedding or something. Since Rachel showed no sign of getting married anytime soon the best he could hope for was Mia, or precious baby Rita, smiling at the thought. Knowing that that was a long ways off, he just continued to look at the suit and his fresh cut and had to give it to Reneea, she was definitely the one with style and she knew how she liked to dress her man and he would sincerely have to agree that the mission was accomplished. Damn BB, what are you out for best dressed award tonight.

Hey Kiddo, I didn't hear you come in.

I guess not you so mesmerized by that reflection in the mirror you can probably only hear the sound of all the cheering that you are anticipating tonight when you walk through the door.

HA, HA, HA very funny little girl. Now you know this ain't me, this all Reneea and her vision for how I should look tonight.

How much that set you back $600-$700?

Nope did not cost me a penny, I told you my baby momma, and more like $1,500.00, realizing what he had said he made a face in the mirror that Rachel caught.

Negro is you serious, $1500.00?

Showing a sigh of relief that she had not lingered on the other comment, he figured he had better elaborate on the suit some more. Yeah, did I mention that it's tailor made that has a lot to do with the price.

253

I see, and what was the remark about the baby momma?

Girl you know that's just me talking shit, stopping to pay attention to his sister, you don't look half bad yourself. You clean up real good Neal. Far cry from your construction get up huh?

Well you know, a sister like to be fly sometimes and from the sound of the invitation dressed to impress was a must. Right, they did stress that didn't they? And you know what I say about us Neal's? What's that? There is no mistaken one, smiling sheepishly. Rick knew exactly where she was headed but he had promised Reneea and Craig both that this information would stay vaulted until such time that they could reveal Craig's true identity.

Rach, can't we just get through tonight? I promise next year I will deal with your suspicions. Uh, uh, don't try that shit, I saw you looking at baby Craigy, you know as well as I do that that baby is your grandson...Come on Rick, don't let them do this.

Suddenly, they heard the door shut and standing directly in front of them both was Reneea, who was not yet dressed which caught them both by surprise. Good evening, don't the two of you look absolutely wonderful, Rick I told you baby that suit would be wearing you, he cut that perfect walking over to touch the fabric, and Rachel after seeing you maybe I should go back and get another dress girl you are sharp.

Hey Nae-Nae, trying to hide the tension in her voice as they were not sure how much she had overheard. Baby why aren't you dressed? Oh I will be I needed to come by and get my ring from upstairs, I left it on the night stand earlier, smiling at Rick devilishly, as his face could not conceal the fact that he was reminiscing over the reason as to why she had managed to leave it, while managing to embarrass Rachael. Well on that note, why don't I go somewhere...hell anywhere but here right now...Rachel stumbled over her words.

Rachel? Reneea called out to her to stop her from leaving the room...I can't pretend that I did not hear you guys, upon coming in and I'm sorry, I don't make it a habit to listen to other people's conversations. I'm afraid that we can't go into detail, but I will confirm your suspicions. Reneea took in a breath and spoke slowly and careful. Rick is Craig's biological father and yes the babies are Neal's. Rick stood there almost paralyzed as he did not know what would come out of his sister's mouth before they had a chance to explain. Rachel just stood there, shaking her head back and forth and for the first time ever, appearing to be speechless. Reneea decided to continue before her opportunity past away. This is something that we just discovered when Craig had the accident and we had to donate blood. Curtis' didn't match, and since I've only slept with one other man in my entire life, your brother was the obvious choice, slapping her hands against her legs. You must know that had I known, I would have never married Curtis or allowed him to think that Craig was his son. As all parties involved have not been informed we promised Craig that we would not disclose the information before he had a chance to speak with Angel and explain everything, which still has not occurred as tonight is to important to rock any boats. Can we please count on your silence, no matter how bad you want to let Curtis have it, and God knows he deserves it, can we count on you for Craig's sake, please, I'm begging you?

Rachel smiled so hard failing to stop the tears that were falling fast and furious… Craig…Craig knows that he's a Neal? They both answered…Yeah, he's mine, and you were right Kiddo. She hugged her brother trying to avoid getting massacre anywhere on him and then turned to Reneea and hugged her. Nae-Nae, again, I believe you and you have my word. I promise. At that moment she excused her self to wipe her face and retouch her make up as Reneea, kissed her lover retrieved her ring and returned to the Limo waiting for her outside.

The traffic was unbelievable trying to get downtown, as it was to be expected after all it was New Years Eve in Detroit and it mattered not the size of the party you were attending, rest assured everyone was trying desperately to get to their destination. There was a Limo scheduled to pick them up as their personal RSVP recording had informed them along with overnight hotel accommodations as they were considered VIP's Tina, Mike, Mia and Troy and of course Craig, Angel, Rick and Rachel who would all be in the same car. Upon entering the Limo there were bottles Champagne that were previously chilled and any other cocktails that their host thought that they would like to have on their ride to the Westin. There were also personalized notes for each passenger that included well wishes for a wonderful new year and for a wonderful time to be had by all attached to a gift bag that contained sterling silver frames with their group photo from

Christmas that Reneea had managed to get Curtis to snap before all of the commotion with an engraving on the frame that read Living Fine in 2009 and they were all impressed.

As Curtis was no longer a welcomed member in this club, he was no where around. He had left the house earlier when he found out that Reneea would not be accompanying him and Craig had no interest in ridding with him. He thought that since Vanessa was attending and it was a company function as practically everyone would be there, that there would be no harm in her riding with him especially since he knew he would end up spending the night with her as she was his only real option for romance as he was told in so many words that Donica would be accompanying Marshall Johnson to a Private Party in the City, and Reneea had made it clear with her absence that she was perfectly fine on her own.

Upon arrival to the Westin and letting the Valet park the car and arriving to the hotel entrance, they were escorted to the ballroom by greeters who were all dressed in costumes like Court Jesters. It was quite circus like but with a touch of elegance. There were several employees there from Rae Enterprise which lead Curtis to believe that this was a party being thrown by an employee of the company as he had originally thought, but why would all of his personal friends and a few family members be there that he had noticed? He looked around and saw Jamison his private investigator who had worked for him over the years and wondered what he could be doing there. Vanessa was just in her element she was dressed to impress and commanding attention from all of the men and even some of the women. Curtis could not help thinking that something just did not feel right, but he couldn't put his finger on what it was. He saw a few business contacts and was shocked to see Marshall Johnson, however, noticed that he was not with Donica Price as she had earlier alluded to. He saw his old friend standing at the bar and decided to walk over to him and say a word as Vanessa was off mingling with the girls at the office who would talk to her. They were the ones that feared she might just marry Curtis and become the head bitch in charge and they wanted to keep their jobs as she always made promises that there would be changes when she was on top. Her dream had always been to fire Charlotte and surely as his wife, he would have to honor her request to keep her happy or risk losing her.

Good evening Mr. Neal.

Good evening Mr. Rae.

This is pretty wild huh?

What would that be?

The party the whole set up.

Oh, oh yeah responding very dry as he really did not want to be in the company of Curtis at all.

Kind of like being back at State when they would throw those Mystery Host Parties, and no one knew who was sponsoring the gig until the end. Yeah, I remember those.

Is Reneea here with you guys?

Nope, I was about to ask you the same thing until I saw you come in with Ms. Winters over there. Yeah, she needed a ride and I thought, what could it hurt now, especially since I thought this was a business type party. With that invitation? Business, really? Naw, I don't think its business? I don't know man whoever it is behind it went through a lot of expense for this to be pulled off. I will say this; it is sho-nuff jumping in here. Yeah that's what's up. The women are out tonight. You better catch you one man. Rick looked at him after that statement and simply replied...Dude, I'm already hooked. Take it easy I'm gonna go holler at Mike and T. Bet give'em my regards. The two separated like strangers as opposed to two men who had grown up together and been friends since either could remember.

Curtis wandered about as he really did know everybody in the room literally, but was becoming board fast. At that moment Jamison a big dude in statue walked over to him. Mr. Rae. Jamison. How's it going man? You know man I can't call it...

What are you doing here tonight?

For starters as I'm off duty, getting my drank on and waiting for my lovely wife to return. Your wife, that's right...She's a Diva of Detroit Society member. For real man, I didn't even know you were married. Yeah, sweet little ole thing, until you piss her off and then, that's your ass in more ways than one.

I heard that. Well look man it was good to see you I'm going to mingle a little bit, before this presentation thing gets under way...Yeah you do that, and Mr. Rae, you should be careful who you kiss, it could get'cha killed. Jamison smiled and walked away from Curtis drinking his beer and laughing. Jamison's comment caught him off guard, who could he be referring to? He brushed the thought out of his mind and took another drink as the Court Jester waitress appeared to appear each time his glass was empty, he blew it off as just being noticed as a VIP and thought he would certainly talk to marketing about hosting something like this for his clients as soon as he returned to work.

All of sudden, Mary J's Fine came on and the whole crowd went wild. A spot light hit the stage and three of the sexiest bitches appeared on the stage that you ever wanted to see. They were wearing tight black sequenced dresses that went to the floor with a split from the floor that stopped just short of their crotch. The glitter on there bare backs showed through the V opening in the center of the opening that shinned like diamonds. Their hair was slicked back, two with long hair one much longer than the other and one with short hair. This he would notice as hair was a real weakness of Curtis, the longer the better. It was his only dislike about Doni, but her screwing made up for all of that. Curtis could not believe his eyes. They were similar in height but there body shapes were damn near identical as they were all tight as hell. And last but not least, they were all wearing a mask that concealed their faces and true identity. They were doing some sort of hustle step and their steps were tight, dancing obviously had to be in their blood, not to mention they had to be related as there were so many similarities amongst them. The crowd was really hyped and appeared to be doing the same step on the ground as they were. Along with being the Party Capital, Detroit was known for its hustle and the crowd was going wild as by now if the Jester's were refilling everyone else's drinks like they were for Curtis, they had to be zonked. There was a Celebrity DJ on the stage that definitely had the crowd hyped, some female from the local radio station on the stage that was certainly worth whatever they paid her to play for the night. Curtis noticed that Rick and Rachael were on the floor in step as was Vanessa and a few of the secretaries that she dealt with. He liked watching them dance when at that moment he notice Craig and Angel off to the side rocking backing forth as he was still not 100% yet, but it was nice to see him up and out. He then saw the ladies coming off the stage and entering the crowd in motion with the other dancers when the one with the longest her danced her way over to Rick's space and began to move in motion with him performing the steps in sequence with him rubbing her body up against him, he appeared to be resistant at first until she flipped her hand around and showed him her ring and he all of sudden appeared relaxed and happy with what she was doing fell right in step with her touching her and rubbing her body sexually. Curtis became jealous watching all the action Rick was getting and began wishing that one of the women would dance his way as one was dancing on Jamison the one with the hair not as long as the one woman, he figured that had to be his wife and the other looked to be making her way over to where he was standing, when the one dancing with Rick kissed him right on the lips and started walking toward him as well. Curtis thought how back in the days of State, they would have sandwiched ole girl up with one of them getting the digits so the other could get the panties and smiled to himself. Finally, the one with Jamison began to follow her friends lead in his directions as well and all three women were now dancing around him and he felt just like he was in heaven as all of their bodies were engaging him to the beat and once again he was King Curtis Anthony Rae. Vanessa took notice and wasn't to thrilled with their little freak show as they were dancing all over her man. As the record was coming to an end and a slow jam was now playing and he remembered hearing it. Before was the Jill Scott cut that Reneea had been playing each woman one by one kissed him on his check, with the last one being the one with the long hair kissed him on his lips and whispered in his ear, *Let's just kiss and say goodbye.* Curtis was taken off his square as all of them were wearing Reneea's perfume and he realized he had yet to see her at the party. Feeling slightly intoxicated, he reached for her hand only to have her pull away gently turning her back to him dropping her mask on the floor behind her at his feet as she walked away not looking back. But the faces of everyone she approached to make her way back to the stage, told a story of shock and unbelief. His son's face was the most perplexed of all. But Vanessa looked damn near horrified, as she stopped directly in front of her and looked into her eyes on her way up the stairs being escorted and shielded by her two twined companions who kept Curtis from seeing her identity.

All of the sudden the house lights went up and the music went down low. One of the masked women was handed a cordless microphone by the DJ and she began to gather the crowd's attention. As everyone had been on the edge of their seats upon receiving the invitation, is wasn't very hard to do.

Good Evening Everyone and Happy New Year in Almost one hour from now. The room exploded in cheers. We want to welcome you our guest to the 2008 Diva's of Detroit Society Ball, we hope that you have found everything to your liking and to our VIP Guest in attendance we trust that you found your accommodations suitable. I am *Big Sister Serve and Protect, a senior member of the Diva's to my right is Lil Sister Gone Bad,* as the woman with the short hair began to wave her hand to the crowd receiving whistles from men in the crowd, and we are pleased that you were good enough to share your New Years Eve with us. And now for our very special guest, Mr. Curtis Anthony Rae, if you would join us it would be greatly appreciated. Curtis heard his name called and was stunned as he had still not figured out why Vanessa looked as terrified as he could not get to her to ask her why. As he is use to commanding and controlling attention he swallowed what was left of his drink and made his way to the stage. Along the way he noticed Rachel Neal smiling in his face as if she had been waiting for this moment to come, however, he continued on as he was just that full of himself and felt he had no worries. Upon arriving to the stage he noticed that the once masked women who had not removed their mask prior were now standing there with their mask in hand and they were glaring at him with eyes that read he was a dead man. The identity of the women was truly unsettling for him as he saw now what he should have seen all a long. To his left was the beautiful Donica Price and to his right none other than Charlotte Williams and with their hair pulled back he noticed that their resemblance was uncanny. He grew ill and new that this was not going to be good. At the moment of his realization the third woman began to speak into a microphone that she had been holding behind the curtain. She emerged from the curtain with Grace and elegance and her beauty was quite a sight to behold, and standing between the two you could see that she had to be the Ring Master and Curtis was by all means a staring cast member in her circus.

And I am Big Sister Got Cha Ass, founding member of the Diva's of Detroit Society as she walked closer into the light he saw his wife and could not believe his eye's.

Welcome Curtis you are our very special guest this evening. Of course you already know my cousin's Charlotte and Donica a.k.a Chucky and Doni. Suddenly Curtis remembered a photo of three little girls in cowboy hats sitting on the hood of a Buick Electra Duce and Quarter that Reneea displayed in the family room with the names and ages written on the back…Re-Re, Chuck and Don ages 7, 5, and 41/2 he felt his heart beating faster. *One might say you know Doni intimately almost as intimately* as you know Vanessa Winters over there, Did you know that Vanessa? You are not the only fuck buddy that Curtis has. How does that make you feel, jilted, hurt, and scorned oh how about this one, embarrassed? Hell because of you I know all of these emotions all to well. Say hello Doni? As she motions for her to speak, Hello Curt, or, should I say daddy like you like me to in bed? Hum? Well, well Curtis you have been quite busy... and then there is Chucky here who just yesterday you tried to initiate into your little fuck club, remember, I don't think her husband, Jamison appreciated that or at least he didn't when we were telling him about it just this afternoon, he'd like to kick your ass, but we asked him to wait, wasn't that so nice of us? I can't promise you that he's not going to though looking over at Jamison who raised his beer bottle to confirm her statement. Say hello chucky. He now remembered that it had been Char who brought Jamison on when he needed to do background checks on a few people. Hey Curt, sorry I'll never know the pleasure of calling you daddy. You could hear the snickers and remarks from a crowd that waited as if they were watching a cliff hanger, well they were sort of just live and in living color. And of course a woman of my status needs no introduction as I am your wife, what a fucking joke. Right? As I haven't been your wife since Vanessa came to work for you what has that been 7, 8, 9 or 10 years or so... Let me see, ah yes Craigy was still in high school that is when my poor son had to witness your infidelities and be played for a fool as if he didn't know the difference between you fucking this woman in my home and conducting business, and girl he just gave you a ring? Damn, you stupid. All of the secretaries in attendance began to laugh at her. See I guess because you could'nt see past your dick, you never noticed how much Chucky...well Charlotte and I look alike. Its obvious, you missed that whole sister thing with her and Donica and they were in the same room together, but in your defense with all that ass and breast flying around, I guess it was pretty hard to look them in the eye, huh baby? See my mom and Charlotte's mom were sister's and our dads which none of them were fortunate enough to have son's had to groom their daughters to be their successor's in business and when your ass latched on to me, I sort of lost sight of the plan that we had to run the companies together, because you wanted a housewife and stay at home mom, never mind that Master's Degree I worked my ass off for, it wouldn't be needed not as long as C.A. Rae, was my man. Remember telling me that sweetie? But what you really wanted was my money, our money, **making reference to the two women in her company**, and with the MAC Foundation you were off to a flying start, you formed RAE Enterprises and forgot those who got you there. This pissed Charlotte off a lot especially when you did away with our Charitable Orgs that our mothers founded along with Bea's Mom. All because you thought that they were not making you enough money, had you read between the lines you would have know better as that was your first mistake. Simply put if you began to sale off divisions your worth to the company would become zero and you would forfeit your rights to any holdings and with your little Merger between the Kirmark Divisions Group and RAE, you have given me 100% of all Rae Stock. Because you were in such a hurry to take that little sweet thing over there to bed that you did not read the fucking fine print. Hell you never read it at all. How the hell did you sign contracts without reading them? You didn't even notice that she used a trick that your little fuck buddy over there perfected, for heaven's sakes Curtis it was your own material right out of your playbook, which you'll find I've studied very well. Curtis I am Kirmark Division Group, simply put Your ass is out and mine is in, along with my Partners Chuck & Don, oh Yeah, our newest Division, **Making to reference to someone standing nearby in the crowd which Curtis could not believe his eyes was making her way toward the stage,** Rachel dear come here please, You remember Rachel don't you Curtis...You should she's your best friends little sister you know the one whose virginity took at age 15, and just the other day on Christmas you felt her up in my house with me in the other room. This little Information Rick is hearing for the first time, so I would really watch my back, he looks pissed. **Curtis looked at Rick who was being held back by Mike and Troy.** Curtis you really are something...In any event, I want you to meet my Executive Vice President of Kirmark Construction Dirision a.k.a Neal/Davis Construction Management. Say hello to Curtis Rachel, **offering her the microphone and bracing herself with what** would be said she looked on as if she had announced the worlds cure to cancer she was so proud of her performance. Sure Nae-Nae...Fuck you Curtis and I told your ass... I would have a front row seat when your shit caught up with you. She surrendered the mic and stepped back never once taking her eyes off Curtis who was standing there a torn and bruised man in disbelief. Well there is so much more that I don't know where to begin. Oh yes I do, the deed to the house that has your Fucking name on it as you so loving told my son who objected to your whore being at my table on Christmas Day, Well baby that too is null and void as it is also a part of RAE Holding Corporation. So I will be taking that as well You betcha! And I want your ass out of it by morning, don't worry about the condo that you have your trash over there stashed in...I will give you time to find another place as I am done paying your bills **looking at Vanessa with a fuck you expression on her face,** I think a week should suffice. And as you almost caused my son his life, you'll be pleased to know that he's not yours, it ought to ease your guilt a little for the way that you have always treated him. Don't get me wrong, you tried to be a good daddy, but as you drilled it into him...Business First. Why do you think he wanted to make his own way in the world instead of working in the family business, he did not want things handed to him of course, but he did not want to become you! That terrified him more than anything...just think even when Rick had road games, when you were to busy with your whores and your money and you had Rick filling in for your absence, he never once let that boy down. Craig, I'm sorry baby you will have to explain a bit faster to Angel than first thought I can't wait. **She received a nod of approval from her son and she continued with a vengeance. The entire room was still with most not able to comprehend what she way saying.** Imagine my shock when the doctor called us back there and told us that? I mean you were in Florida fucking my best friend, which was your best friends girl while my father lay dying in a hospital bed and you two decided that it was best to miss your flight, fuck, get it out of your system and come back the next day. I needed you both so desperately that night. Um, but, Thank God for Rick, who really should have been my man in the first place but thanks to your conniving ass that didn't happen, right? Well that night we conceived Craig an accident occurred and the rubber broke that is the only possible explanation we can come up with as to how that child turned out to be his and we have documentation to prove it, so really all these years I have been staying with you for my son while you have been screwing everything in your path for as long as he has been here. Go figure, I exercise, I eat right, I mean come on everybody, **motioning to the crowd of onlookers for support and validation,** this is a hot body am I wrong, **One man in attendance yelled out HELL YEAH BABY, AND IF YOU FREE NOW, I'LL DAMN SHO TAKE YA,** receiving cheers from the other men in the audience? See, I told you, I'm good, but old faithful over here, had to sprout off with everybody else, but me unless he couldn't get to her that NIGHT, do you know what that does to a woman's self-esteem you bastard? Needless to say that I have taken the liberty of drawing up our divorce papers and I am prepared to offer you an amicable settlement, that is the word your attorny's used, wasn't it I believe he is somewhere in the crowd tonight and dude as I know you are, please encourage your client to sign the documents as soon as possible so he can get on with his life and I can now start to live mine, Thank you so much **acknowledging a gentleman who raised his glass in her direction who was no doubt Curtis' attorney?** Oh and by the way...yes Rick and I are sleeping together so the next time you want bug a room in a house, bug the right one, the Master Suite as no self-respecting woman having an affair with a man that she loves offers him sloppy seconds, and your selection of choice for Jamison to tail me, your trusted Super Snoop, was excellent, I love the fact that your ass is such a creature of habit...but we can't blame all of it on you, how could you have known he was family? You look surprise, yes I made love to Rick each time in your bed, he is so thoughtful after thoroughly satisfying me, he left you several presents, how do we say it Doni, *Daddy* **as the two woman chimed in together to sound like phone sex operators the crowd was by now floored with laughter.** Besides, I'm sure you were pretty disgusted to turn on the television and see a tape of your son and his wife... Oh yeah I know, imagine my shock when I turned it on! Besides, the guest bedroom is reserved for a man I'm not sleeping with and that would be you, remember. You know, I didn't want to do this, this way but you my dear left me no choice. Marshall Johnson, works for me and always has and so do the employees of Rae as most of them were our father's employee's. Is it all coming back to you now? Marshall's companies have always been a stand alone division as Donica has always been the CFO there. Isn't that funny? Reneea found herself laughing out loud. I know, I know, didn't the recording say you would be blown away? Hot Damn, I know I am. Becoming more serious and defined in her tone, listen to me very carefully... I want you and that **Bitch** out of my office by day break and there will a police escort for you both. I guess you can say that I got cha ass, huh? Vanessa, you should read the Bible more and always be careful when someone you consider an enemy kisses you, Vanessa reflected back to Reneea kissing her on the cheek on Christmas and asking her the questions, as they may very well be the Judas that is out to bring you down, I should know, I have been kissed by a Judas for more than twenty years... obviously referencing Curtis.

Reneea, you can't do this shit to me! Curtis was furious he could not believe the embarrassment this woman had caused him and in front of so many people? He had no idea what his next move would be or when he would make one. Suddenly all types of thoughts and memories of obvious things he should have noticed flashed before his eyes that he should no doubt had picked up on and he felt as if he were going to have a heart attack. Striking her was completely out of the picture as that would have brought him certain death where he stood. Finally he heard the Manhattan's singing softly in the back ground a late 70's hit Let's Just Kiss and Say Goodbye, and now he understood what the woman had whispered and why.

And now as it is fifteen minutes to 2009 please grab a glass from the wait staff and get close to the one you love and get ready to help me put out the old and bring in the new....Rick come on baby take your rightful place, by my side. Curtis, get off my damn stage, NOW! We are through...

Curtis could not believe what had just happened and was mad as hell about everything that was taking place. The entire room was buzzing about with people laughing and pointing. Some were grabbing glasses and bottles of champagne and getting close to their significant other as Reneea had suggested, but no one really cared about Curtis or his dilemma because most of the people in the room felt as if he had that and more coming to him. Either he had swindled them out of position or their company and they definitely thought that he was a pig for what he had done to his wife and needless to say that Vanessa was receiving her share of laughs and dirty looks from on lookers as well. Rick resisting the need to knock his ex-friend the fuck out walked up to the stage and simply looked at Curtis and replied, *Shit happens, right Judas?* Curtis had no words as he knew he had been played.

As he continued to walk past the people who had been entertained for the last 45 minutes at his expense he noticed the man who he had just learned was not really his son and his wife standing just in front of him and for him he had no words…Craig looked at Curtis and decided to speak direct and candid. If anything should happen to my mother or father after tonight, I will personally see to it that your ass becomes a memory…and·I always knew that the wrong man got the job as far as my mother and I were concerned, so you can expect me as well as my wife and children, hearing the word children brought pain instantly to his heart, to be changing our names as long as my mother is giving it back to you, I should too. Don't worry, pop's, oops Curtis, *Shit happens, remember?*

5, 4, 3, 2, 1, Happy New Year! The crowd was going crazy as everyone in the room felt as if they had been given a new lease on life and the outlook no longer appeared grim to those who worked in fear and silence at Rae as they felt the King had been dethroned and the wicked witch was dead and it all happened in the worst possible way, imaginable. Curtis managed to make his way to Vanessa, who was standing by the exit crying as he walked up he could see her face was less than pleased. As he begins to speak, Vanessa reached out and slapped him so hard that people standing by took notice. What the FUCK! Have you lost your damn mind? Maybe so Curtis, but it's for damn sure you have. After everything that I have done for you, how could you do this shit to me? We will talk about it when we get home V. HOME! What home, there is no home, no job, no money, are you serious…Oh your ass had better find a hotel tonight sweetie, because I'll be dammed if you sleeping with me. The coat check Jester handed her her wrap, and she left the hotel entering the Taxi that the doorman had held for her. Curtis had nothing left as he glanced around the room, he felt his attorney pat him on his shoulder and they left in silence together.

As Reneea looked on to see Curtis exiting the room she felt an overwhelming sensation come over her and was actually relieved that the whole thing was now over with. She looked at her cousins who were with their significant others raised her glass to them both and smiled as a tear rolled down her cheek, she knew that once again her family honor had been restored and that they could now get back to the business the way it was intended to be. She knew as far as the rest of her core group went by morning she would have a lot of explaining to do but it would all be worth it as she was tired of keeping secrets and the part of her that was dying to live could now start. She knew that restructuring would not be easy, but had no doubt that the Three Amigos would come out smelling like roses they always did. Kirmark, had been undetectable for years as it flew under Curtis' radar thanks to Charlotte who always had a handle on what Curtis needed to know and not to know and it always stayed afloat as Donica, had a good head for business since college. She was pleased with the evening's events and though she knew her son had been put in a tight spot because of it, she had no worries as he did possess his father's, his real father's finesse and charm and by morning he would have smooth everything over for her. She was grateful to Rachel as she looked at her dancing with Davis, who had the gumption to come to her with all the information she needed to put the last nail in Curtis' coffin and knew that the business deal they had made would be one of good financial gain. As she turned to address Rick who was waiting for her patiently she had a feeling of love come all over her body.

Well, well, Ms. Rae.
Ah ahh! She replied alerting him that he had made a mistake.
Oops my bad…Mrs. Soon to be Neal, they both smiled at the possibilities.
You have a lot of explaining to do. She looked down and replied as if she were a child being scolded, I know, I know, I'm sorry Rick, I just didn't…at that moment he put his finger to her lips before she had a chance to begin rambling as he knew she would. Baby, I said you had a lot of explaining to do, but I did not mean tonight…I got other plans in store for you tonight.
Oh, do tell.

I plan on it as soon as we get home.

Oh baby, I can't wait until we get all the way back out to Bingham Farms, I was hoping that you wouldn't mind accompanying me to the Suite, I have reserved for us tonight, here?

Even better, I won't have to wait so long to be inside of you. She smiled at what she knew was going to be an evening filled with pleasure.

They kissed and saw that they had caught the attention of their friends and family who were cheering them on and clapping as, Tina yelled out the loudest. IT'S ABOUT DAMN TIME, YEAH! Tina walked over to them and kissed them both on the check as she too had held many secrets for her to make this night happen all this time pretending not to know Charlotte as well as she did each time she saw her and knowing that Reneea was loaded and not letting on to her own family exactly how loaded that her friend really was. However she was surprised to see that backbone emerge, that she knew all along was there. Tina said happy New Year and rejoined her family who were trying to give Troy the Reader's Digest version of what had just taken place as he pretty much figured out why.

Reneea turned her focus back to Rick as the stream of well wishers had now died down. She looked in his eyes and they said to her everything she wanted them to say and that was that he loved her no matter what. Not bad for my first consulting business venture, huh? Knowing that she was capable of way more than a consulting business he just shook his head and spoke sarcastically, Ah you think? Rick caressed her face and realized that in all the commotion he had not yet told her Happy New Year Properly.

Oh baby, I forgot, Happy New Year, Lil Ms. I'm Doing Fine in 09.

Uh naw baby...Reneea stopped him, Happy New Life, I love you. They kissed each other passionately and decided that it was time for the private after party for two.

Chapter 22

I Win You Lose

Rick and Reneea, made their way from the ballroom onto the elevators as the party was still in full swing and they decided that they would not be missed too much and rather than risk being detained by someone who wanted to give them their regards, or thank her for the party, they just assumed to sneak out unannounced as it was certain that they would see each other for breakfast early in the morning because Reneea had arrange for an elaborate spread for her friends and family to dine on to chase away the hangovers she knew all to well that they would have. As she was talking and reliving some of the night's highlights with much energy, upon arriving to the room she noticed that Rick had slowed his pace and turned around to inquire what the problem was.

Baby, is something wrong?

No, I guess I'm just trying to piece all of this together in my mind, you know?

Which part are you most uncertain of as she was now concerned over his expression?

I would not go so far as to say that I am uncertain of anything, more like in disbelief. Reneea opened the door and instantly saw the beautiful skyline of Canada across the water and as it had snowed a great deal this winter she saw the beautiful white snow and thought how fresh and new everything looked after a fresh coating of snow had fallen, it was sort of how she felt about her life beginning with Rick and wondered if that were his issue. She heard the door shut behind him which brought her out of her gaze. Baby, come on, talk to me we have all night and as a matter of fact, the rest of our lives together to make love, there's no rush no more racing the clock for time alone. See, baby that's just it...I never imagined that you and I would really somehow end up together, I mean I always hoped, and at times, prayed for it yes even though I was praying for another man's wife, but for it to actually happen and the way it happen, it's actually mind blowing for me. Craig being my son and all and better yet wanting to be, not rejecting the two of us together when he very well could have he actually knowing the circumstances gave us his endorsement of approval; Nae-Nae you have to admit that this is a lot for a brother to digest and not feel as if he is in a dream or something?

Curtis has manage to beat me out of everything except sports, I was drafted he wasn't, then I was injured and my career came to a halt. And though I had that experience of traveling all across the country with fame and notoriety, and yes, I had a wife who loved me, when I came home he had still won, because he had you and Craig and there I sat without, wishing and wanting…, Bea was in my life and that should have been enough and I have sought forgiveness over it in the past, but it wasn't because she just wasn't you… Rach was right; he has managed to win everything. But, tonight, I looked in his eyes and thought to myself, *I win you loose* I mean I literally took pleasure in his pain. The thought of all that has me wanting to wait and see if tomorrow I wake up and it was all a dream and he walks past me again with you on his arm laughing in my face. The fact that you love me so much is staggering and Nae-Nae, I am not a perfect man, I have flaws, I can't promise you that we won't ever fight or disagree but I can promise you this… you my loving one, will not enter into another Marriage of Lies.

Reneea, looked at Rick and had so much love in her heart for him that she could not find any words to speak as she sat there wanting to express so much. Rick, I'm not looking for perfection, however, you are pretty dammed close if I must say so. I don't want you to fill as if I will enter our relationship with the baggage of old as you are not Curtis and I know this, I know from time to I will find myself wanting to know if it is still good to you and by that I mean our relationship as whole, but that's when we have to remember that we were once friends who told each other any and everything and allow communication to be key in our life together, I know husbands and wives have their little private secrets that make the marriage work which are private thoughts and I am not asking for you to divulge everything, but to share the things that might be a problem or where you feel we may be lacking so we can fix the problem before one can began. You may be a winner in your mind now right here tonight, but baby you need to know that you were always the winner in my eyes. We will take it slow but I promise we will get to our destination as happily ever after has waited for us to stop by long enough and become a visitor.

Rick pulled her close to him and kissed her repeatedly until he began to tickle her on her neck causing her to pull away in playfulness. Stop it, boy! No, you stop girl come here. They continued kissing until he sat up and interrupted what they were starting. Baby, stand up please. Reneea look at him strange, because she thought the destination was down on the bed at least that was the indication the bulge in his pants was giving her. Standing to her feet he took her by the hand and noticed that she was wearing his ring. He began to remove it with slight protest. Boo, what are doing, give me that I don't want to chance leaving it on the nightstand here!
In a second baby, walking away from her to get two glasses of champagne that he noticed were poured by the room attendant. Returning with the glasses he gave one to her and kept one for himself.

Reneea, when I gave you this ring on Christmas day as a gift and ask you to wear it from time to time so that I could see it as a symbol of our love, I knew that the actual question that went along with it had to be a ways off as you were still and are now, Curtis' wife…however, I believe with everything in me that that's over now and as soon as the ink dries on those divorce papers you my dear will be fair game to have and to hold from that day forward. So, sweetheart I would just like to get the formalities out of the way so that the day we are on that plane to Jamaica…being interrupted by Reneea, *Jamaica,* obviously liking the sound of that? Yes, you heard right it's already arranged. When we land all the Minister has to do is pronounce you *My Wife*.

Rick got down on one knee and took her hand. I love you more than life itself sometimes it seems and I can not imagine my life without you in it for even one moment. So, Reneea Craig, using her maiden name as to not spoil the mood, will you do me the honor of becoming my wife for the rest of our life? Rick placed the diamond band on her finger and she was outdone and head over hills even more than before. Reneea, allowed a single tear to fall and then she responded…How is one week from today, I already have you scheduled in red ink on my planner pull it out of my purse and look for yourself if you don't believe me. Thunderous laughter arose from the two as only she could take a sincere serious moment like that and turn it humorous.

Now see girl, that's why I love you so much.

Oh, I thought it was for my body...

Naw, but it is definitely in the top ten reasons why, in fact, that dress it lovely, I mean what material of it there is…, playfully tugging to the dangerously high split in front, but, how about we see a lot less of it, shall we?

Well Mr. Neal, if you would do the zipper, gravity will do the rest. Reneea looked at Rick taunting him with her natural ability to arouse while swaying back and forth provocatively. She turned her back to him and she could feel his body against her. He was such a passionate lover that the excitement of just thinking about how he would have her tonight made her wet with anticipation of what was to come. He began kissing her on her neck which lead to her back and as he reached the top of her buttock, bending down directly to the level of her vaginal area, he began to turn her around to face him as he slid her lacey black thong down exposing her allowing him to smell her sweet perfume mixed with the scent of her sex, he spread open her lips revealing her clit and began to lick her in a short jabbing motion that was driving her insane, continuing this action for a moment going into a kissing technique that by this time had her begging him for more. As he was still fully dressed he laid her back on the bed as she was so ready for him to come inside her and give her all the love she could possibly stand. As she attempted to assist him in removing his clothing he gently stopped her. No, baby don't move, I want you to see and enjoy everything that's coming your way. How she did love his body, the color of his skin the texture of his hair that lay sweetly on his chest down to the pubic region, the muscles that rippled with each movement he made, Damn she thought hurry up baby! The build up was wonderful and Reneea, though she had made love to this man many times before, knew that tonight would be extra special. Rick, now fully undressed with and erection that absolutely needed pleasing in an attempt to lie down next to his beloved was stopped abruptly as she could no longer take not touching or tasting him. Reneea sat up and clasped his penis with booth hands thinking to herself, how endowed this man was, inserted it into her mouth and began to suck him strong and hard, causing him to cry out. Damn, Nae! Yeah do that shit baby, take it all, don't stop babe… he was gasping for air as he knew that as full as he was if she continued this pattern he would not make it inside of her before he climaxed. Not wanting to cum to quick and knowing this would be the case, he stopped her despite her resistance. Picking his tie up from the floor he grabbed her placing her hands in on another he began to tie them together to her surprise while looking at her in devilment.

What are doing Rick? Baby what's going on here?

Watch and enjoy baby, daddy's going to make you feel so good.

Reneea could hardly stand it the anticipation was killing her she could feel her pussy throbbing and wanted him so badly. As they had checked in earlier his bag had been brought to the room by the bell hop, he just had no idea it would be her room. He retrieved the items and went back to her lying on the bed.

Well, well, it looks like the doctor bought his bag of tricks?

Yes, he did, and they are all for you my love, smiling at her seductively, while laying her back on the bed. Removing strawberries slices from the tray of fruit that accompanied the champagne brought in earlier. He began to place them strategically on areas of her body as she watched in agony and desire. Once all had been placed he began to eat them off one by one making sure to suck on the area sufficiently from where they had been removed to a rousing chorus of oohs and ahhs from his victim. Upon reaching his final location between her legs, kissing and sucking her frantically, he engaged the vibrator that she had enjoyed so much as he had introduced it during their last time together along with his tongue that drove her wild. With her hands tied, all she could do was moan, groan, and scream while grinding her body against his face. This let Rick know that he had hit not only the G spot but any other spots with alphabets as well!

Son of bitch! Rick stop, baby no! Awe shit, shit, shit, yes…fuck me damn it!

Rick knew that she would enjoy it, but he had no idea that she would be this loud. Laughing at the loss of her control, he tried to quiet her.

Baby damn, you are so loud that the neighbors in the next suite will hear you love, taunting her.

Fuck the neighbors, isn't that what you always say, and untie my damn hands so I can touch you!

Uh, uh, tonight you are my prisoner, all you can do is take it…kissing her softly, pouring a little champagne on her navel and watching it run down before it could hit the sheet catching it with his tongue, he commenced his assault a few moments longer seeing that she had cum he pulled her up and she was exhausted from her struggle and pleased as well. Her hair was all over her head as he had long removed the band that was restricting it as it had begun to curl naturally from her own perspiration. Seeing this he sat her atop of him inserting himself gently and stroked her until her eyes rolled back in her head and he knew he had her, still stroking her he untied her hands which she lovingly wrapped around his neck still in rhythmic motion with her lover caressing him and commanding him to cum. As her sweet voice whispered in his ear repeatedly cum baby, oh cum daddy, give me that sweet stuff and he could no longer sustain what had to be. He came inside her which caused him to cry out vowing his love to her while kissing each other softly. As energy levels were low all they could do was fall back onto the bed, looking at one another drifting off to sleep as daylight would have to find them there in all of the night's glory, no one would have to shower first or last anymore, leave and return to places they would rather not be without the other, nor would they ever again be parted.

As the morning found all in attendance from the night before, the core group and a few new comers at breakfast with Rick and Reneea at the head of the table, it was plain to see that a few introductions were needed with Charlotte and Donica and their mates being the newest to arrive. Of course everyone knew Charlotte as she had worked for Curtis for years, no one knew her relation to Reneea with the exception of Tina who of course would tell no one. Donica on the other hand, being Charlotte's sister from her father, Charles Donald Price, who was an investment mogul, who laundered money for Tina's father in the earlier years, thus forth creating the relationship of business between Attorney Matthew Arthur Craig, Reneea's father and his client who would also be Tina's father as also who he later represented in court in lieu of his daughter and states evidence being turned in order to get a sentence that would be lighter than at first expected, Federal Time, and bring a whole slue of corrupted officials down in the process. There was no blood relation between Reneea and Donica except for the fact that her aunt did not blame the child for her husband's indiscretions and felt that family should always know their kin making sure that Charlotte and Donica would be together despite her feelings for what her bigamist husband had done it was the 60's and folks kept family secrets, especially when they were getting a head and had overcome. Reneea had no hard feelings about Doni sleeping with Curtis as it was all part of the plan to bring him down, and as Doni had always been a man eater, it was simply based on business once again. This was also the time that they felt that an explanation was given about the Diva's of Detroit Society. They were simply a group of girls who were the daughter's of women who formed a Charitable Organization and sponsored Debutant Balls for inner city girls and gave to the under privilege families in the Detroit area. As they were to young to become members they created their own team and mimicked their mothers until high school and college when the group took on a whole new meaning of getting even with little boy's who played with their toy's and discarded them when something they thought better came along and they started using the group for revenge against their offenders, which is exactly what happened to Curtis. They were often behind the parties that took place in college that Curtis had mentioned to Rick about, except generally the outing of someone would take place in private as not to disrupt the entire party that many times people paid money to get into, always business women first that was the creed.

As the conversation increased, it was also learned that Craig and Angel had a chance to discuss their new identity and though still reeling from the shock of it all, Angel was finally able to express her true feelings about how she always thought Craig favored Rick much more than Curtis but never wanted to say anything as she did not want to create suspicion in Craig's mind who wouldn't you know thought the same thing all the time. She also understood why Craig did not discuss his concerns of his father with her whom at the time he knew as Curtis as he did not want to cast a shadow of doubt in her mind that he would be the same way. Rachel at this time was thrilled that Craig was really her kin and she openly relayed that to all in attendance. Seeing how important this was to Rachel, Craig got up from his seat went over to where Rachel was seated and hugged his new found Aunt as he had always held a special place in her heart but did not know why in his mind the mystery was solved. As Reneea really did not mind running the company behind the scenes she thought that she would announce the plans for Rae Enterprise' name change along with it's changing of the guards. From now own it would be known as Price Craig Industries with Charlotte becoming and CEO and Craig Allen Neal becoming CFO should he choose to come back to Detroit and except the position and there was no doubt in Reneea's mind that he wouldn't. Kirmark Division Group was still the parent company, but she had no fear as Marshall and Donica had always done and excellent job and with Rachel and Davis on board she was worried even less. Rick and Reneea announced their plans for their wedding which came as no surprise to anyone, but did receive cheers from all in attendance. They would all be in attendance and could not wait to get out of the Detroit snow for the occasion.

Troy who had been taking all of this in felt that there would be no time like the present for his thoughts to come out and as he was feeling like a member of the family and everyone was there he decided not to let the opportunity pass him by. Excuse me if I could have everyone's attention as he stood at his chair. Everyone curious to know what the man had to say stopped instantly and did as he asked.

I just want to say that I have never encounter a group of people like you in my entire life, nor did think that people like you existed. Everyone began to look around as they were not quite sure where he was going with what sounded as if it could be an insult seeing this he continued while he had the chance to explain his statement. By that I mean people who care about one another so much that they would go through great lengths to protect them, to love them and to honor them…I mean what happen to dude last night was unreal and very sobering, because if I was in a jam it would most certainly be the Diva's that I would look up, yaw vicious for sure…Tina interrupted, Did he say Bitches Though, everyone hollered out Vicious while laughing at her question as the alcohol was still playing a role in her hangover process…Oh tell a sister something, I'll have to cut you for real while they all laughed at her remark….May I continue? And I believe that to be case because you know the value of family and friendship. Now I can't lie, I was a little confused but I think I got it. What I know for sure is that I sincerely want to be a member of this crew for so many reasons, but the main reason is that a member of this crew, though we haven't been together long, has made me feel as if I have found the love that I have been searching for, for so long and now with her by my side, I feel my search is over. And if her parents would not mind, Mike, Ms. Tina, I would like to ask for their daughter's hand in marriage. Everyone was stunned as he had shocked everybody and Mia truly did not expect this. I would also like to receive the blessing of her best friend as well as he has made it absolutely clear that her heart is not a playground and I could not agree with him more. At that moment Craig stood up and reached across to give him a pound smiling at Mia while taking his seat. So Mia, if you don't have any other offers, I was wondering if you would marry me, I know it's soon, but we can take our time…just don't say no, especially in front of all these people, he said while winking at her and holding the most beautiful diamond ring she had seen.

Mia was so shocked all she could do was smile and shake her head frantically yes as tears came down. Everyone was excited, congratulating them and hugging one another and with this they raised their glasses of orange juice, and coffee, or glasses of Alka-Seltzer for some of them as Champagne was not an option for any of them as they had consumed way to much the night before.

Chapter 23

The Lies End

The days ahead that followed would be difficult at best there were meetings with attorneys and movers in and out of the house as Craig and Angel had decided together to come back to the city and for him to take the job in the family business as CFO, not to mention with the children it just made sense to live near the family. Craig had began to call Rick dad as it came so natural considering that he had always had a connection with him as such. An occasional *Rick* would come out but it was expected as it was a major adjustment for them all but at least Craig's children would know him as nothing less than Granddaddy. Reneea had major meetings as she was in preparation for her wedding as Curtis did not contest anything as he and his team of lawyers had reviewed all documents and with his signatures applied to every thing that had taken place he hadn't a leg to stand on and the divorce was final as she had paid handsomely to make it happen without haste and as she was amicable in her settlement as she said she would be not making him completely destitute, as many thought she should have, he saw no reason to rock the boat. However, she did keep her promise of one week to Ms. Winter's who had now vacated her condo in the suburbs which had she not the bailiffs were standing by to give her a hand, no problem. She even allowed her to take the furnishing as she wanted nothing there as a reminder of where her marriage had been dissolved to Curtis without so much as any consideration given to her.

They decided to sale Rick's house in the City as it seemed pointless to keep it as he had no problem moving into the mansion that Curtis had built, again thinking to himself I win you loose. Curtis, however, did manage to win Vanessa back as she loved him, however, brought him back on her terms as Reneea had given her all the bargaining chips she

needed and after all that he had been through, the poor self absorbed
creature as he was still, thought that the sun rose and shined on his ass
where she was concerned as of course one women for Curtis Anthony Rae
would never be enough. He had managed to get Sherrie from Mr. Nicks in
his bed somewhere along the line as he could not stand the idea of her
being available and alone especially after the information Rick had shared
with him about her ability to make man very satisfied. Between the two of
them he could maintain until he was back on top in business and making
deals then he would add to his collection again it was only a matter of time
before the right business opportunity presented itself and he would once
again show them all that you could not kept him down. He at times did
agonize over the fact that Craig was not his son and had chosen to take the
Neal name as he had been informed in writing terminating his parental
rights to Craig. This did not bother him to bad as Sherrie was pregnant and
carrying his child and let in be known that this child would come into the
world with or without his permission. This time there would be a junior
and he would see to it that his name was past on, little did Vanessa know.

As she promised one week from today had past and Reneea was preparing
to head to the airport as the Limo was waiting outside when her telephone
rang, looking out of the kitchen window to see Rick rushing her, she
thought twice about answering but she did in case it was something
important as everyone knew that she was leaving the country for her
wedding today. There was a large spread in the Free Press Society Pages
and Chronicle with hers and Rick's photo announcing their wedding.
Hello,
The caller exhaled and started to speak slowly, *Good morning Reneea.*
She knew the voice instantly and held her breath as she knew she had to
respond.
Good morning Curtis.
*Listen I know, I am only supposed to contact you through the lawyers...but
I...*
Curtis really...I'm pressed for time...
Just hear me out Nea, please?
Hurry Curtis my family is waiting for me. Her last statement went through
his heart like a knife and he knew he only had himself to blame.
I'm sorry, for what it's worth, I am sorry.
Sorry for what Curtis getting caught?
I deserve that...but no, I'm sorry for loosing and hurting you most of all.

Reneea took a breath and spoke with strength…Well Curtis, I really do wish you well and I hope that in time you will get some help or at least find something beside yourself to love so that you experience what it really is to have someone who loves you back and you recognize it for all that its worth.

Congratulations on your wedding, I won't lie an say I hope you'll be happy together, there has been enough lying already on my behalf where you are concerned, but I do wish you the best, he should have been the one.

Thank you for you honestly at least, take care of yourself Curtis…she removed the receiver from her ear not allowing his response to reach her and placed the receiver on the cradle. She wiped a single tear from her eye at the moment she noticed Rick coming through the door.

Woman, I have waited 20 years or better to marry you and you are not about to make me miss my flight therefore, causing me hours more delay to hear you say I do. Will you bring you butt outside so we can go. PLEASE! She looked at him and could now see the other members in the car calling them to hurry while pointing to their watches. Okay, Mr. Neal, keep your pants on. Oh I will until tonight. They kissed with the door wide open as the neighbors from the adjacent yard looked on…noticing that they were watching, they both smiled and said *Fuck the neighbors!*

Locking the door and following behind her soon to be husband she thought to herself, Love wasn't really a weird emotion at all, it was an action and the only way to keep it from going past the point of no return was to act on it everyday that we live as though our lives depend on it, after all didn't it? This would be her vow from this day forward, but the difference this time would be that she would love herself in the process a little more, as now the *lies end.*

Sheila Da Lae

The Hatted One

Just who is she?

She is an accomplished published author, who possesses the unique gift of story telling with a twist. She is a Diva in her own rights that enjoys life to the fullest. Sheila Da Lae, is unlike anyone you may have encountered before as she prides herself on being every woman with a voice who may have a story to tell, however, not quite sure as to how it should be told. She enjoys creative writing and creations of fiction that touch the lives of everyday men and women that border along the lines of fantasy and seduction. She has been writing since the age of 16 entering various creative writing competitions and often taking first place as the most creative young journalist. In growing into a woman she decided to follow her dream to see where it might lead. When she learned that this was her passion she decided to pursue it further to turn professionally into what had become of her hobby.

She has been dubbed The Hatted One, as she has chosen to keep her identity a mystery as it allows her the freedom to create without questions. Ms. Da Lae writes about love, lust, lies, desire and romance with a no holds bared freedom. She is a student of life with a flare for the dramatic which allows her to step into the roles of her characters causing them to come to life on the pages while putting you in their shoes to share in their emotions and struggles...and yes their love triangles. Every story unfolds with either a lesson learned or a lesson lived that will cause you to turn the pages one after the next to see where she will end up.

Writing is definitely enjoyable to her as it allows her to create a world of her own where her literary skills can sore to heights unknown. It is her hope that those who dare to venture through her journey filled pages enjoy the experience and share them with a friend. As there are no boundaries or limits to her creating, we invite you to enjoy the flavor. Stay Tuned as surely there is more to come.

Yours Truly,

Sheila

More to come by The Hatted One

Be on the lookout for Sheila Da Lae's
next book entitled,

Diva's Unleashed!

Turn the page and
whet your appetite for the sequel.

Shall We Let the Divas Explain?

My name is **Donica Price**. I am a 27 year old executive who has excelled at everything I've ever attempted, except the area of a meaningful relationship with the opposite sex. I not only need, but I desire the companionship of a man. Often in my haste to get in deep with a brother, I end up with a reject from hell. You know the types, *"Yeah it may look like my mother's basement, but its my sanctuary from the hassle of the world as I'm still finding myself"* or *"It all depends on how you defined together, She's just my wife in name only, we aren't totally together"* and last but never lease; *"Baby, I'm really not looking for a commitment right now, can't we just have a good time?"* No, he's just committed himself to sleeping with you, lounging around on your sofa and eating you the hell out of house and home and if his ass ain't found himself at 40, let his ass stay lost.

Yes, in my time, I've had some real pieces of work, for lack of a better word, but I'm sure you can feel me. It's not that I need a man to take care of me; and believe me when I say I let them know that right from the jump. My father may have been a rolling stone; however, he taught me and my sister the meaning of hard work and how to make a buck. I've been paying my own way since college; I play by my rules when it comes to finances. I don't need a man, *hell...I just want one.* Where is my Mr. Right?

Fayetta Lee Mitchell's the name, and I am a prime example that marriage is not the fairytale that it is often made out to be. I learned all the essentials...The best way to a man is through his stomach! Momma always said... *"Keep his stomach full, his bed warm, his children clean and his home habitable and he will love you for life! Marriage is Key! Be the wife he wants you to be and he won't ever roam from home."* BULLSHIT! My mother did a wonderful job with preparing me to love and care for a man. She provided me with all the tools that would be essential to give him what he needed when he needed it. However, she forgot to equip me with the tools I would come to need to take care of and love myself. She did not give me the basis of finding out about myself, to learn what would be pleasing to me, to explore what it was that I liked, who was Fayetta really? What colors did I like? What made me tick? What were my pressure and breaking points, you know my limits? No, she did not put emphasis on that stuff, it wasn't important. If it didn't pertain to his happiness and well adjustment, it just didn't matter. Come to think of it, every time I would go to my mother with a problem or a disagreement that he and I had, she only wanted to concentrate on pointing out my mistake and what I had done that would have been upsetting to him. I guess that's why when his absence from our home began to happen more and more it was accepted as opposed to questioned and tolerated instead of ended. When his disinterest in our lovemaking surfaced it was easy for me to make excuses for it rather than trouble him as he worked so hard providing the good life that we both enjoyed. Financially that is. I guess it was easy for him to turn to her as I never questioned him about anything. What a sacrifice, I gave him everything mother said I should and in return he gave me heartache, pain, suffering, and grief. What a guy huh?

Rose Marie Carter, I'm high maintenance, Grade A Dime Piece. The epitome of a TEN! I'm gorgeous; damn near flawless if it weren't for my imperfect eye color. My mother used to say I have the eyes of an old soul. I'm sure it meant something to the folks back in the day, but I could have cared less. All I know is that they were too dark for my pretty complexion. However, I can adjust that minor detail with color contacts. Thank God for Bulsh & Lomb, love those people. On any given day, I can go from Hazel to Grayish Blue and carry it all off without a hitch! My almond complexion makes the transition easy with each change. My body… ump, ump, ump, to die for, every inch. I look at myself in the mirror and thank God for making me, me. Yes, yes I especially thank Mr. Roger Mortin, for that wonderful little investment he contributed. Thanks to him being so fixated on me, my career, and my body…I am a perfect perky "C" cup. The $5,000.00 he laid out for that to become my reality was chump change besides he reaped the wonderful benefit of dangling me from his arm for a considerable period of time I might add. I mean, I, from time to time, show him little tokens of my gratitude, what more could he ask for? I let him know going in that we were just friends and nothing more. None of that relationship mumbo jumbo; I do not have time, nor do I desire being committed to any one man. There is just so much of me to spread around, why let one man enjoy what so many could? Besides the fringe benefits I receive from my many talented lovers are too good to let go. There's

Aaron, who wines and dines me at the blink of an eye flies all the way in from Atlanta to do it a lot of times, Mike who keeps me impeccably dressed, Andre who knows how to sooth my beast within, and Nate who pays my bills. Why would I discontinue any of that? My friends harass me all the time about my philandering ways, but I don't care. Seriously, what are my options? Be like Donica and search for Mr. Right only to keep ending up with Mr. Wrong, or perhaps settle down and get married like Faye only to have some joker pump me full of babies, ruin my figure and then leave me for some slut half my age? No thanks! I'll take my chances swinging single; and that other entire headache, a sister don't need. After all, men have done it for years and if you can't beat 'em why not join 'em? Whore? Say what you want to, I'm living large.

Printed in the United States
151685LV00004BA/196/P